"A writer

**Praise for the novels of
Margaret Evans Porter**

Kissing a Stranger
"As rich and savory as a box of fine chocolates."
—Teresa Medeiros

The Proposal
"Impressive! *The Proposal* re-creates the essence of
a bygone era."—*The Literary Times*

Improper Advances
"A winning tale that is sure to become a
subgenre favorite."—*Midwest Book Review*

Seducer
"Wonderful . . . brings to life the exotic world of
the Isle of Man [with] much local color."
—BookBrowser

Road to Ruin
"Cleverly told."—*Library Journal*

Dangerous Diversions

and

Toast of the Town

Margaret Evans Porter

A SIGNET BOOK

SIGNET
Published by New American Library, a division of
Penguin Group (USA) Inc., 375 Hudson Street,
New York, New York 10014, USA
Penguin Group (Canada), 10 Alcorn Avenue, Toronto,
Ontario M4V 3B2, Canada (a division of Pearson Penguin Canada Inc.)
Penguin Books Ltd., 80 Strand, London WC2R 0RL, England
Penguin Ireland, 25 St. Stephen's Green, Dublin 2,
Ireland (a division of Penguin Books Ltd.)
Penguin Group (Australia), 250 Camberwell Road, Camberwell, Victoria 3124,
Australia (a division of Pearson Australia Group Pty. Ltd.)
Penguin Books India Pvt. Ltd., 11 Community Centre, Panchsheel Park,
New Delhi - 110 017, India
Penguin Group (NZ), cnr Airborne and Rosedale Roads, Albany,
Auckland 1310, New Zealand (a division of Pearson New Zealand Ltd.)
Penguin Books (South Africa) (Pty.) Ltd., 24 Sturdee Avenue,
Rosebank, Johannesburg 2196, South Africa

Penguin Books Ltd., Registered Offices:
80 Strand, London WC2R 0RL, England

Published by Signet, an imprint of New American Library, a division of Penguin Group (USA) Inc. *Dangerous Diversions* and *Toast of the Town* were previously published in separate Signet editions.

First Signet Printing (Double Edition), May 2005
10 9 8 7 6 5 4 3 2 1

Dangerous Diversions copyright © Margaret Evans Porter, 1994
Toast of the Town copyright © Margaret Evans Porter, 1993
All rights reserved

 REGISTERED TRADEMARK—MARCA REGISTRADA

Dangerous
Diversions

1

A dancing Shape, an Image gay,
To haunt, to startle, and waylay.
—WILLIAM WORDSWORTH

London, 1810

Force of habit was so strong that Gervase William
Marchant paused before crossing the threshold of the study,
instinctively waiting for permission to enter. His thoughtful
gaze rested on the leather wing chair near the window, now
unoccupied.

Otherwise, the room was unchanged. The mahogany
bookcases were crammed with calfbound editions of classical authors, biographies, travel writing, essays, and political
treatises, and even in the gloom of late afternoon their
gilded spines glittered enticingly. A set of folding library
steps had been left open at the base of the tallest bookcase.
Gervase could remember standing upon them as a boy, examining his surroundings from the superior perspective of
an adult. His wise and patient father had never scolded him
for playing in his well-furnished retreat, or chastened him
for repeatedly spinning the large globes in the corner.

He strode the perimeter of the rich Persian carpet, examining the portraits of his ancestors that decorated the walls.
Among those represented were a Royalist general, ennobled by Charles the First for his valor during the Civil War,
and his Cavalier son, a court wit who had wed an illegitimate daughter of the martyred Stuart's merrier son. The
youthful Gervase had been fascinated by tales of their exploits on the battlefield and at Whitehall, and in later years
he'd read their names in his history texts.

Now, as in childhood, he regretted that he bore no resemblance to his forebears. His eyes were gray rather than romantically dark; he had ordinary brown hair, neatly cropped, not the flowing ebony tresses of the earlier Marchants. The only feature he'd inherited, albeit in a slightly improved form, was that proud and prominent nose. His plain black coat compared unfavorably with their brightly colored satins and velvets; it lacked the broad cuffs so liberally embellished with silver thread embroidery. No lace adorned his white shirt, he didn't carry a silver sword, and the gold signet he wore was not as impressive as the large jewels upon his ancestors' fingers.

He sat down at the writing desk where his father's thoughtful and carefully reasoned speeches had been composed. He nodded in the direction of the bust of William Pitt, mounted on a pedestal on the other side of the room, as if it were animate and might respond in kind. But the marble face of the late Prime Minister remained fixed, and the sightless eyes maintained their unwavering stare.

Opening the top drawer, he took out a sheet of writing paper and laid it upon the olive leather desktop.

At that moment a dark-haired boy bounded through the doorway. "Here you are!" he cried. "I've been searching all over. Parry says you're going to your club tonight!" His intense blue eyes blazed with accusation.

"Yes, that's true," Gervase replied, his hand moving to an oblong footed tray his grandfather had commissioned from Paul de Lamerie, a celebrated silversmith. It held an inkpot and pounce-box, a penknife case, and a compartment for pens, all engraved with the arms of the Duke of Solway. Selecting a pristine white quill from the top drawer, the possessor of that illustrious title began to pare its tip with the tiny knife. "But first I must write your sister. Care to add a line or two yourself?"

"I haven't time," the intruder responded. "Do pay attention, Ger. I've something vastly important to tell you."

The duke laid down his pen. "What is it, Nin?"

"Robert the footman was describing the aquatic show at Sadler's Wells, a grand spectacle called *The Spectre Knight*. I looked in the papers and found out that it's playing tonight," the youth concluded significantly.

"I'm quite sure it will be repeated," said Gervase, his tone as firm as he could make it.

"But you said I might have a treat before you send me back to Harrow."

Unable to deny it, he doubted the wisdom of making so generous an offer to his cousin and ward. "I wasn't specific about *when* you might have this treat."

Without a doubt Ninian Peverel favored the handsome gentlemen of the portraits. In addition to black curly hair, milky skin, and the haughty Marchant nose, he exhibited the stately bearing of one who had inherited an earldom at the age of two. His height was average for a boy of twelve, and Gervase supposed his thinness resulted from incessant activity, for he was a voracious eater. Those persons who had been acquainted with his mother, the great beauty of her generation, never failed to notice that she had passed her remarkable looks on to her son, but Ninian's oval face was saved from girlish prettiness by the impish sweep of his brows and a determined chin indented by a deep cleft.

"You can't say no," he continued serenely, "because I've already ordered the carriage and it's waiting in the street. The theater opens at half past five, and we'll want good places. Don't forget to bring money—a box seat costs two shillings."

When he went to the window, Gervase discovered that his town coach was standing in Park Lane, its caped driver on the box and a liveried footman at the door. He hardly knew what to say, and he missed his father more in that helpless moment than when he'd stepped into the study. Not that Ninian had minded the late duke any better than he did the present one, Gervase reminded himself.

He wore a beleagured expression as he considered his options and his fingers raked his brown hair, disarranging his valet's careful handiwork. This would be his first night in London after an absence of many months and he'd intended to spend it at White's Club in St. James's. And yet he knew it would be risky to leave Lord Swanborough at Solway House without amusement—or adequate supervision.

"You are a pestilential brat," he announced, and resigned

himself to his fate. Apparently there was no way to avoid
passing the evening at a theater renowned for its lavish
spectacles incorporating a famous tank of water. "What are
we to do about our dinner?"

"That's no problem. There's a jolly tavern across from
the playhouse where I went last year with Justin. Or we can
eat at the theater. A man sells food and drink during the intervals."

"Delightful," said the duke, his tone a clear indication
that he regarded the prospect as anything but.

During the subsequent journey from Solway House to
the northern suburb of Islington, Lord Swanborough entertained his guardian with a description of the performance
he had witnessed when his sister's husband had taken him
to Sadler's Wells.

"Don't most boys your age prefer Astley's Amphithe-
atre?" Gervase asked.

"Pooh, dancing horses can't compare with naval battles
and aqua dramas," Ninian said disdainfully.

"I gather Justin took you to the Wells as a favor to Miranda."

"He wanted to go. It was his first time, and afterward he
said Astley's is nothing to it."

"Ever the diplomat," Gervase murmured. "I sometimes
wonder whether Viscount Cavender would have married
into our family if the responsibility of looking after you had
fallen to him."

"Justin likes me," Ninian said blithely. "But I think he
would have wed Mira even if he didn't. When I was at
Cavender Chase for Easter they were always taking long
walks together and kissing in corners when they thought no
one could see. And now she's going to have a baby."

"Are you implying that one necessarily leads to the
other?"

Grinning, the boy answered, "I know better. Lord Phillip
Wanslow got a village girl with child last term. He's six-
teen and has lain with five different women, or so he
claims. He told us everything about it—before he was expelled."

"And to think my father sent you to Harrow to become a proper young gentleman." Gervase, who had attended Eton, was all too aware of the dangerous effects of public schools, yet he blessed the existence of the one in Harrow-on-the-Hill. On the first day of Michaelmas term, he would be rid of his wild and naughty ward, and a welcome peace would then fall upon his bachelor household.

Exasperated though he often was by Ninian, Gervase had to pity one whose relatively brief history was so full of sorrows and tragedy.

The late Lord Swanborough, a famous sportsman, had remained unwed into middle age, when he began his courtship of Lady Hermia Marchant. The earl owned a neighboring estate and was familiar with the beauty's idiosyncrasies: the despondent moods, the persistent melancholy, the frequent fits of weeping. Her fond brother, the Duke of Solway, exhibited scant enthusiasm for the match but hadn't prevented it.

Unfortunately for the couple, the birth of a daughter was not immediately succeeded by the son Lord Swanborough desperately wanted, and regular miscarriages shattered the countess's fragile nerves and delicate health. After a decade of touring spas and watering places, she presented her husband with his heir, an ordeal so detrimental to her state of mind that she withdrew to Bath, hoping to find a cure. The following year the earl died from an excess of drink and disappointment, leaving little Lady Miranda and her infant brother Ninian to the guardianship of their Uncle William. The youngest peer of the realm had inherited a handsome fortune, Swanborough Abbey in Leicestershire, and a celebrated pack of foxhounds, all held in trust for him until he reached his majority.

That happy day, which Gervase desired far more than the person who would derive the material benefit, was nine years off, and he hoped he possessed enough fortitude to meet the difficulties ahead.

Ninian had demonstrated scant respect for his authority during a summer stay at Pontesbury, Gervase's estate in Shropshire. Since their arrival in London earlier that day, the willful youth had managed to tyrannize the Solway

House servants. Parry, the hitherto unflappable Welshman who had been elevated from underbutler to butler when his predecessor chose to remain in the service of the widowed duchess, already exhibited signs of strain.

Too many houses, too many dependents, and entirely too many responsibilities, Gervase thought glumly. As the carriage rolled through the Islington Road turnpike gate he vowed to forget the weighty responsibilities that had devolved upon him at his father's death for the space of an evening. Perhaps, like Lord Cavender, he would enjoy the sort of entertainment offered at Sadler's Wells.

The theater, a substantial brick building with many gables and projecting wings, sat amidst a grove of elms and was enclosed by a low wooden fence and regularly spaced lampposts. It stood on the north bank of the New River, into which several hopeful fishermen were casting their lines. Gervase envied them their peaceful pursuit, for he enjoyed angling and had passed many a pleasant hour outwitting elusive trout and greyling.

After his coachman halted in the yard of the Myddelton's Head Tavern, he and Ninian descended. Observing the crowd at the entrance of the playhouse, Gervase handed the footman eight shillings.

"Secure the best box seats you can find, Robert, and hold them while his lordship and I are dining." With an understanding smile, he presented the man with several more coins, adding, "Find a seat of your own in the gallery, if one can be had, and buy yourself some beer."

Ninian railed at Gervase for choosing a private parlor in preference to the common room, but he said dampingly that he had no desire to eat in the company of actors and tumblers.

"But Grimaldi the clown might be among them!"

"I doubt it very much," Gervase said when they sat down at an unoccupied table. "A player of his stature would hardly risk overeating or drinking too much before going on the stage. It might adversely affect his performance." He passed the bill of fare to his cousin.

Ninian's prodigious appetite prompted him to select the pigeon pie, bread pudding, and a cherry tart. "What's the time?" he demanded as the waiter cleared away the first of his empty plates. "The program begins at half past six, and we mustn't be late."

"We won't be, so stop bolting your food."

Despite his recent elevation to the pinnacle of the aristocratic hierarchy, Gervase hadn't been a duke long enough to disdain a simple meal, so long as it was well cooked and amply seasoned, and that was precisely what the kitchens of the Myddleton's Head offered. Watching his ward chase a morsel of crust with his fork he realized that he was actually looking forward to *The Spectre Knight,* which would surely be more interesting than the droning debates carried on at White's. Several years ago, when his name was proposed for membership in his father's club, he had been suitably gratified. But he didn't yet feel at home there. He hadn't yet determined to what extent he would involve himself in politics, nor was he especially fond of gaming or gossip.

When Ninian and Gervase took their seats in the stage box Robert had hired for them, the opening ballet was in progress. Turgid music rose from the orchestra pit as the dancers glided across the stage. The female soloist, decked out in a diaphanous spangled gown, pirouetted prettily. Her male counterpart carried a trident, which he waved continually; a short tunic revealed his muscular limbs. When the principals retired to the wings, the ladies of the corps de ballet moved forward, all clutching combs and hand mirrors. Twined about their bare shoulders were long greenish vines, and shorter strands were woven into their unbound hair.

"What is the subject of the piece?" he asked Ninian, who clutched a playbill.

"It's an underwater ballet," the boy replied. "I *think* those girls are meant to be mermaids, and the stuff wrapped around them must be seaweed. The man with the pitchfork thing is Neptune, and the lady is his Queen. Her real name is Madame Louis. Do you suppose she's French?"

"All the best dancers are French. Or Italian."

"I wonder why."

His dread of unanswerable questions caused Gervase to

sigh. "I'm sure I can't say. But I do know that our actors are reputed to excel those of all other nations."

Neither of them was sorry when the dance ended and the pantomime began. It was a humorous piece with a simple plot, and featured London's most popular comedian as Clown.

In one scene Josepsh Grimaldi delivered a sharp kick to old Pantaloon's rump, and the audience roared with laughter. A gentleman in the pit shouted, "That's our Joey! Give 'im another one!"

"I wonder how much time Grimaldi takes to clean his face each evening," Ninian said during the ensuing interval. "All that white and red paint must be a bother to wash off."

Gervase shifted in his seat. "Having a good time, Nin?"

With a shrug, his ward replied diffidently, "The ballet was nothing great, but the panto was amusing. I wish the aqua-drama would begin—that's what *I* came to see." He gripped the rail in eager anticipation and described the vast water tank that the manager of Sadler's Wells had built beneath the wooden stage. Upon this artificial lake, he informed his cousin, miniature boats were floated, villains met their doom, and valiant heroes rescued lovely ladies from drowning.

Charles Dibdin, the author of nearly all the plays he produced and the lyricist for the songs, had based *The Spectre Knight* on Sir Walter Scott's popular poem "Marmion." The result was highly melodramatic, and its climactic scene was set within Fingal's Cave on the Isle of Staffa, faithfully depicted by an ingenious scenery painter. A sentimental conclusion had a powerful effect upon the females in the crowd, and many a handerchief was in evidence by the time the curtain dropped upon the final tableau.

"How I should love to watch them fill the tank," Ninian commented. "The water is pumped in from the New River, you know. D'you think we might go under the stage and have a look at the waterworks?"

Gervase examined his timepiece. "It's eleven o'clock already, Nin, and well past your bedtime."

"Do let's stay till they've cleared away the scenery." His

eyes darkened to blue-black and he thrust out his chin stubbornly. "I don't wish to go yet."

"Stop trying to bully me, you young devil."

"Don't be such a stick, Ger. Say yes."

For the second time that day, Gervase's resolution failed him. "We'll stay for a little while, if you promise not to get in anyone's way and agree to leave when I say it's time—with no argument."

Ninian's mouth had flown open in instinctive protest, but after a pause he said instead, "Oh, very well."

Curious stares from players and stagehands followed Gervase and Ninian as they prowled the labyrinthine corridors behind the stage. One harassed-looking individual, upon being informed of their desire to have a look around, offered to fetch Mr. Harris or Mr. Dibdin from the treasury, where they were counting up the night's receipts.

Gervase replied that this wouldn't be necessary, and his steely eyes dared Ninian to protest.

"But don't you want to see the water tank?" the boy asked plaintively as the man hurried down the hallway.

"Not if it entails disturbing the manager or the proprietor. I suspect all of these busy people are as eager to go home as I am."

"If anyone objects to our looking about, you can tell them who you are," Ninian suggested. "There's a door at the end of the hall," he crowed when they rounded a corner. "I'm sure it must open onto the stage."

"Are you?" Gervase asked wearily. His sense of direction had deserted him long ago. "I'll try this one."

The door nearest him lacked a handle, but a single shove was sufficient to open it. The chamber, dimly lit by a flickering taper on the high mantelshelf, was occupied by a young woman in a gauzy green gown. She stood beside a window, her hand resting on the sill as she stretched one leg out before her. The instant she saw Gervase, she lowered it hastily and regarded him with dismay.

"Forgive me," he said, "I didn't mean to intrude."

Before he could withdraw, she moved in his direction,

her heart-shaped face showing alarm. "You won't tell any-one you found me here?" she asked softly.

"Of course not," he assured her.

"Mr. Dibdin won't let us have a proper green room," she explained, "and he would fine me if he knew I came here to practice my steps." Her voice carried a faint accent, and she tended to lisp her sibilants.

It was too dark for Gervase to determine the precise color of her enormous eyes, which were set beneath arching brows and fringed by dark lashes, but he perceived that the fluffy hair tumbling about her shoulders was light brown. She was small and slim, but her fragile appearance was be-lied by a nicely rounded figure, much of which was re-vealed by her insubstantial draperies.

"The devil's in it, Ger," announced Ninian, stepping into the room. "That door at the end of the hall is locked."

"The custodian has already bolted it," the girl told him. "There's nothing much of interest behind the scenes, only the pipes and water cisterns."

"I *wanted* to see them," Ninian informed her loftily.

"By now Mr. Wheeler will have made his way to the at-tics," she said apologetically. "Perhaps you and your father can come back another time."

Gervase hastened to make it clear that he was the boy's guardian, not his parent. "We had hoped to have a look at the pumps and the stage machinery, but if the person in charge has departed, then we must do the same."

Ninian, peering curiously at the young woman, asked suddenly, "Weren't you a mermaid in the ballet? I remem-ber! You're the one who climbed on the rock to do that lit-tle jumping step. How d'you keep your balance?"

"Not very well, most of the time," she answered on a laugh. "The *entrechat* is almost impossible to perfect, and is even more difficult when one perches on a cliff."

"Come along, Ninian," Gervase urged his ward. "We mustn't keep the lady from her practice, lest she make a mistake the next time and blame you for it."

But his cousin had no intention of departing just yet. "I'm an earl," he stated impressively. "Wouldn't that convince the custodian to take me under the stage to look at the tank?"

."Not necessarily" was her frank reply.

"D'you think we might arrange a tour?"

Her expression was thoughtful as she regarded her inquisitor. "The men who work inside the tank during the performances have been complaining that the water has gone bad—it smells after a few weeks of use. Would your lordship like to watch the stagehands pump the old water out and replace it with fresh?"

"Wouldn't I just!" Ninian declared fervently, gazing at her as if she were a fairy who had granted his dearest wish.

"Mr. Garland, the machinist and stage carpenter, is a particular friend of mine. I'm sure he'd let you observe his operations and would also show you whatever else you wish to see. I'll speak to him tomorrow."

Gervase bestowed a grateful smile upon her. "If he is willing to oblige us, you may send a message to Solway House to let us know the day, Miss—" He paused for her to supply the surname.

"My name is Rosalie."

Ninian, demonstrating his impatience with proper introductions, asked her whether she'd ever gone into the tank herself.

Rosalie shook her head. "Some of the actors use it when the water is clean, which it rarely is, but I've never done so. Mr. Dibdin would disapprove of mixed bathing parties." Her eyes twinkled. "He's very strict with the company, and even conducts prayers before each performance."

"What a bore," Ninian responded.

"Nin," said his guardian, "thank Miss Rosalie for offering to make the arrangements for your tour, and bid her farewell. It's nearly midnight."

"Is it?" the dancer asked in surprise. "I'd best hurry home, else my landlady will think the worse. She waits up until all of her lodgers from the theater return, and I'm always the last."

Gervase had already extracted a calling card from his case and he presented it to her, admiring the graceful curve of her arm as she held it up to the candlelight. "Is your lodging house very far from the theater?"

She returned his gaze warily, patently suspicious of his motive for asking so personal a question. "I live quite near, your grace."

Her defensive attitude precluded an offer to see her safely to her door. "Come along, Ninian," he repeated in his sternest voice.

His cousin bowed to the young woman, saying with un- characteristic gallantry, "I'm vastly pleased to have met you."

With similar formality she executed a curtsy. "Your lord- ship is most kind."

"You'll let us know soon about seeing the water tank?"

"Indeed I shall," she promised, smiling at his zeal.

Gervase laid one hand on his cousin's shoulder and steered him toward the door. Before exiting the room he cast a backward glance at the pretty dancer and saw that she was biting her lower lip as if to stifle a laugh. He could only hope it was Ninian who amused her, and not himself.

In the morning Gervase was able to eat his breakfast in peace. According to his Welsh butler, Lord Swanborough had departed for Hyde Park at an early hour with his cher- ished miniature sailboat tucked under his arm.

"He went alone?" Gervase inquired.

"I made sure that a footman accompanied his lordship," Parry said calmly. "Robert is most popular with him be- cause his brother serves in the Royal Navy. And Robert himself witnessed Lord Nelson's departure from Portsmouth before the Battle of Trafalgar."

"Did he? Well, I only hope he can keep my cousin away from the docks. The duchess lives in fear that he'll run off to sea."

"I hardly think so, your grace, now that Robert has in- formed him about ship's rations. My lord Swanborough is very particular about his food."

Gervase had heard Ninian's criticisms of the Solway House cook, and surmised that he had also aired his griev- ances to the butler. "Only one week more," he said heavily, wondering if he would survive it, "and I shall turn him over to Dr. Butler and the masters of Harrow."

A short time after deserting the breakfast room, Parry returned with the silver letter tray. "This was just delivered for your grace."

The direction inscribed on the square of folded paper was written in a feminine hand, one unfamiliar to Gervase. He tore through the seal and flattened out the single sheet. "My lord Duke," it read, "Mr. Garland of Sadler's Wells will be honored to receive both your grace and Lord Swanborough on Saturday at midday. Your obedient servant, Rosalie de Barante."

"Did the lady bring it herself?" he asked the butler.

"The footman will know. Shall I inquire?"

"Never mind, it makes no difference."

He returned to the study to carry out yesterday's uncompleted tasks. After seating himself at the leather-topped writing desk, where a stack of letters awaited his attention, but he ignored them in order to write Lady Cavender in Wiltshire. His pen moved steadily, producing line upon line of news, until he heard a curious noise from the hall. When it was repeated he was able to identify it as a moan from the housekeeper, warning him that Ninian had returned from his outing in a less than respectable state.

A moment later his ward appeared, and the muddied clothes and tangled black curls confirmed that he'd spent a busy morning.

"What a grand time I had," Ninian declared. "But I desperately need a larger boat than *Victorious*."

"Soon you'll be at school," Gervase pointed out wryly, "where I trust you'll spend your time more productively."

"I suppose I can bear Harrow, if I'm allowed to view the waterworks at Sadler's Wells before I go back." When Gervase handed over the note that had arrived in his absence, he snatched it greedily. "Her writing is pretty," he commented after reading the brief message. "It looks like she trims the point of her quill very fine. What sort of name is de Barante?"

"French."

Ninian's face fell. "D'you really think so?" he asked in dismay. "I like her. I don't want her to be *foreign!*"

"It might not be the case," Gervase said soothingly. "Many dancers take stage names."

"You said all the best ones come from France," Ninian recalled. "Though I suppose she might want the public to believe she's French." He tucked the paper into his pocket and made an unceremonious exit.

Gervase completed his final paragraph and signed his name. Setting the letter aside, he examined the morning's post and found nothing more interesting than some invitations which he would probably refuse, with false regret.

Conscious of his new and unwelcome prominence, he had no desire to remain in town longer than was absolutely necessary. At some future time, perhaps after he'd wed some lady as yet unknown, he might learn to enjoy balls and routs and exhibitions. But for the present, he wanted only to hasten back to the country.

He'd passed his summer of bereavement in peaceful seclusion at his Shropshire manor house, dividing his time between riding his acres and studying newly published works on modern farming methods, free from all social obligations save a twice-weekly visit to his mistress in Shrewsbury. It was autumn now, the season for shooting his well-tended preserves, fishing the streams, and chasing foxes with the Swanborough Abbey huntsmen, all of which pastimes he could enjoy at Haberdine Castle, his ancestral estate in the heart of the shires.

London represented temptation and trouble, besides being a reminder of a time when Gervase had seriously disappointed his fond parents. For most of his life, Solway House had been no more to him than a superior hotel with a well-organized staff and excellent food, and he would not be sorry to leave it.

Politics and society could wait, he told himself. In his opinion, they were the business of older and wiser men.

2

On Saturday morning Rosalie Delphine de Barante woke from a dream of Paris, the city of her birth. Her subconscious mind had carried her back to a past she seldom dwelled upon, to days filled with laughter and frolic. To a distant time when her mother, also a dancer, had been the darling of the French nobility.

Nothing, she thought dully, was a greater contrast to the lost grandeur of the ancien régime than her present abode, an upper floor apartment in Owens Row. The tiny chamber in which she slept and the cramped parlor made her long for her childhood home, a spacious suite of rooms in the Rue du Hazard, conveniently near the Paris Opéra.

Rosalie climbed out of bed, and the floorboards protested as she crossed to the washstand. She was conscious of the persistent pain in her right ankle, always at its worst early in the day. The demanding entrechat admired by Lord Swanborough several evenings ago had compounded an injury that refused to heal. Even so, she continued to perform the step.

After bathing her face with cold water, she put on a silk dressing gown edged with some of the rich Valenciennes lace brought over from France and went into the adjoining room. She'd tried to make it attractive as well as habitable, for her soul cried out for beauty, but her lack of funds hadn't permitted any drastic alteration. The chintz curtains were so faded that their pattern was barely distinguishable, and she regretted her inability to replace them, or refurbish the worn sofa, its seat cushion flattened from overuse. She'd acquired a pretty hearth rug and the chipped vase in which she kept fresh flowers from a street market. A few colored theatrical prints hid the worst of the marks scarring the walls. Upon the shelf of the mantel stood a porcelain figurine modeled after her mother.

While she was extracting a few wilted blooms from the vase, a maidservant arrived with her breakfast.

"Lawks, miss, I was sure you'd be dressed by now," Peg Reilly declared, depositing the tray on a low table between the sofa and the fireplace. "The other ladies went down an hour ago, to do their shopping, I s'pose. It's a scandal how they waste so much of their money on fripperies!"

"They have more of it to waste," Rosalie said. "Actresses are better paid than dancers."

"Don't you be jealous, now," the girl remonstrated as she tied back the curtains. "They've none of 'em performed at an opera house, or any other grand theater. And for all their fine airs and graces, nary a one has ever lived in France!" With quick efficiency she dusted off the tabletops, then went into the next room to make the bed.

Rosalie was glad to have a friend in the house, for the landlady was militantly disapproving of her theatrical lodgers and the performers were themselves disinclined to confide in each other. The fact that she'd come from Paris was a marvel to the downtrodden servant, who never tired of hearing about her adventures and listened avidly to harrowing tales of the Great Terror, her pale eyes round with amazement. Peg was thrilled when she learned that Rosalie had actually seen Napoleon Bonaparte, not once but many times, although she refused to believe that he bore only a slight resemblance to the hideous monster so regularly depicted in print shop windows.

Rosalie's breakfast consisted of a boiled egg, bread and butter, and a small pot of coffee so black and strong that Peg, whom she'd taught to brew it to her taste, wondered how she could drink it. Her profession required that she take good care of herself, for food and rest were essential for preventing the illnesses and fatigue which destroyed many a dancer's career. Thus she lived a Spartan life, eschewing all personal luxuries and many of the pleasures she had known in happier, more prosperous times.

The new day promised to be busier than usual, despite the fact that she had no rehearsal. She intended to visit the theater and remind Mr. Garland of his appointment with Lord Swanborough and the Duke of Solway. She had accepted a rare invitation to a social function, an afternoon party at the home of a former opera dancer now respectably wed to a man of fortune. And most important of all, she was scheduled to perform in the ballet that evening. Out of consideration for her feet—and her aching ankle—she would have to travel to Golden Square and back in a hackney. Coach fares, like food, depleted a significant portion of her income.

When she finished her meal, she went back to her bedroom to begin her toilette. Successfully taming her golden brown curls, which had a tendency to escape pins and combs, she arranged them in a simple knot at the back of her head and coaxed the short, wispy strands into decorating her temples and forehead. She opened the door of the wardrobe, wincing at the loud complaint from the rusty hinges, and looked over her dresses, seeking one that would be appropriate for her various activities. Her choice, a jade cambric gown with a pink bodice and trimmings, made her changeable eyes appear more green than blue. She completed her ensemble with a simple straw bonnet designed and trimmed by a fellow emigrée, her reticule, and a pair of kid gloves which had seen better days.

Leaving her lodging house, she followed the footpath beside the New River. The weather was bright and clear, not uncommon for late September, and her walk to the theater was pleasant. She rather looked forward to another meeting with the duke and his ward. Although she seldom encountered aristocrats, she was far from being discomfitted by them. In her infancy she'd sat upon the silken lap of Marie Antoinette, the martyred Queen of France. And her mother's patron, the exquisite Duchesse de Polignac, had doted upon her, providing such tokens of affection as silver apostle spoons and a coral teething ring.

When she approached the grounds of Sadler's Wells she heard the cries of children as some or all of the manager's eight offspring played in front of their house. The prolific Mrs. Dibdin occupied a prominent place in the company as both leading lady and premier songstress, and she appeared on the boards as regularly as her frequent confinements permitted. Her antipathy toward the other female players was rooted in bitter jealousy. Each season saw the departure of the very best singers, for none could dare to outshine the lady and expect to remain in her fond husband's employ.

A man was seated upon a low bench near the stage door, filling the bowl of a clay pipe with tobacco. "Good day, Wheeler," Rosalie greeted him.

"A fine one it is, Miss Rose, every bit as sunny as midsummer."

"Has Mr. Garland arrived?"

Mr. Wheeler nodded. "He's inside with the stagehands—they'll soon be pulling up the floor."

When he questioned her presence, she explained, "Some acquaintances of mine are coming to examine the waterworks."

The doorman gave her a sour look. "Shall I give them my opinion of our manager's famous innovation? You won't remember, 'twas before your time, but Sadler's Wells used to be renowned for clever pantos and pretty ballets and daring rope walkers. Nowadays it's all aquatic spectacles, and if not for them the theater would likely fail."

"People also come to see Mr. Grimaldi," she pointed out.

"Aye," he agreed. "Clown Joey and that tank of putrid water—that's why Mr. Hughes gets rich, and Mr. Dibdin and his wife can give their fine dinners and parties. Not that they're any worse than their partner Mr. Barfoot, who chases after all you ladies." Mr. Wheeler frowned and shook his gray head. "This theater brings in a full two hundred pounds a night when all the seats are taken, yet those fine gentlemen pay their golden goose of a clown a mere twelve pounds a week."

"Oh?" Rosalie earned less than half that amount and felt she was lucky to get it.

"Don't never say 'twas I who told you. And bless him, he's worth far more than that to the managers, for he's as hardworking as he is popular." Glancing in the direction of the turnpike road to London, Mr. Wheeler said, "Here's a carriage now—must be your friends coming." The handsome coach was drawn by four fine horses, and both the man holding the reins and the servant perched beside him wore gold-braided livery. "Fine company you're keeping these days," he commented, not unkindly.

Lord Swanborough, the first to emerge, rushed toward Rosalie.

The duke followed at a more sedate pace, and greeted her by saying, "We didn't expect to find you on the premises, Mademoiselle de Barante."

"Have you a rehearsal?" the earl demanded. "Will I be able to watch it?"

"No rehearsal today, my lord," she answered. "I've come to introduce you to Mr. Garland, if you will but follow me into the theatre."

She led both visitors to the auditorium. The lamplighters were replacing the old candles of the lowered chandeliers with new ones, and portly Mr. Wren busied himself with replenishing the stock of food and drink he would sell to the playgoers that night. On the stage, workers had already begun raising the platform with ropes and pulleys, revealing the tank of water beneath it.

Lord Swanborough couldn't wait for Mr. Garland to be presented, but began a conversation as readily as though they were lifelong acquaintances. The gentleman listened patiently as the young peer bombarded him with eager questions. "Come along with me, my lord," he said in his friendly way, "and I'll show you how the pumps work, and many other wonders."

"Don't you wish to go also?" Rosalie asked when the duke remained by her side.

"Not in the least," he replied bluntly.

"Lord Swanborough was talking so fast that I never had

an opportunity to make Mr. Garland known to your grace,"
she said sorrowfully.

He consoled her by replying, "It's just as well, for I've
no desire to compete with Ninian for his attention." Smiling
down at her, he added, "I'm sorry you felt it necessary to
come. You must have other more important things to occupy you today."

"I'm entirely free until this afternoon," she assured him.
His impeccable manners and elegant attire were as impressive as his height and his good looks, and his physique was
sufficiently muscled and athletic to command the respect of
a dancer. But he seemed very much out of place in the
murky, empty theater, prompting her to say, "I believe your
grace will be most comfortable in Mr. Barfoot's box while
you wait for his lordship. It overlooks the stage and is high
enough that you can watch the tank fill."

He accompanied her to the box lobby. "Unlike my
cousin, I care very little for the mysteries of the water
tank," he said, coming to a halt, "and on a day so fine I prefer to be outdoors. I've always heard about the tea gardens
at Islington but can't recall ever visiting them. May I take
you there?"

The offer was flattering and tempting, yet she didn't feel
she ought to accept. "Lord Swanborough won't know
where to find you," she pointed out.

Gervase didn't regard this as an impediment. "I'll leave
word with the doorkeeper, and he can tell Ninian where
we've gone."

Without much difficulty he managed to overcome her reluctance, which he considered unusual in a dancing girl—
his limited experience had taught him that the majority of
her kind were all too eager to consort with noblemen. Recalling her wariness at their first meeting, he hoped she
wasn't nervous of him. But as they walked together to the
gardens, she gave him no real reason to suppose that she
was.

His initial impression of her beauty survived the merci-
less glare of the sun. Her long-lashed eyes were greenish
blue, and the fringe of curls hanging over her brow was
light brown. She was as tiny as she was lovely—her head

didn't even reach his shoulder—with a slender waist and perfect posture. He also noted that her attire was neither new nor fashionable, proof that she hadn't yet made her fortune on the stage.

As soon as they reached the gates of Islington Spa, he paid the requisite entrance fee. When he commented on the absence of pleasure-seekers, his companion said knowingly, "Tomorrow there will be a crowd. On Sundays it is very busy and gay."

"Do you come often?" he asked, taking her down a serpentine pathway bordered by late-blooming flowers.

"Less often than I'd like," Rosalie replied. "*Il faut de l'argent*—it is necessary to have money, and only when I'm reasonably plump in the pocket can I afford to come here. If I'm in the mood for a ramble, I generally go to Sadler's Wells Field, for that costs nothing."

Here was another indication that she was poorly recompensed for her labors. "How long have you danced at Sadler's Wells?" he asked.

"This season is my sixth," she responded. "I hadn't planned to return but changed my mind because the ballet master desperately needed me to fill out his corps. Last year Miss Gayton left to marry a clergyman, and now we have a problem with poor Miss Bates, one of the small-part dancers." Her voice lowered to a confidential murmur. "Mr. Barfoot, who owns a share of the theater, *preys* upon the females in the company. He has a child by Miss Bates, whose place I must fill whenever his wife attends a performance. As long as she continues living under Mr. Barfoot's protection, Mr. Dibdin can't dismiss her, which Mrs. Barfoot is forever demanding that he do. It's an awkward situation."

"I can see how it would be," Gervase said sympathetically.

The surrounding landscape was thickly wooded with elm, laburnum, and shrubbery and rendered even more picturesque by classical urns and pedestals. At a bend in the gravel walk they came upon the spring of mineral water that had given birth to the spa, and he suggested that they make use of a strategically placed stone bench.

He could tell by the way she perched beside him, as though she might bound up again at any moment, that inertia was an unfamiliar state. Her rapid speech and dancing eyes made up for the fact that her body was at rest, and her answers to his questions were punctuated with hand gestures, a Gallic habit which he considered quite charming.

"I gather you've been a performer for quite some time," he said.

"All of my life," she responded matter-of-factly. "I began as an opera dancer in Paris—I was born there."

"You haven't much of an accent."

"I once did," she said with a laugh. "My mother was a *soloiste* with the ballet of the Paris Opéra, and when I was still a very young child I danced there, too, in the great patriotic spectacles that were produced in the aftermath of the Revolution. I portrayed pages and Cupids and cherubs until I was old enough for the corps. During the Peace of Amiens we came to London. Papa was an Englishman, a violinist and composer, and he'd heard that the theaters here were eager to acquire foreign artists—he regarded himself as such after twenty years in France. He joined the orchestra of the King's Theatre, but by that time Maman had stopped performing. Mr. d'Egville, the ballet master, hired me in her stead, but as a coryphée rather than a principal dancer. I was thirteen."

She fell silent and gazed down at her feet, the points of which poked out from beneath her skirts. Gervase noted that they angled outward; having received instruction in the rudiments of dance for purely social purposes, he recognized the first position.

"At so young an age most girls are in the schoolroom," he commented. "Did you mind working so hard?"

"I was thankful that I was able, especially when Papa became ill and had to resign his position. After he died I was my mother's sole support. Her health also declined and I lost her in 1805, a year of many trials. Mr. d'Egville left the opera house—the mangers, and especially the critics, disapproved of his using the children from his dancing academy in his ballets. He found employment at Sadler's Wells and encouraged me to join him, in the belief that Mr. Dibdin's theater would be safer and more suitable for a girl still in her teens and alone in the world. But I haven't been as happy here as I was there and I mean to go back, if I can."

Gazing at her profile, Gervase said, "It is no less dangerous now than it used to be."

"That makes no difference," she told him firmly. "My career as a dancer may last only a decade more, if as long, and I'd prefer to spend it with the best ballet company in London. And the pay at the King's Theatre is better than at the Wells. I'm twenty-one years old now, and have no interest in the gentlemen who frequent Fops' Alley. Entanglements of that sort are not for me."

It was a great pity, he thought, that a girl so young and lovely should be concerned about sordid matters like making money and eluding backstage gallants. He deemed her integrity all the more remarkable because it contributed to her poverty. She could live far more comfortably as the pampered plaything of a male admirer, for she was enticing enough to have her share of offers. When he remembered how he'd found her hiding in a dark room late at night, practicing her steps as if her life had depended upon it, he was glad he'd invited her to come to the spa gardens for a brief respite from work and worry.

"I hope you will excuse my making a familiar remark on such short acquaintance, Mademoiselle de Barante, but I imagine that the life you lead can be a lonely one."

She bowed her head in acknowledgement, and the brim of her straw bonnet hid her expression when she replied, "I can't deny it. I do have some friends—the Grimaldis are very kind to me, and Mr. d'Egville—but none of the dancers in the company are close. There's too much jealousy in our ranks."

They soon abandoned the bench and Lord Swanborough found them wandering through a shady arbor.

After describing the many wonders Mr. Garland had shown him, he suggested that they order some tea. "I'm thirsty as the devil."

"It's no wonder, if you chattered to your guide as ceaselessly as you've been doing for the past few minutes. Mademoiselle de Barante, will you join us?"

"I'm not sure I can, your grace. What is the time?"

Extracting his gold watch from the pocket of his silk waistcoat, he answered, "Half past one."

"I do have that engagement in town," she admitted, "though it's the casual sort of party where people drift in and out. I don't suppose the hostess will feel slighted by my tardiness."

Ninian, who had preceded them along the path, suddenly spun around to say, "Gervase and I will take you in the carriage."

"*Non, non*," she protested, her cheeks pink. "Your lordship is most kind, but it isn't necessary."

"You *can't* refuse."

"I agree," Gervase said, and her troubled eyes met his. "If not for you, my cousin wouldn't have seen the waterworks. You must let him repay his debt and reciprocate your generosity by providing you with transportation. Where does your friend reside?"

"In Golden Square. But—"

"It's settled," he interrupted gently. "Ninian is determined to befriend you, and I'm so very reluctant to trample his first charitable impulse that I really must insist upon your accepting his offer."

Her grateful smile was a sunbeam lighting up her lovely face, and Gervase regretted that Ninian was its recipient.

Of the dozen persons scattered about the sunny drawing room, Rosalie was acquainted with no more than half, yet she felt quite at ease among them. Hearing the language of her native country, she could easily imagine herself at an artistic salon, an institution which had survived the turmoil of the Revolution, the Reign of Terror, and the many changes imposed on France by the Directory and the Consulate. Last night she had visited Paris in her dreams, and now she fancied she was there again.

"How glad I am that you are here at last, petite," Rosalie's hostess said warmly.

At the height of her fame, Mademoiselle Parisot had been the toast and the scandal of London, adored by the public and condemned by the clergy for wearing costumes that revealed more of her charms than they concealed. Since her marriage to the wealthy Mr. Hughes she had kept herself covered in public, but she smiled no less constantly than she'd done from the stage of the King's Theatre.

"James d'Egville has been asking about you for the past hour. See how eagerly he comes to greet you!" Mrs. Hughes indicated a swarthy, well-dressed gentleman moving toward them. He had wavy dark hair and long side-whiskers, and the pronounced arch of his eyebrows gave him a look of perpetual surprise. "I promised you she would be here, *mon cher*," the former dancer told him triumphantly.

Rosalie held out her hand to James d'Egville. "How have you been, sir?"

"What's more important," he said gruffly, "is how you are going on."

"*Très bien, merci.*" Her right ankle throbbed in contradiction, but she knew better than to mention her aches and pains to any former or prospective employer.

"*Pauvre petite,*" her hostess sighed, placing one hand on her famed bosom. "I want to weep, knowing that you dance for the *canaille* who visit the Sadler's Wells. Delphine would never have permitted it."

"You are forgetting, Parisot, that I used to be ballet master of the Wells," d'Egville interjected, "although I share your belief that our Rosalie is destined for better things. What are your plans, my dear? Will you spend the winter season at Astley's theater in Wellclose Square?"

Rosalie shook her head. "I mean to try my luck at the new playhouse in Tottenham Street."

"But why not at the opera house?" Mrs. Hughes clutched the gentleman's arm. "Please, you must convince Signor Rossi to have her in his company."

James d'Egville studied Rosalie, his brows moving higher still. "Is that your wish?"

"There can be no question!" Mrs. Hughes cried. "You must meet the signor, petite—I will introduce you *maintenant*. He does not make ballets as lovely as *mon cher* James, and I hear complaints that he favors the Italian dancers, but you will not mind that. At least you will again perform before audiences of true taste and style, and for an artiste anything else is *insupportable*! Come with me."

With a backward glance at d'Egville, Rosalie allowed herself to be borne to the other side of the room. Three persons stood before the window, a gentleman of middle age flanked by a vivacious brunette and a stocky young man whose vacant expression became animated the moment he spied Rosalie.

He darted forward to take both her hands in his own and went down on one knee, raising them to his lips in homage. "*Ma belle*, I dare not hope you remember me, but I have not forgotten my first partner. How many years it has been!"

"More than I care to admit," she declared, smiling down at him. "You haven't changed, Armand Vestris. In our student days you were as famous for your *galanterie* as for your *grands jetés*!" She noted the jealous sparks flying from the brunette's black eyes, further proof that the Frenchman still had the habit of choosing his partner of the season for his mistress.

When Armand rose, he faced the frowning lady and said softly, "Fortunata, you must not be alarmed. She was never my sweetheart, she had not enough courage to go walking with me when I begged and pleaded. For her, it was always work, work, work. *Chère* Rosalie, I present Signorina Angiolini, the *première danseuse* of the opera ballet." Turning to the other gentleman, he explained, "I knew Mademoiselle de Barante in Paris, Signor Rossi. She was a pupil of *mon père*, and of Dauberval."

The ballet master inclined his head. "The name is familiar."

"*Bien sûr*, you will have known her mother, Delphine de Barante."

"*Sí, sí*," the Italian replied, examining Rosalie more closely and with heightened interest. "You are the dancer d'Egville has mentioned to me so often, a coryphée of great promise."

But the ballet master did not engage her in conversation. Addressing his countrywomen in their own tongue, he escorted her to a nearby sofa, leaving Rosalie and Armand together.

"All winter and spring, and last year *aussi*, Fortunata and I have danced together at the opera house," he told her. "Did you not see us?"

"I'm afraid a ticket is beyond my means," she answered candidly, "though I sometimes read about your performances in the newspapers." The critics had been unkind to the Frenchman at first, but he'd won them over with the athletic power of his dancing and his ability to spin on one foot like a top.

"When Parisot told me your parents had died, I was so sad for you."

"I've been without Maman for five years now."

"Last season, a French gentleman came backstage to ask me if I'd been acquainted with La Belle Delphine. He had followed her career in Paris, I think, and was *très désolé* when he spoke of her. I cannot recall his name. Remercier? *Non*, it was something else." After a pause, he shrugged. "It matters not. So tell me, *ma belle*, why do you not dance at the opera house?"

"I left when d'Egville moved to Sadler's Wells and was never invited to return. I hope he'll recommend me to Rossi, should there be a vacancy in the company next season. And Oscar Byrne would probably vouch for my ability, if I asked him."

"I, too, will have a word with the signor," Armand promised her. "And you may also rely upon Deshayes."

"Didn't his wife retire from the company?" Armand confirmed this with a nod, and she begged him to tell her all the gossip. "I've been buried in Islington and hear so little news from the King's Theatre. Is it true that Monsieur Boisgerard opened an academy and is training young opera dancers?"

"He did, but *les enfants terribles* were banished from the stage not long after they first appeared. The English do not like to see the little ones kept awake so late at night!"

"Nothing has changed, then, for the public used to object when d'Egville introduced his own students into the corps."

Rosalie sighed. "It is strange to me, for no one complained when I appeared in ballets as a child."

"In Paris," said Armand loftily, "there is altogether more appreciation for true art. At the King's Theatre the audience talks through the opera, they hiss when they dislike a character, and they interrupt with their clapping at the most inappropriate times—*ils sont bêtes sauvages!*"

Laughing, Rosalie told him, "You would despise the Sadler's Wells audiences far more, I fear. And the salary."

"Come back to my theater, *chérie*, and you will soon be rich enough to buy silk gowns, and jewels to match your eyes," Armand said extravagantly. "Parisot made over twelve thousand pounds during her career, not all of it from her lovers. The managers would pay you well, at least three hundred in your first year."

"As a coryphée?"

"*Mais non*, you will be a *soloiste!*"

The vision conjured by his eager words was most appealing. The Opera season lasted from late December to early August, not quite eight months, and three hundred pounds was triple what Rosalie earned for the nearly the same period at Sadler's Wells. To resume her interrupted career as an opera dancer was her dearest dream. If it ever came true, she would be able to afford a pleasant and comfortable lodging, preferably within an easy walking distance of the theater. No more hackney coaches, she thought exultantly.

Her spirits soared as high as her hopes, and while she circulated among her former colleagues she prayed that she would soon be able to rejoin them on the stage of the King's Theatre in the Haymarket. Bearing in mind that she was supposed to perform in a matter of hours, she watched the clock, and when it was time to return to Islington she sought out her hostess to make her excuses.

"Departing so soon!" Mrs. Hughes said in dismay after Rosalie expressed her heartfelt thanks for a delightful afternoon.

"I really mustn't linger, madame, for I'm dancing this evening."

"Ah, then I won't try to keep you. But wait, there is

something I want you to see—can you guess what? Come with me to my boudoir."

As Rosalie followed her friend up the staircase to a small room furnished with a dressing table draped in pink silk and several French rococo pieces. A large oil painting in a gilt wood frame hung upon one wall. It depicted a slim female in Gypsy costume, her arm forming a graceful arc as she held a tambourine decorated with crimson ribbons high above her head. The scene, a Paris street, was also familiar to Rosalie.

"I thought you would like to look at it again," Mrs. Hughes said quietly.

"*Oui*," Rosalie whispered, focused on her mother's laughing face. "It was a great relief to me that you wanted to own it. So many of her pictures went to collectors."

"She didn't sell them all?"

"We kept the other Fragonard, and most of the portraits Monsieur Greuze painted of me when I was a child. Maman was quite sentimental about those, and they weren't especially valuable."

"You must never let them go, or the other things Delphine left to you. Any exquisite object—a painting or a porcelain ornament, or even a tiny scrap of lace—can be a source of joy."

"I know."

"And never forget, you have the power to make others happy by performing. Remember how you used to feel hearing your papa play his violin, or watching Delphine dance? They were so talented. And so proud of you, as are all of us who knew their hopes for your success. *Chère* Rosalie, do not make the mistake of wasting such a valuable legacy."

"I won't," she promised. Looking at the colorful canvas one last time, she added, "I can't."

3

Sends Nature forth the daughter of the skies
To dance on earth, and charm all human eyes.
                                        —WILLIAM COWPER

Despite his unwillingness to dance and his preference for
the sober colors of protracted mourning, the Duke of Solway received cards of invitation from all of London's
prominent hostesses. He accepted only a fraction of them,
for he derived no pleasure from standing about in overheated ballrooms, feigning interest in the young ladies trying so desperately to attract his notice.

But his peace of mind was no longer disrupted by his
ward, whom he had delivered to Harrow. He was now free
to devote himself to his favorite solitary pursuits—reading
the papers and writing letters to his steward at Haberdine
and to his mother in Shropshire. When the weather permitted, he drove in the park, and if he had no social commitments he visited one of his clubs or dined with his closest
friend, the Marquis of Elston.

Lord Swanborough had been at school for less than a
week when Gervase received a scrawled note of despair.
Harrow was a prison, the masters were brutes, and he'd
been flogged twice without cause. Knowing Ninian's talent
for provocation, his guardian was inclined to doubt this, but
he resolved to pay a Sunday visit to Harrow-on-the-Hill.

He wrote to inform Ninian of his intent and received a
brief missive in response, demanding that he bring Mademoiselle de Barante.

His ward's admiration of the dancer perplexed Gervase
as much as it frustrated him. He didn't know where she

lived, or whether she might be willing to call upon a rude schoolboy she'd met only twice in her life. But the probability that a disappointed Ninian could create an unpleasant scene was reason enough to find out if she had any objections to the scheme, and to overcome them if necessary.

After penning a note of regret to Lord Elston, with whom he had made a tentative pact to attend a ball, he dispatched a footman to Sadler's Wells to hire a stage box. Sitting through a ballet performance, he decided, would be less tiresome than to an evening of insipid small talk with those damsels who had failed to snare a husband the previous spring.

He had just finished dressing for the theater when Parry announced Lord Elston's arrival. "Tell Timothy to bring the carriage around in ten minutes," he instructed the butler before going downstairs to face his friend's criticism for the abrupt change of plan.

The blond gentleman waiting in the green salon had already supplied himself with a glass of port. "I'm sure your new fellow fills his position admirably," he said, "but I do miss old Richards."

Taking up the decanter, Gervase replied, "My mother's need is greater than mine, and I had no wish to rob her of a faithful retainer. Richards trained Parry, so the house runs as smoothly as it ever did. I've no intention of entertaining anyone but you."

"Yet you spurn my company with no explanation. Have you an assignation with some fair creature?"

"I'm going to Sadler's Wells."

This announcement startled the marquis out of his customary composure. After a restorative sip, he said, "You must be joking."

"Not at all. This is a favor to Ninian, who has become attached to one of the ballet dancers."

"He's rather young to begin his career as a rake," Damon Lovell commented. "And when one considers the sterling example of conduct set by his guardian, the circumstance is even more incomprehensible. Your interest in carousing was singularly short-lived, as I recall."

"My appetite for wine, women, and so forth certainly never matched yours," Gervase said lightly.

"Oh? i wonder. it seems to me that your restraint arises more from consideration for your family's feelings than from disinclination. Although a disappointment in love could also be responsible for your monkish existence."

"A certain fair female in Shrewsbury could refute that characterization of me."

"How intriguing. Has someone finally eclipsed Georgiana in your affections?" Observing the duke's frown, Damon said, "We needn't talk about her if you'd rather not, though I admit I'm curious to know what caused the rift."

"I suppose you deserve to know," Gervase replied. "You are her friend. You even introduced us."

"Did I? Do forgive me, for I meant no harm to either of you." Wagging his golden head, the marquis commented, "That affair was a nasty business from the beginning."

"And Georgiana's final affront was decidedly the worst," Gervase volunteered. "After concealing my guilty pleasures from my parents for a considerable period, I bravely informed them of my desire to marry the twice-widowed Lady Titus, whose second husband died after dueling with one of her former lovers. Although they accepted the news stoically, I know it broke their hearts."

"You never proposed to her," Damon said gravely.

"Fate conspired against me on the very night I intended to make my offer. We'd arranged to meet at a party, but I was detained and arrived much later than I expected. Whereupon I learned that my beloved had departed in the company of another. I went to her house in Clifford Street straightaway, but the maid refused to let me in. She did, however, confirm my worst suspicions. My response to an act of infidelity so flagrant that it sickened me was to return to Solway House and make myself profoundly drunk. As it happened well over a year ago, I'm fairly certain my recovery is complete."

"Evidently, if you keep a mistress in Shrewsbury and are chasing after this creature at Sadler's Wells," said his friend. "I always believed that you had more in common with your Stuart ancestors than you let on. Charles the Second was notorious for his amours with play actresses."

"I told you, Mademoiselle de Barante is Ninian's friend." With a sly smile, Gervase added, "You could come with me and see her for yourself. Or is mixing with the common herd too far beneath your lordship's dignity?"

"Not if the dancers are pretty enough," Damon replied, draining his glass.

Spectators, laughing and chattering as they waited for the performance to begin, crammed the pit and gallery of the playhouse. One of the seats in Mr. Grimaldi's box, which commanded an excellent view of both stage and audience, was occupied when the two noblemen sought their places. The stranger's fashionable but flashy attire and the cheerful, hearty way he welcomed their arrival told Gervase that he was a scion of the prosperous middle class. His sandy hair was curled and pomaded in the newest and most fashionable style. His waistcoat was a riot of color, a number of fobs and seals dangled from his watch chain, and his plump hands were weighed down by heavy gold rings.

"Thought I would be sitting here all alone," he greeted the gentlemen. "Name's Benjamin Beckmann. How d'ye do?"

"Quite well, thank you," Gervase responded. Damon's aloof silence and his rigid features expressed his distaste at sharing the box with a social inferior. "I'm Marchant, and this is Lovell," he said, using their family names rather than their titles to preserve anonymity.

"Pleased to make your acquaintance." Mr. Beckmann embarked upon a long commentary in which he praised the manager of Sadler's Wells for the introduction of water dramas and stated his admiration of Clown Grimaldi. "And the dancing—well, my friends, wait till you see those pretty girls in their little short skirts." Angling his florid face toward Gervase, he added, "I've got my eye on one of 'em, I confess."

From his cheerful admission that he'd come into money upon his father's death, Gervase inferred that he was dissipating it on expensive diversions. Knowing all too well that

Damon was capable of snubbing the vulgar, voluble young man, he was relieved when the curtain began to rise.

The audience murmured approval of the setting: a leafy arbor with a real waterfall in the background. Seated beneath the dome of a small white temple was a female in classical attire, and as she raised one arm the orchestra began to play.

A trio of performers wearing pastel gowns floated out of the wings, followed by a pair of men in tunics and flesh-colored tights who sported about in a manner more athletic than graceful. A tiny boy costumed as a cherub appeared and joined the lady on the dais. The last dancer to join the revels was Rosalie de Barante, her arms filled with pink and white roses which she presented to the lady as an offering. Her curling hair was unbound and she wore a coronet of blossoms; her draperies were pale green, embroidered all over with leaves and flowers.

As she danced a *pas de trois* with the two men, Mr. Beckmann elbowed Gervase. "That's Mamselle de Barante, the very one who's taken my fancy. A real dasher, ain't she?"

Damon, seated on his other side, spoke for the first time. "It's Botticelli's 'La Primavera' brought to life. Venus, Cupid, the three Graces, Mercury, Zephyr, and Flora. Which is young Swanborough's inamorata?"

"Flora," Gervase whispered.

He suspected that their slight acquaintance had prejudiced him in her favor, but in his opinion her performance was superior. The beauty and fluidity of her body in motion was impressive, and she seemed to live and breathe the music. While dancing she looked so joyful, so free—altogether a different being from the earthbound girl who had candidly admitted her troubles to him at their last meeting.

When the performers froze in a final tableau, Mr. Beckmann clapped loudly. Grinning, he said, "Don't mind telling you, Marchant, I'm smitten. Look at that figure, those legs!"

The young man's raptures were wearing thin with Gervase. Damon interrupted them by pronouncing, "A charming pastoral, almost worthy of an opera ballet. A pity that the audience appreciates the attributes of the dancers more than the dance itself."

As they waited for the pantomime to begin, Gervase listened absently to Mr. Beckmann's discourse, wondering all the while whether it was a good time to seek out Rosalie de Barante and where he might find her. He rose and excused himself, carefully avoiding his friend's accusing blue eyes.

By now he was familiar enough with the theater to make his way from the box lobby to the backstage corridor. A hopeful visit to the room in which he'd first seen the dancer was disappointed, and he continued the search. His persistence was rewarded by a timely encounter with the stage doorkeeper.

"Hullo, sir," the man said, recognizing him. "Come to see the panto?"

"Actually, I need to speak with Mademoiselle de Barante. Could you help me locate her?"

"Miss Rose?" Leaning forward, Mr. Wheeler said in a conspiratorial hiss, "She wanted to practice, so I let her into the scene painting room—though Mr. Dibdin would sack me if he ever knew it. Wait here and I'll fetch her for you."

A few minutes later Rosalie joined him. Her wobbling steps caused the silk flowers sewn to her costume to quiver and prompted Gervase to ask if she had sustained an injury.

Disregarding his concerned query, she said softy, "You shouldn't be here. Mr. Dibdin doesn't permit us to receive visitors backstage. We aren't even supposed to speak with each other during the performance."

"Then don't say another word," he told her, keeping his voice low, "because you can answer me with a nod or a shake of the head. My ward—and I—would be very much obliged if you'd consent to visit Harrow School on Sunday. Ninian insists that you accompany me when I go to see him. Can you, or is it too great an imposition?"

A faint laugh escaped her rouged lips. "Your grace makes it difficult to reply, pelting me with so many questions at once. Yes," she said with a brisk nod, "I'll visit him. And no, you aren't imposing."

Gervase smiled his relief. "I'm glad."

"I can't imagine why Lord Swanborough should ask for me. I thought he cared only for the waterworks."

"I confess I'm a bit surprised myself," he admitted. "In general he dislikes strangers."

"You don't object to my going?" she asked curiously.

"Why should I?"

"Because—well, because I am a stage performer, and not at all the sort of female his lordship's family would wish him to befriend."

"Do you know," he said, his sober expression belied by the light in his gray eyes, "it never even occurred to me that you might be a bad influence. In truth, it's far more likely that Ninian will corrupt you."

Again she laughed. "I'll be on my guard against it." After glancing over her shoulder, she said nervously, "Mr. Dibdin sees us—I cannot stay, else he'll fine me for talking." She turned to go, then faced him again, her head cocked sideways. "At what time on Sunday must I be ready?"

"I'll come at noon. Where should we meet?"

"At my lodging in Owens Row," she whispered. "The fifth house down."

When Gervase returned to his seat the pantomime, *Bang Up, or Harlequin Prime,* was in progress. He answered Damon's curious look with an inscrutable smile, and turned his attention to the stage. Although he and his friend were members of the Four-in-Hand driving club, neither of them took umbrage when the piece satirized the coaching mania. Mr. Beckmann laughed the loudest, slapping his knee at Mr. Grimaldi's antics.

The clown wore a skullcap to simulate baldness, and his motley consisted of a short tunic, its brightly colored dots contrasting with the striped shirt underneath, thigh-length spotted trousers, and white breeches tied at the knee with ribbons. His winking, rolling eyes served him well, and he could provoke laughter merely by screwing up his whitened face.

The audience cheered when he stepped forward to sing "Tippety-witchet," a popular ditty Mr. Dibdin had composed for him.

> This very morning handy,
> My malady was such,
> I in my tea took brandy
> And took a drop too much!

After a few drunken hiccups, he warbled the next verse.

> Now I'm quite drowsy growing,
> Because this very morn,
> I rose while cock was crowing,
> Excuse me if I yawn.

Drawing a snuffbox from his pocket, he held it up.

> But stop, I mustn't chatter hard,
> My head aches if you please,
> One pinch of Irish blackguard,
> I'll take to give me ease.

He mimed taking snuff, inhaled deeply, and immediately let out an explosive sneeze. After two more verses he bowed to the appreciative crowd and exited the stage.

Gervase, having succeeded in his errand, was prepared to depart, but Damon persuaded him that they ought to stay for the aqua drama. "After all," he said, "it's the form of entertainment Sadler's Wells is so famous for."

The first scene featured a revolving model of the planetary system, and a transformation in which the man in the moon became the Harlequin of the piece. The clown's return inspired boisterous applause, and he leaped and pranced across the stage, playing his usual pranks on the other members of the company. In a departure from his characteristic laziness, he sought employment with an astrologer.

"Oh," Grimaldi cried to his public after the wise man had offered to cast his horoscope, "he's going to tell my fortune!"

"Thou wert born under the planet Mercury," the ancient gentleman intoned, "and therefore by disposition thou'rt a *thief*!"

"Who d'you call thief?" Grimaldi demanded, his eyes bulging with outrage.

"Thou wert not in the sign of Taurus born, nor Leo, Virgo, or Libra."

"Go to the *library*?" the Clown repeated, to the great amusement of the crowd.

"Pisces, Aquarius, Capricorn disown thee, also Scorpio and Sagittarius."

"Sausages? Oh, I likes to eat *them*!"

Mr. Beckmann let out an explosive guffaw, and Lord Elston's face was softened by an amused smile.

The troop of dancers, Rosalie de Barante among them, made a brief appearance while the wooden platform of the stage was raised behind the curtain for the final spectacle: an illuminated temple floating upon the water.

"You'd best warn young Ninian that he has a rival," Damon advised Gervase when they left the theater.

"Are you referring to that overdressed mushroom?" he asked.

"I'd call him a blustering bag of wind but won't dispute your description, for it is similarly appropriate. After your mysterious disappearance, he entertained me with a recital of his plans for the little dancing girl. He intends to have her for his mistress."

"He's got no chance of winning her favors, of that I'm certain."

"Your confidence raises certain questions about your earlier claims of indifference," Damon drawled. "Did you really come to Sadler's Wells on young Swanborough's behalf, or your own?"

Annoyed by his friend's damning assumption, Gervase made no reply.

"What does Napoleon look like?" Lord Swanborough asked, lifting a forkful of meat pie to his mouth. "Did you know him well?"

"The first time I saw him, I was a little girl and he was a young general," Rosalie answered.

Immediately after their arrival, his lordship had lured his visitors to the King's Head, a tavern in the High Street. So far all Rosalie had seen of Harrow was the exterior of its buildings, and she doubted she would see much more. The earl had made it quite plain that he abhorred his school.

"Where did you meet him?" he prompted her.

"In my godmother's home. She owned and managed a popular theater—all of literary and artistic Paris flocked to her rooms above the Café de Chartres. Famous politicians frequented her salon as well: Danton, Robespierre, Marat. Bonaparte and his friend Barras were great admirers of the tragic actor Talma, as famous in France as Mr. Kemble is here, and knew they could meet him at Madame Montansier's. In those days the Emperor was a thin, pale, awkward man in a uniform. Since then he has filled out, but when I last saw him he still had the same dark hair and very black eyes."

Ninian lifted his head. "When was that?"

"In 1801, the year before I came to England. I was dancing at the Paris Opera that season, and occasionally he and his wife attended the performances." Rosalie accepted the cream pitcher from the duke and followed his example by pouring a dollop over her trifle.

"Tell me about Napoleon's wife."

"Ninian, you really must give Mademoiselle de Barante an opportunity to eat her dessert."

Rosalie assured the duke that she didn't mind his lordship's questions. "Josephine was no more beautiful than her husband was handsome, for she had the sallow complexion of a Creole, and bad teeth. But she always wore such perfect gowns. All the women of Paris tried to dress as elegantly as she, but few succeeded."

"Will you return to France someday?"

Rosalie considered the earl's question briefly, then shrugged. "I can't say. But I've no relations in Paris nor any friends—so many of the dancers from the Opera are also living in England now. I suppose I'd go home if there were a Restoration, although that doesn't seem at all likely."

Ninian reached across the table for a plate of cakes. "Cousin Edgar is fighting in the Peninsula, and he thinks Boney will be routed soon."

"My brother serves on Lord Wellington's staff," Gervase explained.

"How lucky you are to have family," she said.

"Am I?" He directed a pained glance at his ward.

"I always longed for brothers and sisters and cousins. Except for Armand Vestris and the other students at our dancing academy, I knew no one close to my own age, and we were too busy working to have much time for play."

"What did you do for fun?" Ninian inquired.

"We thought dancing was fun. When we had the time, and if the day was fine enough, we strolled in the Jardin des Tuileries. Sometimes in the evening we made up a party and went to the Tivoli Gardens—rather like your Vauxhall. Monsieur Greuze, the painter, was a friend of mine, practically a grandfather to me. I used to accompany him on his promenade from his apartments in the Louvre to the Palais Royale. I would put on my very best dress, and he wore his black coat trimmed with gold lace. We always stopped at Café Frascati for ices, and afterward he'd let me choose whatever I wanted from the bookstalls."

"I *hate* to read," her inquisitor said venomously.

"That," Gervase interjected, "explains your lamentable lack of progress in Latin and Greek."

"What are your favorite books, mademoiselle?"

Blushing, she fidgeted with the cream pitcher and butter plate, realigning them and then changing them back to their original positions. "Your guardian might prefer that I not tell you."

"Nasty books?"

"Well, French ones," she admitted, not quite daring to meet the duke's amused gaze. "Novels and poetry." Desperate to change the subject, she began to question Lord Swanborough about his favorite pursuits.

"I like rowing my boat on the lake and sailing my miniature ship, *Victorious*. In summer I bathe in the pond near Haberdine, and in winter we go skating, if the surface freezes hard enough."

"What is Haberdine?"

"Ger's castle in Northamptonshire. I've got a house, too," Ninian informed her proudly. "It's called Swanborough Abbey. He administers the estate and manages my foxhounds. I quite like hunting, but I'd rather have my own sailboat than a dozen horses! If only I weren't an earl I could go to sea and no one would care."

"You wouldn't wish to if you'd ever crossed the Channel," Rosalie told him with conviction.

Gervase broke in upon his cousin's demands for an explanation. "I daresay Mademoiselle prefers not to discuss her experience, if it was an unpleasant one."

"How could it be?"

"Well," said Rosalie, striving for delicacy, "not everyone is comfortable being on the water when the waves are rough. Neither I nor my parents, or any of the other passengers on the packet from Calais to Dover, *enjoyed* the journey."

A short time later the threesome exited the King's Arms. When the duke excused himself to confer with the headmaster, Ninian offered to take Rosalie to the Fourth Form room, where pupils past and present had carved their names or initials into the wood-paneled walls and on the backs and seats of the benches.

"How many boys attend this school?" she wondered aloud.

"I don't know," he said diffidently. "Two or three hundred."

"You must have many friends."

"My best mates were taken away two years ago. We organized a great rebellion—I stole the key from Peachey the custodian so we could open up the birch cupboard and put the whips they flog us with on the fire. The older boys managed to blockade the road to London. None of the post coaches could reach the school and the masters couldn't write to the parents for days! But after they restored order they became much stricter with us. Now there's no blanket tossing, and we aren't permitted to throw bread at the new boys if they try and enter the hall. That's our private club, where we plot against the masters, and tell jokes. Shall I tell you the one I heard the other day?"

She nodded.

"What man shaves more than ten times a day?"

Rosalie pondered this. "I can't imagine."

"A *barber*," he announced triumphantly, and waited expectantly for her laugh. After she obliged him, he said, "Here's a puzzle for you to solve. Suppose a man standing on the bank of a river has with him a wolf, a goat, and a basket of cabbages. He wants to take them all across with him but his boat is only big enough to carry him and one other thing. Therefore, he must take them over one at a time and in such a way that the wolf has no opportunity to devour the goat, and the goat cannot eat up the cabbages. What should he do?"

"Nom de Dieu," she said helplessly. "It will make my head ache to think of an answer. I'm afraid I'm not very clever."

"Shall I tell you? First, he takes the goat over. Then he returns and takes the wolf, leaving it on the other side. He carries the goat back and leaves it to take his cabbages. Lastly he goes over again to fetch the goat. That way, the wolf is never left with goat, or the goat with the cabbages."

His sudden desire to show Rosalie the lake and games field saved her from another such trial.

The persistent throbbing in her ankle had not troubled her all day, and she suffered no pain during their walk. Though she was gradually warming to the aristocratic youth, she considered him less engaging than Joe Grimaldi, the studious and well-conducted son of the comedian. Lord Swanborough's erratic behavior indicated that he had little in common with her friend Joe.

Some lads tossing a ball near the water's edge waved at him, but he ignored them. "They're in the First Form," he informed Rosalie, lifting his cleft chin in disdain. "Little babies, who cry for their mamas and their nannies."

"What do you do to make them cry?"

"The same things the big boys did to me when I first came here."

"You and your fellows are a pack of bullies," she commented in a voice of disapproval.

"The masters are the bullies," Ninian contradicted, his azure eyes flashing defiance. "The only Trojan at Harrow is Jem Martin, who arranges things for us. He'll find a horse if someone wants to slip away for some hunting, and he looks after *Bluebell*. He just finished painting her for me."

He took her to a small building where cricket bats, footballs, and fishing tackle were stored. In the middle of the unswept floor was a wooden rowboat glistening with a fresh coat of blue paint.

"Next time you come to visit, I'll take you out on the lake," Ninian promised when she'd had ample opportunity to admire his most prized possession.

They found the duke waiting for them in front of the brick house where Ninian lodged. The phaeton was in readiness; the liveried groom held the team of four gray horses.

Although Gervase presented his ward with a half guinea as a parting indulgence, he said sternly, "Your housemaster's story was most damning, and Dr. Butler is so displeased that he gave *me* a lecture. If you hate floggings, Nin, I advise you to conform to the rules of discipline. Your deportment had better alter significantly, or I'll remove you from school and consign you to a tutor's care. I doubt if you'd enjoy that."

"Not much I wouldn't," Ninian growled. "You won't tell Aunt Elizabeth what Dr. Butler said?"

"I haven't decided about that yet."

The duke offered Rosalie his hand, and when she was comfortably settled she said farewell to Lord Swanborough.

"Do come again, mademoiselle," the boy sang out as the carriage rolled along the street.

After successfully negotiating the steep hill upon which the school and village were situated, Gervase said, "I hope he didn't weary you with his tiresome questions."

"Not in the least," she answered promptly. Seeing his frown, she stifled an inquiry about the headmaster's report. His face was so grim that she feared his dissatisfaction with his ward extended to her. She folded her hands in her lap and waited for him to speak again, reluctant to intrude upon his reverie.

Until now he'd exhibited an affability so unforced that she judged it to be habitual; as at their previous meetings, he had treated her courteously and kindly. If she hadn't been aware of his name and title, she would have cause to doubt that he was her social superior. For the first time she was conscious of their differences in background and modes of living, and she marveled that she had ever felt relaxed and easy in his exalted company.

They had traveled a considerable distance in silence when he finally said, "Ninian never had much respect for authority at the best of times. With my father gone and my mother living in Shropshire, he thinks he needn't mind anyone."

"How long has Lord Swanborough been an orphan?"

"He isn't one." Looking over at her, he explained, "Despite the fact that his mother is living, he was left to my parents' care when his father died. Lady Swanborough suffered a mental decline shortly after Ninian's birth and resides at Bath in the care of an eminent physician. Although she has steadily improved, she'll never return to the Abbey or be able to take care of herself—or her son. My cousin Miranda, who married Viscount Cavender at the first of the year, is fond of her brother, yet I can't foist him upon a pair of newlyweds in happy expectation of their first child."

"He is an odd boy," Rosalie acknowledged.

"And always was. Mother and Father ruled me and Edgar and our sisters with a firm hand, but they spoiled Ninian. I've been his guardian since last spring, and at first I believed I would be the one to put a stop to his naughty tricks and curb his tendency to ride roughshod over everyone he meets, but so far I've failed miserably. He still has his way in all things. As you have seen, he's fearfully persuasive."

Eyeing his strong profile, she said, "And yet you don't seem to be a person who is so easily persuaded."

"Not easily, but inevitably." He heaved a sigh. "Have you any advice for me?"

With a regretful shake of her head, she replied, "I never had any brothers or sisters, and my experience of little boys is limited to Joe Grimaldi, who is very good. I am slightly acquainted with Mr. Dibdin's children," she added direly, "and have no desire to know them better. They are all so horrid and noisy that I try to avoid them, and I wish *they* would go away to school."

"Ninian is turning me old before my time," he confided. "He has made himself so odious at Harrow that I shudder to think what sort of mischief he'll tumble into at Oxford or Cambridge."

When he returned her to the house in Owens Row she regretted having to bid him farewell and hoped her feelings weren't apparent to him. His cousin had injected some much-needed excitement into her life, and the duke was the most distinguished gentleman she'd met since coming to England.

Though she judged it unlikely to happen, perhaps they would meet again somewhere. When trying to stage their next encounter she decided it should take place at the opera house, after the most brilliant performance of her career. Her arms would be filled with floral offerings, testimony to her talent and popularity, and he would be exquisite in his evening attire. The sea of her male admirers would slowly part, permitting him to approach her. . . . And then she remembered that such ambitions, professional and personal, were hopelessly unattainable.

She would never succeed in becoming a famous and popular dancer because she lacked her mother's artistry. She might possess a pretty face and a good figure, but she viewed her own charms as less than dazzling and hardly sufficient to attract a handsome duke. And even if they could, in her heart she knew that she would never welcome his advances.

4

A lovely apparition, sent
To be a moment's ornament.
——WILLIAM WORDSWORTH

The leading players at Sadler's Wells enjoyed the traditional perquisite of a benefit performance at the close of the season, and the profits they derived supplemented their weekly earnings. In October the most popular pieces in the repertory were repeated for the purpose of enriching Mr. Grimaldi, Mr. Ridgway, and Mrs. Dibdin. Rosalie maintained an easy friendship with the two actors and hoped their nights would be successful, but her wishes with regard to the manager's wife were rather less charitable.

One day, after her dismissal from rehearsal for a new dance, she was accosted by the company's premier comedian, whom one critic had called a living jest book.

"Miss Rose, I hope you will let me take you home with me for tea and a visit with my wife. I promised her I'd ask—oh, a week ago at least, but till now I've not had the chance." Years of constant grinning had etched deep lines around his mouth and eyes, and they were particularly noticeable when he said soberly, "Our paths seldom cross at rehearsals, and soon as the curtain comes down after the panto I must dash away to the Covent Garden playhouse."

"You'll wear yourself out if you don't take care, sir."

"My Mary says the same—not that she doesn't work just as hard, looking after our young Joe and playing small parts at Drury Lane."

Rosalie gladly accepted his invitation, for she owed Mrs. Grimaldi a visit. Throughout the long walk across the fields, Joseph Grimaldi spared no effort to amuse, and if he was as weary as she was he gave no sign of it.

He'd known many a tragedy during his thirty-two years, the worst of them the loss of his beloved first wife Maria, who died in childbed. In his desperate grief he'd been comforted by the actress Mary Bristow, and she now presided over their modest but comfortable dwelling in Baynes Row. Despite Joseph's reputation for penny-pinching, both he and the second Mrs. Grimaldi tended to live above their means. Their combined salaries from three theaters—Sadler's Wells, Drury Lane, and Covent Garden—barely covered the expenses of a town house, a country property, the horse and gig, and the education of their only son.

Mary ushered her husband and their guest into the parlor and gave the servant orders to bring food and drink. Young Joe, a miniature version of his father, shook hands with Rosalie in his polite fashion. As well as being dark-haired and small for his age, he was agile and quick-witted.

Although Rosalie's envy of her friend's elegant silk gown was tempered by the suspicion that the dressmaker hadn't yet been paid, she was quick to compliment it. Within a short time the tea tray arrived; accustomed to solitary meals, she reveled in the Grimaldis' merry jokes and lively discourse.

Eventually the comedian excused himself and retreated to the room where he kept his butterfly collection and at his mother's urging, Joe scampered back to the nursery. The two ladies then passed a pleasant half hour devoted to theatrical gossip.

After they had voiced their mutual dislike of the Dibdins, Mary said, "Has Joey told you that he has been engaged to perform at the Theatre Royal in Birmingham next month? I was afraid he might miss our son's eighth birthday, but it turns out he needn't leave till after the celebrations. You're coming to Joe's party, I hope?"

"Of course. And you must depend upon me for any assistance you require."

"Thank you, I'll keep it in mind. Well, I daresay the provincial audiences will be delighted to have my husband in their midst, and goodness knows we need the money.

I'm also eager for some news of my sister Louisa. She's with the Birmingham company this season."

"We miss her at the Wells," said Rosalie. "She is by far a better Columbine than Mrs. Dibdin, and charmed her Harlequin off the stage as well as on it. Will Miss Bristow and Jack Bologna make a match of it, do you think?"

The other woman shrugged. "I wish I knew, for I'd like to see her married. And you, too, Rose—it troubles me that you live so alone. But I suspect your circumstances might improve, having heard some intriguing reports of fashionable gents lurking backstage."

With a shake of her head, Rosalie replied, "You were misinformed. It was but one gentleman, far too grand for me, and his ward, only a few years older than your Joe."

Unwilling to boast of so slight an acquaintance, she hadn't discussed the Duke of Solway and Lord Swanborough with anyone and was reluctant to begin now. She had already accepted the unlikelihood of meeting that noble pair again. His lordship's curiosity about her theater had been satisfied, and he had other diversions now that he was at school. And the Sadler's Wells entertainments were not sophisticated enough to turn his guardian into a regular visitor.

Continuing their discussion of professional matters, Mary asked, "Where will you be dancing this winter?"

"I've already found a place at the New Theatre in Tottenham Street and begin rehearsals there within a fortnight. In fact, I'm having a costume fitting with Madame Ferrier this evening. The first ballet is *Flora's Sports*—a pastoral not unlike the one I danced at the Wells this autumn."

"So you won't have to leave Islington after all?"

"It appears not. As yet I've received no summons from Signor Rossi, not any word from d'Egville about returning to the King's Theatre. So you needn't seek another French teacher for Joe," Rosalie added brightly, to cover her disappointment. "Does he still make good progress in his studies?"

Mary Grimaldi beamed her pride in her son's attainments. "Indeed, and he likes his school, which is the same one his papa attended as a boy. He often talks of the time you visited our farm at Finchley to speak French with him, and hopes you will again. Did you know that we're calling the house Tippety Cottage now, after Joey's song? Oh, I *do* hope we can keep the place, being there is so good for him—and all of us."

After promising to return soon, and often, Rosalie left Baynes Row for her appointment with the elderly female who sewed her costumes. Darkness had fallen by the time she reached Madame Ferrier's lodging, a dilapidated house in Pentonville Road. The building was occupied by a variety of tradespeople, and its rooms were as dim and uncomfortable as Rosalie's.

The Frenchwoman, formerly a dresser at the opera house, helped the dancer out of her clothes and into a partly finished stage dress. Constructed from pale green muslin, it had a stomacher front and emerald-colored piping at the seams.

Twitching the full skirts, Rosalie commented, "A modest garment for the ballet. I'm not used to so many petticoats, or so conservative a décolletage."

"Is this not as you wanted, mademoiselle?"

"*Absolument*," she assured the seamstress, "for the audiences at the Tottenham Street theater aren't accustomed to naked limbs and bare bosoms."

"Ah," sighed the Frenchwoman, "I remember well the dresses I made when you were at the King's Theatre. The material thin enough to show *le corps et les jambes,* and draped so one breast was exposed." Her hands moved to Rosalie's waist and she pinched the loose fabric. "You have become thinner."

"Have I?"

The gray head bobbed slowly. "I sewed to your measurements—or as they were in the spring. How shall this be finished? Some gold lace to trim the neck, *peut-être*?"

"I think a tiny cluster of silk flowers just here," said Rosalie, indicating the top of her bodice.

"*Bon.*" Madame's swift, impersonal fingers began unlacing the front panel.

"When will it be ready?" Rosalie asked when she slipped her own gown over her head.

"Within two days. Do you wish a glass of wine before you go, mademoiselle?"

She declined, saying apologetically, "This has been too busy a day. *Je vous assure,* I will stay longer when I return for my costume."

During her solitary walk homeward, she found the Duke of Solway intruding upon her thoughts, as he sometimes did when she was too weary to consider her work or her uncertain future. Apart from being handsome and wealthy, his grace exhibited only a few of the qualities she associated with French noblemen. Rather than flirting with her as though she were a potential conquest, he'd treated her as a rational being, worthy of respect despite her profession. British aristocrats, it seemed, were more democratic in their outlook than the dispossessed nobility of France, because so many of their titles and fortunes were of comparatively recent origin. The present generation of peers had abandoned the rigid social code of their fathers and grandfathers. They made friends of actors, consorted with prizefighters, copied the attire of their grooms, and admired radical politicians. Not unlike the *jeunesse dorée,* the gilded youth of the Directory, who had flaunted the latest fashions in clothing and haunted the Paris theaters as patriotic fervor inspired a greater appreciation for the arts.

Her consideration of the duke gave way to memories of her musician father. He'd instilled in her an appreciation for the rights of all men at a time when his adopted nation had struggled with a concept so alien. For the past eight years she'd lived in his land, one of peace and plenty—and inconsistency. The English admired French clothes and furniture and art, yet to them French people were objects of distrust and ridicule. And even though she was no longer sensitive about the satiric caricatures lampooning France's victorious leader, she hadn't relinquished her innate national pride—or her national guilt.

One of her earliest memories was of the sad, worried face of Marie Antoinette. The most painful one was her mother's tearful announcement of the poor Queen's death.

So many people had perished, and when the horrors of the Revolution were succeeded by the still more heinous acts of the Terror, it had seemed to Rosalie that the end of the world was imminent. Her heart and mind had been loyal to the Royalist cause, even though she had frequently personified the republican spirit on the stage of the Paris Opera. A few creative artists, her mother among them, had flourished: ballets, operas, plays, and paintings had effectively communicated political ideals and rhetoric. Anyone wise or desperate enough to follow the lead of the party in power had been allowed to live and work without hindrance. Thus Rosalie and her parents had managed to survive.

Circumstances had forced her to be a hypocrite, and her conscience was still uneasy about her inability to choose a single side and support it to the death. As she crossed Waterhouse Field, she mourned those who had paid the ultimate price for their convictions. And she feared her failings would disappoint that attractive duke with the wise gray eyes.

"What the devil have you been doing?" Gervase demanded of the individual standing on the threshold of his study.

"Swimming in the Serpentine," replied Ninian, who resembled someone salvaged from a shipwreck rather than a juvenile peer of the realm. He was wet from head to toe, and his thin frame was wrapped in the dark blue coat of a Solway House footman.

"In October?"

The boy shrugged and the coat slipped from his shoulders. Righting it, he replied, "It wasn't so cold as you might think. When the *Victorious* capsized I had to rescue her, and after I was in the water there wasn't much point in coming out straightaway."

Gervase transferred his gaze to Robert the footman, in whose charge Ninian had departed for Hyde Park. "While his lordship changes into some dry clothes, you will explain how this disaster came about."

"It wasn't *his* fault," Ninian stated emphatically before retreating.

Lord Swanborough's expulsion from Harrow had

marked the beginning of the most disruptive and disheartening week of Gervase's experience. He had put off writing an explanatory letter to his mother, not knowing what to tell her. His home was rife with contention; thus far Ninian had offended the chef, frightened the housekeeper, and created an unpleasant scene in a bookshop. Now he'd made a spectacle of himself in Hyde Park.

"Your grace, I would've gone for the boat myself if I'd realized his lordship meant to go in the water. 'Twasn't till I heard the ladies scream that I knew what had happened, he was that quick. They thought he was drowning. One was so shocked that she fainted on the grass. The park keeper tried to make the earl come out, and so did I, but as your grace knows—"

"I know all too well," Gervase said grimly. "I'm sure you did your best, Robert."

"Yes, your grace, and I'll do better next time."

"Grateful though I am for your good intentions, I devoutly hope there won't be a next time."

The footman backed out of the room, his face a study in despondency.

After mulling over the problem of his ward, Gervase concluded that the only way to ensure Ninian was sufficiently prepared for university was to engage a private tutor. Harrow had been his playground and his platform, and during his brief career at that hallowed institution he'd distinguished himself only in his ability to infect other pupils with his waywardness. Loathing all subjects equally, he'd so stubbornly resisted any effort to educate him that his knowledge of Latin and Greek was a disgrace for a boy his age, and his deplorable deficiency in history and mathematics needed to be remedied.

"How does one go about hiring a tutor?" he asked Lord Elston that night when they met at White's Club in St. James's.

"I haven't the foggiest notion," the marquis replied blandly, wandering toward a table in the coffee room. "I should think you advertise. But I can't believe a pastyfaced parson will be able to control young Swanborough any better than you do. Clearly he's a hopeless case—you had better foist him upon the masters of Eton."

"I thought of that," Gervase admitted, "but I should find myself in exactly the same predicament a few months hence. Besides, as an Etonian, I am reluctant to inflict Ninian upon *my* school."

"What about marriage?"

Startled, he stared at his friend. "Whose marriage?"

"Yours, of course. A drastic measure, I agree, but females have a way of imposing order and discipline—so I have inferred from observation."

"I thought you gave up matchmaking after you paired my cousin Miranda with your cousin Justin," Gervase commented, his tone neutral.

"I'm not proposing any particular young lady. I trust you to know who'll suit you best."

Gervase chuckled. "I don't dare leave Ninian unsupervised long enough to go looking for a wife. Besides, there's no certainty that he would approve of my choice. The only female who has ever taken his fancy is that opera dancer, Mademoiselle de Barante. He talks about her all the time. For years he refused to learn anything useful or necessary, but all of a sudden he's adamant about studying French. Says he wants to converse with her in her native tongue so she won't feel homesick. Admirable of him, but quite unnecessary, as she has lived in England for nearly a decade."

Damon commented, "You are rather well informed for one who consistently denies any interest in the lady."

Shaking his head, he replied, "I know next to nothing about her, only that she and Maman danced at the Paris Opera. She uses her mother's surname rather than her father's English one, so I presume she was love-begotten." Seeing his friend's frown, he said in quick defense, "It's not as if it was her fault."

"I quite agree."

"Then why are you scowling?"

"I was remembering how you dragged me to Islington, a vicious act for which you're not yet absolved."

"I didn't notice that you were so very bored," Gervase

retorted. "You said the ballet was as good as you've seen at
the King's Theatre."

"*Almost* as good," Damon corrected. "The experience
might have been a pleasanter one had it not been soured by
that chap Beckmann, who talked me into a stupor."

"Not that I need one, but that's another reason to hire a
tutor. He would take on the responsibility of accompanying
Ninian to the playhouse. You'll let me know if you hear of
a promising individual, won't you?"

"You may depend upon it," the marquis said cordially.

But it was Miranda, Lady Cavender, who discovered the
ideal candidate. Gervase, after informing her by letter of
her brother's latest scrape, received a reply in the next post.
Her ladyship reported that the local vicar's son had taken
orders; he was a brilliant scholar who would be without
preferment until his father retired from the living. Because
Viscount Cavender had no other parish in his gift, and she
wondered if Gervase might employ the estimable young
man as a secretary or librarian.

Gervase penned a summons to Mr. Jasper Duffield, trusting Miranda to warn him about Lord Swanborough's character and shortcomings, and he provided a bank draft to
cover the costs of a journey from Wiltshire to London.

His mind free of care, he spent a pleasant evening at
White's, dining and drinking and conversing with his father's friends, who had accepted him into their circle. They
were congenial company, if a trifle dull and sedate.

He left St. James's for Solway House close to midnight,
and he was astonished to find the senior members of his
staff gathered in the entrance hall as if waiting for his arrival. When he relinquished his hat and gloves to Robert, he
noticed that the footman's hands were shaking. Parry appeared to be slightly more at ease, but he had a habit of
concealing his emotions.

"Your grace," the butler said quietly, "I deeply regret
that I must impart some disturbing news."

Gervase's disquiet, which had been in abeyance for several hours, instantly revived. "What has Lord Swanborough
done now?"

"He ran away, your grace." Parry dismissed the gaggle

of footmen and housemaids watching from the top of the service stairs, and followed his master to the salon.

"When did you discover that he'd gone missing?" Gervase asked.

"His lordship went up to his room after dinner, carrying your grace's newspaper. Susan, the chambermaid who waits upon him, came to me about an hour ago to report his failure to answer her knock when she wanted to turn down his bed. She and Robert searched all the upstairs rooms. The earl wasn't hiding in the cellars or the mews, or in any of the places we thought likely. I'm afraid he must have left the house on foot, slipping out while the staff and I were dining belowstairs."

"I expect so. Did you say he'd been reading my paper?" After considering this possible clue to his cousin's whereabouts, he said heavily, "Send a message to the carriage house, that John must not unharness the horses yet. I believe I know where Lord Swanborough has gone."

The first item on the Sadler's Wells program that evening had been the ballet. Rosalie, after completing her performance, was pressed into service as dresser to the actresses appearing in the principal entertainment, *The North Briton*. It was a new drama written by Mr. Ridgway, one of the company's leading actors, whom she liked well enough to help in any way he required.

She ignored Mrs. Dibdin's constant carping about an ill-fitting gown, and busied herself by pinning up the lace trim that dangled from Miss Jellet's bodice. For some time afterward, she tried to keep Master Aubun the Infant Phenomenon and little Miss Worgman from getting in the way of the adult players.

When the play was finally over, she helped the ladies out of their dresses, staying behind to hang each costume on its peg. By the time she emerged from the stifling canvas enclosure that served as a dressing room, she looked forward to the day when she'd have one place of employment rather than two. Until Mr. Dibdin dismissed his company later in the week, she must divide her time and her energies between ballet rehearsals at the New Theatre in London and her performances at the playhouse in Islington.

She bade Mr. Wheeler a weary good night at the stage door and left the building. The coachyard was deserted, for the playgoers and the performers had long since departed. To make up for lost time, she diverted from her customary path along the river and took the quicker way across the lawn, pausing occasionally to draw a refreshing chestful of cool air. The stars sparkled and danced in the clear autumn sky, and the elm leaves dislodged by the light breeze wafted gently to the ground.

"Mamselle de Barante!"

Upon hearing a shout behind her she halted abruptly. Turning around, she saw that a gentleman was following her. When he came closer she discovered that he was a stranger, despite his knowledge of her name. His substantial frame was squeezed into a fashionably cut coat and pale, tight pantaloons, and a high collar framed his full face.

Lifting his hat to her, he revealed a crop of fair, curly hair. "Ben Beckmann, your most obedient servant. Pray let me escort you home—so fair a creature shouldn't be walking alone at this hour."

"I'm safer than you imagine," she countered. "The watchmen from the Hatton Garden Magistrate Office patrol the theater grounds at regular intervals."

"Only let me walk with you for a little way then, as far as Islington Road," he pleaded. "I've been wanting to meet you for many weeks. I'm your greatest admirer."

Hoping to dissuade him, she answered, "I'm too fatigued to be good company, sir."

"Oh, I don't care about that. I'll do the talking—in fact, I waited just so I could speak to you. For weeks I've been wanting to ask if I could call upon you. You're my favorite dancer in all London." He paused, then blurted, "Damn it, m'dear, I'd like to be your friend, your very special friend." His pudgy fingers closed around her arm.

The avid light in his eyes alarmed her, and his bulk was intimidating. "Mr. Beckmann, please be kind enough to release me."

"I'm hoping you'll be kind to me. Just one kiss, m'dear, that's all I ask."

As his arm circled her waist, a shadowy figure emerged from the trees and raced forward to deliver a swift and brutal kick to his shin.

"Let her go, or I'll do it again!" the Earl of Swanborough cried militantly, holding up his clenched fists.

A bewildered Rosalie stared at her rescuer. *"Mon Dieu,"* she gasped. "What are you doing here, my lord? You should be at school!"

"The headmaster expelled me."

"No wonder," Mr. Beckmann huffed. "Young devil, I'll teach you go about kicking people!"

"Just try it, you fat baboon," Ninian retorted. "If you move one step closer I'll have you thrown in prison—and don't think I can't. I'm an *earl*!"

Rosalie nearly laughed at the ludicrous expression of chagrin on her admirer's face.

"Call off your watch pup, mamselle," he muttered. "I meant no harm. I just thought we might—" Glaring at Ninian, Mr. Beckmann fell silent.

"If you don't want trouble, you'd better go away now," the boy warned him.

"Indeed he should," agreed a gentleman whose low, controlled voice was familiar to both Rosalie and Ninian. "Or I, too, may resort to violence."

5

The duke's arrival alarmed Rosalie no less than had the earl's attack upon her infatuated swain. *"De mal en pis,"* she muttered under her breath, for the situation had most definitely shifted from bad to worse.

To her surprise, he greeted the other gentleman as an acquaintance, saying coolly, "Good evening, Mr. Beckmann. We meet again."

"Oh, hullo there—sorry, but I've forgot your name. Lovell, ain't it?"

"That was my friend. I'm Marchant, and I'm curious to know what you did to excite my cousin."

"He was being nasty to Mademoiselle," growled Ninian, his fists clenched purposefully.

The duke placed a restraining hand upon his shoulder and glanced at Rosalie. "Is that true?" he asked her.

"Lord Swanborough exaggerates," she replied as calmly as she could, thankful that the darkness hid her blush.

"But he tried to kiss you," Ninian protested, "and I knew you didn't want him to. He's too ugly."

Replacing his tall hat upon his woolly head, Mr. Beckmann said, "I'll leave you now, mamselle. But I look forward to continuing our discussion at some other place and time, when we can be more private. Good night, Marchant." He retreated with undignified haste.

Ninian frowned at his guardian and asked with intense displeasure, "How the devil did you find me?"

"Parry told me he'd seen you with my newspaper, and I deduced that its account of some spectacle enticed you here. Have you been enjoying yourself?"

"Not as much as I expected to," the boy said bluntly. "There wasn't a water show tonight, only a melodrama. But Mademoiselle danced."

"My carriage is in the yard of the Myddelton's Head. Wait for me there."

Ninian shook his head. "I want to talk with Mademoiselle."

"Do as I say—*now!*"

The earl's hunched shoulders and hanging head aroused Rosalie's pity and emboldened her to plead for merciful treatment. "Please don't be too severe with him, your grace. He meant well."

"I daresay, but his method of rescue was unnecessarily rude and crude." He studied her silently, then asked, "Have you known Beckmann long?"

Did he suppose she'd courted the gentleman's attentions? Seeking to clarify her integrity, she told him, "I never met the man before tonight. Is he your friend?"

"Hardly that," he replied, his expression grim. "Lord Elston and I shared a box with him when I last had the pleasure of visiting Sadler's Wells."

Rosalie attempted a smile. "Maman used to warn me that attracting unwanted followers was one hazard of our profession."

"Beckmann is not likely to return, but Ninian and I will see you home nonetheless." Before she could protest, he said firmly, "You must let us do what we can to save your precious feet."

He must have been conscious of her discomfiture, for during their walk through the grove he said no more about Mr. Beckmann. As if trying to put her at ease, he asked a few questions about her life in Paris.

"My parents made regular visits there before the unfortunate upheavals made travel to France too dangerous. I wonder if they ever saw your mother dance."

"It is possible. She was many years with the Opera, and so popular a performer that all the most famous artists invited her to sit for them." Looking over at him, she confided, "I am called Rosalie in memory of Monsieur Fragonard's daughter, who died as a child. Like Monsieur Greuze, he was a friend of Maman's and painted her several times, dancing in a grove *en le style de* Boucher. One such picture was very well received—in it she wears a gown like a pink cloud and a garland of roses in her hair. It was titled 'La Belle Delphine.' After my father's death, Maman had to sell all but one of the Fragonards. We needed the money."

"Who has them now?"

"Madame Parisot took one, and Sir George Beaumont bought the other to add to his collection."

"The next time I visit his house in Grosvenor Square, I shall look out for 'La Belle Delphine.'"

"Oh, do you know him?" Coming to a halt, she placed her hand upon his arm. "Perhaps your grace would do me a favor."

"Anything in my power," he responded gallantly.

"I am quite anxious to know whether Sir George also possesses a certain Greuze painting, one called 'Mischief.'"

"What is the subject?"

"Me," she said simply. "As a child I posed for a series of works in which I personified innocence, grace, purity, and mischief. Monsieur Greuze always referred to them as 'La Petite Bergère,' 'La Petite Danseuse,' 'La Petite Ange,' and 'La Petite Gitane.' The critics regarded them as sentimental, and when none found buyers he offered them to my parents. When Maman died and I had to pay her funeral expenses I delivered 'Mischief,' the Gypsy picture, to Mr. Christie. I'm certain it sold because I received a bank draft with his signature. I've always wondered if Sir George acquired it, and I would be so very grateful if you could find out for me."

"I will."

"How kind you are! I can't imagine what it would be, but if there's anything I can ever do for you . . . " As he gazed into her eyes, she ran out of words, and it dawned upon her that he might expect a more tangible reward than mere gratitude.

When he placed his hands on either side of her face, her

heart raced. Then it seemed to cease beating altogether when he leaned closer and gently kissed her lips.

"Now you're thinking I'm as bad as Beckmann," he said, his voice tinged with amusement. "Come along, lest my cousin accuse me of monopolizing you—which I am, to my shame."

This casual apology only made her feel worse. Deeply wounded by his apparent assumption that kisses like the one he'd bestowed were commonplace to her, she accompanied him to the waiting coach.

Lord Swanborough insisted that she take the place beside him, forcing her to sit directly across from the duke, whose speculative gaze was singularly unnerving. At the end of their short drive, the earl bounded out to unfold the steps for her, holding out his hand to assist her descent.

Still flustered by his grace's watchful presence, she misjudged the distance from the bottom step to the pavement and lost her balance. Her right foot paid the price.

Immobilized by pain, she summoned a false, stiff smile in response to his lordship's effusive farewells. After waiting for the carriage to turn the corner of Islington Road, she hobbled over to the area railing, which provided necessary support as she began a slow and agonizing progress toward the door.

Worse than her physical discomfort was the blood-chilling realization that if she couldn't walk, she would definitely be unable to dance.

The effort of entering the house made her weak and queasy. The looming staircase presented a trial she was not at all prepared to meet, for her ears were ringing and tiny pinpoints of light had begun to cloud her vision. Sinking down upon the bottom step, she closed her eyes. How could she ever rehearse that new ballet at the Tottenham Street theater tomorrow?

From far away she could hear Peg's panicked shriek. "Come quick, someone—oh, do *hurry*! Miss Rose has fainted away!"

The Tower guns fired at midday on the twenty-fifth of the month, which concluded the King's fiftieth year on the throne.

The celebrations marking His Majesty's achievement
were less ostentatious than those of the previous October. A
commemorative medal had been struck and festive bunting
was draped in public places; patriotic persons stuck wreaths
of laurel on their hats, and children gathered in the park to
set off squibs and firecrackers. But most of the shops remained open, and the King's failure to show himself in
Windsor or London lent credence to the rumor that Princess
Amelia, his most beloved daughter, was gravely ill.

In the evening the Duke of Solway and Lord Elston attended a Jubilee Ball at the Argyle Rooms and discovered
that the sad story making the rounds of the ballroom had
cast a pall over the event. Gervase was more perturbed by
the arrival of Lady Titus, the widow with whom he had dallied the previous year.

Her spectacular beauty had helped her to overcome the
defects of common birth and an early marriage to an obscure army officer, and during her first widowhood she'd
been mildly notorious for her liaisons. Eventually she enticed the elderly Sir Algernon Titus to the altar, only to lose
him a few weeks later when he was mortally wounded in a
duel with Lord Blythe—her former lover—who had subse-
quently wed Gervase's cousin Nerissa.

Even though she was no less lovely than he remembered
and her brown eyes were still soft and inviting, the lavishly
endowed body tempted him no longer. Her betrayal of his
trust had slain his passion and his affection in one terrible
blow. When he saw her coming out of the supper room on
the arm of her latest cavalier, a uniformed Guardsman, he
was comforted by his indifference and accepted it as proof
that his recovery was complete.

He made no attempt to avoid meeting her in the over-
crowded ballroom, and even entered into a discussion about
the royal family.

According to Lady Titus, who had heard it from her
Guards officer, a London jeweler had been dispatched to
Windsor Castle by royal command. "Princess Amelia
wished to have a choice stone set in a ring as a last gift to
her poor papa, with the inscription, 'Remember me when I
am gone.'"

The musicians struck up the tune of a popular dance, and she regarded him hopefully, prompting Gervase to say, "You must ask Damon to partner you. I still mourn my father."

"It makes no difference," she said tartly, "for I lost my taste for dancing after you deserted me."

"No reproaches, Georgiana."

"But you never allowed me to explain, or to defend myself."

"I don't need explanations."

"Gervase," she continued relentlessly, "I feared that your parents had persuaded you to cast me off!"

"And rather than waiting to find out the truth, you took advantage of an opportunity to be unfaithful to me. Are you so determined to review what happened that night? You never used to care for ancient history."

She lifted her golden head, saying pensively, "I have never ceased to regret my actions, and would welcome the chance to make amends."

"I'm afraid you'll have scant opportunity, for I won't be in town much longer. I'm departing for Northamptonshire immediately after my debut in the House of Lords and don't expect to return before spring."

Her chin shot higher, and in a threatening tone she declared, "Then I shall rely upon Lord Elston for consolation during your absence."

"Be warned, Georgiana, he also requires fidelity from a mistress. You don't want to make that fatal mistake again."

Accepting the failure of her attempt to rouse his jealousy, she said with artful carelessness, "Have a pleasant journey, your grace. I daresay we shall next meet during the season."

He related the substance of this conversation to the marquis later while they shared a bottle of cognac from the Elston House cellars.

"She's a damnably attractive woman, despite her lack of sound judgment," Damon opined. "I've always been fond of Georgiana, but I do pity her. To think that she might have been your duchess, had she behaved herself!"

Gervase shuddered. "I was a fool to consider marriage."

"It's no wonder she was casting out lures tonight. You are a very notable *parti*—there are so few bachelor dukes below the age of fifty. But your fortune is probably a greater attraction to Georgiana than the title. She has very little money and far too many debts, with only her house in Clifford Street as a token of Algy's misplaced affection."

Determined to change the subject, Gervase asked, "Are you still so friendly with that set of art connoisseurs as you used to be?"

"I only tolerate Thomas Hope, but remain on reasonably good terms with Sir George Beaumont. Why should you want to know?"

"I'm trying to locate a Greuze painting of a young Gypsy titled 'Mischief.' I'd like to buy it."

"If you're setting up as a collector of French pictures, I can put you in the way of acquiring a charming Watteau that will soon be offered for private sale. It's a better value than some insignificant Greuze."

"I'm not making an investment." Meeting his friend's curious stare, Gervase explained, "I intend to restore it to the former owner." Precisely why he was so determined to spend heaven only knew how many hundred guineas on a gift for a dancing girl, he wasn't prepared to admit. He didn't entirely understand it himself.

By organizing and regulating Lord Swanborough's days and nights, Mr. Jasper Duffield had earned the respect of Gervase and all his servants. The hitherto ungovernable youth rose at a respectable hour—earlier by far than his guardian did—and spent two hours at his studies before having a late breakfast. He and his new tutor were generally absent from Solway House during the afternoon, and by evening his energies were sufficiently depleted to make him an unexceptionable companion.

Arriving in the dining room one morning, Gervase cast a benign smile upon the bespectacled young man who had restored peace to his household. "Good day, Mr. Duffield. I'm eager to hear your report of yesterday's edifying excursion."

Ninian speared a large portion of bacon with his fork.

"We saw the Elgin marbles. Antiquities are terribly important, aren't they, Jap?"

"Indeed, my lord, and I'm happy that you've learned to share that opinion." The brown-haired gentleman laughed more often than might be expected of a tutor, one reason that his first week as Lord Swanborough's preceptor and chief companion had been a triumph. By dispensing with formality he'd been able to keep his pupil's attention, and the instructive rambles in and around London had been both entertaining and enlightening.

"Just remember," Ninian added slyly, "I only went because you agreed to take me someplace *I'd* like to visit. I've made up my mind to take you to Sadler's Wells so you can meet Mademoiselle."

"The theater has closed for the season," said Gervase.

His resolution unimpaired by that bit of information, Ninian responded, "Then Jap and I will take her to the spa gardens." Turning to Mr. Duffield, he added, "Mademoiselle may be French, but she's very nice. *And* pretty."

"So I understand, my lord. If you've finished your tea, you may return to the schoolroom to continue writing your essay."

After a final swallow, Ninian set down his empty cup and abandoned the table. He not only obeyed the gentleman's instruction, he did so without argument and that, thought Gervase, was a great improvement.

"Am I permitted to take his lordship to Islington, your grace?" Mr. Duffield asked his employer. "It would certainly be possible to combine a tour of the New River waterworks system with a lesson about Roman aqueducts."

"How inventive," Gervase said approvingly. "No, I don't object to Islington, but Ninian mustn't disturb Mademoiselle de Barante. If he insists upon visiting her, you might remind him that she rehearses during the day."

Gervase, sharing his ward's preoccupation with the dancer, had also been tempted to call upon her. His failure to do so was rooted in guilt over his behavior at their last meeting. Kissing her had been no great crime, he argued to himself, but he couldn't quite shake off the suspicion that she'd regarded it as one. Finding her precious painting and returning it to her, whatever the cost, seemed the most suitable means of making amends.

He retreated to his library, where the morning paper awaited him. All the news from Windsor was bad, for the King, after receiving the engraved ring from his dying daughter's hand, had succumbed to sobs and tears. Since then he had reportedly been "unwell"—a suspicious epithet and one alarmingly reminiscent of his former spells of madness.

The royal physicians issued regular bulletins describing His Majesty's health, and as the week progressed they abandoned any attempt to conceal the unhappy truth. The fearsome malady had recurred, and the King's anxiety about Princess Amelia had plunged him into a dangerously volatile state.

Parliament convened at Westminster on the first of November, despite the fact the monarch was unable to sign a commission to extend prorogation, or carry out the duty of addressing both houses. The government crisis intensified on the following day, when Princess Amelia's sufferings ended. Her father's illness was by then so far advanced that his recovery was in doubt, and the Lords and Commons could only vote upon a proposed adjournment of a fortnight. In the interim the Whigs closed ranks around the Prince of Wales and clamored for a Regency bill, while the Tories interviewed the doctors again and again in the hopes that they would give the favorable report that might forestall so drastic a measure.

Denied his formal presentation to the Upper House and lacking a strong motive for remaining in London, Gervase fell prey to the long-suppressed urge to travel to Haberdine Castle. The political debates being waged in the gentlemen's clubs and the ladies' drawing rooms could not compete with the bucolic delights of Northamptonshire. Privately he believed that a Regency was inevitable, but he preferred to keep his opinions about it to himself until he was required to cast a vote.

One gloomy afternoon while he was out exercising his grays, a whim prompted him to drive in the direction of Islington. As the phaeton approached Owens Row, he wondered about the chances of finding Rosalie de Barante at home.

Gently twitching the reins, he guided his horses into a turn. Seeking to justify the visit to himself, he decided that he required some additional information about the missing Greuze canvas to assist his search.

He halted before her lodging house and left his team in the groom's capable hands. He approached the door, tapping it with the silver butt of his whip, and after a lengthy interval a pale, scrawny maidservant appeared.

"Can you tell me if Mademoiselle de Barante is receiving visitors today?" he inquired.

"Miss Rose? She's gone away, sir."

"When do you expect her to return?"

The girl stared at him blankly. "She never said she would. I'm hoping she *does* come back, but I don't think she'll want to, not if she can't dance anymore."

"Is she ill?"

"That's what I feared when I found her lying at the bottom of the staircase," she replied obscurely. " 'Twasn't till after the mistress sent for the doctor that we learned Miss Rose had sprained her ankle. She never told us how. After keeping to her bed for a week or more, she made me pack up her trunks and send them to the mail coach office. As far as I know, she left town that very evening, with her right foot still wrapped in a bandage."

If only he'd allowed Ninian to visit her, Gervase thought with dismay, or done so himself, he would have learned about this tragedy. "Haven't you some idea where she may have gone?"

"Not I, sir. The clown's wife—Mrs. Grimaldi—sometimes sat with her, she might know. The other performers living here weren't that friendly to Miss Rose, so she wouldn't have told them nothing."

"If you don't mind, I'd like to come inside and talk with you. What's your name?"

"Peg Reilly," she answered as he entered the vestibule. "I always carried Miss Rose's breakfast to her, and looked after her rooms. They've not been let to no one else yet, if you'd like to have a look."

"I would, thank you."

"She took away all that was hers—the flower vase and the prints and the little china statue of her mum." Peg preceded him up the narrow staircase. "She was French, you know—*is* French," she corrected herself. "I mustn't speak as if she's dead, though I do think she wanted to be at first. Once I found her crying, and it wasn't just from the pain. I never saw her look so sad, not even when she used to tell me about the guillotine."

Gervase halted on the topmost step. "The guillotine?"

"And the murders. When she lived in Paris, one of her friends was stabbed with a knife when he was sitting in the bath—at least, I think she knew him. Some of them she knew, and some she didn't." Pausing before a door halfway down the corridor, she opened it and said, "You may go in, sir."

He was appalled at the small sitting room and the meanness of its furnishings—a scarred tea table, a couple of plain chairs, and a sofa with faded upholstery. Floorboards creaked beneath him as he moved about. After a cursory examination of the only other chamber, in which he found a bed, a cracked mirror, and a wardrobe that had seen better days, he returned to the shabby parlor.

It pained him to discover that the lovely, vital dancer had lived in such drab and dismal surroundings. The relief of knowing that she had escaped the squalor would have been great if he could be sure that she'd found a more comfortable refuge. The concern that it might even be worse gnawed at his conscience.

The expression on Peg Reilly's plain face was sad and worried, corresponding exactly with his own emotions.

Feigning absolute confidence, he declared, "I'll find her, never fear, wherever she has gone. And now, if you please, I'd like to know where Mrs. Grimaldi lives."

6

Fallen from her glory, and too weak to rise.
—WILLIAM COWPER

Rosalie eyed the knitting needles hopelessly, trying to summon the courage to pick them up again. Her unfinished handiwork was lumpy and ill-formed, resembling something altogether different from the stocking it was meant to be. Not even the most desperate mendicant, she thought glumly, would welcome such a gift.

Drawing her shawl closer about her shoulders, she realized that the parlor seemed colder because the fire was dying. She grasped the poker and wielded it with the energy of one who had been sedentary for a fortnight, but her efforts produced more smoke than flame. In Gloucestershire wood was cheaper and more readily available than the coals she'd been accustomed to in London; ensuring that the logs burned properly could be a tricky business.

Her ineffectual stabbing and prodding ceased when a middle-aged woman whose white cap concealed most of her graying blond hair entered the room and intoned, "What do you think you're doing?"

"Stirring the fire," she answered meekly.

"I left you that handbell for a reason, Rosie."

"But Annie is too deaf to hear it, and I refuse to summon my only aunt like a servant."

"Better that than setting the house afire, which you're in danger of doing. Give me the poker."

After Rosalie surrendered it, her relation knelt down to remedy the damage. "There now," she said with satisfaction as she worked the bellows. "If you aren't warm again in a few minutes, I can fetch a blanket."

"Thank you, Aunt Tilda." With a regretful smile, Rosalie held up the lump of coarse wool. "You see how poorly I'm getting on with this. Should I pull it apart and begin again?"

Shaking her head, Matilda Lovegrove answered, "Best give it up as a bad idea. You needn't repine, because I never expected you to take on my work. This is supposed to be a holiday."

Rosalie made a face.

"You need a good rest, Rosie. If you'd taken better care of yourself, that ankle wouldn't have been damaged so severely. Didn't the doctor say that you aggravated an earlier sprain which never healed properly?"

"The doctor said a great many things." She studied her right foot, bound with a strip of linen and resting on a hassock.

Matilda patted her shoulder. "There's no need to fall into one of your despairing moods just because I'm determined to keep you chairbound for another few days. I know I sound like a crotchety spinster, soured by too many years of teaching flighty, ignorant young women, but I believe you should stay off that ankle for as long as possible. You're young and strong, and you'll dance again."

"But not in time for the opera season." Rosalie could feel tears of frustration gathering. During her long period of inactivity she'd had time to think too many gloomy thoughts, mostly about the seeming impossibility of rejoining the prestigious ballet company belonging to the King's Theatre.

Her dismal journey from London's General Post Office had begun at eight o'clock one cold November evening. After rocking and jolting past innumerable towns and hamlets, the mail coach reached Oxford, and two hours later a sleepy Rosalie had boarded the Bristol coach for Gloucestershire. The early morning fog had filled the valleys between the Cotswold hills, and her despair had deepened at the sight of bare tree limbs, and the clouded sky; even the sheep along the roadside had looked gray and unattractive. Half faint from sitting up all night, she had hired a post chaise in Fairford, where the mail set her down, and during her journey to Bibury she had wished for a hot brick to warm her feet.

She had astounded her aunt by limping up to the door, pale and tired. Chilled to the marrow of her bones, she had desperately needed Matilda's firm, fond embrace and repeated assurances that all would be well.

Both ladies were descended from a prosperous landholder who left his farmhouse early in the last century and settled in Bibury, where he acquired a dwelling appropriate to his social and financial standing. When Mr. Lovegrove's grandson David demonstrated an aptitude for the violin, he'd sent the boy to the best teachers he could afford, first in London, then in Paris. Matilda, blessed with a golden voice, also received musical instruction but her parents had opposed her plan to sing professionally. In her girlhood she'd been allowed to perform at private gatherings, eventually accepting the position of voice instructress at a select female seminary in Bristol.

Her acquaintance with her niece began when David Lovegrove first brought his French wife and thirteen-year-old daughter to Bibury to meet his family, and subsequent encounters had taken place in sickrooms and at funerals. Matilda hadn't resigned her teaching position until after both her parents were dead, at which time she took possession of their house on the banks of the River Colne. She'd offered to share it with her widowed sister-in-law, but Delphine de Barante, entirely devoted to furthering Rosalie's dancing career, had been reluctant to leave London for a remote Cotswold village. So the spinster lived alone, supported by her own savings and the annual rents from the Lovegrove farms. On Sundays she walked to St. Mary's Church to take her place in the family pew, and during the week she kept busy gardening and calling upon her neighbors, and each year she invited friends from Bristol to join her for the Bibury Races.

"I don't want you to make the same mistake I did when I was about your age," the older woman went on. "I was supposed to sing at a party, and when I took a cold in the head I only made it worse by continuing to practice. I was able to perform, but not as brilliantly as I'd intended. Let that be a lesson to you."

"Signor Rossi *does* expect brilliance in his dancers," Rosalie interjected. "A few weeks ago I might have convinced him that I could meet the standard of perfection set by Armand Vestris and Oscar Byrne and Signorina Angiolini. Not now. Perhaps never. Oh, I wish I'd never become a dancer!" she cried pettishly.

"Do you think you would prefer the humdrum existence of most married women, or being an old maid like me?"

"I don't know, but I wouldn't mind having a *soupçon* of your Lovegrove respectability," she admitted.

"Whatever can you mean?" her aunt wondered.

"I've become a target for presumptuous gentlemen," she confessed. "On the night of my accident I was preyed upon twice. First by a rude stranger, and then by—by an acquaintance of mine. You can't imagine how distressing it was."

"Well, my face never inspired any painters, but I had my fair share of admirers. Lord, how long ago it seems." Moving to the window, Matilda pulled back the wooden shutters, then turned to say with fond pride, "Lovely as you are, I can't be surprised that a pair of bold young bucks would court your favors. Who were they?"

"The rude one was Mr. Beckmann. Fortunately Lord Swanborough, the boy I've been telling you about, chased him away. As for the other man—well, I may have been partly to blame for what he did." Rosalie's lips curled in a reminiscent smile. "*Entre nous,* I haven't much experience managing gentlemen. Maman scarcely let me out of her sight when we first lived in London. She accompanied me to classes and rehearsals and was always backstage during performances at the opera house. In Islington I've been fairly safe, because Mr. Dibdin is so opposed to his actresses and dancers having followers. Not that I want any," she added. "I intend to keep my promise to Papa."

"You haven't been tempted to break it yet," Matilda said shrewdly.

"*N'importe.* My will is very strong, and I learned early the discipline of keeping a vow. I attended a convent school, until it was burned down, and my godfather was an *abbé*."

"By all accounts he was a shockingly worldly man, despite his calling."

"True," Rosalie acknowledged.

"David really should have taken you to church after he brought you to England."

"Sometimes he did—so I could hear the organ music!"

"As far as I can tell, despite your vow of chastity you're not a proper Papist, and you're a most improper Anglican. To you, the only difference between a Roman priest and an English parson is that one can't marry and the other can. The result of your religious upbringing is deplorable."

"Papa was a freethinker," Rosalie said in defense. "He used to say that good and evil were concepts, not absolutes, and that what is right for one person could be entirely wrong for another."

"Evidently his morals became muddled after so many years of living in a country run by radicals and atheists."

"But he did believe that some sort of religious faith was better than none at all. He also said any document outlining the Rights of Man should grant a person the freedom to choose his church as well as his government. It's a wonder he was never thrown into prison," she said thoughtfully, "for he wasn't one to keep his opinions to himself."

Matilda laughed. "A Lovegrove trait, I'm afraid. And here's my opinion—you should put that pitiful piece of knitting aside. Your spirits need lifting, not lowering, so I'm going to fetch that novel one of my neighbors loaned me."

Rosalie did as she was told. But her troubled mind refused to concentrate on Miss Owenson's tale. For a long time the book lay upon her lap untouched while she stared at the flames leaping in the grate.

For too many weeks she'd ignored that recurring pain in her ankle, hoping regular exercise would have a beneficial rather than harmful effect. Now she was forced to acknowledge the truth of Matilda's accusation that her injury was worse and her recovery slow because her joint had been in poor condition. And the cure was even more dangerous than the sprain itself, because prolonged inactivity was a dancer's greatest enemy. Already her arms were growing weak from disuse, and when she flexed the muscles of her thighs and calves, they were no longer taut and firm.

Yet even if she never performed again, her body would retain the structure imposed upon it by years of training. Her legs were permanently and unnaturally turned out from the hips, forcing her arched feet to point diagonally rather than straight ahead.

The quiet and calm of Bibury made her restless, and the foretaste of her future depressed her. Day after day she sat in her invalid's chair by the parlor window, and when she wearied of gazing at the view of river and corn mill she watched the arrivals and departures in the adjacent innyard. She pined for the excitement of London—the busy streets crammed with carriages, the shops whose goods were beyond her means, the theaters where she had performed.

Frowning down at her bandaged ankle, she prayed that a few more years of dancing were left to her. To give up her work, to lose her only talent at twenty-one, was a fate too dreadful to contemplate.

Bibury, which lay at the center of a triangle formed by the larger towns of Northleach, Fairford, and Cirencester, possessed a Jacobean manor house, an ancient church crowned by a square bell tower, and a tidy inn. The Swan and its outbuildings stretched along one bank of the slow-moving River Colne, spanned by a solid stone bridge with a triple arch.

The landlord, impressed by the private traveling carriage at his front door, stated his hope that Gervase would be stopping for the night. "Or do you require horses for the next stage to Gloucester, sir?" he inquired, proudly indicating his large stable and coach house.

"I'm not positive about my precise plans," Gervase replied. "But my postilions require food and drink, also my valet."

"And for yourself, sir?"

"I want nothing at the moment, for I must first call upon Mademoiselle de Barante. Perhaps you are acquainted with her?"

The landlord shook his balding head. "Can't say I know anyone of that name."

"Has *any* young lady lately come here from London?"

"Miss Lovegrove has her niece to stay, and I've heard she lives near London. Works at a theater, though you wouldn't think it to look at her. Such a quiet little thing she is. Always was."

"Where might I find Miss Lovegrove's house?"

The man directed Gervase to the dwelling adjacent to the inn, which was built from the same pale weathered stone. It had tall chimneys at either end, sash windows, and a slate roof. Trusting the efficient Webster to reveal his identity to the proprietor of the Swan and its staff, he left the inn.

Well-tended shrubbery encroached upon the Lovegrove door, and the brass knocker gleamed from a thorough polishing. The spare, elderly female who answered his determined rap had difficulty hearing or understanding him. After he repeated his request to speak with Mademoiselle de Barante, she bade him enter and mumbled that she would fetch her mistress.

Despite its simplicity, the furniture was well made, with the patina that resulted from decades of careful attention. In the parlor, a cosy room with thick wooden beams and a colorful Persian carpet, he found substantial proof that he'd come to the right house. Four oil paintings hung upon the walls, and three were studies of a girl whose delicate features, golden brown curls, and melting eyes were so accurately limned that she was instantly recognizable.

In one oval-shaped portrait the young Rosalie cradled a lamb, her draperies arranged to reveal one budding breast. Another canvas depicted her as a pink-cheeked cherub with fluffy white wings. The third was a full-length portrait of her in a ballet costume.

Gervase recognized the fourth and largest painting as the work of Fragonard. A smiling brunette lady whom he knew to be Delphine de Barante held up her frothy blue skirts to show off her shapely ankles and pointed toes.

Hearing footsteps, he turned hopefully toward the door.

A tall woman stepped into the room, her expression not entirely welcoming. "I am Matilda Lovegrove," she informed him. "Annie says you asked to see my niece. May I ask how you knew she was here?"

"Her friend Mrs. Grimaldi told me."

"Pray be seated, sir," she said in a dry voice. "There is something I must make you understand."

Her eyebrows drew together, reminding him of the stern governess who had terrorized his sisters, and he did as she commanded.

"As my only brother's only child, Rosie is very dear to me. She is neither friendless nor helpless, and I warn you, I won't stand idly by and let some unprincipled man of the town plague her half to death. Yes, she confided in me, I know very well how distasteful your advances are to her. If you seek a mistress, sir, you would do better to court a less respectable dancer."

"I don't—and I didn't follow her to Bibury to make advances," he said adamantly.

"I'm not finished," she interrupted, her eyes glinting. "I can tell from your dress and your demeanor that you were born a gentleman. Let me tell you, sir, lurking in the dark and *pouncing* on a young female is hardly my notion of gentlemanly behavior!"

"Before you reach for your birch rod, ma'am, let me assure you that I am not Benjamin Beckmann. Mademoiselle de Barante can corroborate it."

"In this part of the world she is called Miss Lovegrove," Matilda corrected him. "Who are you, then?"

"Gervase Marchant, but like your niece I often employ a different style. I'm also known as the Duke of Solway."

The effect of this speech was not what he had hoped or expected, for Miss Matilda Lovegrove continued to frown at him. But the violence of her antagonism abated, and gave way to a semblance of civility. "I hope your grace will overlook my rudeness, not that your rank would excuse your behavior if you *had* been chasing after her."

"I'm not," Gervase said smoothly. "My interest in Mademoiselle de Barante—or Miss Lovegrove, as you prefer—is charitable rather than dishonorable. I feel a certain responsibility for the accident which caused her to lose her place at the Tottenham Street playhouse. My cousin, who is also my ward, precipitated it."

"Her ankle is much better, and I trust she'll be back on the stage by Candlemas. Sooner, if she has her way."

"But I didn't come only to inquire about her recovery," he went on. "I'd rather tell her the other reason in private, if you will permit."

She pressed her lips firmly together as she considered his request. "I suppose I can't object to that," she said at last, "so long as Rosie doesn't mind. She's lying down in her room just now."

Climbing to his feet, Gervase said, "I don't wish to disturb her rest. Should I return later?"

For the first time, the woman smiled at him. "That is most considerate, your grace, but I can't imagine she would thank me for sending you away. If your grace will excuse me for a moment, I'll tell her you've come."

Within a few minutes she was ushering him up the staircase and into a spacious chamber that was a vast improvement over the cramped rooms of the Islington lodging house. The green curtains at the windows and around the bed complemented a set of tapestry-covered chairs. Rosalie occupied the windowseat, a patchwork blanket draped across her lower body. Loose brown curls framed a face much paler than Gervase remembered, or could approve.

"Here's your visitor, Rosie," Matilda Lovegrove announced before withdrawing.

As the young woman began to rise he said quickly, "Please don't get up."

Complying with his wish, she sank back against the pillows. "I regret that your grace felt it necessary to journey into Gloucestershire on my account."

"As I'm on my way to Pontesbury, my Shropshire estate, it was easily arranged. But had it required a much greater effort, I would have found you." After accepting her invitation to be seated, he said, "I wish I'd learned about your mishap sooner than I did."

"In truth, I was reluctant to tell anyone," she replied. "If James d'Egville or Signor Rossi heard about my sprain they would consider me spoiled goods, to the detriment of my future career. So I left London as soon as I was able to travel."

"Yes, I found that out when I visited your lodging house. Peg Reilly was ignorant of your whereabouts, but she directed me to Mrs. Grimaldi. I understand that you were hurt when Ninian helped you down from my carriage."

"I should have been more careful."

"That you weren't is partly my fault, I think," he told her gravely. "I distressed you that night, didn't I?" When she looked away, thereby confirming his conjecture, he went on, "My pride has received blow upon blow since then. I accept that you might conceal your acquaintance with a duke from Peg, and I don't know to what extent Mrs. Grimaldi is in your confidence. But the fact that you failed to mention me to your aunt is only slightly less wounding than her suspicion that I was Benjamin Beckmann!"

Still avoiding his eye, she toyed with a corner of the blanket. "To link your name with mine, however innocently, was too great a risk. Gossip, even when untrue, can do a great deal of damage."

"I commend your good sense, Miss Lovegrove." When she glanced up in surprise, he said, "I've been told I must call you so, here in Bibury."

"This was Papa's home, and the local people would think it odd if I didn't acknowledge my parentage. Maman was always Mrs. Lovegrove whenever we came here to visit. It used to make her laugh whenever she heard her rightful title, she was so unaccustomed to it."

"They were married, your parents?"

"But of course."

"Yet you use the surname de Barante."

"I did so at the urging of my mother, who wanted me to benefit from her fame. Your grace isn't the first to assume that I'm baseborn. Several Sadler's Wells performers are— Mr. Grimaldi, Master Carey, even our strict and stuffy Mr. Dibdin." Eyeing him curiously, she said, "Aunt Tilda told me you wanted to discuss a private matter."

"I do—thank you for the reminder. Miss Lovegrove, I have a proposition to lay before you. When Mrs. Grimaldi told me, among other things, that you have been teaching

French to her son, it occurred to me that you might take on the task of instructing Ninian in that language."

"Does his lordship *wish* to study French?"

"He has said so, provided you consent to be his teacher."

"But I've never been bookish, and I'm not at all clever. I can't imagine that I would be very effective in a schoolroom."

"This wold be a temporary appointment," he elaborated, "lasting only until you are well enough to rejoin the ballet company. Ninian and his new tutor, an excellent man, are presently at Haberdine Castle and will remain there through the winter. Naturally I would cover the expenses of your journey to Northamptonshire to join them, and also pay for your return to London when you feel ready to dance again. And you'll receive a generous salary."

"Hardship pay?" she asked suspiciously.

Smiling, he answered, "I won't deny that Ninian can be a difficult charge, but I feel sure you'll be a good influence on him. He said I must tell you that he'll *try* to behave himself. Because he and I are largely responsible for your present difficulties, we decided that we owe you an alternate form of employment. I ask only that you consider my offer, for I'm not here to press you into making a hasty decision. May I call upon you tomorrow—not to hear your answer necessarily, but to see how you go on?"

"If—if you wish," she said hesitantly. "It is your grace's intention to remain in Bibury, then?"

"Judging by appearances, this is a charming place to break a journey."

"It is certainly quiet," she conceded.

"That will suit me very well. During my university days I visited this district on a fishing holiday, and we spent a most enjoyable week at Fairford. I suspect there's equally fine sport to be had in your river, provided I can beg or borrow some tackle."

Her gaze wavered again at his approach, and faint color tinted her cheeks when he extended his hand, saying, "Till tomorrow, Miss Lovegrove."

A quarter of an hour later Gervase was installed in a comfortable chamber in the quiet wing of the Swan Inn, which had the added advantage of facing the windows of Rosalie Lovegrove's bedroom. He recognized her green curtains.

The landlord, discomposed by his guest's exalted title, sought assurance that the accommodation was satisfactory. "I had the great honor of serving tea to the duchess, your grace's mother, several years ago," he informed Gervase proudly. "She stopped for refreshment and a change of horses."

"I should like to cast for trout tomorrow, if the weather permits. Would it be possible to arrange the loan of a fishing rod?" Gervase asked him.

"Indeed, your grace, I'd be honored if you used mine," the man offered. "And my lures as well."

"You are most generous, but I prefer tying my own. I rely on you to direct my man Webster to a shop where he can procure the necessary materials."

After a respectable supper of roast capon and pigeon pie, Gervase set to work. Webster had obtained silver and gold thread from the village seamstress, and the landlord's wife had provided needles, scissors, sealing wax, and some rust-colored feathers plucked from the fowl she had sacrificed for his dinner. Gervase applied himself to the familiar task, his eyes unwavering and his brow furrowed in concentration as he assembled the bits and pieces into careful copies of plain hackles and great duns and palmer flies.

His mind was as busy as his fingers. A thoughtful assessment of his brief interview with the dancer led him to the conclusion that she would probably turn down the position he'd offered. And that one imprudent, impetuous kiss would, he suspected, be the reason for her refusal. Somehow he must find a way to allay her concerns about his intentions.

She hadn't admitted to holding him or Ninian responsible for her plight, but he'd read the truth of it in her mobile face. And though she had maintained her composure at his false impression of her illegitimacy, she had surely been pained by it.

So much of her life, past and present, was still a mystery to him, but to court her confidences would be to risk involving himself. She was a curiosity, and a beautiful one at that, but for both of their sakes he would have to remain detached, he told himself, replacing the unused hooks in the landlord's well-stocked tackle box.

After extinguishing the branch of candles, he moved to his window to stare at the one across the way, curtained and lit like a miniature stage. He stood there until he caught a tantalizing glimpse of Rosalie in her nightgown, then backed away so she wouldn't see him spying on her.

Did she braid her hair before retiring, or did she bundle it into a bedcap? While he readied himself for his own repose, he pondered the insoluble question, which teased him until he finally drifted off to sleep.

7

Footing it in the dance that fancy leads.
—WILLIAM COWPER

By the following morning the Lovegrove ladies were still discussing the Duke of Solway's remarkable visit, and its purpose. Matilda shared Rosalie's view that his grace's offer of employment was an act of charity but disagreed that as such it should be refused outright.

"After you went to bed I studied his family in my father's old *Debrett's*," she said, her knitting needles clicking busily. "The Marchant lineage is most impressive, going back to the Tudors and the Stuarts. Your duke is eight-and-twenty, with a brother, Edgar, and two sisters called Imogen and Ophelia. Do they also live at this castle of his?"

"The sisters must be married," Rosalie replied. "Lord Edgar Marchant serves in the Peninsular army."

"I also found an engraving of Haberdine Castle in a book of views, and it looks to be a grand old pile. I must admit, it would be a nice change of scene for you. The little earl may not be a model of deportment, but he can't be much worse than the stage children you've known. And afterward you'd be entitled to an employment reference, which might be useful."

"Signor Rossi won't care for that."

"One never knows," Matilda said sagely. "Of course, you needn't work at all if you don't care to, for I'd gladly keep you here with me. This house and all the tenanted farmland will belong to you someday, and I can think of no good reason why you shouldn't enjoy the benefits during my lifetime. If you want to stay, that is, and I don't think you do." Watching Rosalie flex her foot, now free of its bandage, she added, "The dance has ever been your obsession. I remember Davey used to say you wanted to dance before you ever learned how to walk."

"He spoke the truth," Rosalie admitted, almost apologetically.

"Still," her aunt went on, "you should go to Northamptonshire, if only till the New Year. Look on it as a holiday, your chance to see more of the world than the interior of a theater or an opera house. You cannot reasonably expect to dance before then, not even if Signor Rossi invited you to join his company."

"I don't know what to do," she sighed, thinking only of the thing she was meant to do and couldn't.

At midday a servant from the Swan delivered a rush basket containing a brace of trout and a large grayling and presented them with his grace's compliments. Matilda ordered Annie to prepare them for the evening meal, and penned a note to the Duke of Solway inviting him to dine.

Rosalie was as indecisive about what she should wear as about accepting or turning down his offer.

Matilda, after changing into a gown normally reserved for Sundays, approved her choice of rose-colored kerseymere with creamy lace at the collar and the cuffs.

"You'd better go into the parlor and light the candles," she advised. "It's growing dark already, and our guest will soon be here. I must take the best wineglasses out of the china cupboard and dust them off. Annie is too busy in the kitchen to do it herself."

With everyone occupied elsewhere, the scullery maid had the honor of showing the Duke of Solway into the parlor, where Rosalie was hastily plumping the sofa cushions. The formality of his attire surprised her; his white neckcloth was beautifully arranged, and silver buttons adorned his black coat.

"Thank you for the fish," she said, and his amused smile made her wish she'd chosen a less prosaic opening remark.

"November isn't an ideal month for angling, but here it seems not to matter. I've already considered returning in

May. My host at the Swan says he has taken trout as large as ten pounds during the spring and summer." When Rosalie moved to draw the curtains, he told her, "I'm delighted to see you on your feet again, Miss Lovegrove."

"I scarcely limp now," she said with pride, "though I'm not steady enough yet for *tendus* and *développés*. And I have no stamina at all."

Matilda, entering the room in time to hear this, frowned at her niece. "You've made a fine recovery, Rosie, but you're at least a month away from practicing your dance steps."

Said their guest, "She might accompany me on my next fishing expedition. I mean to try my luck at that wide bend in the river, north of the village, so she wouldn't have far to walk."

"If this dry weather holds, I see no harm in it." Matilda turned to Rosalie. "But you must dress warmly and sit upon a blanket or two, because the ground will be cold from the frost."

"I'll be careful," she promised, cheered by the prospect of an outing after so many days within doors.

But when the duke's gray eyes met hers, communicating his pleasure at her agreement, her soaring spirits abruptly descended. Rather than being flattered, as she ought to have been, she was reminded of the time he'd kissed her, and fear obscured her delight. Were his visit, his offer of employment, and his invitation to watch him fish the beginnings of an elaborate and devious seduction plot?

Although an overcast sky disappointed Rosalie, Gervase informed her that the weather couldn't be better for his purposes. "The breeze is in the proper quarter, too," he said brightly. "As my father always said, 'Wind out of the south blows bait to the fish's mouth.'"

In his brown coat and beige twill trousers, he bore no resemblance whatever to the elegant beau of the night before. He carried a long, single-handled rod with a butt made of ash wood and a brass reel and a landing net; a willow fish basket with a leather strap was slung over his shoulder.

Their short walk to the chosen place was more exhausting than Rosalie had expected, and she was grateful when he stopped to let her rest. While sitting upon the edge of the stone bridge, she explained that it had been built by subscription, and her grandfather had contributed to the funds.

The duke's interest in local landmarks resulted in several questions about several attached houses with sharply gabled fronts, which she identified as Arlington Row. "The buildings were built several centuries ago to store wool and were later converted to weavers' cottages," she explained.

When they reached their destination he helped her spread some blankets upon the grass, well beyond the shadows cast by the willows, and she sat down to watch his preparations. Attached to the long silken line was a shorter one made of gut, to which he fixed an artificial fly before dipping it into the river to take out the curl. Then, keeping the point of his rod upright, he sketched a broad circle in the air and flung the line forward. The fly drifted down to settle upon the water.

His lean body was taut and his eyes focused on the river as he stood upon the grassy slope. Rosalie, recognizing his passionate intensity, was amazed that so ordinary an activity could be its inspiration. The fanaticism of the sportsman, she thought, equaled that of the dancer.

He addressed her in an undervoice, saying, "One should always cast upstream, so the current will carry the line along. I'm keeping it on the stretch, and every so often I'll pull back to twitch the fly."

After several minutes of silence, he said even more softly, "Ah, a rise."

Holding her breath in anticipation and sitting very still, she studied his maneuvers.

He jerked the pole upright and cried triumphantly, "He's caught now, so I can let him run a little." Soon he began to wind his reel, walking backward as he did so. "A heavy one. Pass me that landing net, I'll need it presently."

She hurried to his side with the requested article, and when he pulled his catch out of the water she exclaimed, "It's larger than those you caught yesterday!" Unable to watch him stun the fish, she shut her eyes, and afterward held the basket open so he could place it inside.

"I usually get good results with my red-brown flies. I may try a palmer fly next time—that's how I caught the grayling. They're fatter and better at this season than trout."

The duke's first catch was his best one, but he brought in two grayling and another trout so small that he returned it to the water. After he admitted to feeling a trifle hungry, Rosalie unpacked the generous meal of cold chicken, bread, cheese, and chilled wine pressed upon him by the landlord's wife. While they dined together, seated upon the thick pile of blankets, she felt oddly at peace despite the uncertainty of her future—and his precise intentions.

"Yours is splendid country," Gervase declared.

Smiling, Rosalie replied, "My trips to Bibury have been so infrequent that I'm only slightly less a stranger here than you, your grace."

Leaning closer, he asked, "Couldn't you perhaps call me Gervase when we're alone together?"

"Non, non," she protested nervously, lapsing into French. "You are a duke, it would not be—*convenable*."

"Why not, if I've given you leave? I don't much like to hear 'your grace' from anyone, as I inevitably associate that mode of address with my late father. Try my name, just once," he challenged her.

"Gervais," she essayed, eliminating the final consonant and giving strong emphasis to the second syllable.

"Sher-vay," he repeated. "It sounds far nicer in your language."

"Most words do." She wondered if he was about to kiss her again, and what else he might do if she let him.

"Paris must seem very distant when you are here," he said idly. "Do you miss it?"

"Occasionally."

"I gathered from my conversations with your Islington friends that you were there throughout the Revolution."

"I was born the year it began, on a hot summer day a fortnight before the Bastille fell. As a very young child, I witnessed the evil done in the name of liberty, fraternity, and equality."

His sympathetic questioning elicited many a secret she'd kept locked away. She related the harrowing tale of her godfather, the Abbé de Bouyon, who had been seized by a mob and hanged from a lamppost. She told him about the actors of the Théâtre Française, arrested and thrown into prison to await trial and certain death. But a clerk in the Prosecutor's Office, a former player himself, had intervened; he destroyed the indictment papers, and eventually all were released.

Her voice softened when she spoke of her beloved godmother, Mademoiselle de Montansier. "Although she had enjoyed the favor and patronage of Marie Antoinette, after the fall of the monarchy she embraced the cause of the people and produced plays promoting Republican virtues. But her patriotism couldn't save her, for she was falsely accused of being part of a Royalist plot to burn down the Bibliothèque Nationale. She was denounced to the Commune by an enemy and was sent to prison by some of the gentlemen who had frequented her salon above the Café de Chartres."

"Did no one step forward to defend her?"

Rosalie shook her head. "She spent nearly a year in Petit Force. We went to her, Maman and I—the Committee of Public Safety permitted visitors. I was terrified that the guards wouldn't let us leave when our hour was over, that we'd be trapped inside. I still have nightmares about it." She looked down, startled, when his hand covered her own.

"It was a difficult and painful time to grow up," he said gravely.

"Fear was everywhere, it ruled the city. My parents were also under a cloud of suspicion. Maman had so often performed in the royal theater at Versailles—so beautiful, she used to tell me, all gold and ivory and blue. At heart she remained faithful to the monarchy, though she pretended otherwise. As long as the Opera remained open she continued to work, and I remember her coming home in tears many nights, in despair about having danced for the very men who had ordered her Queen's death. Republican, Bonapartist, the *jeunesse dorée*—she pleased them all, and her popularity kept us alive."

"What about your father?"

"In theory he supported the Rights of Man—by British

standards he was a radical—but the atrocities committed by the politicians disgusted him. And in his own way he was a patriot. When Francoeur, the manager of the Paris Opera, staged an anti-English pantomime, Papa resigned his place in the orchestra as a protest. But we didn't starve, because he made money by composing and giving violin lessons, and Maman received a large salary. By that time I was dancing, too."

A sudden gust of wind showered them with golden willow leaves, and he reached out to pluck one from her hair. "You've led a most interesting life, Rosalie de Barante. Mine seems dull and tame by comparison."

She gazed back at him silently, envious of that calmer, easier existence.

As he rose from his recumbent position he declared, "I'm going to teach you how to cast a line, mademoiselle. You should learn quickly enough after watching me all morning." Evidently he took her acquiescence for granted, because he immediately handed her the rod.

Holding it helplessly, she asked, "What must I do?"

"Don't worry, I'll show you." He opened his leather pocketbook and removed an artificial fly with red feathers and a black body wound with silvery twist. While he attached it to the line he explained, "This is a lesser hackle."

"They've got such silly names," Rosalie commented.

"Grasp the rod here, just above the reel." In helping her find the proper position on the butt, his hands touched hers intimately and his breath fanned her cheek. "There, that's right. Remember to keep your back against the wind. Good. Now try to cast—yes, that's fine. Don't jerk the pole, but let your line drift downstream."

Nothing happened.

Gervase encouraged her to reel in and begin again. "Keep your eye on the fly at all times, and if you get a—"

"It moved!"

"Steady now, the fish is likely to nibble once more. Can you feel him yet?"

"I think so."

"Let him run, not too far, and then I'll help you bring him in."

"But he's gone," Rosalie wailed, tugging at the road. Nearly half of the line had disappeared.

"The devil! He took the fly, and the hook as well—the only Number Six." Looking down at her woebegone face, he added kindly, "A minor annoyance, but no harm done. I can make a hasty repair, and then you must try again." He sorted through the tackle box for a spool of horsehair and anther of gut, then lengthened the remaining line. "This Number Eight hook will serve," he announced, and began to tie it on.

Patience, Rosalie decided, was a necessary virtue for the angler. Following her instructor's example, she quickly recovered from her disappointment and before long was casting sufficiently well to win a commendation.

Her delight was boundless when she managed to catch a small chub, which she landed with Gervase's assistance.

"I hope you aren't tired of dining on fish," he teased as she placed it in the basket.

She laughed. *"Jamais!* Besides, I've not had the pleasure of eating one I caught myself." Several unruly curls had escaped their pins, and her cheeks were flushed from excitement and the effects of the chilly air. She didn't care about the mud stains on her gown or the willow leaves clinging to her shawl. She felt truly alive for the first time since the night of her accident.

They argued over who should carry the basket, and all the way back to her house they congratulated each other profusely on the success of the outing. Matilda was in the parlor, head bent over her knitting, and after she had listened to them boast of their achievements, she announced that a letter had just come for Rosalie.

"It's so weighty that I had to pay another eight pence," she said, passing it to her niece.

The duke declined her invitation to take a chair. "I've just remembered that I have some necessary letters to write today myself." With a smile and a nod for each of the ladies, he departed for the Swan, leaving the basket of fish behind.

"I think this is Mary Grimaldi's hand," Rosalie reported after studying the writing on the cover. She sank down upon the footstool and broke the seal of missive. "Two letters!" she exclaimed when a second sheet of paper fell into her lap. "By two different people, both strangers." She scanned the shorter one. "This comes from an attorney, writing on behalf of a gentleman who wishes to arrange a meeting with me," she reported.

"Not that nasty Mr. Beckmann, I hope," said Matilda darkly.

Rosalie shook her head. "He's called Lemercier, and wrote the other letter. The lawyer gave both to Mary Grimaldi to be forwarded. Poor woman—half of London has turned up on her doorstep since I left town. Monsieur Lemercier has wanted to meet me ever since he came to England last year, and requests that I contact him or his *avocat* when I return to London. He knew my parents in Paris." Looking up from the sheets spread across her lap, she murmured, "Etienne Lemercier."

"Are you acquainted with him?"

"The name seems familiar, but I can't think why. I don't suppose I owe him any reply. I hope not, for I've no desire to begin corresponding with every Frenchman who remembers Maman and Papa, or is suffering from *mal du pays*. Homesickness," she translated for her aunt.

While Rosalie continued to study her letters, Matilda asked, "What answer did you give the duke about the position he offered?"

"He never asked for one," she said absently.

"Have a care, Rosie. Don't offend him with your capriciousness."

"Of course I won't. When I refuse him, I'll be gracious and civil." Glancing up at last, she heaved a small sigh. "You still think I ought to accept."

Matilda resumed her knitting. "I do. Certainly I would have difficulty turning down an opportunity to spend Christmas at a duke's castle. If it's your career you're so concerned about, how much harm can a few more restful weeks do?"

"More than you realize, Aunt Tilda. My time would be better spent in London. James d'Egville is capable of preparing me for any ballet, however complicated, and—"

"And before you know it you'll be laid up with another sprain," Matilda predicted.

"If you think I mean to give up dancing now," Rosalie said with rising impatience, "you're deluding yourself. Not yet. Not until I've proved to d'Egville and Rossi and Armand Vestris and—and the rest of the world that I'm talented enough for the opera ballet!" On that defiant note she stalked out of the room, her clenched fist mangling the letters.

Early the next morning Rosalie, covered by her warmest pelisse and wearing a sturdy pair of shoes with two pairs of thick stockings to keep her feet warm, left the house. Determination to increase her strength with exercise motivated her every step, but before she reached the center of Bibury her heart was pounding and her legs ached.

The Church Road led her first to the peaceful cemetery where her grandparents rested and on past the grassy village common, occupied by a flock of gray geese. She nodded to the servant girl scattering corn for the vicar's hens and continued along Packhorse Lane until she reached the Pigeon House, so called because of the medieval dovecot adjacent to it. Pausing to catch her breath, she heard the mournful cries of the birds within.

Never had she felt more earthbound or less like a gravity-defying sylph. Her chest heaved, she could barely lift her leaden feet, and her knees were wobbly and unreliable. Matilda had suggest Ladyhill Covert as a pleasant place to roam, but Rosalie knew she would have to put off going so far until another time. She faced an equally taxing journey home.

She turned back, covering ground less rapidly than when she'd set out. The thorny hedgerow along the road and the blasted tree in a meadow were neither as pretty or picturesque as those she'd seen on painted canvas backdrops, she thought gloomily.

In an effort to elevate her spirits, she hummed the minor accompaniment to the mermaid ballet she often performed at Sadler's Wells but lacked the energy or the daring to attempt the *bourée*, *glissande*, and *arabesque* in the middle of the High Street. Not that anyone would have noticed. Even at that ridiculously early hour the men were working at their looms or opening their shops or cutting wood, and the cottage women were occupied with their various tasks.

The only other person abroad that morning, she soon discovered, was the Duke of Solway, who stood upon the older of the two bridges across the Colne, gazing down at the slow-moving water below.

"Come and look at this water vole," he said at her approach. When she joined him he pointed to a small brown rodent scurrying through the fallen leaves along the riverbank.

"Just like a *petit rat*," she commented when the creature darted into its muddy burrow. Realizing that the duke was without his rod and tackle, she asked, "Why aren't you fishing this morning?"

"Because I intend to depart for Shropshire within the hour."

She was so unprepared for his announcement that she stared mutely back at him.

"I wish I might stay longer, but my mother expects me at Pontesbury by tomorrow or the next day, and I mustn't disappoint her." Facing her, he asked whether she'd reached a decision.

At that moment, frustrated and discouraged by her own frailty, she was tempted to accept his charity. "Aunt Tilda urges me to say yes," she admitted.

"From the outset of our brief acquaintance, she struck me as an astute woman."

"But," she went on, "I am more inclined to refuse."

"Allow me to present some enticements that might persuade you. The castle has a ballroom where you can practice your dancing. Its servants, who have been with my family for many years, will treat you as they would any guest. Ninian has promised not to be naughty, but if you should be unhappy or uncomfortable, you'd be free to leave. The appointment will last only as long as you want it."

She could think of no arguments to counter his, nor did she remember just why she'd been so reluctant. "If I found out about a place at the opera house, or another theater, I'd have to go to London."

"Of course. That is understood." He withdrew a leather purse from his coat pocket and removed five ten-pound notes, interrupting her protests and reminding her of his earlier promise to pay her posting fees. "I suggest Banbury as a good place to stop for the night, as it's forty or so miles from here, nearly half the distance to Haberdine. The Red Lion is the best inn."

Rosalie stared down at the fortune he had pressed into her gloved hands. Fifty pounds—the largest sum she'd ever seen at one time, enough to live on for at least half a year. "I'm accustomed to traveling in the mail coach," she said, her eyes growing larger as he began counting out additional banknotes. "It's less expensive than a post chaise."

"Keep these for your return fare to London." Smiling down at her, he added, "You'll be glad to have some running away money if Ninian troubles you with his tricks. Write to me if you encounter any problem at all, though I doubt you will. This piece of paper has my direction in Shropshire and also the name of my London solicitor, who will know where I am at all times. Have you any questions?"

Striving not to drop the riches he had showered upon her, she gazed back at him in confusion. "Dozens, only I can't recall what they are."

He touched her cheek. "You've no cause for concern, Rosalie. Remember, you survived the Revolution and the Reign of Terror. By comparison, teaching my cousin to speak French should be easy enough." After replacing the purse, he extended his arm, saying, "Permit me to walk you home, for I must say good-bye to the other Miss Lovegrove. And I'd like one last look at those Greuze paintings."

Rosalie took him to the dormant garden behind the house, and when he'd addressed his farewells to her aunt, they went into the parlor. His thorough and thoughtful examination of the three canvases, two of which showed her in a state of partial undress, made her self-conscious.

"You must have been a well-behaved little girl to sit still

for so long," he commented. "I once had my likeness taken, and it was an excruciating experience."

"It was never easy," she answered. "When Monsieur made the initial sketches for 'La Petite Ange,' the halo kept falling down over my eyes, and the angel's wings were quite heavy. The lamb in 'La Petite Bergère' looks sweet and gentle in the finished picture, but I was all over bruises from his sharp little hooves. Posing for 'La Petite Danseuse' was almost a pleasure, because I was dressed in ballet costume and could pretend that I was Maman."

"Tell me again about 'Mischief,' the one you sold."

"It was an oval portrait, painted at about the same time as the angel and the shepherdess. I held my head *comme ça*," she said, illustrating, "and wore a scarlet cloak. But I was much too fair to make a convincing Gypsy."

"I must reserve judgment until I see the result, but in my opinion you are the perfect gamine." His voice was devoid of any inflection, so detached that his remark hardly seemed to be a compliment.

After he left her, Rosalie went upstairs to her room and watched from the window seat until she saw his travelling coach roll by.

Absence and distance would alter the easy relationship that had developed during his stay in Bibury, perhaps even destroy it, she thought sadly. By taking his money she had accepted him as an employer, and now she found it impossible to regard him as anything else. He'd never really been her friend, and she had always known he couldn't be her lover.

Their temperaments were so different—his was calm and steady, her own was emotional and variable. In addition to lacking the refinement and the social graces he expected in a female, she was shamefully uneducated. He was a duke, descended from dead kings and queens; royal blood flowed in his veins. She was only a dancer, her gowns sewn with false gems, consorting with imaginary lords and ladies in an endless masquerade.

However kindly and generously he treated her, they would forever inhabit separate realms. The fact that he'd invited her to live at his castle for several weeks wouldn't alter that harsh and disturbingly hurtful truth.

8

When you do dance, I wish you
A wave o' the sea, that you might ever do
Nothing but that.

—WILLIAM SHAKESPEARE

"Tell me how to say, 'That woman is ugly,'" Lord Swanborough urged his governess. "If you please," he added
with an engaging grin.

Having learned how persistent he could be, Rosalie
promptly answered, *"La femme est laide."*

"And fat."

"Elle est grosse aussi." Frowning at him, she said severely, "The duke did not send me here to teach you insult-
ing expressions, my lord. Have you studied the list of
words I copied out for you?"

"Yes." Ninian shoved at the thick fringe of black curls
obscuring his brow.

They were wandering through the west wing, which contained spacious, elegant apartments and a magnificent ballroom decorated with plasterwork friezes and medallions. It
was the most modern part of the castle, and the abundance
of marble and gilding and pale silk draperies reminded
Rosalie of Parisian splendors.

Nodding briskly at the earl, she said, *"Commencez, s'il
vous plaît."*

"Now?" he asked in dismay.

"C'est obligatoire."

He began his recitation in a bored monotone, correctly
translating the words Rosalie had assigned the previous
day. Her efforts to impart the rudiments of French weren't

always so successful, but her pupil was so bright and quick that she didn't entirely despair.

As soon as she had arrived at Haberdine Castle, she had conferred with Jasper Duffield. Despite his profession he was neither dull nor pedantic, but she was awed by his passion for ancient languages and his detailed knowledge of obscure history. He didn't seem to disapprove of her true calling, unlike the prosy chaplain and the provincial couple who filled the positions of steward and housekeeper, and thus she was able to maintain an easy rapport with him.

The tutor had searched among the books in the schoolroom and the library until he found a French phrase book for travelers and a grammar text, formerly the possessions of the earl's sister, Lady Miranda Peverel. Armed with these, and her own well-thumbed copy of Jean Georges Noverre's treatise *Lettres sur la danse et les ballets*, Rosalie had become a governess.

Accepting Mr. Duffield's advice, she gave Lord Swanborough informal, unstructured lessons. The castle itself provided a wealth of ordinary, everyday objects for vocabulary sessions. She taught her pupil the vagaries of irregular verbs during long walks in the terraced gardens; he learned his numbers by counting the hundreds of steps from the cellars to the attics. The kitchen staff had provided assistance, admitting her into their domain for a study of food and drink.

With no previous experience of English country houses, she was astonished by the grandeur and antiquity of Haberdine. According to the scholarly Mr. Duffield, who haunted the muniment room, its foundations dated from the reign of William the Conqueror, the only remnants of the original royal hunting lodge. In medieval times the building had been converted to a fortress by the addition of the two solid bastion towers flanking the entrance gate; the oldest part of the castle still possessed a thick, nail-studded wooden portal. A minstrel gallery, tapestry-hung chambers, and suits of armor recalled the days when knights and their ladies had roamed the corridors, and one meadow continued to be called the Tilting Ground. The Marchants had purchased the castle directly from the crown, but their own occupation had been far from peaceful. At the time of the Civil Wars, the original Norman keep was irreparably damaged by Parliamentary forces and the stones now formed the chapel and the steward's house.

Scowling in concentration, Ninian continued, "Ballroom. *La grande salle de la danse.* Box. *La boite.* Button. *Le bouton.* Butter. *La beurre.*"

"*Le beurre,*" she corrected him.

"Is it? *Diable!*"

Startled by his unexpected talent for swearing in French, she demanded to know where he'd learned the expression.

"From you," he said blithely. "You lost your balance yesterday when you practiced that bouncing step, and that's exactly what you said."

"You must never repeat it, my lord!"

"Sometimes I've heard you say *sacrebleu,*" he added, his blue eyes sparkling with mischief. "And *peste.*"

"I should never have taken this position," she moaned.

Ninian grasped her hand. "Please don't leave me, mademoiselle! I'll be good, I won't say those words again."

His lordship's attachment to Rosalie had increased during her month at Haberdine, and she was worried that he wouldn't easily let her go. "I cannot remain indefinitely," she pointed out as gently as she could.

"Why ever not? Don't you like living here?"

"Very much. But I'm a dancer—I need a stage and an orchestra and an audience."

"When I come into my inheritance, I shall build a theater for you," the boy said grandly. "The finest in all the world!"

His offer made her smile, but she believed it was sincere. "Let's go to the Elizabethan wing," she suggested. "I've thought of another way to test your knowledge."

A row of paintings lined the wood-paneled walls of the gallery, and when Rosalie pointed to the silk gowns and velvet doublets and fine jewels of Ninian's Marchant ancestors, he identified their colors.

Pausing before a particularly fine portrait of a young lady with long, dark tresses and deep blue eyes, he said soberly, "This is my mother. She looks like that still, though she seldom smiles. She lives in Bath with a doctor, and before he cured her she was mad—*dérangée*. She's called Hermia."

"How pretty."

"It's a family tradition to name daughters for Shakespeare heroines. That's why my sister Mira's new baby is Juliet." He led her past the Countess of Swanborough's image and halted again when they came to a full-length study of a brown-haired youth with a gun under his arm and a spaniel at his feet. "That's Ger, with his dog."

It was an excellent likeness of Rosalie's employer. The artist Hoppner had captured the warmth of expression she knew so well, and the portrait conveyed the approachable quality so much at odds with his grace's exalted position. Reluctant to make any sort of comment that might reveal to Ninian how much she missed his guardian, she led him to the next picture and continued quizzing him.

On Christmas Eve the castle staff gathered in the chapel to hear Mr. Penfield read the daily collect. Garlands of holly decorated the brass altar rail, the scarlet berries brightening the somber vault of stone and wood. Rosalie shivered through the service; her fingers and toes were so numb with cold that she felt as stiff as the marble effigies of the entombed Marchants.

Fortunately the schoolroom, which doubled as her private parlor, possessed a large fireplace and a well-filled coal scuttle. After giving Ninian an abbreviated lesson, she dismissed him and began writing a holiday message to her aunt. Her task was interrupted when the upper housemaid, patently excited about the festivities belowstairs, brought her a letter from London.

Rosalie, spying Mary Grimaldi's familiar script, eagerly unfolded the page. But when she finished reading, her expression was pensive.

It wasn't that her friend's news was bad—quite the opposite. The Christmas pantomime at Drury Lane was extremely popular, and Clown Joey's portrayal of the fierce Vegetable Man had been acclaimed by all of London. His latest character appeared in more printshop windows than portraits of the Prince of Wales, and his innovative antics were discussed as often as the proposed Regency Bill.

Rosalie rejoiced in the actor's success, but not when she read the newspaper clipping enclosed with his wife's cheery note, a review of the first opera of the season. The critic vilified the management of the King's Theatre for presenting the plump-faced, matronly soprano as the tragic heroine Zaira. And he ridiculed Signora Bertinotti mercilessly, pointing to her girth as proof that she had greater talent for wielding her knife and fork than the prop dagger. Her performance had so displeased the exacting and anonymous gentleman that he neglected to comment on the ballet, which followed, merely noting that it had been *L'Épouse Persane*, a Rossi creation dating from the previous spring.

The descriptions of Grimaldi's triumph and the signora's failure not only rekindled Rosalie's desire to perform; they also prevented her from enjoying the servants' dinner and ball that evening. While footmen and maids were engaged in a rowdy country dance, she mentally composed a speech to Lord Swanborough to explain her immediate desertion.

But by the time she climbed into her bed she'd decided that she couldn't spoil his lordship's Christmas as hers had been spoiled. The news that she must return to London could be delayed for another day or so.

Ninian, granted a respite from his less than arduous studies, spent his holiday playing games—billiards, cards, charades. In the evening he and Rosalie and Mr. Duffield dined on roast goose and braised partridges, stewed carrots, salsify pie, and a plum pudding. After eating himself into a stupor, he went up to bed, saying he must be up early to meet the hounds.

At daylight he and his groom rode off to the Boxing Day hunt at Swanborough Abbey. He returned late, consumed another hearty meal, and after withdrawing to the library with his instructors he sought additional sustenance from hothouse oranges, sweetmeats, and roasted chestnuts.

Wiping his fingers with his handkerchief, he said in his abrupt and determined fashion, "Let's play Snapdragon."

"I don't know how," Rosalie replied.

"Easiest thing in the world," he assured her.

The student became the teacher, and soon she was leaning over a bowl of flaming brandy, deftly plucking out hot currants. Ninian, who had suggested the game, was the first to tire of it, but Rosalie and the tutor remained at the fireside to continue the contest long after he had stretched out upon the sofa with paper and pen.

A few minutes later he looked up and asked, "What's the French word for ravishing?"

"Ravissante," Rosalie answered absently, her attention fixed upon the hazy blue flame before her. Knowing that a quick, bold action was the best, she thrust her hand into the bowl and snatched up another hot currant, bravely placing it in her mouth.

Ninian lifted his head again. "What color are your eyes, mademoiselle?"

"Bluish green," Mr. Duffield offered.

"In French, please."

"Bleu-vert," Rosalie translated.

The Duke of Solway, who had stepped into the room unnoticed, declared, *"Elle a les yeux turquoise."*

"Gervase!" Ninian shouted gleefully.

As the tutor and governess rose from the hearth rug, their employer encouraged them to proceed with the game. "But 'Take care you don't take too much, be not greedy in your clutch! Snip! Snap! Dragon!'" Turning toward the sofa, he asked, "Why aren't you playing, Nin?"

"I'm writing a poem. In French," the boy announced impressively. "It's about Mademoiselle."

Rosalie gave up her futile attempts to smooth the creases from her skirt and explained, "I assigned the task to his lordship, though I never dreamed that I should be the subject of his verses." With a Gallic shrug, she concluded, *"On essaie de faire des progres."*

"It appears that you've made considerable progress," Gervase commented, "if Ninian is willing to spend Boxing Day engaged in studious pursuits."

"Where's Aunt Elizabeth?" Ninian asked. "Did she stay at Cavender Chase?"

"She's visiting in Derbyshire now, with Ophelia and

Hethington and their half-dozen children. We left Miranda and Justin immediately after the christening, and reached Hethington Hall on Christmas Eve."

"What does Mira's baby look like?"

"She's very tiny," Gervase reported. "Her eyes are blue like yours and nearly as dark."

"When will I see her?"

"There is talk of your visiting the Chase again at Eastertide. May I read your poem?"

Shaking his head, Ninian thrust the paper into his pocket. "Not till it's finished."

Sitting down beside his ward, Gervase asked, "Did you take my place at the servants' dinner?"

The youth nodded vigorously. "It was a grand feast! Afterward we all sang silly songs, and the footmen tried to kiss the maids under the mistletoe. There was dancing, too. I partnered Mrs. Brinkworth, but not because I wanted to. She asked me."

"How else have you been passing your time?"

"Learning French. And translating Latin." Ninian's black brows drew together in a frown. "Caesar's *Gallic Wars*."

"Rough going?"

"Agony! Oh, I went hunting with Jap last week, and by myself today. We had some pretty fine runs. I'm at liberty from my lessons, and will be on Twelfth Day, too, for our party. I've been telling Mademoiselle about the ball Aunt Elizabeth and Uncle William used to give, and about the cake."

Gervase sighed. "Do you think of nothing but food? I'm not opposed to having a cake, but with the household still in mourning I doubt that celebrations would be appropriate."

"We needn't invite anyone else, it will be just ourselves—you and me and Jap and Mademoiselle. If we wear fancy dress we can call it a masquerade. A *bal masqué*," Ninian added with a triumphant glance at Rosalie.

"There won't be much mystery about our identities."

"I don't care about that," his cousin replied. "*I'm* going to be Sir Francis Drake. Will you help me make a costume, mademoiselle? With so many boxes of cast-off clothes in the attic, I daresay we can find materials."

Rosalie glanced at the duke, whose thoughtful expression gave nothing away. "If his grace permits."

Ninian turned to his tutor. "What character will you be, Jap?"

"Oliver Cromwell, I think. Most of my clothes are black."

"Oh, but we can't have him here," the boy objected. "The Marchants were Royalists. You should be a knight— we've got helmets and swords and armor all over the castle."

Gervase curtailed the ensuing debate by saying that Mr. Duffield would make an admirable Cromwell. Then he asked Rosalie, "Have you made your choice?"

"There are two dancing costumes at the bottom of my trunk, so I have the choice of being a fairy or a shepherdess."

"You must come as Titania," Ninian said decisively. "The queen of the fairies. And what about you, Ger?"

"I'm keeping my character a secret," Gervase responded, "in order to provide one surprise on the night."

Assuming that he would wish to consult Mr. Duffield about his ward's studies, Rosalie convinced Ninian that he should go up to bed, and excused herself. To her surprise, the duke followed them into the great hall.

"Ninian," he said, "the length of your hair is a disgrace. In the morning I expect you to submit yourself to Webster's scissors."

"Must I?"

"I've already told you so." Watching his cousin climb the carved oak staircase, Gervase addressed Rosalie. "Tell me frankly, how does he get on with his French?"

She answered ruefully, "He's no worse a student than I am a teacher. He seems to enjoy our lessons and has acquired some useful words and phrases. When I leave Haberdine, as I must do soon, I won't consider myself a complete failure."

"You agreed to take part in our Twelfth Night revels," he reminded her.

"I did so in the hope that my participation will reconcile Lord Swanborough to my imminent departure."

Glancing up at the brass chandelier hanging above their heads, he asked her, "What has become of the kissing bough that usually hangs here?"

"The only one I've seen is in the servants' hall."

"A pity. This is exactly the place for it." Smiling, he said in a more intimate voice, "To assure myself that my ward has been behaving is not the only reason I've come to Haberdine. I've thought about you often, and I—" After abruptly breaking off this statement, he asked, "Has your ankle given you any trouble?"

"It's strong enough that I'm able to spend a part of every day twirling about your ballroom."

"Without any music? Or do you keep it here?" His forefinger grazed her brow.

She nodded in affirmation. His gray eyes were as near to blazing as she had ever seen them, and this light kindled a fire in her cheeks. Awkwardly she murmured, "It grows late, your grace."

"One more question, and then you may retire. Are you glad that I've come, or would you rather I'd stayed away?"

His question aroused an emotion she dared not define. Nor could she give him an answer. Alarmed by the tension between them, she broke away, moving wordlessly toward the ornate staircase. Not until she attained the safety of the upper landing did she recall that she'd failed to wish him a happy Christmas.

When Rosalie realized she was in love with the Duke of Solway, she did not immediately perceive the danger of her situation. Dancing, her primary concern for the whole of her life, had consumed her thoughts and directed all her actions to the exclusion of all else. Her tender regard for the Duke of Solway was so novel that at first she reveled in it. The physical manifestations—an erratic heartbeat and hectic pulse—were not unlike those she felt before stepping on the stage.

Her dancing was unaffected, but mental disquiet had a disastrous effect upon her ability to sleep and eat. However

fatiguing her daily practice sessions, at night she lay awake
for hours at a time, reliving every encounter with her employer, however insignificant. Increasingly rigorous exercise demanded adequate nourishment, but despite a
noticeable improvement in the dishes since the duke's return her appetite faltered, especially in his presence.

When the weather permitted, he and Ninian rode off to
join the Swanborough Abbey hunt. Upon their return,
which usually occurred around midday, Ninian settled
down to his Latin studies, followed by a French lesson, and
Gervase conferred with his steward. He rarely received
company, and his only dinner guests were other sportsmen
from neighboring estates in Rutlandshire or Leicestershire.
On those occasions Lord Swanborough and his instructors
were served their evening meal informally, in the schoolroom.

Rosalie, Ninian, and Jasper Duffield spent one rainy day
in the attic rooms, hunting for suitable raiment for Sir Francis Drake and Oliver Cromwell. All were so caught up in
the pleasures of opening trunks and trying on discarded
garments that they forgot to watch the clock, and the ring of
the changing bell caught them unawares. Scurrying to their
rooms, they washed smudged faces and combed out tangles
and replaced soiled clothes with clean ones.

Rosalie joined the small group assembled in the great
hall, avoiding the stern and disapproving eye of the chaplain when he wondered aloud about what had detained Lord
Swanborough. She was relieved that the duke appeared to
be unconcerned about her tardiness, or his ward's.

Later that night, after the dour cleric retreated from the
library, Gervase drew a chair close to hers. "I heard the
laughter coming from the garret this afternoon."

"Were we so noisy?" she asked, meeting his gaze uncertainly.

"Yes, and I hope you will be again. This house isn't as
gay as it should be at this season."

When he asked what kind of celebrations she'd been accustomed to in France, she answered, "Very few. Although
religious rites were discouraged when I was very young,
Maman did take me to Mass on Christmas morning. And

we had a *bûche de Noel* with our dinner. This time of year is the busiest for stage performers, with so many pantomimes and spectacles and ballets. Until now I've never been at leisure to enjoy the festivities."

"Haberdine was bustling with wedding preparations a year ago," he told her. "My cousin Miranda and Viscount Cavender were married in the chapel on New Year's Eve, so all our family were together. My father wasn't well, but he concealed it from us—I suspect he knew it would be his last Christmas. I've never felt his absence more acutely than I have done this week. This house harbors so many memories that the prospect of coming here was more than my mother could bear. Very likely she'll remain with my sister at Hethington Hall until the London season begins, when she removes to Solway House."

Ninian growled, "I can't think why she'd want to do that. Except for Sadler's Wells and the Serpentine, London is detestable."

"I'm not especially fond of it myself," Gervase said.

"But why not?" asked an incredulous Rosalie. "I think it's a splendid city. The houses may not be as grand as some in Paris, but the shops are every bit as good, if not better. There are so many parks and gardens and theaters and exhibitions that one can never be bored—there's always something to do. On holidays there are processions and illuminations, and every night all the streets are lit up so beautifully."

"And by day are nearly impassable because of all the carriages, drays, and hackney coaches," Gervase countered. "I grant you, Mayfair and Kensington are pleasant, but in too many districts you'll find criminals lurking behind every corner and hear beggar children crying from hunger. The workhouses are overflowing, as are the houses of correction, and there's scarcely an empty cell in the debtors' prisons." Smiling at her, he asked, "Haven't you discovered yet that the town cannot compare with the country?"

She was hurt by his apparent disdain for her opinion, and reflected that the disparity of taste matched the inequality of their stations. How foolish it was, she chided herself, to yearn for someone so far removed from her in birth, intellect, and experience. Instead she should concentrate upon the more attainable of her dreams, returning to the opera house stage.

The oppressive fog on New Year's Day could not deter Ninian from his hunting.

"The scent will lie high today," he explained to Rosalie when she took her place for breakfast. Bounding out of his chair, he urged his tutor to hurry. "Tom Webb must have our horses ready. We're frightfully late—the hunt will be halfway to Stoke End covert by now—and I'm not waiting for Ger. He can catch up to us later."

Rosalie toyed with her food, consuming very little, and drank a cup of coffee far too weak for her Continental palate. Not so long ago she had been accustomed to taking all her meals alone; now it depressed her.

Going to her room, she put on a hooded cloak her aunt had provided and the half boots she'd procured locally, from a cobbler so charmed by her dainty dancer's feet that he begged the privilege of making her a pair of kid slippers as well. Hoping to banish her cares, she strolled down the hill to the village, a long street of solid stone buildings: cottages crowned with thatch, a church, several shops, and the Solway Arms. From the number of horses, carts, and gigs in the innyard, she surmised that a number of people were inside, toasting the arrival of 1811.

She decided to explore the remnants of the ancient forest of Haberdine. Mr. Duffield had explained that most of the trees had been felled centuries ago to create farms, but a few small tracts of woodland still formed the boundaries of the duke's vast estate. Coming to a broad, open field grazed by sheep, she saw a medieval barn which brought to mind the tutor's observation that the landscape continued to reflect the feudal system which had shaped it.

Because the cart track winding through the trees was the shortest and swiftest way from Great Melden to Little Melden, she encountered several pedestrians. A man and a woman accompanied by a large brood of noisy, red-cheeked children. Then a pair of lads and their dog hurried by, calling out wishes for a joyous New Year.

The sky had darkened to a deeper gray, and the air

seemed to grow more frigid as a result. To avoid walking all the way back to the village, she followed a narrow footpath which she hoped would lead directly to the castle. But her sense of direction was so poor that she sought assistance from the next person she met, a shabby individual carrying an axe.

"If you walk on," he answered gruffly, "you'll soon find yourself at the old tilting ground." Narrowing his eyes, he said, "You must be that Frenchwoman, the young lord's governess."

"I am."

"My boy was killed in Holland more'n ten year ago. He was fighting the French."

Striving to moderate his resentment, she said sympathetically, "He must have been very brave."

"He was that," the man corroborated, continuing on his way.

Rosalie proceeded along the path, shivering from the intense cold, but she halted once more when she saw Gervase coming toward her. Startled, she cried, "I thought you went hunting!"

"I've been hunting for you," he responded. "Parry said you left the house nearly an hour ago, and I was worried that you might be lost."

"*Mais non,* your grace." She hoped he would think her breathlessness a natural result of a long walk. The wind blew harder, causing bare branches to scrape against one another. "Such a mournful sound," she murmured, flexing her frozen fingers.

Staring intently at the treetops, he said exultantly, "There it is."

"What?"

"The very thing I've been searching for. Come closer and I'll show you."

As soon she carried out his request she was drawn into an embrace that was firm yet gentle, passionate yet tender. His arms held her more securely than any of her dancing partners, and at the touch of his lips upon hers a searing warmth replaced the wind's icy sting. This kiss was quite unlike the one she had received that long-ago night at

Sadler's Wells. Then she had been desperate to escape him—now she dreaded that he might let her go.

Without releasing her, he said softly, "Look up."

Rosalie tilted her head back, and tiny white flakes settled upon her brow and cheeks. "It's snowing!"

"Keep looking, it's on the highest limb."

"I see nothing. Only a—a clump of something."

"That's mistletoe," he told her.

"Are you sure?" she said, disappointed. "The kissing bough in the servants' hall is so pretty, with its red velvet ribbons and gold tassels."

"Clearly I must teach you to appreciate the starker beauties of a wood in wintertime, my little opera dancer."

But Rosalie, missing the gauze and tinsel, the soft lights and painted screens of her own rarified realm, doubted that he could.

He was smiling, as if pleased with himself, or with her. "You are surely thinking this season has a strange effect upon me, and I can't deny it. How cold it has grown! If this weather continues, Ninian will be able to go skating on the pond. But don't let him persuade you to try it—we can't risk another accident." Touching her on the shoulder, he said with a hint of regret, "We'd best go back to the house."

His words and actions, as disturbing as they were gratifying, seemed to prove that her feelings were requited. But what if he was only trifling with her out of curiosity, to determine how receptive she was to his advances? The uncertainty tortured her.

They separated in the great hall, Gervase going to the library and Rosalie hurrying up to her room. She needed privacy to recover her equilibrium, for their encounter in the woods had been singularly unsettling.

Hoping that work would bolster her spirits, she changed into a multicolored dance costume and pink hose, and made her way to the ballroom. At first its size had intimidated her, and more than one slip had taught her the dangers of the highly polished floor, but otherwise it was an ideal place for rehearsing.

As was her habit, she started by copying the poses of the bas relief gods and goddesses. Then, using a chair back as a makeshift barre, she began her preliminary exercises, her eyes watching for mistakes in a tall pier glass framed in giltwood.

Moving to the center of the room, she performed Lison's "Ribbon Dance" from *La Fille Mal Gardée*, her favorite ballet. Its plot was refreshingly simple, and she was particularly fond of its characters, not the allegorical or mythological beings of most ballets, but ordinary humans entangled up in a dispute over an arranged marriage. She hoped one day to repeat the role of lovely Lison, who renounces her betrothal to a rich and foolish young man favored by her mother and plots with her sweetheart Colas to avoid a marriage of convenience.

Jean Dauberval had first staged the ballet in Bordeaux, the site of his celebrated dancing school, and the debut performance had taken place two weeks before the fateful storming of the Bastille—the very day of Rosalie's birth. The celebrated choreographer had created his heroine with Delphine de Barante in mind. He had expected her to perform his promising new work in Paris after recovering from her confinement, but the dancer never had an opportunity to interpret the part she had inspired. By the time Delphine returned to the stage, the Revolution had brought more serious, politically significant ballets into vogue.

The first time Rosalie had danced Lison, Armand Vestris had been her Colas. He'd been an engaging youth in those days and popular with his fellow students. But Delphine, an exacting critic, informed her daughter that he lacked the greater talents of his father Auguste and his grandfather Gaetano, forever known as *Le Dieu de Danse*. She would have been even less impressed with the mature Armand, thought Rosalie, who was now a self-centered, overly confident performer, determined to trade upon his famous name.

But, she reminded herself, she had a similar motive for calling herself de Barante. It was unfair to condemn Armand out of envy, just because he'd achieved a success which eluded her.

Pleased with her execution of an *entrechat six*, she concluded that the long weeks of rest had done no harm, only good. Her former flexibility had returned; she was capable of soaring *battements*, deep pliés, and graceful *ronds de jambe*.

Her dancing was good enough for the opera ballet, she had no doubt of it. She would be satisfied with any available position, however lofty or lowly—*première danseuse*, *soloiste* or *coryphée*. For just as she had promised her dying father that she would guard her virtue, she had assured her beloved mother that she would continue to perform.

Gervase entered the ballroom quietly and stealthily, concealing himself in an alcove so he might spy upon the girl whose poppy red skirts swirled with her gyrations, revealing a petticoat the color of coral.

In the months since she had danced into his life, he'd often wanted to kiss those alluring lips, to hold her small body against his pounding heart. Now he deeply regretted the impulse that had prompted him to take advantage of the mistletoe. Kissing her a second time had been both unwise and unfair. But in future, when she was no longer Ninian's governess, he need not be constrained by the restrictions of an employer. He would then be able to speak freely about his feelings, and discuss the arrangement he had in mind.

During his stay in Shropshire she had persistently invaded his thoughts. Their separation confirmed what he'd first suspected while visiting her in Bibury. He wanted her. So much that he had risked offending her with that impulsive and ill-timed overture.

"*Peste!*" The dancer, oblivious to his watchful presence, pounded her forehead with her palm and muttered, "*Chienne stupide, et gauche!*"

Gervase hadn't noticed her error and could not fathom why she'd called herself a stupid, clumsy bitch. Slowly rising upon her toes with one pink leg stretched out behind her, she was the personification of grace.

But her labored breathing and fleeting grimace of pain warned him that she'd passed the limit of her endurance. Lacking the authority—and the right—to make her stop, he slipped out of the ballroom unnoticed.

The apology he owed her, like his declaration, would have to wait.

9

Thy mummeries; thy Twelfe-tide Kings
And Queenes; thy Christmas revellings.
——ROBERT HERRICK

Six days of unceasing snowfall kept the duke's household
indoors, and by the twelfth day after Christmas the castle
grounds were buried beneath a thick white blanket. Vague
rumors about delayed mail coaches and tales of stranded
travelers were communicated to Haberdine by the servants,
who heard them third or fourth hand. Ninian, hoping that
Rosalie's departure might be delayed indefinitely, made no
secret of the fact that he desired a continuation of the cruel
weather.

Unable to ride with his hounds, he'd kept busy organizing the festive dinner and masquerade, which would take
place in the evening. All that day he sought his governess's
approval of the last-minute additions to his menu and relied
upon her to help him decorate the room he'd chosen for
their party.

Mr. Duffield found Rosalie in that tapestry-hung chamber late in the afternoon and sat down to watch her attach a
pair of wings fashioned from gauze and wire to a spangled
frock. Firelight illuminated her face as she bent her tawny
brown head over her work.

Breaking their companionable silence, he said, "Haberdine won't be the same without you, mademoiselle. I trust
we'll meet again one day, for I intend to see you dance. But
his lordship's aversion to London is so violent that I can't
say how soon I'll be able to go there."

"Peste!" Rosalie muttered when she stabbed herself with

the needle. Removing a lace-edged square of linen from her
pocket, she dabbed at the spot of blood on her finger. "Did
you find any theatrical news in the papers?"

Mr. Duffield shook his head. "I was reading the accounts
of the proposed Regency Bill. A change of government
seems unavoidable. The King's Tory ministers are so inim-
ical toward the Prince of Wales that he'll want to replace
them with Whigs if he comes into power."

"Is he so political? I thought he preferred gaming, and
chasing middle-aged matrons and building expensive
houses to state affairs." She reached for her scissors and
snipped the silvery thread. "Finished at last."

"With the paste tiara we found in the attics and the wand
his lordship made from the shaft of a broken candlestick,
you'll be a splendid Queen of the Fairies." Mr. Duffield
cleared his throat, as he often did when he wished to make
a serious observation. "The earl is greatly attached to you,
Mademoiselle de Barante. He tries not to show it, but he's
fretting over your decision to leave."

"I will miss him," she admitted. "But he has his Latin
and Greek and history to occupy him, and after the snow is
gone he'll be able to hunt again."

"The Duke of Solway also holds you in very high esteem."

Avoiding his gaze, Rosalie studied the gauzy material
spread across her lap. "I am honored by his grace's good
opinion, though I've done nothing to deserve it."

The tutor was intelligent and perceptive enough to guess
her secret. He must also be aware, as she was, that her
hopeless and impossible love for the Duke of Solway
would result in heartbreak and remorse.

Her final preparations for the evening party included col-
oring her cheeks and lips with rouge and darkening her eyelashes with a burnt cork, as she did before a stage
performance. The sparkling tiara made her feel regal, and
she promenaded before her dressing table mirror, admiring
herself. Recalling her conversation with Gervase just after
he had kissed her, she thought again that she was entirely
susceptible to fantasy—her existence was governed by it.

Gervase Marchant, titled and wealthy, could afford his

preference for reality. The treasures of his country had not been plundered by angry, hungry people, or sold to wealthy foreigners. No angry mob had attacked the palatial homes of his friends, or flung them into prison to await an appointment with the guillotine. The scales of his conscience had never been weighted down by innate loyalty to aristocratic patrons and the opposing need to placate the agitators who had replaced them in society and the government.

To aid her recovery from the agonies of her past, she'd allowed herself to be seduced by that imaginary world she inhabited on the stage. Beauty, however artful or illusory or transient, was more desirable than ugliness. She needed the gentle glow cast by oil footlights, the heavenly music of the orchestra, and all of the seductive theatrical magic.

When she joined Lord Swanborough in the tapestry room, he complimented her extravagantly. "I say, Jap, won't Ger be pleased when he sees Mademoiselle?"

"Undoubtedly, my lord," the tutor replied. Meticulous research had enabled him to put together a costume suitable to the Lord Protector. He had put on the black gown from his university days and wore a round hat with a wide brim, to which Rosalie had affixed a silver buckle.

While waiting for his cousin to appear, Ninian speculated on what character he'd chosen. Adjusting his false beard and moustaches, he said, "I told Ger he should wear armor—the breast plate and helmet that belonged to an ancestor, the one who trounced Oliver Cromwell's army at the Battle of Solway Marsh."

But Gervase had spurned his ward's suggestion. He had robed himself in a floor-length garment of green velvet, loosely bound at the waist by a gold sash. Beneath it he wore a lawn shirt and red satin breeches. A heavy chain encircled his neck, and jeweled rings adorned his fingers, and his head supported a pinchbeck crown.

After a painstaking inspection, Ninian was still at a loss. "Who *are* you?"

"I've guessed," Mr. Duffield announced. "His grace has come as Oberon."

"How clever of you, Ger! I wish I'd thought of that!"

"You are quite magnificent in doublet and hose," Gervase comforted him, "and the sextant completes the portrait. However, you failed to seek my permission before removing it from the glass case in the muniment room." With a smile at Rosalie, he added, "Shall we take our places at the table, fair Titania?"

Accepting her consort's outstretched hand, she let him escort her to her chair. He had entered her realm of make-believe, and for this one night they were equals.

During the meal Ninian's companions teased him about the disproportionate number of sweets he had included with every course: gingerbread, fruit tarts, lemon custard, macaroons, and glasses of whipped syllabub. The last item to appear was the Twelfth Night cake borne by Parry. At his master's command, he set it down before Rosalie, who was invited to cut it.

"This is so pretty I can't bear to spoil it," she said mournfully, gazing at the spun sugar icing and the candied cherries. *"Eh bien,* if I must."

"Divide it into four equal pieces," Ninian instructed, handing her the knife. While she quartered the cake he exchanged a complicitous glance with his cousin, and when he passed the plates around he examined each slice carefully.

"It tastes as delicious as it looks," Rosalie said after her first bite. She raised another forkful to her mouth, lowering it quickly. Embedded in the cake was an unidentifiable object, something green which resembled a tiny pebble.

"You've found it!" Ninian cried excitedly. "A pea is always hidden in the cake, and the lady who finds it is queen for the night."

"But I'm already a queen." Watching him stab his own piece with a knife, she asked suspiciously. "What other items are concealed?"

"A bean," said Gervase, holding it up.

"Diable! I wanted it." When Ninian realized that the others were staring at him, he mumbled an apology.

"You promised not to use that word again," moaned Rosalie, her face hot with chagrin. "I never *taught* him to say it," she defended herself to the duke.

He chuckled and said, "As Pope observed, a little learning is a dangerous thing."

"Which pope?" she wondered.

Mr. Duffield shook his head. "Not the prince of the Roman church, mademoiselle. His grace refers to the great English poet, Alexander Pope."

Mortified by her ignorance, she blushed again.

After dinner they moved to the tapestry room. Ninian, who had adorned the mantel with holly boughs, led the master and mistress of the revels to their thrones, a pair of ornately carved and gilded chairs. He explained to Rosalie that possession of the pea and bean conferred the right to decree the evening's entertainments.

"Which game would *you* most like to play?" he asked.

"Snapdragon," she answered promptly, remembering that it was the duke's favorite.

Afterward they derived considerable enjoyment from forfeits, followed by speculation. Gervase persuaded a reluctant Rosalie to favor them with a pantomime. While her audience shouted out characters, she personified Queen Charlotte, the butler Parry, and lastly a drunken sailor, Ninian's mischievous suggestion.

To ensure her pupil's satisfaction, she insisted upon playing Blindman's Buff. After he completed a brief turn as Blindman, his cousin and his tutor succeeded him. Rosalie, swiftly captured by Mr. Duffield, was the last to submit herself to the blindfold.

Tying the silk scarf over her eyes, Gervase asked solicitously, "Too tight?" She shook her head, and he spun her around, slowly at first, then with greater speed until he finally released her.

Dizzy and off balance, she waited for her senses to be restored. The room was not large and there were only three players, so she anticipated no great difficulty.

Hearing frantic footsteps, she moved forward. Her outstretched hands brushed the damask curtains, and when she ascertained that no one was concealed behind their folds, she continued her sightless search.

A soft laugh made her pause, but while she was trying to determine its origin, a muted commotion from the hall confused her. Someone emitted a sharp gasp, followed by a low groan which broke off abruptly.

The sound of the door opening prompted her to cry out, "*Arrêtez!* No one is permitted to leave while the game is in progress!"

"Pray forgive my intrusion," said a cool, unfamiliar voice, unmistakably that of a female.

Disconcerted, Rosalie ripped away the blindfold. She was horrified to see a middle-aged woman standing directly in her path.

The candlelight lent a sheen to her sable mantle and muff. Her lavishly plumed bonnet was black, as was the skirt visible beneath the dark furs, both indicative of fullest mourning. She stared down at Rosalie from a superior height, her silvery eyes clouded with anger, and her arched brows expressive of aristocratic disdain.

When Gervase approached her, crown in hand, she asked him, "Who is this person?"

"Mademoiselle de Barante. She is teaching Ninian to speak French."

"Is she capable of doing so?"

The earl popped up from behind a sofa. "*Certainement, ma chère tante.* She made my costume, too. Can you guess who I am?" He replaced his drooping beard and brandished his sextant.

The Duchess of Solway's expression softened. "The suspense of knowing whether I've guessed right or wrong would be more than I could bear. An illustrious naval hero, I should think, from the look of you. Raleigh?"

"Sir Francis Drake!"

"And who might this be?" she asked, glancing at the gentleman standing in the corner.

"Jap is my tutor. He's Oliver Cromwell. Ger and Mademoiselle are Oberon and Titania."

Not knowing what else to do, Rosalie knelt down for a plié in the fourth position, the traditional stage curtsy. "*Je suis enchantée de faire votre connaissance,* Madame la Duchesse."

"I daresay." Tugging at her gloves, the lady addressed her nephew again. "Ninian, come and give me a kiss before

I go up to my room. And Gervase, I must ask that you come with me. We have *much* to discuss."

"As you wish."

The duke's parent maintained her disapproving silence even after they entered her upstairs suite, where a fire was being hastily kindled by a chambermaid. After placing her gloves on a console table, she removed her bonnet and wrap. The hovering abigail took them from her and immediately withdrew into the dressing room, motioning for the maid to follow her.

Not until she was alone with Gervase did the duchess address him. "What sort mischief have you been getting up to? And who is that painted, half-dressed creature downstairs? You can never convince me that she is a governess."

"She's an opera dancer," he said baldly. "Her given name is Rosalie Delphine Lovegrove, but she is known professionally as Mademoiselle de Barante."

She shook her graying head. "If that is meant as a jest, I don't consider it an amusing one."

"It's the truth."

"Then I can only conclude that you've taken leave of your senses."

Sensitive to any remark about madness, which had plagued his father's family, he moved away from her. "Had I been informed of your intention to come to Haberdine, I would certainly have provided a full explanation beforehand."

"Do so now." She sat down upon a chair, her chin remaining high and her back erect.

From earliest childhood Gervase had been close to his mother, but since becoming a man he'd concealed from her those aspects of his life that were likely to provoke disapproval. With regard to Rosalie, his efforts had succeeded all too well. Choosing his words carefully, he explained how he and his ward had become acquainted with her.

"Her mother was a Parisian dancer and her father an English violinist—lawfully wed," he added, lest she make the same erroneous assumption he had initially. "Both are dead now. Mademoiselle de Barante has supported herself by performing at the King's Theatre, and more recently at Sadler's Wells. Because I inadvertently brought about the injury which caused her to lose her place, I felt honorbound to provide temporary support. The only way I could to do it logically, and respectably, was to employ her as a French teacher until she resumes her work."

"It would surprise me greatly if she ever chose to work again," his mother said caustically. "Your chivalry is laudable, but in my estimation you've carried it to excess. From what I saw of her—which was entirely too much for my comfort—she has made a full recovery. Yet she is still living with you."

"It is her stated intention to leave within the week."

"She will go tomorrow," the duchess declared.

Gervase shook his head. "I cannot allow that while the roads are so bad."

"I traveled here from Hethington Hall without mishap," she countered. "The London turnpike is in a fair state, and the mails and stagecoaches are running again. I don't dispute your right to befriend whomever you please, but I refuse to associate with a dancing girl, or countenance her presence in this house. Give her money, promise her an expensive trinket, but get her away from Haberdine."

"She's not my mistress," Gervase stated firmly.

"Thank heaven for that," his mother breathed. "She would be far worse for you than that atrocious Titus woman."

Her criticism of his taste offended him, and only through a concerted effort did he maintain his composure. "You should save your lectures for Ninian, who has taken quite a fancy to her."

"I'm sorry to hear it. My dear, I don't mean to dictate to you, for you are your own master. But I must implore you to do as I've requested."

Reluctantly he said, "I'll speak to Mademoiselle de Barante in the morning."

"You'd better not wait," she advised him. "And don't look so tragic, my dear. Females of that sort always land on their feet."

When Gervase returned to the tapestry room, Ninian reported that Mademoiselle had retired. "Is Aunt Elizabeth angry because of our party?" he asked.

"She's weary from the long drive," Gervase replied. He knew he should prepare the boy for Rosalie's immediate departure, but he couldn't bring himself to disappoint another person that night. "There is something I must attend to, but you may stay up for as long as Mr. Duffield allows."

Going directly to the steward's office, he gathered together as many banknotes as he could find and stuffed them into the deep pockets of his velvet robe. Slowly he made his way to the distant part of the house traditionally allotted to the family governess, and tapped gently upon the door of Rosalie's room, his heart heavy with regret.

He knew she'd just been washing the paint from her face, for it was still dewy with moisture and damp curls clustered at her temples. "Meet me in the schoolroom," he said in a low voice, "and bring your candle."

Going to the dark chamber across the hall, he waited until she arrived with a flickering taper. He took it from her and placed it upon the scarred table where he and his siblings had learned their lessons. "Please sit down. I won't keep you long."

"I can guess what you are about to say," she told him, "and I can save you the trouble. I've already made up my mind to leave in the morning."

When she shivered, he realized that her shoulders and back were exposed to the chilly air—she was still wearing the diaphanous fairy costume. He removed his heavy velvet robe and wrapped her in it, saying, "I bear full responsibility for that unfortunate scene a short while ago. When I informed my mother that I'd engaged a lady to instruct Ninian, I left out certain details of your history. I also concealed the truth of your profession."

Smiling faintly, she said, "Many weeks ago I warned you that I'm not a proper person for Lord Swanborough to know. Has the duchess been telling you as much?"

"I disagree with both of you. Your success as Ninian's governess has been considerable, far greater than I thought possible. He has minded you and Duffield better than any member of my family. Not only does he admire and respect you, I believe he is also fond of you." After a pause he continued, "My mother is less concerned about your influence on Ninian than the danger you pose to me."

One white hand flew to her cheek in dismay. "I didn't think of that!"

"No? How could you not think it?"

"But you are a duke, and—and I'm only a dancer."

"That didn't prevent us from becoming friends."

Her gaze was steady and her voice calm as she said, "I believe you seek more than friendship."

"Yes," he confessed, relieved that he could finally speak openly and candidly. "From the night we met I've known that you are as virtuous as you are desirable, Rosalie. I didn't have seduction in mind when I persuaded you to come to Haberdine. And not until I joined you here on Boxing Day and saw you again did I become aware of the nature of my regard for you. But because you were my employee, I couldn't court you in the way I wanted to."

"You did in the wood," she reminded him.

"I don't regret kissing you, I'm not that honorable."

"You mustn't talk that way—not tonight!"

"If not this night, when?"

"Never! Because I cannot give you the answer you expect." Her subsequent words came fitfully, in short bursts. "I don't want to become your *chère amie*. My profession is too demanding and fatiguing. Every day I attend classes, and rehearsals, and the performances sometimes continue past midnight. I couldn't give parties and entertain your friends. I'm not witty or dashing or fascinating. And I don't know anything about pleasing a gentleman."

When she had exhausted her objections, he said quietly, "I don't require that you become a slave to my whims. It's my habit to avoid social gatherings, so you needn't serve as my hostess. I've got only one good friend, and he's such a handsome fellow that I'd just as soon you *didn't* entertain him. The qualities I demand in a mistress are constancy and honesty, nothing more or less." But her sad eyes and wistful face were proof that his speech had failed to move her. Kneeling beside her, he took both her hands in a firm grip. "Rosalie, I'd try so very hard to make you happy."

"But you wouldn't be happy with me. We have nothing in common. I spent but a few months at a convent school, and dancing is my sole accomplishment. I read only novels and poetry. You are educated, your ancestors were kings and generals. I'm descended from English farmers and French lawyers." She drew a long, sobbing breath and bowed her head. "But there is another reason that I must refuse you, and I don't know how to explain."

"Try," he urged, tightening his hold upon her. "You can tell me anything—everything."

"I suppose the place to start is with Maman," she began tentatively. "She was the daughter of a respected attorney in Rouen, who was rich enough to provide her with dancing masters. Her talent was such that Madame Montansier, the proprietress of the local theater, decided to take her to Paris and when she agreed to go her family disowned her. She never saw them again, or tried to communicate with them, though they must have been aware of her success. She performed at Versailles and won the favor of the Queen."

"Yes, so you've told me."

"She was young and beautiful and popular, the toast of Paris. My father was one of her many admirers, but she scarcely noticed him. She'd fallen desperately in love with another man and was to him what you ask me to be. They lived together, and though their affair lasted several years, he did not treat her well nor was he *fidèle*. She expected to become his wife, and when he abandoned her, she was destroyed by grief."

Gervase broke in at this point. "I can guess what happened next. She sought comfort from your father."

"*C'est vrai*. And she was so grateful for his kindness that when he proposed she agreed to marry him. Theirs was a hasty union, but it turned out to be a happy one. My mother's gratitude became a love so strong that she forgot the other man. In addition to receiving acclaim as a dancer, she was revered for being a dutiful wife and a devoted mother—a shining example of the virtues of the new republic."

When she paused, Gervase asked, "How did you learn

about her unhappy past? I can't imagine that she told you about her lover."

"Papa did, when he thought I was old enough to know. It was his way of explaining the facts of life for opera dancers."

Now comprehending the deeper meaning behind her story, Gervase said, "I can understand that you might be reluctant to live as your mother did before her marriage. But surely you know I'm not so heartless as to desert you?"

"It isn't that." Her greenish eyes locked with his. "I won't be your mistress because of my *father*. When he lay on his deathbed, I promised him I would never give myself to any man but my husband. That, Gervais, was my sacred pledge, and I will not break it. Not even for you."

There was little comfort to be had from her wistful conclusion, which indicated that she was not entirely indifferent to him. Staring down at her fingers, still entwined with his, he heard himself say, "I'm sorry—sorrier than you can imagine."

"*Moi aussi.* You aren't angry?"

"Only disappointed." Releasing her hand, he dipped his hand into the deep pocket of the robe and withdrew the money he'd collected.

"You gave me what I need for the journey to London before you left Bibury," she reminded him. "I've still got all of it and I know there's more than enough for a post chaise."

"You must take this as well—consider it your salary if you prefer."

"*Non,* it is too much."

Ignoring her protest, he continued, "You can hire lodgings in town and live comfortably until you find another situation. Should you require anything at all, I want you to let me know. Will you?" He expected resistance and was glad that she nodded.

He slipped his arms beneath the folds of velvet and pulled her close. Her body was yielding, and when he kissed her mouth he discovered that his longing for her, if not his love, was indeed reciprocated.

"Go to bed," he said at last, separating himself from her.

Her lips, now warmed by his, brushed against his cheek. "*Adieu,* Gervais."

She took the candle with her, leaving him equally bereft of light and hope.

10

Each step trod out a Lover's thought,
And the ambitious hopes he brought.
—RICHARD LOVELACE

Rosalie stood before the building that occupied the corner of Haymarket and Pall Mall, her fingers curled around a pair of dancing slippers. The arches and pediments of its facade reminded her of a temple and she, an aspiring vestal, doubted her worthiness to enter. During her years as a humble coryphée, she'd always used the stage door.

"What are you waiting for?" asked James d'Egville impatiently. "We cannot linger, for Rossi is waiting. And nothing could be worse for your muscles than this brisk wind and chilling damp."

London was caught in the frigid grip of winter. The Thames waters were frozen, enabling intrepid pedestrians to walk on ice from Battersea Bridge as far as Hungerford Stairs. In the days since Rosalie's return, the weather had moderated slightly: the heavy snowfall of last week had been succeeded by rain showers.

Rosalie hurried through the sacred portals of the King's Theatre in d'Egville's wake.

Recent events had demonstrated that fate could be generous as well as cruel. A soloist in the ballet had requested a leave of absence necessitated by pregnancy, and Signor Rossi needed an immediate replacement. The term of employment would last for the remainder of the opera season, which ended in August, but as her mentor had pointed out, a temporary appointment often became a permanent one.

Together they had worked diligently to prepare her for

today's examination. Determined to make up for the weeks she'd lost, Rosalie had visited d'Egville's dancing academy. He'd spent the better part of a morning supervising her exercises at the barre, barking out intricate combinations of steps, and hadn't stopped until her entire body was shiny with moisture. Then she had listened stoically to his critique of her performance, so scathing that she was reluctant to return the following day.

Her mother had often warned her that the dancing profession was one of practice, sweat, rehearsal, and worry, and the past week had proved it.

Somehow she'd found the time to locate a lodging in Panton Street, only a short distance from the opera house. And she'd engaged Peg Reilly, the downtrodden girl who had waited upon her in Islington, as her servant. The princely sum Gervase had provided was largely intact and would keep her in comfort until Easter, when the Sadler's Wells theater opened. For if Rossi deemed her unsuitable, she would have to return to Islington and Mr. Dibdin.

"I've already discussed the terms of employment with Michael Kelly," James d'Egville told her as they proceeded through the lobby. "He agrees to a salary of eight pounds a week, and you'll have a dress allowance of fifty pounds." Opening a door, he ushered her into the cavernous auditorium. "Remember to hold your arms high for the arabesques," he said under his breath, "it will make you appear taller. And don't forget to smile."

Although Rosalie was familiar with the theater, its proportions were overwhelming after six years at the more intimate Sadler's Wells playhouse. The auditorium, vast enough to accommodate over two thousand spectators, seemed even larger when empty. Only the chandeliers nearest the stage were lit, and after her eyes had adjusted to the darkness she discovered that the decor was different from what she remembered. The alterations included new upholstery for the seats which matched the scarlet curtains of the boxes. The lighter hues of the frescoed ceiling were completed by the panels of the box fronts. The ones on the ground level had been painted gray with decorative medallions, those directly above were embellished with trompe l'oeil marbling, and the next highest had bas relief figures on a silver ground. The fourth and fifth tiers and the gallery above were unadorned.

A pair of gentlemen stood in Fop's Alley, a broad central aisle separating the rows of red-cushioned benches, conversing with each other in rapid Italian. One was Signor Rossi, who turned his head to say, "Here they are. D'Egville, I have decided to revive your ballet *Le Jugement de Paris*, and it must be ready in only two days!"

Rosalie's friend answered calmly, "Mademoiselle de Barante is already familiar with the piece, for she danced it several years ago. I've been teaching her the role of Juno."

"Molto bene." The ballet master acknowledged the aspirant's presence by saying, *"Signorina*, you will be showing me that you dance as well as your mother, no?" When she removed her heavy cloak to reveal a thin muslin gown and pink stockings, he said approvingly, "You do not need to make the change of clothes—d'Egville has warned you how much I am misliking any delay. I summoned Vestris, but he takes so long a time in the dressing room."

Relieved to know that Armand would be her partner, Rosalie felt this was a favorable omen. She was putting on her slippers when he materialized, clad in tunic and hose.

After kissing both of her cheeks in the French fashion he said gaily, "What a prophet I am, *chérie*—now I see you in the place you belong. We perform together again!"

They made their way to the stage, already arranged for the first act of the current opera, and he explained that the side pieces and painted backdrop represented an Oriental palace. Taking her position, Rosalie was content to be back in her own comfortable setting, where castles were built of wood and canvas rather than stones and mortar.

A pounding heart and a dry throat were the first signs of her habitual stage fright. As she waited for the music to begin, the larger purpose of reestablishing herself in the company suddenly seemed less important than proving that d'Egville's faith was not misplaced. She knew her *épaulement* was intact—her head, neck, shoulders, and arms moved as gracefully as ever—but her jumps were sadly *terre à terre* and her footwork was less accurate than either of them liked.

Rossi angled his dark head toward the other Italian, now seated before the harpsichord. "Signor Pucitta, it will be the *pas de deux* of the shepherd Paris and the goddess Juno."

The sound of her feet brushing the wooden floorboards threatened to drown out the soft strains wafting from the orchestra pit. She concentrated on the music, matching her movements to its rhythm, her performer's smile growing more genuine with each success of her will over the laws of gravity. She placed her hand upon Armand's outstretched arm, letting the other rest upon his firm shoulder, and raised one leg behind her for the *arabesque penchée*. A moment later she darted away from him, her toes skimming the stage, and he pursued her by vaulting himself into one of his celebrated *jetés*.

Inspired by his brilliance, Rosalie completed a tricky *bourée* without cheating, as she'd done when practicing with d'Egville. Armand's eyes flashed as his stocky, muscular form left the earth yet again, and it occurred to her that when he danced he was almost handsome.

His next feat, an *entrechat huit,* provoked a sharp comment from Rossi, whose disembodied voice called out from the front row, "Allegro—faster! No, no, try again. You want to be quick, lively! We will attend to it later. Signor Puccitta, continue."

The coda was grand and stately, demanding less energy from the dancers, and the pas de deux ended with another supported arabesque.

While Signor Rossi and James d'Egville conducted a whispered dialogue, Rosalie stood beside Armand, her chest heaving. She was too weary to think clearly, but instinct told her that she'd performed reasonably well for a dancer who had been away from the stage for two months. Her technique hadn't entirely deserted her, and the troublesome right ankle remained wonderfully steady and free of pain.

"I am satisfied, *signorina*," the ballet master announced, "even though you are small to be Juno. Go down to the tiring room and someone can make the costume fit. I will advise Signor Kelly to draw up a formal contract, if you accept our terms."

Exultation deprived Rosalie of speech, but before withdrawing to the wings she managed a nod signifying assent.

"Wait, Vestris," Rossi commanded as Armand followed her off the stage. "I am wanting to see the *entrechat* once more. Your elevation is not what it could be."

The Frenchman's scowl indicated that his professional pride was offended by the comment.

As Rosalie peeled off her leather slippers, their insides damp with perspiration, she puzzled over Armand's displeasure. A true artist, her mother had often said, must strive to vanquish the ego and recognize those weaknesses which required improvement. Distressed to discover that fame and adulation had altered her friend, she made a silent vow never to let vanity impede her ability to learn, especially now that her dream had become a reality.

A chorus of London church bells were striking the hour of two as the Duke of Solway's town coach and the vehicles bearing a Parliamentary delegation reached the columned forecourt of Carlton House.

A mere two days after Rosalie de Barante's departure Gervase had also deserted Haberdine Castle, citing his need to take his seat in the House of Lords. It had been an act of rebellion, a demonstration of his unwillingness to be ruled by family expectations. He hadn't stated his intention of seeking out his inamorata, and if his mother had guessed that duty was not the only reason for his journey she'd been astute enough not to make any comment. Perhaps she didn't care, so long as he refrained from conducting his amours in her presence or beneath his ancestral roof.

He already knew that Rosalie had not returned to the Tottenham Street theater, the one she'd left so abruptly after her October accident. His hopeful visit to Islington had been similarly unrewarding: Sadler's Wells remained closed until Easter, and Mrs. Dibdin was quite certain that her husband hadn't engaged the French dancer for his summer season. Mary Grimaldi had been unable to help him, and she'd seemed so preoccupied by some private concern that he regretted troubling her with questions.

It was imperative that he find Rosalie. While he didn't expect to overcome her scruples by admitting the depth and strength of his attachment, he wanted her to know that his proposal had been prompted by more than a transient physical desire. He had cheapened his offer of protection by failing to explain that he was in love with her. Madly, fiercely, agonizingly in love.

Before joining the group of officials, he gazed across Pall Mall at the Italian Opera House. To dance there had been Rosalie's stated ambition—possibly he could solve the mystery of her whereabouts by seeking her there.

Reluctantly he'd interrupted his search for the dancer to participate in the frenzied political debate being waged by the Government and the Opposition over the proposed Regency. Without understanding how it came about, he had become embroiled in a conflict rife with intrigue.

Spencer Perceval, the Prime Minister, was determined to restrict the powers of the Prince of Wales. The Whigs, anticipating a swift rise to prominence in a new ministry, were eager to placate His Royal Highness and protested the limitations. Gervase, taking his seat in the House of Lords some days after the final division on the question, had followed his father's example of enlightened Toryism in subsequent votes, thereby endearing himself to the party. His new and unsought prestige had resulted in Lord Camden's invitation to join the deputation of Lords and Commons bound for Carlton House, where they were about to hear the Prince's response to the provisions of the Regency Bill.

Grey and Grenville, the Whig lords most likely to head the next government, were brimming with self-importance and ill-concealed triumph when the doors were opened by a footman in the Prince's livery. As a crowd of noblemen and ministers assembled in the octagonal vestibule, the major domo intoned, "My lords, gentlemen, His Royal Highness is prepared to receive you now."

From his position at the rear of the procession, Gervase cast a fleeting glance at a marble bust staring down from a pedestal. It was Charles James Fox, the Prince's political hero, who had labored for a Whig supremacy but hadn't lived to enjoy it.

Entering the circular drawing room in the wake of his illustrious companions, he discovered that their royal host had summoned his friends among the Opposition to witness this momentous occasion. Richard Sheridan and Lord Moira were present, as was the Duke of Cumberland, whose scarred face was more grim than the proceedings seemed to warrant.

Presently in his forty-ninth year, George, Prince of Wales was less handsome than in his youth. An excess of French food and French spirits had broadened his figure, and his features were rapidly vanishing beneath fat. His bulging blue eyes scanned each member of the party, and when they fell upon Gervase, he said, "It is my pleasure to welcome you to Carlton House this afternoon, cousin. You have never been here, I think."

"I've not been so honored, Your Highness."

"Some other time you must permit me to show you my many treasures. I deeply regret that the business at hand prevents my doing so today."

Conscious of the stares of all the other gentlemen as they puzzled over an obvious overture, Gervase made a deep and reverent bow. He could not account for it himself, having encountered the Prince but a few times in his life. By tradition all peers above the rank of baron were officially designated as cousins by the King, but the present monarch had only the remotest blood connection to the aristocracy. Was the Prince's familiarity an early attempt to establish himself as his father's substitute?

After a brief exchange of civilities, Lord Camden began reading Parliament's final resolutions. For the term of one year, the Prince could create no peers. The Queen would be responsible for the care of His Majesty, assisted by a council, and crown property would be administered by trustees.

Gervase, feigning attentiveness, examined the towering columns of red prorphyry and the blue silk draperies. Now he understood why many people referred to Carlton House as the grandest palace in all of Europe. The Prince had certainly created a suitably royal residence for himself and an appropriate repository for his most precious works of art.

When Lord Camden reached the conclusion of his address, his voice increased in volume. "The lords spiritual and temporal express their hope that His Royal Highness, out of regard to the interests of His Majesty, will be prepared to undertake the weighty trust proposed to be vested in him, subject to such limitations and restrictions as might be provided."

The attention of every person in the room turned toward the portly individual in the blue coat and tight white breeches.

The Prince dutifully recited the acceptance composed by his Whig advisers. "Being determined to submit to every personal sacrifice consistent with the regard I owe to the security of my father's crown and the welfare of his people, I do not hesitate to accept the office and situation proposed to me." He paused, then added, "My lords and gentlemen, you will communicate this answer to the two Houses, with my most fervent wishes and prayers that the Divine Will may extricate us and the nation from our present position by the speedy restoration of His Majesty's health."

At the conclusion of the ceremony, Gervase stepped aside so the others might precede him out of the room.

Upon reaching the courtyard the distinguished gentlemen scattered in several directions, some departing for Westminster, others hastening toward such Whig strongholds as Holland House and Melbourne House to report on what had passed. There would be no rejoicing in Tory circles; it was almost certain that after his swearing-in the new Regent would topple his father's ministers from their lofty perch.

The rain showers of the morning had abated; the heavy clouds were lifting. Gervase sauntered purposefully across busy Pall Mall to find out if Rosalie had returned to the King's Theatre.

He posed this question to the box keeper, who shrugged and replied helplessly, "Mr. Taylor is confined to the Rules of the King's Bench Prison, and 'is secretary Masterson doesn't tell me nothing. One of the ladies of the ballet was given leave for a lying-in, but whether a Frenchie replaced 'er I can't say. Most of our dancers are Italian—Angiolini,

Mori, Peto. But that Madame Nora is a Portugee, so is Monroy."

"Mr. Read, would *anyone* here know if Mademoiselle de Barante has applied to the management?"

The man shook his head. "The stage manager—that's Mr. Michael Kelly—will very likely be at Drury Lane today. And our treasurer Mr. Jewell departed after the midday rehearsal. Tomorrow is an opera night, so you might come back then and see if she's dancing."

Gervase, having already decided to do so, was dismayed to learn that his own box might not be available. "How can that be? It's my personal property. My father purchased it twenty years ago, when the theater was rebuilt."

His informant gave a guttural laugh. "Aye, in theory it's yours. But last year, when 'er grace stopped attending, she gave Mr. Ebers permission to let the box. Any member of the public can 'ire it by going to a certain bookseller in Bond Street. It may be too late to recover your seats, for they're 'ard to come by for a Saturday performance even if the Cat—when Madame Catalini isn't singing."

As Gervase retreated, Mr. Read called after him, "Your grace might take this, if you're interested in backstage matters." Turning around, he saw that the boxkeeper was holding out a newspaper. "It's the *Examiner,* crammed with gossip about stage performers. Mr. Jewell left it behind, and I was going to throw it out with the rubbish."

Gervase left the theater, the paper tucked under his arm. His carriage was waiting at the corner, and before climbing inside he commanded his coachman to take him to Elston House. Damon, he knew, retained possession of his opera box and would no doubt oblige him with a seat.

The vehicle moved forward. Gervase, who relied exclusively upon the *Morning Post* and the *London Gazette,* settled back against the cushions to study the unfamiliar newspaper. He was scanning the back pages absently when his eyes fell upon a promising paragraph beneath the heading "New French Dancer to Perform."

Mr. William Taylor and Mr. Michael Kelly, managers of the Italian Opera House, announce that they have engaged

MADEMOISELLE DE BARANTE to perform in the opera ballets for the remainder of the season. On Saturday, 12th January, she will essay the role of Juno in Mr. d'Egville's popular ballet *Le Jugement de Paris*. The new soloist is the daughter of the celebrated *danseuse* Delphine de Barante, who formerly graced the stage of the Paris Opera.

Smiling, Gervase removed a penknife from his coat pocket and cut out the notice. He wasn't sure which made him happier, the prospect of seeing her again, or the knowledge that she'd found her way back to a theater where her talents would be recognized, and appreciated.

The Duke of Solway and the Marquis of Elston navigated their way through the crowded lobby of the King's Theatre until they reached a box located on the bottom tier, on a level with the pit and slightly lower than the stage.

In common with the other gentlemen attending the opera, they wore long-tailed coats, embroidered waistcoats, and satin breeches. Their cravats were tied in the most intricate styles, and snowy ruffles extended from the sleeves of their coats, falling over their white kid gloves. Diamonds studded Gervase's silver knee buckles, and a dress sword hung from the crimson sash at his waist. He, like his friend, carried a *chapeau bras* under his arm.

Gervase studied the female component of the audience, equally splendid in low-cut gowns and flashing jewels, with far less interest than Damon. The marquis ogled the ladies, who waved their fans to and fro as they chattered to one another or flirted with their elegant escorts.

When the first act ended, Gervase asked if the soprano was a superior artist, or merely adequate. "She isn't much to look at," he commented.

"Nor are many other opera singers, with the notable exception of Angelica Catalini," Damon replied. "Bertinotti's voice hasn't the power of the Cat's, but it has a quality of sweetness. In my opinion, the management have chosen an inappropriate piece for her introduction to the public—I should think she's better suited to comic roles. I believe her prospective husband, a musician, has been commissioned to create a new work for her."

The opera dragged on to its tragic finish and Gervase, eager to see the ballet, was relieved rather than saddened when the suicidal heroine raised her dagger for the last time. He wondered whether Rosalie was nervous as she awaited her entrance. Had she found friends in the company, or did the others treat her as an outsider, a newcomer? Did she ever think of him, or remember their times together in Bibury and at Haberdine? Before the night was over, he hoped to have the answers to those and many other questions.

During the ensuing interval, Damon moaned softly, prompting Gervase to ask, "What's amiss?"

"That bovine fellow we met at Sadler's Wells is parading up and down Fop's Alley. What was his name?"

Gripping the padded rail, Gervase said grimly, "Beckmann."

"Can that man in the powdered wig be his father? By his appearance he is a gentleman of the old school, although a green velvet coat seems a bit excessive even for the opera."

"His father is dead, that's how he came by his money," Gervase recalled. He glowered in the direction of the young fellow who had discomfitted Rosalie on the night of her accident.

He clenched his gloved hands, tense with anticipation. The curtain rose to reveal three goddesses and their respective courts posed before a backdrop of Mount Ida, its peak obscured by pillowy painted clouds. The soloists performed a lively *pas de trois,* each one striving for the golden apple, and when the shepherd youth Paris appeared, they pantomimed an appeal, begging him to choose the fairest.

Armand Vestris danced first with Rosalie, who made an enchanting Juno in her sleeveless Grecian tunic. Narrow bands sewn with pearls supported a high-waisted bodice, artfully draped to reveal one bare breast. The elaborate arrangement of her hair made her appear exotic and unfamiliar to Gervase—curling tongs had imposed strict order upon her shorter curls, and the longer ones were crimped into ringlets.

The *scène d'action* continued, with the *danseur* partnering Mademoiselle Monroy, a warlike Minerva. His last and longest *pas de deux* was with Venus, the lovely Fortunata Angiolini, to whom he awarded the apple.

Although the spectators applauded graciously when the ballet ended, the occupants of the boxes and the pit abandoned their seats immediately after the curtain dropped. Damon explained that they were eager to take part in one of the most exclusive assemblies in London, a postperformance supper in the concert room.

"Do you intend to pay your compliments to Mademoiselle de Barante?" he asked Gervase as they skirted the multitudes of people in the box lobby. "As the holder of a ground level box, I am entitled to move freely behind the scenes. My guests also."

"Does she have her own changing room?"

"No, she hasn't the seniority for any perquisites. There's so little space backstage that the choristers of the opera and the ladies of the corps de ballet, poor souls, must share quarters. Never fear, I'll help you find your pretty friend— Lord Swanborough's friend, I should say," he added slyly.

Gervase accepted the offer of assistance politely but unenthusiastically, for he would have preferred a private reunion with Rosalie. They joined the other bucks and beaux thronging the subterranean corridors, chatting up the female performers. After peering over many a shoulder and being jostled more than once, Gervase glimpsed Rosalie. Benjamin Beckmann and his well-dressed companion had already cornered her.

"Blubbery bastard," Damon muttered.

Beckmann's bulk made the dancer appear more fragile than ever, and Gervase fancied there was a hunted expression in her wide eyes.

"Your invitation to dine is most generous, sir," he heard her say in a strained voice, "but it is so late." She fidgeted with the pearl trim at her waist.

"Don't refuse me," Mr. Beckmann pleaded. "You won't be sorry—and we'll not be entirely alone. See, I've brought someone who wishes to talk with you. Come forward, Lemercier, let me present you to Mamselle de Barante."

Turning to the man in the green velvet coat, she asked, "You are Monsieur Lemercier?"

He bowed his powdered head in confirmation.

"I received your letter," she said, oblivious to the presence of the duke and the marquis as she stared at the Frenchman. "I am happy to meet any friend of my mother's."

"*Pauvre* Delphine," he sighed, swaying slightly. "How like her you are, *ma belle*—I hoped it might be so."

Rosalie reached out to him, placing her hand on his arm. "Monsieur, you are ill."

"*Non, non,*" he protested. "*Je suis hébété*—I am dazed to look upon your face at last, after so many years of wondering what happened to you. And to her."

She gazed at him in confusion. "Have we met, then? *Je regrette,* but I do not remember. Was it in Paris?"

Large tears slipped down the man's shadowed cheeks as he replied, "*Non,* for I was in Vienna at the time you were born. It is so—so *difficile* to explain to you a secret my Delphine concealed for so long, and with success. I am not bitter that she married her Englishman. She had no other choice when I left Paris, but she was always mine and so are you." Gripping her hands, he said, "*Ma chère* Rosalie, I must kiss your sweet face—that is my right. For I am your true father, Etienne Lemercier."

11

I know not how t'attain the wings that I require
To lift my weight that it might follow my desire.
                                                —SIR THOMAS WYATT

"But this cannot be—*c'est impossible!*" Mrs. Hughes exclaimed, her thin face incredulous. The former dancer had come to Panton Street to hear Rosalie's report on her performance only to find her preoccupied with what had happened afterward. "Delphine must have married Mr. Lovegrove many months before you were born."

"She did," Rosalie agreed. "But that in itself doesn't disprove this gentleman's claim. Maman had a lover before she was wed—I expect you even knew him."

"*Certainement.* It was *une grande passion.* She used to be so angry when her *cher* Etienne flirted with me." Seeing Rosalie's dismay, the Frenchwoman asked sharply, "Is that the name of this man?"

"Etienne Lemercier."

Mrs. Hughes stiffened. "So he is here in London? But I thought—" Breaking off, she regarded Rosalie speculatively. "His willingness to acknowledge you is unusual, for most men deny paternity."

Rosalie had hoped her mother's friend might discredit Lemercier's assertion, but instead she was confirming her worst fears. "Not this one. He announced that I was his love child in the presence of the Duke of Solway and Lord Elston. And I should not be at all surprised if that horrid Mr. Beckmann spreads the tale all over town."

Shock had blunted her recollection of all that had transpired after she emerged from the emotional Frenchman's embrace. Gervase, whatever he may have thought, brought the uncomfortable scene to an abrupt end, removing Mr. Beckmann with a curt command to procure a hackney. With consummate gallantry he'd escorted her to the waiting vehicle, nodding his understanding when she refused to let him see her safely home.

Not that she would be ashamed to have him visit her lodging, of which she was justly proud. The large bedchamber contained everything necessary to her comfort, and the sitting room was tastefully arranged, with dark blue curtains and a handsome Turkish rug. Delphine de Barante's porcelain image smiled approvingly from the mantelpiece ledge, as if satisfied with her daughter's new abode.

The pantry was spacious enough to admit a cot for Peg Reilly, whose chief duties were brewing tea, cooking simple meals, and the daily marketing. The girl wore her fresh white cap and serviceable olive green gown with a pride that had been notably absent when she'd worked at the shabby house in Islington.

As her maid carried off a tray of food and drink, none of which Rosalie had touched, she told Mrs. Hughes about her intention of receiving Monsieur Lemercier that afternoon. "He begged me to, and I couldn't refuse."

"*Non,*" the other lady said ruefully, "that would be unwise. But you need not meet him alone, *chérie.* Shall I ask my husband's lawyer to advise you, or do you rely on your protector for assistance?"

Disliking her friend's implication, Rosalie said hastily, "But his grace of Solway is nothing to me, madame."

"*Bien sûr,* that is not my business, and I know you will conduct your *affaire d'amour* with great discretion—as Delphine did hers." After a thoughtful moment, the Frenchwoman continued, "If Lemercier should be telling a lie, he might be persuaded to recant. Especially if you have the support of this English *duc.* I am convinced he ought to be present."

"I'd rather not ask him."

The plumes of Mrs. Hughes's bonnet swayed when she shook her head in reproof. "*Quelle sottise!* Is a foolishness to be so timid. Begging favors of gentlemen is an important and necessary task. How else does one manage to survive? The opera paid me well, *c'est vrai,* but my lovers were more generous. From each I received a large settlement."

"The duke is *not* my lover," Rosalie repeated.

But she had accepted money from him, she reminded herself. Her cosy, handsomely furnished flat was proof that French practicality had outweighed any English prudence she possessed.

Reluctant though she was to impose further upon her benefactor, she also respected the opinion of her worldly-wise friend. Shortly after Mrs. Hughes departed, Rosalie sat down to compose a note to Gervase, glancing occasionally toward the figurine occupying the mantelshelf as though it could provide the answers to her many questions.

When Peg left to perform her usual errands, she carried with her the note bound for Solway House. Rosalie, not altogether certain that its recipient would respond to her summons, sat down to wait and worry.

Gervase arrived in less than an hour, his promptness earning him a warm and grateful welcome. Her relief at seeing him again was so overpowering that she could not spurn the comfort he offered.

While he held her close, she burrowed her cheek into his white muslin shirtfront and murmured, "Thank you for coming, Gervais." But his strong embrace had revived a deeper misery and reminded her that he had expectations she could never fulfill.

"I'm glad you wanted me to," he said, encircling her waist with a firm arm and leading her to the sofa. "When do you expect Lemercier?"

"At any time," she told him, sitting down.

He remained on his feet, observing her silently for several seconds before saying, "Since last night I've thought of you constantly, considering all that occurred at the theater. And I remembered what you told me on Twelfth Night about your mother's lover. Isn't there a possibility that the Frenchman could be he, and that you could be his daughter?"

"As much as I would like to say no, I cannot. Lemercier wrote to me—his letter was the one that arrived the day I

went fishing with you. In it he said only that he knew
Maman and Papa in Paris, and wished to meet me. His
claim may turn out to be false, though one cannot doubt his
conviction. And even if he speaks the truth, at least this
awful uncertainty will be over. My being baseborn won't
harm my career."

"From what I observed last evening, nothing could do
that." His praise brought a fleeting smile to Rosalie's troubled countenance. "It is a pity that your triumphant return
to the opera has been overshadowed by this event." He
went on to voice his concern that her new position might be
too demanding physically.

"Signor Rossi does work us very hard at rehearsals for
his new ballet, but I need to discipline myself after practicing on my own for so long." When asked if she found the
members of the company congenial, she nodded. "Oscar
Byrne's father used to direct the ballets at Sadler's Wells,
so we were already acquainted. I met some of the other
male dancers years ago, during my earliest days in the
corps, or knew them in Paris. Nearly all are French—Armand Vestris, Boisgerard, Deshayes, Bourdin, Moreau—
and when I return home at night, poor Peg has to remind
me to speak English!"

"What about your female colleagues, have they treated
you well?"

"Not very," she admitted. "Most of them are Italian, and
all are inclined to be wary of newcomers. I have made one
friend, little Charlotte Dubochet, the youngest member of
the ballet company. I daresay you've heard of her sister,
Harriette Wilson, the courtesan."

"And Fanny and Sophia. All three are notorious."

"Charlotte is a pupil in Boisgerard's dancing academy.
When I watch her practicing the role of Cupid, she reminds
me of myself at that age, for she truly loves to dance and is
quite talented."

"You seem to be drawn to children," Gervase commented. "It amazed me that you could manage Ninian so
easily."

"I trust he's well."

"When I left Haberdine, he was still struggling with Caesar's *Gallic Wars*. My mother was agreeably surprised by his proficiency in the French language."

Rosalie had not forgotten how insignificant she'd felt in the presence of the haughty, disapproving duchess. And the knowledge that the parent of the man she loved considered her a wanton would forever be a source of pain and regret. One week only had passed since her conversation with Gervase in the dark schoolroom, but so much had happened since then that it could have been a year ago.

She suspected him of trying to divert her from her problems when he encouraged her to tell her impressions of London's rival prima donnas. She preferred plump Bertinotti, recently engaged to a violinist from the orchestra, to the beautiful Angelica Catalini, whose greedy French husband demanded huge sums for her rare appearances. Her description of Signor and Signora Cauvini, a tempestuous married couple, made Gervase laugh.

"They squabble constantly, in very rapid Italian, during rehearsals for the new opera. Signor Pucitta composed the music for *Le Tre Sultane,* which is quite lovely, and Catalini sings it with the voice of an angel. I hope it will be acclaimed but expect our largest crowds next month, when she repeats *Semiramide*. It's one of her most popular parts."

Her discourse was interrupted by a knock at the door, followed by Peg's hasty tread in the hall. She rose swiftly, her eyes meeting Gervase's, then she crossed to the looking glass above the mantel to make sure her hair was in order.

When she turned around, she saw that Gervase was smiling. "What amuses you?"

"You looked so very French just then, patting your curls and adjusting the lace at your throat."

"I may well turn out to be more French than I knew," she said, striving for a cheerful rather than a despondent note.

Etienne Lemercier entered the room. Rosalie judged him to be in his middle to late fifties, but the powdered wig and the deep crevices about his eyes and mouth made him appear somewhat older. His attire, albeit less formal than the previous night, conformed to Continental fashion and was characterized by elegant ostentation.

With as much aplomb as she could muster, she presented him to Gervase.

"You were at the opera last night, Monsieur le Duc?" he asked. "At the time I had eyes only for *ma belle fille,* but I recall seeing you."

"Pray be seated," said Rosalie, indicating the chair nearest the fire. She returned to her sofa, expecting Gervase to join her there, but he moved to a window. "Monsieur Lemercier, because I've always believed myself to be the daughter of Richard Lovegrove, your insistence that you are my father is difficult to comprehend."

"I intend to explain, then it will be clear to you. I lived with Delphine de Barante in Paris, and for more than two years she was *une maitresse fidèle.* Often I angered her with my own transgressions and dissipations, and there were scenes. Eventually I became so impatient that I ended our affair, never guessing that she was *enceinte.* Her pride, or her shame, must have prevented her from telling me then, and later she did not know where to find me. I had wealth enough to travel, so I left Paris for Vienna, and within some months the Revolution broke out. I was a careless young man, too fond of my pleasures and expensive diversions to return to a land of strife and death."

"It is as well you did not," Rosalie murmured.

"Not until the year before last did I journey to Paris. A sentimental desire to know what had become of my Delphine took me to the Opera. I met there a lady who remembered me, one of the character dancers, and from her learned about my mistress's hasty marriage to the Englishman, and of the little daughter they passed off as his. *Mais, ce n'est pas possible,* if your mother gave birth in 1788."

Encouraged by the discrepancy, she informed him that in fact she hadn't been born until July of the following year.

"Are you so positive, or is that what Delphine and the musician told you?"

She sank back against the sofa cushions. "I can't imagine they would have lied."

"Out of consideration for your feelings, they could have concealed the truth," Gervase suggested.

"I bring no proof of what I believe," Lemercier continued, "for my search produced none. I even visited Delphine's church, but the register of marriages and births had been removed or destroyed. Many who might have confirmed my suspicions had vanished. I learned that Pascal Boyer, the editor of the *Journal des spectacles*, was a victim of the guillotine. And I was unable to locate Madame Montansier, who must have guessed whose child you were, or the Abbé de Bouyon."

"My godfather." Rosalie's hands clenched involuntarily. "He was killed during the Great Terror. The *canaille* dragged him from his house and hung him from a streetlamp."

"*Chère* Rosalie, how I wish I could have removed you from all the danger and destruction." After a pause, he continued, "I do not doubt that the violinist was good to you, or that he treated you as his own. But he has been dead many years, and cannot be hurt by your accepting me as your father. You did not even take his name."

"Occasionally I use it in my private life," she informed him, looking to Gervase for corroboration.

He stepped forward and asked, "Monsieur Lemercier, what was your motive for contacting Mademoiselle de Barante?"

The Frenchman regarded him blankly. "Motive? I only wished to meet the child of my mistress Delphine, to know her. Is that not permitted?"

"Now that you have succeeded in your object, what are your intentions? Will you return to France?"

"England is now my home, Monsieur le Duc. For almost a year I have lived here, all the time trying to trace Delphine's child. Other emigrés will confirm this—Monsieur Beckmann, *aussi*."

Rosalie, curious about his association with that gentleman, asked how they had met.

"I went to the Sadler's Wells a few months ago, after hearing that it had a ballet troupe. My stage box was the one rented out by the *bouffon* Grimaldi, and that night I shared it with Monsieur Beckmann. When he described to me a Mademoiselle de Barante who had been part of the company, my heart filled with joy. After the performance I asked the actors and dancers for additional information, and they referred me to Madame Grimaldi. Though she would not tell me or my *avocat* exactly where you had gone, she kindly offered to forward our letters." With a sad smile for Rosalie, he concluded, "If you desire that I keep away and tell me so, I must comply. But I hope you will not, for I am a lonely man in a strange country, without wife or children or family."

Rosalie responded, "Your story raises more questions than it answers, and it is too soon for me to give you any answer."

She could not dislike him, nor was she impervious to the easy charm that must have captivated her mother so many years ago. But she could not yet acknowledge him as her parent, despite the increasing probability that he was.

"If I really am his daughter," she told Gervase after the Frenchman's departure, "I don't know how I shall bear telling Aunt Tilda. She won't love me any less for not being her blood relation, but I am her last tie with Papa— that is, we *thought* so," she concluded pensively. "I have always called myself de Barante, yet I always knew that I was equally a Lovegrove. Now it seems my name could be Lemercier. Difficult though that is to accept, it is even worse to imagine that I might be a full year older than I supposed. For a dancer, that is a fearsome discovery!"

Even in February, the meticulously landscaped grounds of Solway House provided their owner with a pleasant refuge. The water in the marble fountain behind Solway House was turned off for the winter and the branches of the ornamental trees were still bare, but the gardeners were busily pruning the banksia roses growing along a high wall. Although the erratic sunshine failed to warm Gervase as he wandered along the evergreen yew hedge, it raised his spirits. So did the white and yellow crocuses blooming in the borders.

During the past month he's seen Rosalie several times, most often from his box at the King's Theatre. Because the House of Lords sat late into the night, he invariably missed Tuesday night performances, but every Saturday he was there, sitting through hours of operatic tragedy or comedy in order to enjoy the dancer's brief appearance in the ballet.

His initial hope that Rosalie might no longer feel constrained by the deathbed promise she'd made to David Lovegrove was exceedingly short-lived. Integrity and honor were her most notable virtues, apart from virtue itself. She would not become his mistress, she'd told him so quite plainly, and he cared too deeply for her good opinion to enact some ruthlessly persuasive seduction.

As yet he'd found no opportunity to inform her of the powerful feelings that had him soaring to heights of happiness and tumbling back down into the depths of despair every hour or so. His first visit to Panton Street had been twice repeated, with disappointing results. On one occasion Mrs. Grimaldi had been with Rosalie, and the next time he encountered a former colleague of David Lovegrove's, an elderly musician from the King's Theatre orchestra.

The most recent attempt to see her had been the least successful. Hoping to amuse her with a description of a solemn ceremony he had witnessed in the Crimson Drawing room at Carlton House, he'd gone to her house at midday. After Peg Reilly informed him that her mistress had just departed to attend a rehearsal, he had returned to Solway House to prowl the garden pathways.

Lord Elston found him there, and took him to task for his failure to attend an evening party the previous night.

"But unlike my beauteous hostess, *I* didn't really expect to see you. Georgiana Titus was desolated by your absence, for which I hold myself partly responsible. I should have warned her not to give it on an opera night. However, I didn't come to tease but to discuss a matter of importance. Two of them, in fact."

"Oh," Gervase said indifferently, his mind still dwelling upon Rosalie.

"You might have told me about your most recent encounter with royalty rather than letting me read it in the newspapers. I wish I'd known you mean to attend the Regent's first levee. I'm your best friend, your crony, your boon companion, yet you said nothing at all. After affronting me so grossly, you don't deserve my advice, but

I'll offer it anyway. As one whose experience of our Prince
far exceeds yours, I warn you to be cautious in your deal-
ings with him."

"I intend to be," Gervase assured him.

"He is notoriously demanding and dangerously fickle.
Just ask Grenville and the other Whigs, who were engaged
in forming their new administration when they learned that
their hopes and efforts were all in vain. But I'm sure that
you, His Royal Highness's newest confidant, know all
this."

Gervase nodded as they passed beneath the intertwined
branches of the laburnum arch. "The political status quo is
preserved, and the King's Tory ministers will keep their
places."

"And the Prince is always motivated by self-interest, to
say nothing of pure selfishness. He wants something from
you, and everyone knows it. Speculation has been rife from
the day you went to Carlton House with the Parliamentary
delegation. Do you know what is being said?"

"I'm not sure I want to," he said grimly.

"Yours is a family of distinction, but even more to the
point, Tudor and Stuart blood flows in your veins. The
Prince Regent is known to have an abiding interest in the romantic rulers who were supplanted by his plebian forebears
from Hanover. He also has a daughter approaching marriage-
able age. An English duke, one with a royal heritage, would
be a more popular choice as her husband than any German
princeling."

Gervase emitted a sharp laugh. "Are you implying that
the Prince regards me as a prospective son-in-law? If that's
the role the gossips have chosen for me, they've outdone
themselves on absurdity! I've never met Princess Charlotte
of Wales, and considering all I've heard about her I don't
particularly wish to. Besides, her grandfather's madness
combined with my Aunt Hermia's mental instability must
be regarded as serious impediments to an alliance."

"Nevertheless, keep on your guard against palace in-
trigues. Unless, of course, you aspire to the position of consort."

"I can think of nothing more distasteful to me—or my

family. Mother would be appalled, and I've worried her quite enough lately."

Damon exhibited his most wicked smile. "Your obsession with the opera dancer alarms the duchess, does it? And while we're on the subject of Mademoiselle de Barante—"

"I'm in no mood for another of your warnings," Gervase said firmly.

"I wouldn't presume to interfere to that extent," said the marquis, wagging his golden head. "Do you remember asking me last autumn if I was familiar with a work by Jean-Baptiste Greuze?"

" 'Mischief,' " Gervase said quickly. "Yes, I did."

"I thought you might like to know that just such a painting is on view at Mr. Christie's rooms in Pall Mall. I noticed it there earlier this week and recognized the subject immediately. That was the other important thing I came to tell you."

Gervase ordered his carriage at once, unconcerned about exposing himself to mockery from Damon, who insisted upon accompanying him to the auction house.

But his friend exhibited remarkable restraint, merely saying in his languid way. "I perceive that your interest in Mademoiselle de Barante is more than casual."

"I refuse to discuss my connection with her," he stated as they were borne southward along Park Lane. But he thought better of it, not wishing Damon to draw an incorrect conclusion. "Trust me, she is undeserving of any censure. And whether or not she permits me to become something more, I am forever her friend."

"Obviously you wish it could be more than friendship. Poor Gervase—with all the opera dancers who would welcome your attentions, you had to choose the only one who is unattainable. But your taste, I must admit, is in all other respects impeccable."

When the two noblemen entered Mr. Christie's showroom, one of the employees stepped forward to offer assistance.

"I believe this establishment has acquired a painting by Greuze, and I should like to examine it," Gervase announced.

"Ah yes, the little Gypsy girl. I would have been most happy to show it to your grace, but I fear it went under the hammer yesterday and was sold."

"Sold?" he repeated.

"It failed to fetch the price we had hoped," the gentleman explained. "Even so, the seller, who had acquired it from the original owner, made a substantial profit. The painting had an interesting history, for it was formerly the property of a Parisian lady who posed for several notable artists, including Fragonard. I understand that she was a famous dancer."

"I'm interested in knowing the identity of the purchaser," Gervase said.

"If your grace will grant me but a moment, I shall examine the record."

Damon drifted away to inspect a framed landscape displayed on an easel, while Gervase waited impatiently for Mr. Christie's assistant to return. He wished he'd learned about the painting sooner, for then he could have attended yesterday's sale and placed a bid high enough to secure it for himself. For Rosalie, he amended, because it was on her behalf that he'd wanted the elusive picture.

The man returned to report that the Greuze had been acquired for two hundred guineas.

"Is that all?" Damon asked over his shoulder.

"It is not regarded as one of the artist's better efforts, my lord."

"But a charming study nonetheless. I daresay you could still have it, Gervase, if you offered the new owner three hundred."

The assistant shrugged. "I can't say with any certainty that he would be willing to relinquish it so soon after adding it to his collection, but your grace could inquire."

"I intend to do so," Gervase said with decision. "Who is he, this admirer of Greuze's lesser works?"

"A French gentleman, now a resident of London," their informant replied. "His name is Lemercier."

12

"You are dismissed. And remember, everyone, tomorrow evening it is necessary to dance *con brio, con spirito!*"

Rosalie, her confidence shaken by one of Signor Rossi's sharp rebukes, was relieved that the morning rehearsal had ended. Utterly dispirited, she followed the other soloists to the lower regions of the theater, retreating to a dim, out of the way corner to repeat the intricate *enchainement* she'd muddled on the stage.

She didn't care that the bodice of her muslin gown clung damply to her heated flesh, or that her feet ached, and she ignored the twinge in the small of her back whenever she elevated her leg. Only by improving could she maintain a place in the company and keep her part in *Asiatic Divertissement,* a new ballet with music by Michael Kelly, in which she would portray an Asian court lady.

Armand Vestris and Oscar Byrne exited their dressing room and paused nearby to continue an ongoing conversation. She listened to them absently as she attempted a *pas de basque.*

Said Byrne, without lowering his voice, "Concern about his debts greatly impaired his judgment. He and his wife made up their minds to share a dose of poison in order to escape their financial troubles."

"A sad end for *le bouffon* Grimaldi," was Armand's comment.

Rosalie's body went rigid when she heard the comedian's name. "Grimaldi can't be dead!" she cried.

In a calming voice Byrne replied, "No, he still lives. But
he attempted suicide, and so did his wife. They swallowed
some laudanum before going to bed t'other night, but didn't
even mix enough to put themselves to sleep. When Mary
asked, 'Joey, are you dead yet?' he replied, 'I don't think
so—are you?' and both began to laugh. To hear him tell it,
'twas a great joke. After eating a good supper and drinking
quantities of wine, they felt a great deal more cheerful and
decided to live on."

This tale was followed by some gossip about Grimaldi's
regular visits to a Clerkenwell pawnbroker. Armand was
clearly amused by it, but Rosalie regarded both of Byrne's
anecdotes as pathetic rather than humorous. Her last chat
with Mary Grimaldi had been some weeks ago, and she felt
guilty about neglecting someone who might require a
friendly word and possibly monetary assistance.

She returned to her lodging house for a hasty wash and a
fresh gown, and set out for Baynes Row in a hackney
coach. Along the way to Islington she spied comforting
signs of spring's approach—a clump of wild primroses
whimsically planted in the windowbox of a town house,
and the waving daffodils in Clerkenwell churchyard. When
she arrived at the Grimaldi residence, she gazed across Waterhouse Fields toward the New River, Islington Spa, and
Sadler's Wells—reminders of her earliest encounters with
Gervase and his cousin.

Mary Grimaldi, delighted by Rosalie's unexpected visi-
tation, welcomed her with a warm smile and a fond embrace. "Just look at you!" she exclaimed. "Such a modish
bonnet, and quite a pretty shawl—you're doing very well
for yourself, I see. No regrets about leaving the aquatic theater?"

"Only one, that I so seldom see you and your family."

"And we also miss you. Don't we, Joe?" Mary smoothed
her son's dark hair, then returned her attention to Rosalie,
saying, "You must tell us what it's like, dancing in the
opera ballets, and about all your admirers."

"I'm not here to talk of myself," she objected. "I want to know how things are with you, Mary."

Her hostess expelled a heavy sigh. "You've been hearing rumors about us. I'm not surprised—my husband *will* tell tales on himself to provoke a laugh. Joe, my dear, why don't you amuse yourself while Mama and Miss Rose are talking, and in a little while we can have tea and cakes." When her child resumed his play, Mary said quietly, "We're buried in debt. Between us, my husband and I have three salaries yet are quite unable to meet all our expenses. I do try to economize, but when it comes to Joe I find it very hard not be indulgent."

Rosalie studied the little boy as he manipulated a mechanical monkey; a turn of the key at its back made the head bob from side to side. It, like the other playthings scattered upon the hearth rug, must have cost Joe's fond parents a considerable sum.

"I greatly fear we shall be forced to let Tippety Cottage go, and that will break our hearts. Joey discharged his groom and gave up the horse and gig. Now he has forbidden me to make any alterations in this house or hire more servants. In the hope of settling with our creditors, he will put his affairs in the hands of a solicitor, who will doubtless demand additional sacrifices from us."

"But at least it might help you out of your difficulties," Rosalie said encouragingly.

"Joey and I share the blame for managing so badly," Mary acknowledged. "We both committed our resources to our son's education, our primary expense. First we sent him to the local school, then we provided French and Italian lessons, and now he has a private tutor. Lately we've engaged a music master—he plays the violin beautifully for a boy so young. The Byrnes and the Fairbrothers, who put all of their lads and lasses on the stage, think us mad to bring him up a gentleman instead of a theatrical performer. But he's very clever, is our Joe, and could make something of himself."

The child, hearing his name, looked up.

"Come and sit by me," Rosalie invited him, patting the cushion of the settee. "Now tell me, what do you most want to be when you grow up? And don't say you aren't sure, because I made up my mind before I was eight years old."

Joe grinned. "I'm going to be a clown in the panto, just like my pa." He wound up his toy again, and made it bow to her. "Papa was younger than me when he went on the stage—he played the part of a little monkey. I can, too. Watch!" Pulling at his ears, he copied the simian's expression.

"Don't make faces," his mother reproved him gently. "Be a good lad now, and tell Cook to make us some tea. Perhaps later Miss Rose will talk French to you. Dear me," she moaned softly as he scampered out of the room, "suppose he really *does* become a player? It's such a hard life, not the one Joey wants for his child."

"It's only natural that he should want to perform. When I was young and saw my mother dancing, I longed to do it, too."

"And I was just the same," the clown's wife acknowledged. "I come from a family of actors and actresses. So does Joey. Old Grimaldi set him to stagework as soon as he could toddle about. I'll speak with him tonight," she said decisively. "Perhaps he will agree that it's foolish to beggar ourselves turning Joe into a gent if he'd rather train to be a comedian."

When Rosalie returned to London, she instructed the hackney driver to convey her to Piccadilly. She spent the rest of the afternoon in the shops on both sides of that fashionable thoroughfare, searching out dress materials for a forthcoming role.

She rejected velvets and satins as too heavy and stiff, and silver tissue as too expensive. After finding a turquoise gauze woven with strands of gilt thread, she chose a length of white sarcenet for an underskirt. The same establishment sold ribbons and other trimmings, and she was tempted by a spool of shiny gold braid and matching silken tassels. Her seamstress, Madame Ferrier, regularly performed miracles and with such items at her disposal would certainly create a costume to arouse envy in all the other dancers.

The shop assistant was already sweeping the floor in

preparation for closing when Rosalie paid for her purchases. The proprietor tied up her last parcel and asked if she wanted her goods delivered. She declined; she lived so near that it was no trouble to carry them herself.

Rounding the corner of the Haymarket and Panton Street, she noticed a curricle and pair waiting at the curb. To reach her door she had to walk past the groom holding the horses, and he leered at her, winking slyly. Despite a strong inclination to put out her tongue, she disregarded him.

Her feet dragged as she climbed the two flights of stairs to her floor. Monday always seemed the longest day of the week, and she was glad to be spared the effort of a performance. Before the next rehearsal she would perfect the *enchainement* for Rossi, and dance it faultlessly at tomorrow's performance.

Recalling that this was Peg's afternoon off, she shifted the packages to one arm and reached into her netted reticule for her key. While she was fitting it into the lock, a large figure moved out of the shadows.

"Mr. Beckmann!" Her startled cry was followed by the sound of her key hitting the wooden floor.

He stooped down to recover it. But when she held out her hand, he only grinned and held it just out of reach.

"If you please, sir, let me have that key."

"Allow me."

When he had unlocked the door, he followed her into the cramped vestibule. She placed her parcels on the parlor table, silently praying that Peg would soon return.

Before she could ask the gentleman's purpose in coming, he stated proudly, "That's my new curricle in the street. I happened to be tooling it down Haymarket, past the opera house, which made me think of you. I'm here to invite you on a little excursion I have in mind. High time we became better acquainted, so what do you say to a drive out to Salt Hill? The Windmill is a snug inn, and its dinners are fine enough for the chaps in the Four-in-Hand Club."

"I'm not able to go away with you, Mr. Beckmann," she said firmly. As much as she disliked him, she couldn't bring herself to be rude.

"My horses can cover thirteen miles in an hour, and we'd be there within two, maybe less. We'll lie abed as late as we please tomorrow morning, and I'll get you back to the theater in time to dance. I'd like to take you down to Brighton, too, but that can wait till the opera season ends."

"You misunderstood me. To put it more plainly, I do not *want* to go. Not to an inn, and definitely not to Brighton."

"Come now, don't play the coquette with me," he said impatiently. "We both know you've got no other prospect but me, not now that your fine duke has deserted you for that royal wench. That's who Solway's chasing, didn't you know? Young as she is, the Regent's daughter is as troublesome as her mama, and the only way to be rid of her is to arrange a marriage as soon as possible. But don't break your heart over his grace, for I'm here to take his place in your affections—and your bed. I may not have a golden coronet or a castle, but you can depend on me to stick by you."

At the end of this preposterous speech he put a pudgy hand upon her arm. Unnerved by the hot, greedy light in his pale eyes, she edged away. "Come no closer, Mr. Beckmann," she warned, flattening herself against her bedchamber door.

"I'll wager you're not so damned skittish with Solway," he said grimly. "Why are you set against me? I'm rich enough, you'll live in grand style under my protection. I should've thought you'd be grateful to me for helping your old father find you. It's more than the duke ever did."

Rosalie groped behind her back for the brass doorknob, twisting it surreptitiously. "I am not grateful at all," she declared with considerable heat, "nor will I be your *fille de joie. Jamais!*"

He came to an abrupt halt, and she seized the opportunity to make a swift escape. She slipped inside her room, slammed the door in his face, and slid the bolt into place with shaking fingers.

Her pursuer let out a loud, derisive laugh. "What a sly one you are, mamselle—like all the Frogs. I don't object to playing games, if that's what you prefer."

Rosalie did not reply.

His heavy tread made the floorboards creak. "I'm going now, but I'll be back. Remember, I've still got your key!"

His arrogant assumption that she would welcome his advances had alarmed her as much as his implication that the Duke of Solway had been her lover. And now, if Beckmann told the truth, Gervase was involved with the Prince Regent's daughter. That could well account for his failure to call upon her in recent weeks. Not so long ago he'd stopped by often, albeit at irregular intervals, to show her a letter from Lord Swanborough or vent his growing frustration with his political allies and adversaries.

Peg Reilly returned at dusk and found her mistress locked in the bedchamber. Outraged by Rosalie's tale of persecution, she offered to sleep on the sitting room sofa in case Mr. Beckmann should make good his threat to return.

"You must send for a locksmith first thing tomorrow, Miss Rose. And if that nasty, thieving man tries to get at you again, he'll discover that you're much cleverer than he *thinks* he is!"

Spring had come early, but in the first week of April its rapid progress was inhibited by a chilling easterly wind. The dismal change in the weather matched Rosalie's low spirits. Mr. Beckmann had not approached her again, but he continued to prowl Fop's Alley. And backstage gossip confirmed his allegations about the Duke of Solway and Princess Charlotte of Wales.

Rumors of a royal engagement had supplanted the Regent's retention of the King's ministers as a favorite topic of conversation in theatrical as well as social circles. The Heiress Apparent was only fifteen, and some performers professed to be shocked by the duke's apparent courtship. Armand Vestris, whose roving eye had lighted upon the fourteen-year-old Lucia Bartolozzi, a recent addition to the dancing academy, could not understand this objection.

No one bothered to ask Rosalie's opinion, which was just as well. She preferred to keep it to herself.

Because the King's Theatre suspended its performances during Passiontide and Easter Week, she faced a fortnight of inactivity during which to mourn Gervase's defection. In an effort to divert herself, she sent a letter to her aunt in Gloucestershire, begging her to visit, and was disappointed when Matilda regretfully refused; a string of social commitments would tie her to Bibury until summer.

On Easter Day, Rosalie went to the Roman Catholic chapel near Golden Square, where she joined a crowd of emigrés. Many were strangers; others, like the hedonistic Armand, she knew quite well. The priest's singsong Latin and the heady scent of incense carried her back to her early childhood, when attendance at Mass had been regarded as a dangerous act of defiance. During the service her attention was caught by a gentleman wearing a white wig. When he turned his head to gaze back at her, she saw that he was Etienne Lemercier.

"So much I have heard about your English *duc*," Mrs. Hughes told her after the service. "*Pauvre petite*, you should have snared him when you had the chance. If he marries *la princesse*, her stuffy relations will be careful to keep him away from the opera!"

Her dismay was heightened when Etienne Lemercier approached her to ask if she would dine with him that evening, accepting her polite refusal with a nod, as though he'd expected it. She regretted causing him pain but was still unable to offer him the filial companionship he desired.

Although she had hoped to sleep luxuriously late on Easter Monday, she woke with the sun and lay in bed brooding until Peg brought her breakfast tray.

She forced down mouthfuls of boiled egg until the shell was half empty and swallowed a piece of buttered toast, but the food seemed to stick in her throat. For the remainder of the morning she altered the white tunic she'd worn for her debut as Juno, which she would use again in *The Loves of Mars and Venus* later in the month. Never fond of needlework, she was glad to set it aside for a titillating novel. All afternoon she lounged upon the parlor sofa, her stocking feet supported by a cushion, and devoured *Les Liaisons Dangereuses*. She was so absorbed in her reading that for long periods she was unaware of the incessant chopping sound coming from the pantry, where Peg was preparing cabbages for soup.

An abrupt tap on the door recalled Rosalie to the real world. She sat upright, tense and wary, and reminded herself that Peg had instructions to send Mr. Beckmann away should he return.

"It's you," she breathed in relief when Gervase entered. His habit of appearing just when she was convinced that he'd never return bewildered her. And past experience had taught her that the peace of mind his presence bestowed was transitory, and would not outlast the visit.

He handed his hat to the beaming Peg and asked, "Are you displeased to see me?"

"Of course not, only I'm embarrassed that you've come at a time when my rooms smell of cooked cabbage." Instinctively her hands flew to her tumbled hair, although his broad smile indicated that disheveled appearance appealed to him.

"The soup is ready, Miss Rose," her servant announced, "and I've sliced the bread. Shall I lay two places?"

Rosalie turned to her guest. "I've dinner enough to share with you."

"I accept with pleasure. But you weren't expecting a guest, so you must permit to let me make some additions to the meal." Turning to Peg, he presented her with a handful of coins. "Go to the pastrycook shop across the way and purchase some meat pies and hot cross buns and fruit tarts. I prefer gooseberry, if any are to be had. Choose whatever you like for yourself."

Peg bobbed a curtsy. "Aye, your grace, and thank you."

"Sadler's Wells playhouse opens tonight," he told Rosalie when they were alone.

"Yes, I know."

"I've sent my footman Robert there to secure a pair of box seats. May I escort you to Islington to see how well Mr. Dibdin is managing in your absence?"

She knew it was folly to accept but lacked the strength to do anything else. Conscious of a painfully intense longing to be in his arms again, she knelt down to search for her slippers.

He sat down on the sofa and picked up her discarded

novel. "By Choderlos de Laclos. I know his name but never read this work. What is your opinion?"

"It's a troubling tale. And a tragic one."

"And shocking, *n'est-ce pas*?"

"Only to the English," she retorted.

Throughout dinner, she managed to stifle her nagging questions about his budding relationship with Princess Charlotte. Surely if he was about to enter into an engagement, he wouldn't have visited her—unless, she thought in sudden panic, he had come to announce his marriage plans. The suspicion that he intended to break off their loose and ill-defined connection grew ever stronger, and she decided that his invitation to the playhouse was a characteristically thoughtful attempt to give her some pleasure before shattering her heart. Except that he could never know how deeply she cared for him, she reasoned with herself.

Her appetite, which had flagged of late, deserted her altogether. She was unable to finish her portion of the Perigord pie, a concoction of meat and truffles in a light pastry, and the play of candlelight across his aristocratic face was of greater interest to her than hot cross buns from the cookshop.

When he complimented the cabbage soup, she told him, "It is made from the recipe of *ma marraine*, my godmother. Because she was childless she mothered her actors and dancers and provided them with sustaining food, not trusting them to take proper care of themselves. She often served this soup—and a good thing she did. It helped to make her fortune."

"How?" he asked curiously.

"It has a heavy aroma, as you will have noticed. One night when the Queen was in attendance she smelled cabbages and was told that the manageress had made her famous soup. Her Majesty, who had not dined, sent a footman to ask if she might have a bowl of it herself. That is how Mademoiselle de Montansier won Marie Antoinette's favor and friendship. After the encounter she was invited to the *petits levées*, and eventually became *directrice* of the theaters at the royal palaces of St. Cloud, Marly, Fontainebleau, Compiegne. And Versailles."

"Where your mother sometimes performed," he said with a fond smile.

As Peg began clearing the table, Rosalie excused herself and left the duke to finish his wine.

Going to her bedchamber, she changed into a gown more appropriate for an evening at the theater. Standing before the looking glass in her chemise, she wondered if she might alter her destiny by inviting Gervase to come to her. She imagined his hands caressing her body, his gray eyes smoky with desire. But there was no certainty that she could keep him beside her for longer than a single night, and afterward she would be doubly shamed. Her guilt over a broken vow would be as hard to bear as the loss of her self-respect.

She took pains with her hair, piling the curls high and securing them with the gold combs she'd been given on her sixteenth birthday, after her mother had sold the Fragonard canvas. Inspired by Delphine de Barante's shining example of strength and dignity in the face of adversity, she prepared herself to accept Gervase's engagement as any friend would, with felicitations. She was a dancer, not an actress, but she trusted in her ability to make her best wishes sound genuine.

Her finest gown was rose-colored silk, its low neck adorned with creamy Valenciennes lace. In future, if he should think back to their final hours together, she wanted him to remember that she had looked beautiful.

During their drive to Islington, to give the impression of being gay and lighthearted, she said brightly, "What a pity Lord Swanborough isn't here to share the treat."

"He and Duffield are in Wiltshire—they spent Easter at Cavender Chase," Gervase told her. "Ninian's mother is also there, so they'll have another opportunity to improve their acquaintance."

"I'm glad." Rosalie recalled the day in the Elizabethan gallery at Haberdine, when the boy had shown her Lady Swanborough's portrait. "The only time he mentioned her to me, he said he'd met her but once."

"Yes. But her condition is much improved, and she wishes to be reconciled with her children." Looking at her,

he said quietly, "I believe the French regard melancholy as
a singularly English malady."

"*C'est vrai.* Even your King suffers from it. Our King,"
she amended, unwilling to appear wholly foreign.

"His Majesty's recoveries from previous spells have
been remarkable, but this time he appears to be more
gravely ill than ever before. When I was at Windsor with
the Prince Regent I was privy to a gloomy report from the
royal physicians."

Rosalie's blood ran cold at his acknowledgement of a
growing intimacy with the court.

"My visit received a great deal of publicity, far more
than was warranted. Fortunately it served to conceal the
truth of why I went to Windsor—just as well, I suppose, for
I did so in connection with what could become a serious
royal scandal. I'll tell you as much as I can, if you promise
never to breathe a word to anyone."

"No, never," she murmured through stiff, pale lips.

"Princess Charlotte has developed a strong attachment to
her tutor. Not surprising, really, for the poor girl is constantly surrounded by females, dull ones at that, and the
only gentlemen she's allowed to see are her royal uncles
and the Regent's ministers. The Duke of York was the first
to suspect her feelings. He told his brother the Regent, who
was appalled to learn that his fifteen-year-old daughter regarded a commoner with affection. Remembering that I had
attended both his swearing-in ceremony and the first levee,
he summoned me to Carlton House and requested that I accompany him to Windsor."

"For what purpose?" Rosalie asked around the lump in
her throat.

"I was excluded from his private discussion with his
mother, but I believe he sought her permission for me to
call on the princess. As best I can determine, in his mind I
represent a more suitable alternative to a scholarly clergyman. But the Queen adamantly opposed him. Not long afterward, she visited Warwick House herself to scold her
granddaughter for her waywardness. Princess Charlotte,
who is as headstrong as she is volatile, took her revenge by
drawing up a will leaving all her jewels, her books, and

other private property to the tutor as a pledge of her high regard for him. She told me about it herself."

"Then you have been visiting her?"

"Not officially. Perceval, the Prime Minister, hopes I can counsel her to abandon her quarrel with the Queen before it becomes public, so I'm forewarned on those occasions when she takes exercise in the gardens of Carlton House. And I've escorted her and her governess, Lady de Clifford, to Blackheath, where she goes every Saturday to dine with her mother. The last time we were all entertained by some singers from the opera."

Rosalie nodded. "Naldi and Tramezzani—I heard of it, but not that you were there. Is Princess Charlotte pretty?" she asked, careful to keep her voice steady.

"Her skin is fair and her hair is reddish gold, like her father's. She has his large blue eyes, too. Her features are very expressive, and her figure voluptuous for her age."

This favorable account, coupled with the earlier description of the harsh treatment the Heiress Apparent received from her relations, reminded Rosalie of the heroine of a romantic fairy tale. And any lonely and persecuted princess would look upon Gervase, the head of the nation's most prominent and pedigreed family, as the perfect cavalier.

The duke's servant had acquired a pair of box seats which provided an excellent view of stage and auditorium, smartened up by a fresh coat of paint and chandeliers of gleaming brass. The crowded theater was typical of the first night of the season, but Rosalie was so preoccupied that she felt no satisfaction on behalf of the management.

There was no ballet that night, so she could not discover who had replaced her in the *corps*. The evening's entertainment began with a new harlequinade, *Dulce Domum, or England the Land of Freedom*. The curtain opened upon a cottage *ornée*, the honeymoon dwelling of Columbine and Harlequin. Bored with their quiet life, the newlyweds journeyed to foreign lands, a device which permitted Mr. Dibdin to draw comparison between Britain and enemy nations and turn the piece into a form of political propaganda. Joseph Grimaldi, as a strutting and bombastic Napoleon Bonaparte, was loudly hissed by the patriotic crowd.

The comedian reappeared later in his customary guise of Clown, to sing a merry ditty. When finished, he declaimed, "Oh, give me little England, where a man's head is his own freehold property, and his house is his castle. And whoever touches a hair of the one, or the latch of the other without leave, is sure to get the door in his face!"

The people cheered, ladies waving their handkerchiefs and the gentlemen their hats. Rosalie and Gervase joined them, similarly inspired by partisan sentiment.

The finale turned out to be *The Spectre Knight,* the popular aqua-drama from the previous season. Turning to her escort, Rosalie whispered, "I'm sick to death of this play and doubt it has improved since last autumn. Do you mind if I slip away for a little while? I'd like to speak to Mr. Grimaldi, before he departs for the Myddelton's Head."

"I'll meet you outside the stage door," Gervase replied.

The renovation of the theater had not included the areas most familiar to her; the narrow, twisting hallways were as dim and dirty as ever. Grimaldi, his swarthy face washed clean of the white and red paint he'd worn onstage, greeted her with surprise.

"How are Mary and young Joe?" she asked, eager for news of his family.

"Both are very well. Now that my son has made plain his inclination for a career on the stage, I've begun instructing him in tumbling and mime. It's not what I'd have chosen for him, Miss Rose, but I cannot deny a vain desire to see my success repeated. The Grimaldi name has been synonymous with pantomime since my father's time, so I'm not altogether displeased that the association will continue for another generation."

She exited the building, pausing to speak with Mr. Wheeler, gently puffing on his pipe as he guarded the door.

Gervase was waiting for her, and when he recommended a stroll through the grounds she readily assented, for the weather was pleasant and mild. She let him lead her across the greensward and farther away from the glow of the oil lamps marking the carriageway. A gentle breeze stirred the branches of the towering elms and caused the daffodils along the paths to tremble.

Gervase said softly, "Listen to that nightingale. It's the first one I've heard this spring." Speaking over the songbird's trilling aria, he added, "The ideal accompaniment for a love scene, don't you agree?"

Her shining eyes and upturned face expressed her willingness to oblige him. A few kisses under the stars were all she could aspire to, and she was determined to have them before it was too late. His exploring lips helped her forget that they were soon to part, and in his sheltering arms she felt entirely weightless, capable of soaring over the treetops.

"Would you fly away with me tonight?" he murmured against her cheek. "For the rest of the week you're at liberty from the opera house. Like Columbine and Harlequin, we might hide ourselves away in some secluded, secret place, where no one knows us and no one could find us."

This invitation was far more appealing than the similar one tendered by Mr. Beckmann. How difficult, how terrible to give him up without sampling the passionate pleasures his eyes and mouth and seductive words promised her.

"Don't ask me again, Gervais, unless you wish to break my heart."

"Keeping your precious heart intact is more important to me than anything in all the world." He looked as if he might speak again, but when he did it was only to suggest that they return to the carriage.

Throughout the return journey to London they said very little. Rosalie, understanding that the time for words was behind them, wondered what their fate might have been were he not a duke or she a dancer.

All too soon they reached Panton Street. He assisted her out of the vehicle, and when he pressed her hand in farewell she was more certain than ever that she'd been given her final chance to refuse his increasingly tempting offer.

Rosalie knelt upon the unrelenting wooden floor, holding her portion of a long floral garland supported by a line of white-clad nymphs. Tonight she was part of the corps; only one female soloist was needed in this new ballet about Mars and Venus.

Armand Vestris and Fortunata Angiolini, lovers on the stage as in life, skipped and swayed before her. The dancer's diminutive body matched the movements of her stocky and athletic partner, and her pretty face testified to her rapture at their togetherness.

The music, so light and bright, clashed with Rosalie's somber mood. From her position she had an excellent view of the royal box and its occupants. The Prince Regent sat in the center, flanked by his current favorite, Lady Hertford, and his brother the Duke of York. Behind them were two individuals unknown to Rosalie, and one whom she knew much too well for comfort. The Duke of Solway's presence would doubtless lend credence to the popular belief that he was the Prince Regent's chosen candidate for the hand of the Princess Charlotte.

Not even Rosalie's devotion to her precious art had enabled her to forget the nobleman she loved no less for having lost him. It was a terrible strain, dancing as though she hadn't a care and smiling brilliantly all the while, when her well-trained body felt utterly leaden with despair.

13

Stay near me—do not take thy flight!
A little longer stay in sight!
—WILLIAM WORDSWORTH

Rosalie stood in the wings drinking in the sublime notes of the lovelorn Fiordigili's lament. She thought it a great pity that the fashionable people avoided benefit performances, for this new production of *Cosí Fan Tutte* was one of the season's best.

Therese Bertinotti-Radicati's portrayals of tragic heroines had not been well received by the critics, who compared her unfavorably to Madame Catalini, but Rosalie suspected that they would praise her in this lighter work. The singer's voice was particularly well suited to Mozart's comic opera, but even so she'd excised two bravura arias that she deemed too demanding.

Signor Naldi performed the *buffo* role of Don Alfonso with his usual zest. Rosalie, who admired his vocal abilities, was also exceedingly fond of him. Despite his legendary hatred of France and her people, he never failed to treat her kindly. And his wife, a former dancer, had been acquainted with Delphine de Barante.

The popular tenor Tramezzani, with his manly figure and dignified manner, made a romantic Guglielmo, and Signor Cauvini sang Ferrando's ardent arias with a heart-wrenching pathos. His magnificent but volatile spouse was perfectly suited to the part of Despina, the meddling maid, and the mezzo soprano Madame Collini rounded out the cast as Dorabella.

The gaiety and fun of the opera had infected all of the

performers, and merriment reigned backstage. Even the dancers had set aside their characteristic jealousy for one night, chattering to one another in the dressing room, and even Rosalie had laughed at some of the jests and pranks.

Because the company was small in number, she and her colleagues were needed to swell the crowd scenes. In the first act she'd made a brief and anonymous appearance as a villager, and now she was awaiting her cue to go on as a household servant in the final scene.

Her dress, pale green with emerald piping at the seams, was the one Madame Ferrier had made last autumn in the days preceding Rosalie's accident. The addition of an apron had transformed it into a maid's costume, and in place of a chemise she wore a creamy gauze shift. She had only to remove her overdress and tear away the kerchief covering her hair to be ready for the *divertissement* that would conclude the evening's entertainment.

As the trio of gentlemen finished their merry chorus of *"Cosí fan tutte!"* she moved aside to make way for their exit. The scene shifters went to work, transforming the sisters' bedchamber into the grand salon, and Rosalie took her place with the other supernumeraries. When the lilting music started, she spread a large square of brocade cloth upon the table where the marriage settlements would be signed, lighted some candles, and generally tried to look busy while Despina trilled her orders.

Her duty done, she darted back to the wings. Squeezing past the curtain and a web of ropes, she rushed to the wooden staircase and descended carefully, relying on the handrail. A broad figure at the bottom blocked her way, so she called out, "Move aside, if you please—I have a costume change!"

"Not so fast, my beauty."

She was too consumed with her mission to question Benjamin Beckmann's presence. "Pray excuse me, sir, for I cannot stop to talk." She tried to brush past him, but he grasped her arm.

"You won't snub me tonight." As he pulled her toward the stage door he said gruffly, "Hurry along now."

Rosalie resisted with all her might. "You're hurting me," she gasped and struggled to free herself.

"I wouldn't if you'd stop wriggling."

Her dread of another accident was so great that she let him drag her up the rain-slick stone steps to the carriage yard. A hackney waited, its door gaping open. "You can't do this!" she protested. "I'm dancing in the ballet. Don't you understand, you *must* let me go!"

Shoving her into the vehicle, Beckmann growled, "Not yet. We're going for a little drive together, you and I." He plopped down beside her.

His face, pink and bloated from good living, repulsed her and she edged away. "You're mad!"

"If I am, it's your fault," he retorted. "You've toyed with me for months, and now it's my turn to choose the game." He pounded the roof with his cane and the carriage lurched forward.

"This crude attempt to suborn me will not succeed," she said furiously. Staring out the rain-splashed window, she watched the King's Theatre grow ever smaller. "Take me back to the theater now!" she demanded. "If I fail to appear in the ballet tonight, I'll be dismissed from the company."

Mr. Beckmann stroked his curling side whiskers. "You've been flying too high, m'dear—the Duke of Solway was bound to become jaded in time. And perhaps you expected too much of him. Surely you didn't think so grand a fellow would stoop to wed the bastard daughter of a French opera dancer?"

Rosalie's cheeks flamed and her eyes blazed. A sharp crack on the head with his walking stick might restore his reason, but it was beyond her reach. So she struck out at him with her balled fist.

He ducked just in time to avoid the blow. "What a spitfire!" he crowed. "And just my taste. I prefer a lady who is every bit as lively as she is pretty."

She tried to direct her chaotic thoughts into useful channels. Somehow she had to escape, for the prospect of being ravished by this man was sickening. He thought he could overpower her, but agility of mind and body would surely win out over brute strength.

When the jarvey negotiated the sharp turn from Pall Mall to St. James's, she gripped the leather strap to prevent contact with her abductor's encroaching form.

"Why do you pretend to dislike me?" he asked plaintively, capturing her hand. "My pockets are deep, and I'm a generous man. I'll give you jewels and an allowance—you won't have to dance for your keep. You can go with me to all the race meetings, and to Brighton. You'll have such a pleasant time that you'll soon forget your duke."

Her flesh crawled when he stroked her arm.

His thick fingers roamed the front of her bodice, then fumbled with the dark green ribbons of her stomacher. With a groan of impatience, he tugged and ripped the thin fabric.

Preferring possible injury to certain rape, Rosalie gripped the handle of the door and wrenched it open. The moving pavement aroused even greater panic, and just when her nerve failed her the jarvey slowed his horse to avoid pedestrians in the street. Before he picked up the pace again she tumbled out of the hackney.

Stunned and breathless, she sprawled upon the wet cobbles, certain that the fall had shattered all of her bones.

From a great distance above came a stern command to lie still.

"Don't try to speak yet," someone else advised her.

Ignoring the advice of the two gentlemen who had witnessed her escape, she tried to sit up. She blinked to clear the tears from her eyes and examined a long, raw scrape on her arm. The thigh on which she had landed felt badly bruised. "I must go," she panted, fighting for the breath that had been jolted out of her. "He—he might come back."

"I hope he does," one man growled. "I'd like to teach him a lesson. Look at that, Rupert," he said, pointing down at Rosalie. "Her gown is torn!"

"Yes, Allingham, I see that it is."

The group of onlookers expanded as other gentlemen exited the club. Rosalie wondered what they must think of her painted face and scanty attire.

"I've never seen anything like it," said the man called Allingham. "Harburton and I were just crossing over to

White's when this female fell out of a moving hackney coach!"

When his friend helped Rosalie to her feet, she discovered that her precious ankles had survived. "What's the time?" she asked desperately.

"Past midnight, I should think."

By now the ballet had begun—it might well be over. With that realization her aching body sagged, and had the stranger not supported her she would have fallen again.

"Can't we escort you to your home?" he asked, his owlish countenance matching the concern in his voice.

"*Non*—oh, no," she said hastily. She dared not return to Panton Street; Benjamin Beckmann might be waiting for her.

When she had thanked the gentlemen and assured them that she was capable of walking unassisted, she limped up St. James's Street. The thin-soled dancing shoes hampered her ability to maintain her footing on the greasy pavement, and she made a slow and agonizing progress.

In missing a performance she'd committed the unforgivable sin and the punishment would be exceedingly harsh. In all likelihood Signor Rossi would banish her from the stage of the King's Theatre. No one, not even James d'Egville or Armand Vestris, would intercede on her behalf. Her career as an opera dancer was over.

She walked on, though she didn't even know where she was going, constantly watching out for the hackney bearing Mr. Beckmann. She contrasted his brutishness with Gervase's unfailing chivalry, and a sob escaped her. Even though his intentions were once the same as her abductor's, how happy she could have been with him—if she hadn't given her word to Richard Lovegrove never to become what her mother had been to Etienne Lemercier. She was often teased by the irony of her position: she had managed to keep the respect of the man she loved only by giving him up. And with all her heart she wished that she could have shared her life with him and become a part of his, and preserve her honor at the same time.

On reaching Piccadilly she found it occupied by an endless line of carriages, their lamps creating a trail of light that extended as far as she could see. The coats of the horses drawing the nearest coach glistened with moisture, and the caped coachman on the box regularly adjusted his three-cornered hat in an effort to keep the rain out of his face.

Two persons were seated within. Rosalie spied the flash of diamonds on the lady's white breast, and snowy ruffles at the neck of the gentleman seated across from her. They were obviously annoyed by their delayed departure from Devonshire House.

Had the Duke of Solway attended the ball? For some reason it hurt her to think that he might have been drinking champagne and dancing and flirting throughout her ordeal. But it wasn't his habit to flirt, she corrected herself, he disliked large parties. In all probability he'd spent the evening at home, composing a political speech. Or writing a letter to his mother, who so despised opera dancers.

Even though she knew he couldn't really help her—there was no remedy for the variety of blows she had suffered tonight—to her he represented security and decency. An insistent voice in her swimming head urged her to find him.

But Mayfair was alien territory, so she had to seek directions from a passing watchman. He held his lantern close to her face, his voice heavy with suspicion when he asked, "Wot would the loikes of you be wantin' with the Duke of Solway?"

"My uncle works in the stables," she improvised, "and my aunt sent me with a message."

Although the man shook his head in patent disbelief, he pointed the way. "You keeps goin' down this street and turns roight at Park Lane—if you gets to the Hyde Park turnpike, you've walked too far. A little beyond Lord Dorchester's house, on the corner of Park Lane and Mount Street, you'll foind a great white building with gardens behind." Grinning, he added, "The mews, if you *really* wants 'em, are at the back."

She knew he expected a token of appreciation but she had no coins to give him, only her heartfelt thanks. She broke into a run, her battered limbs rebelling with every step.

The duke's mansion was more imposing than she had expected. She paused at the bottom of its shallow front steps and gazed up at the shadowed facade and dark windows. Having come so far she couldn't turn back, but she feared what she was about to do would be viewed as a serious transgression by the sort of people who lived in this exclusive neighborhood.

Summoning the necessary fortitude, she approached the house and pounded upon one of the glass panes framing the door with her fist.

A wrinkled visage appeared immediately. "Who goes there?" its owner asked suspiciously.

"I must speak to the Duke of Solway," she replied, her heart pumping furiously from the combined effects of nervousness and exhaustion. When she heard him draw the bolts she let her breath out in relief.

The man did open the door but after studying her from head to toe adamantly refused to admit her. "His grace has retired," he said frostily.

"Tell him I've come," she pleaded, "for I'm certain he'll agree to receive me."

He twisted his head to say in aggrieved accents, "Mr. Parry, this—this *painted* person is asking for the duke."

"Oh, is Parry there? He will know me." She boldly stepped past him and walked up to the butler.

"Mademoiselle de Barante?" Parry's carefully neutral expression never altered, but his eyebrows twitched slightly as he took in her bedraggled appearance. "Step into the green salon, and I will inform his grace of your arrival."

He conducted her to a sumptuously appointed chamber and left her there with a branch of candles. She was too sad and anxious to care about her surroundings, but she couldn't help noticing a vaulted ceiling decorated with a frescoe of sportive gods and goddesses, green damask hangings, and the towering marble chimney piece at one end of the room. She doubted that the elegant room had ever sheltered so forlorn and pitiful a creature as herself.

When his butler first roused him from deepest sleep, Gervase was reluctant to rise. After he heard the reason his mind was still too groggy and dazed for speculation, but he scrambled into shirt and breeches.

The hall porter standing stiffly at the foot of the marble staircase regarded him with disapproval. "Return to your post," Gervase said curtly before he entered the salon.

The lingering fog of sleep dissipated entirely when he saw Rosalie. Her full skirts were splattered with rain and dirt, and part of her bodice was torn, revealing the white shift beneath. "What the devil happened to you?" he demanded.

"Oh, Gervais, such a night I've had!"

Answering the appeal in her anguished eyes, he wrapped his arms around her, laying his cheek against her wet curls. "Don't worry, you're with me now. You're safe."

"I know. It's why I came." In a firmer voice she said, "I will *not* weep, for if I do I'd never be able to stop."

Gervase led her to a hassock and sat upon the floor at her feet, chafing her cold fingers as he said, "Tell me, as calmly and slowly as you can, what has distressed you."

He listened in horrified silence to her fractured account of all that had occurred after Benjamin Beckmann took her away from the opera house. His grip tightened involuntarily when she explained that she'd eluded him only by leaping from the carriage.

"I was dazed, but not hurt," she assured him. "Some kind gentlemen came to my assistance—they even offered to take me home. But I couldn't go back to Panton Street, I was too afraid Mr. Beckmann might be lurking somewhere near my house. I did change the lock on my door, but—"

"You did *what*?"

"Mr. Beckmann stole my key."

After extracting the story of her importunate admirer's visit to her lodging house, Gervase said harshly, "You should have told me."

"What could you have done?" she responded wearily.

A cold rage possessed him as he reviewed Beckmann's tactics. He should have guessed on that long-ago night at Sadler's Wells that the man could be dangerous.

Rosalie, living alone, her movements regulated by her performing schedule, had been an easy target for a sly and determined individual like Beckmann. Unlike Gervase, he'd been too dense to perceive at a glance that the dancer's morals were not as light as her little feet. And he had been too puffed up with his own consequence to accept that she might spurn him.

"I suppose I'll have to swear a complaint against him tomorrow," Rosalie said. "Can you tell me how to go about it?"

"I don't want you worrying about that now." A pity, he thought, that he had no legal grounds to prevent Beckmann from troubling her again. Only a father or a brother could lodge a petition in the courts.

Or a husband.

Pushing that thought aside, he went on, "My housekeeper will prepare a room for you here. No," he said firmly when she shook her head, "you mustn't refuse. It's quite late and you're utterly exhausted. I want a doctor to examine you in the morning, to confirm that you've sustained no lasting injury."

Rosalie stared at him. "But I can't sleep in your house, Gervais. The man who answered the door wouldn't even let me in, and I'm sure Parry disapproves of my coming in the middle of the night."

With a chastening frown, he replied, "Rosalie, my servants are employed to wait upon me, not dictate to me. And for the time being, I refuse to concern myself with anything so mundane as what they might be thinking about either of us."

The Duke of Solway spent the following morning alone in the study. The only member of his staff to intrude upon his solitude was Parry, who kept him informed of Mademoiselle de Barante's activities. At midmorning the Welshman informed him that she had awakened, and an hour later he announced that one of the maids had just removed her breakfast tray.

When Gervase went to the room in which his lady love had passed the night, he found her sitting up against the pillows of the mahogany fourposter. Her unbound hair massed about her shoulders in tangled waves.

"You shouldn't be here," she reproached him, drawing up the sheet to cover herself. "If I'd known you were bent on creating a scandal in your own household, I wouldn't have let you keep me here overnight."

"There's no scandal in visiting a sickroom," he pointed out, sitting down on the edge of the bed. "How are you feeling today?"

"I won't let myself feel yet," she said with what he recognized as forced humor. "*Vraiment,* Gervais, you mustn't be caught among the sheets with an opera dancer." Her faint smile faded when she concluded, "But I was forgetting—I no longer have a right to that title. Last night saw the end of my brief association with the King's Theatre."

In his most teasing voice he said, "Surely it isn't so bad as all that. You can't expect to give a perfect performance every time."

Shaking her head, she said sadly, "You don't understand. I must not have been very clear last night. I never *did* perform—Beckmann dragged me away just before the ballet began. I was there for all the crowd scenes of the opera, so no one will believe me if I pretend I suddenly fell ill, much less if I explain what really occurred. The management will remember what happened last autumn. My hasty resignation from the Tottenham Street playhouse will be dredged up as further evidence of unreliability."

"Nonsense. One small mishap won't matter so much."

"But it will," she told him earnestly. "Mr. Kelly will fine me, and Signor Rossi is certain to dismiss me, for nothing is more unprofessional than failing to go onstage. I'm only a temporary replacement, not really a member of the company, and therefore expendable. James d'Egville will turn his back on me forever, and so will Dibdin. It could be years before another theater manager will take a chance on hiring someone with so tarnished a reputation as mine is now. And," she concluded with a catch in her voice, "no dancer has years to spare."

The tears filling her eyes reminded Gervase of how very young she was. She had begun preparing for her career practically in her infancy and became a professional before she ever learned her alphabet letters. She hadn't experienced a normal childhood or adolescence because her theatrical upbringing had forced her out of them so quickly.

She might not realize it now, while her pain was so fresh, but she had no cause for regret—he would make sure of that. He intended to comfort and cosset her, this tiny, brave girl whom he loved.

"If it would make you feel better," he said, blotting her cheeks with his handkerchief, "I'll speak with Kelly. I'll even visit the King's Bench Prison and tell Mr. Taylor himself why you were absent last night."

"It will do me more harm than good," she prophesied bleakly. "And if you become too much involved in my affairs, there's bound to be gossip. Think how dreadful it would be if your friends or family found out I'd slept here last night!"

Gervase abandoned the bed and went to stand by the window. "Have you considered what you will do if you can't dance at the opera?"

"I've thought of little else this morning." She managed a lopsided smile. "Lord Swanborough once said he would build a splendid theater especially for me when he comes into his inheritance, but I'm afraid I can't wait that long. My only recourse is to return to Paris."

"Paris?" he echoed.

"If I leave at once I could be there before word of this frightful mess leaks across the Channel. Etienne Lemercier can help me acquire a French passport." She walked her fingers slowly across the counterpane, her eyes following their scissorlike motion. "My mother's name will be my entrée to the Opera."

Fiercely he said, "You aren't going back to Paris."

"But if I don't find work soon, I'd have to creep back to Bibury and spend the rest of my days pining for—for something that can never be."

He sensed that she referred to something other than the ballet, and his suspicion gave him the courage to admit, "I'm grateful to that cur Beckmann for cutting your connection to the opera house so neatly. I can't bear the prospect of waiting until you wear out your knees or sprain another ankle. Rosalie, couldn't you learn to live without dancing?"

"Someday I'll have to. No career lasts forever."

He continued, "It is wrong for you and me to remain forever apart, yearning indefinitely. Rosalie, do you care for me? Enough to let me look after you for the rest of your life?"

She bowed her head. "Yes to the first question. And to the second one—if it were possible for me to be with you always, nothing could make me happier. But it isn't, Gervais."

"You think not? Then I will tell you how I spent my time while I waited for you to wake up. I've been writing letters—to my mother at Haberdine, to both of my sisters, to my cousin Miranda and her husband. I even wrote one to my brother Edgar, though God only knows when it will reach him in Spain. But I couldn't post them yet. They all announce that I'm madly, intensely, irrevocably in love, and I wanted you to know it first. I also explained to my relations that I hope to be married very soon. If you'll have me."

She stared back at him with wide, unfathomable eyes. "*Je suis danseuse.* Your family will wish for you *la grande alliance avec la princesse,* or to an aristocratic lady."

"Rosalie," he said softly, joining her on the bed, "I adore your habit of speaking French in moments of strong emotion, but I object to your talking such drivel. Marriage is the one way we can be together. If you cannot feel right about being my mistress, then be my duchess instead." He pressed her back against her pillows, and his eager mouth covered hers.

Then he touched her cheek, her shoulders, the rounded contours of her breasts, and discovered that her skin was marble-smooth and deliciously warm. Her blushes delighted him, as did her soft sighs and startled cries.

Gripping her forearms, he said, "Now that I've presented you with a highly honorable proposal, are you still so eager to go to Paris?"

Apparently too shocked to speak, she rolled her head from side to side.

"Good." He resumed his caresses.

"Gervais, you are too naughty!"

"Be quiet," he commanded. "Most men would have compromised you first and then proposed, rather than the reverse. You can lie back and enjoy this—and I hope you will. I've dreamed of doing it for months."

"Have you?" she breathed. Smiling up at him, she asked, "What else did you want to do to me?"

"All sorts of wicked things, which I'll be happy to demonstrate in a moment. But first, Miss Rosalie Delphine Lovegrove de Barante, or whatever you call yourself, I want an answer. Will you now make another of your unbreakable vows, and promise faithfully to become my wife?"

14

And having danc't ('bove all the best)
Carry the Garland from the rest.
—SIR THOMAS WYATT

Tomorrow night, Gervase thought exultantly as he exited Rosalie's bedchamber, he would finish convincing her how thoroughly he adored her. Before descending the marble staircase, he swiftly tidied his garments and smoothed his hair.

More than a little disoriented from the haste of his betrothal, he forced his muddled brain to consider his next course of action. Meeting his butler on the middle landing, he smiled dreamily and said, "Please be the first to felicitate me, Parry. I'm going to be married."

The Welshman smiled. "You have my most sincere wishes for future happiness, your grace. I know the entire staff will be gratified by the news."

"Thank you. Mademoiselle de Barante and I have agreed that the ceremony will take place in the morning, at Grosvenor Chapel. I'm off to speak with the parson, and also to procure a special license." Extracting his pocketbook, he studied the contents. "Just when I'm in need of cash, I find myself short. By any chance have you got five pounds about you, Parry?"

His butler reached into his pocket and produced a single note. "If your grace requires additional funds, I can open the strongbox."

"This will serve for the time being. I'll be wanting the town coach this afternoon, and there are some letters on the desk in the study—they must be posted without delay.

The footman who takes them should also go to Mademoiselle de Barante's lodging in Panton Street and bring back her maid. And you might inform the kitchen staff to begin preparing for the wedding breakfast. Nothing too elaborate, but there should be meats and cakes—and plenty of champagne." Gervase continued down the stairs, then turned back to ask, "Am I right in thinking that Richards has a relative who keeps an inn somewhere on the road from London to the west country?"

"His youngest brother lives at Overton, beyond Basingstoke, His house is called the Peacock. Quite respectable, as I have been informed, and popular with the gentry."

"Yes, yes, that will do nicely. I'll send Webster down to Hampshire to make the necessary arrangements for me. For us," he added beatifically.

Before leaving Solway House, he drank a tumbler of brandy to calm his nerves. He had made a momentous decision—not a difficult one, but he couldn't overlook the fact that the immediate future would not be easy. His love for Rosalie was unwavering, deep and strong enough to sustain him in the face of public censure and familial outcry. But what of her? Would her feelings withstand the troubles ahead?

Shoving that uncomfortable question aside, he set out in his town coach for Grosvenor Chapel, just around the corner in South Audley Street.

"No need to walk them, Tim," Gervase told his coachman when he climbed out. "My business here will take but a few minutes." His servant's vigorous nod and toothy grin told him the tidings of his forthcoming nuptials had circulated in the mews.

The brown brick chapel was dark and empty and silent, but he found the warden in the lower regions. Yes, he assured the duke after consulting a leatherbound volume, the priest would be at liberty to perform a marriage ceremony on the morrow. But, he warned, his grace might have some difficulty obtaining a license on such short notice, as the gentlemen of Doctors' Commons were notoriously slow.

It seemed to take forever to reach St. Paul's. Gervase,

now afraid that he would be unable to secure the essential piece of paper, fretted and fumed throughout his journey, hands clenched tensely around the knob of his walking stick. He scarcely noticed the traffic clogging the Strand, and by the time he arrived in the churchyard he was in a fever of impatience.

He passed beneath the Dean's Court archway and begged directions to the Faculty Office from a stranger, who obligingly took him to the stone-paved hall. A crowd of other hopefuls were seated upon benches and standing about in small groups.

"Did you wish to speak with one of the advocates?" inquired a squat gentleman swathed in a long scarlet robe.

"I'm not sure," Gervase answered frankly. "Is this the Court of Faculties and Dispensations? I expect to be married tomorrow, and I've come for a special license."

"You must wait your turn, then."

"It is a matter of some urgency," he said loftily, presenting his card.

The man accepted it unwillingly, but after reading the inscription his attitude of disinterest was replaced by one of respect. "I can be of assistance, if your grace will follow me."

They removed to a smaller room. Sitting down at a table covered with green baize, the gentleman took a paper out of an upper drawer. Reaching for a pen, he asked, "What is your grace's full name?"

"Gervase William Marchant."

"In which London parish do you reside?"

"St. George's, Mayfair." He watched as the official wrote this down, then added, "The lady lives in Panton Street, but I don't know which parish that might be."

"St. Martin's. Her full name, please."

"Rosalie Delphine Lovegrove."

"Are you both of legal age?"

"Indeed."

When he had finished writing, the man sanded the document. "That will be five pounds," he said, curt and businesslike, and Gervase tendered Parry's banknote. "In general, applications for a special license do not receive such prompt attention. Your grace is fortunate that you chanced to meet me on my way in."

"I suspect I'm equally fortunate in possessing a title," Gervase said wryly, accepting the coveted paper.

His next destination was Number 32, Ludgate Hill, occupied by the noted jewelers and diamond merchants Rundell and Bridge. His assumption that he was unknown by the proprietors was refuted as soon as he entered their establishment.

The gentleman standing nearest the counter bowed exceedingly low. "Good day, your grace," he intoned before introducing himself as Mr. Bridge.

Not entirely pleased to be recognized, Gervase made a civil reply and expressed his intention of establishing an account with the firm. "As my father had."

Again the jeweler bowed. "From time to time my partner Mr. Rundell and I undertook commissions from the late duke. We should deem it an honor to serve his son in the same way." Moving behind the counter, he asked, "Is there anything in particular your grace wishes to look at today?"

"I've come to purchase a ring. For a lady."

Mr. Bridge's eyes sparked with interest. "We have many fine gems in gold settings. Which stone would you consider most suitable?"

Regretting his failure to ascertain Rosalie's preference, Gervase answered, "Something rare, and of the best quality."

The proprietor removed a velvet-covered tray from his shelves and set it down before his customer. "I have here pearls, diamonds of various sizes, some emeralds, a single fine ruby, and a rare sapphire." He presented the latter for inspection.

Gervase tried to imagine it on one of Rosalie's small, childlike fingers and decided that it was much too large. Shaking his head, he said, "I'd like to examine that ruby." Mr. Bridge took back the sapphire ring and handed him the other. The stone was a dark, clear crimson, and a delicate pattern of rose leaves was engraved upon the golden band.

"A recent acquisition, your grace, and worthy of the most discriminating buyer. It is known as the Rose of India and was cut in Antwerp. One of our own goldsmiths fashioned the setting to Mr. Rundell's design."

"Charming," Gervase opined. And splendidly appropriate for a lady called Rosalie.

In a single afternoon he had acquired a bride, a license, and a ring. The ceremony was arranged, and the accommodating Webster had orders to plan the wedding journey. Thus he returned to Solway House with a strong sense of accomplishment.

Greatly though he wanted to relate his activities to his betrothed, they had agreed to keep apart until the moment they would join hands before the altar of Grosvenor Chapel. Half afraid that she might change her mind, he would be careful not to grant her any opportunity to tell him so.

He learned from Parry that she had remained in seclusion all afternoon, and the news that Peg Reilly had arrived with her mistress's trunk and bandboxes struck him as a favorable sign. Apart from packing his own bags there was but one thing left to do, and that was locating a pair of witnesses. Preferably close friends, and discreet ones.

He conducted his search that evening at White's Club. Although some of his acquaintances were there, he saw none that he liked well enough to request their presence at his wedding.

While taking dinner in the coffee room, he overheard the party of elderly gentlemen at the next table bemoaning the proposed rise in the club's subscription fee.

"Eleven guineas? Pshaw," one fellow said, "what man among us cannot afford that?"

"A great pity that everyone should have to support the alteration to the facade," commented another. "We're all paying for that damned bow window, even though that upstart Brummell regards it as his own. The only chap who dares make use of it in his absence is young Elston."

"He has impudence enough for anything, that one. Takes after his father."

"Careful how you speak of him—he's here now, with Harburton. Drunk as a lord, by the look of him."

Gervase turned around and saw his friend standing on

the threshhold, one hand gripping the doorframe for support. His companion, dwarfed by his superior height, surpassed him in elegance of dress.

Advancing unsteadily into the room, the marquis cried, "Hullo, Ger! We'll join you."

As his friends sat down at his table, Gervase commented, "A bit early for you to be in this parlous state of overindulgence, isn't it?"

"It's my butler's fault, damn him. Said the vintage red port that my father laid down in '88 desperately needed to be drunk, so we imbibed as much as we could in one sitting, Rupert and I." When a waiter brought the duke's bill, Damon regarded him sunnily and said, "A pot of strong coffee for Mr. Harburton and myself, Mackreth."

"As you wish, my lord."

"You really ought to eat something," Gervase advised. "Bring a plate of biscuits, and some fruit."

With a brisk nod, the man absented himself.

Rubbing his brow, Mr. Harburton complained that he had a devilish headache.

"It'll be much worse tomorrow," Damon predicted. His blue eyes sought Gervase. "You'll never believe what Rupert saw on his way here last night. He was crossing the street with someone, I forget who—"

"Allingham," Mr. Harburton supplied.

"With Allingham, when the damnedest thing happened! A female leaped out of a passing hackney coach and fell at their feet. Imagine—right in the middle of St. James's! He'll dine out on that tale for a week at least."

Gervase frowned at the other gentleman. "I sincerely hope you won't, Rupert. I know the identity of that lady and would be very sorry if her adventure became widely known."

Damon's eyes narrowed in suspicion. "Would you indeed? Then she must've been your little opera dancer."

"An excess of wine has definitely hot hampered your thought processes," Gervase observed.

"And," his friend continued triumphantly, "I'll wager she was trying to avoid that beast we first met at the Sadler's Wells playhouse."

"Yes. But I'm not going to reveal more than those essential facts."

"Challenge him to a duel," was Damon's advice. "Can't have some crass *bourgeoise* plaguing the girl to death."

"Beckmann won't trouble Mademoiselle de Barante in future. Not after tomorrow morning, when she and I are to be married."

"Married!" Damon crowed. "D'you hear that, Rupert? Ger's getting married."

"Of course I heard," Mr. Harburton retorted. "I'm drunk, not deaf."

"Well, well, this is an unexpected turn of events. Will it be a private affair?"

"Extremely, but I would be very happy if both of you would stand up with me. The wedding will take place at Grosvenor Chapel, with a breakfast at my house immediately afterward."

"And then the long-anticipated pleasures of the honeymoon, eh?" the marquis asked slyly.

"We'll spend a fortnight by the seaside, at Weymouth."

"Look at him, Rupert—he's love-bitten!" Damon ran his fingers through his golden hair. "Where's that coffee? I've got to get sober—can't disgrace Ger at his wedding."

"I think we ought to have a toast," Mr. Harburton said solemnly.

Laughing, Gervase said, "Perhaps you'd better save the toasts for tomorrow."

"I've just decided what my gift will be," Damon announced. "A dozen bottles of my '88 port. I'll have Mimms pack it up and send it round to Solway House. What are you going to give him, Rupert?"

"I'm damned if I know. He's a blasted duke, and has far more than he wants or needs. Ah, here you are, Mackreth." Mr. Harburton sighed thankfully as the waiter poured out a cup of steaming coffee. Gripping the handle, he held it aloft and said grandly, "To the bride and groom."

Gervase had made it exceedingly plain to Rosalie that he expected her to remain at Solway House until their wedding. Before parting from her he'd suggested that she busy herself with writing the happy news to her aunt, and she had obediently requested pen and paper from the chambermaid. She sat down at a Sheraton dressing table and scribbled a hasty note to Matilda Lovegrove, investing it with all the joy one would expect of so fortunate a being as herself.

But grave doubts overshadowed her joy in announcing that she was the future Duchess of Solway. An abiding love for Gervase and a powerful desire to be united with him body and soul could not blind her to several painful facts. Her unworthiness for the position to which he would elevate her chafed at her. Her parentage was questionable and might remain so. Her experience of society was restricted to the highborn gentlemen who had sometimes ogled her at the opera. And she worried that the Marchant family, the Duchess of Solway in particular, would suspect her of entrapping him by some devious stratagem.

For most of the afternoon she wondered why she hadn't refused his offer, just as she had the previous one, finally acknowledging the lack of reasonable justification. No promise precluded her becoming his wife, no scruple stood in her way. And if she didn't marry him, what else could she do but carry out her threat to go to Paris? She had no desire to separate from him again, or to spend the rest of her life alone.

The arrival of Peg and the accompanying boxes gave her thoughts a new direction.

"You're going to be a duchess," the maidservant said over and over, as if unable to accept either the inevitability or desirability of it. When Peg recovered her composure she asked Rosalie which clothes should be packed for the wedding trip.

"I haven't even considered that," she answered abstractedly. "*Bien sûr*, I'll want my jade green cambric to travel in and the rose silk for evenings, and whatever else is clean and in good repair. I need as many of my chemises and petticoats as you can fit into the trunk, and all my shoes and slippers. Except the ones I wear—wore—for dancing. The duke said I might choose something out of his cousin's wardrobe to be married in. Most of the gowns she left behind are out of style, but I found this white silk." She reached for a garment draped over the back of a chair.

At Peg's urging she tried the gown on, but because it had been made for a slightly taller, slimmer woman it turned out to be a trifle tight in the bodice and too long in the front. Her maid was confident that she could remedy these faults and immediately set to work.

While Peg sat in the corner busily hemming, Rosalie sipped tea and sampled some of the sweets from her tray to please Parry, who had come to consult her about the wedding breakfast. The senior staff already treated her as the mistress of the house, which was endearing yet disconcerting.

Glancing over the menu the butler had prepared, Rosalie noted one omission. "The duke is especially fond of gooseberry tarts," she reminded him. "As for the other cakes, I suspect the cook knows his preference better than I." She handed back the list.

After he left the room she wandered to her window and gazed in the direction of Hyde Park, her eyes following the line of smart carriages rolling toward Stanhope Gate.

Mayfair was such a new and different world. Islington and Sadler's Wells were no longer a part of her life, and in future she would return to the Haymarket as a member of an audience rather than the company.

Never again would she undergo the rigors of a rehearsal, dancing to the accompaniment of a poorly tuned harpsichord, contorting her body as commanded in the singsong French ballet masters used when calling out instructions. But she had the comfort of knowing that she'd achieved her ambition: her career had ended where it had begun, on the stage of an opera house. And she did not regret being finally and forever free of that ruling compulsion to emulate her mother's greater success.

Cruel Mr. Beckmann, though he might not realize it, had precipitated an improvement in her circumstances. But it would take time to grow accustomed to so many changes all at once.

Still wounded in body and spirit, she went to bed at an early hour, half afraid she might not be able to sleep. But the variety of emotions she'd been experiencing had wearied her more than she knew, and the scented sheets and fat goosedown pillow were not only comfortable but wondrously soporific.

She was gently wakened by the chambermaid who brought her morning coffee. The promise of hot water for the copper bath roused her even more successfully than her favorite beverage, for her limbs seemed stiffer on this second day after her fall from the hackney.

When she removed her nightgown, she was mortified by a large dark bruise marring her thigh and the unsightly scrape on her arm. Gervase, she thought ruefully, was acquiring a sadly disfigured bride.

Her nervousness was nearly exceeded by Peg Reilly's, whose shaking fingers fumbled with the fastenings at the back of the white gown. But Rosalie was accustomed to dressing for a performance and no stranger to the fluttery anticipation she felt while preparing for her wedding. When she inspected her reflection in the mirror, she commented that she looked like she was on her way to a ball rather than a church. The silvery lace and shimmering silk looked odd in the bright sunshine of the new day.

She was ready when Parry came to conduct her downstairs to Lord Elston's waiting carriage. "The household staff have already lined up in the hall to see you pass by, which is the custom in his grace's family."

While making her way down the staircase, she smiled shyly at the servants. Some of the women were weeping sentimental tears; the men's faces conveyed polite interest. She was startled to find two footmen carrying a large and weighty packing case through the front door, and her progress was impeded by another pair with a similar burden.

Said Parry apologetically, "The port is a gift from the marquis. It would have been sent around to the tradesmen's entrance had he not brought it here himself."

Rosalie exited the house through the door she'd entered two nights before and made her way to his lordship's splendid equipage. Parry handed her inside, then shut the door upon her and Lord Elston.

"A delightful day for a wedding, Mademoiselle de Barante," her handsome escort commented as the team pulled away from Solway House. "The sun smiles upon this happy occasion."

Uncertain how to reply, she simply nodded.

"What a charming gown. White becomes you well."

"I'm afraid it's borrowed finery," she admitted. "I hope Lady Cavender won't mind that I was married in her cast-off clothes."

"Knowing Miranda as well as I do, I can assure you that she'd be delighted," he told her with one of his brilliant smiles. "You must be sure to tell her when you meet." They rode in silence until he said quietly, "You aren't anxious about what lies ahead, I hope. There's no reason to be, for Gervase has loved you a very long time. Longer than he dared admit to me, and I'm his closest friend."

"He is also close to his mother, I think. She will not be happy with his choice, my lord."

"That needn't concern you. Her greatest desire is for Gervase to take a wife, and the fact that he wed a lady both beautiful and virtuous should gratify her."

This was such a blatant attempt to soothe her alarms that they increased. "I pray your lordship may be right," she murmured.

He patted her hand. "When you know me better, you'll discover that I always am. Well, my dear, here we are. That's Rupert Harburton standing at the church door."

The name was familiar, and when he introduced her to the short, nattily dressed gentlemen she recognized him instantly.

"We meet again, mademoiselle," he greeted her. "But the least said about your trials the other night the better, eh? Come, the bridegroom awaits."

She preceded the two gentlemen into the chapel. Gervase turned away from the black-gowned cleric standing before the altar and came down the aisle to meet her. He wore a dark blue coat with large gold buttons, a white satin waistcoat, and pale gray breeches.

"How lovely you are," he said, gripping both of her hands.

The enormity of what they were about to do suddenly swept over her. "You are quite sure this is what you want to do, Gervais?"

"I want *you*," he replied. "I always have, and I always will."

The quiet calm of early evening had settled upon the Hampshire town of Overton, situated some fifty-two miles and seven furlongs from Hyde Park Corner. Long before the Duke of Solway's traveling chaise reached the Peacock, his grace's valet had already bespoken a private parlor, the best two bedchambers, and a dinner.

"Well done, Webster," said Gervase as he handed his bride across the threshold of their suite.

The upper parlor was comfortably appointed and scrupulously clean, and a chambermaid was there to wait upon Rosalie and unpack her trunk. Fatigued from the combined effects of a busy morning and the long afternoon journey, she was relieved when Mr. Richards, the landlord, informed her that no one else was stopping there that night.

"I shall leave you for a little while," Gervase told her. "You should rest before dinner, if you can."

"I'll try," she promised.

The maid helped her out of her traveling gown, taking it and the rose silk away for ironing. Rosalie stretched out upon the bed and closed her eyes, reveling in the stillness and silence after the incessant swaying and dipping of the chaise and the thunder of horses' hooves.

Her enjoyment of the wedding breakfast had far exceeded her expectations. Lord Elston's effusive merriment had been tempered by Mr. Harburton's calm graciousness, and their easy acceptance of her as Gervase's wife had quelled her instinctive fear of their disdain. The Solway House servants were granted a holiday in honor of the occasion and provided with food and drink belowstairs. Gervase presented each of them, from the lowly footboy to housekeeper with a gold half guinea.

Despite her pleasure in the day, the unknown, uncertain future was never far from Rosalie's thoughts. As she lay upon the bed, she wondered whether her mother-in-law, now a dowager duchess, would receive her letter from Gervase tomorrow or the next day. Her reaction was easier to predict.

Benjamin Beckmann would learn of the marriage from the duke's lawyer, who would also present him with a writ requiring him to keep his distance.

Later in the week an announcement would appear in the London papers, doubtless leading to cruel gossip and unpleasant speculation. Possibly it would rouse the anger of the Prince Regent, for she hadn't quite trusted Gervase's blithe assertion that His Royal Highness hadn't been serious about that rumored match with Princess Charlotte.

Her wedding day, which brought her the greatest joy of her life, would cause so many people to feel anger and pain and resentment. However much she wished it otherwise, she had to face that uncomfortable reality.

From the moment the priest had declared her to be Gervase's wife, she had embarked upon an uncharted journey. The rules and rituals her mother had laid down for her as a dancer were useless to her now. No longer would she consort with the performers from the Wells and the opera house, although she hoped to maintain her relationships with Mary Grimaldi and Mrs. Hughes. But neither had been her confidante, and she suspected that she was going to need one. If only, she thought drowsily, there was another female to whom she could confide her feelings, simple and complicated, and go to for advice. Her Aunt Tilda would be sympathetic, but she'd never been married nor had she moved in fashionable circles. And Rosalie doubted that any aristocratic lady would befriend a former opera dancer. She would suspect the motives of one who did.

Eventually she rose to wash and begin preparing herself for dinner. When she sat down at the dressing table to rearrange her hair, she saw her pale face gazing back, her shadowed eyes reflecting inner turmoil. Gervase, she told herself sternly, deserved much better than a wan and worried bride.

The chambermaid returned with the rose gown and helped her to put it on. The color warmed Rosalie's complexion slightly, in her silk and lace she felt rather more like the duchess she must become and less like a frightened coryphée only seconds away from her debut.

She stepped into the parlor. A tall branch of candles in the center of the table cast its light upon Gervase, already seated and holding a glass of wine in his hand. He gave her a reassuring smile as she took her place across from him and signaled to Webster to begin serving. An array of covered platters adorned the sideboard, and the aromas were tempting enough to encourage Rosalie to sample nearly everything set before her.

"More wine, your grace?" the valet inquired.

When she realized that he was speaking to her, she nodded, wondering how long it would take to become used to the unfamiliar form of address.

"How many miles are we from Weymouth?" she asked her husband.

"A little over one hundred and twenty—rather a lot of ground to cover in a single day. I'm thinking that we might take the time to look around the cathedral at Salisbury, and stop along the road tomorrow night as well. Webster will continue traveling ahead of us, and engage our rooms at an establishment Mr. Richards suggested, Woodyates Inn. It lies just over the Dorsetshire border, and he assures me that it's greatly improved from what it once was."

After a sip of wine Rosalie stated her approval of this plan.

"I'm glad you agree, for travel by easy stages is far more civilized than dashing about in a great hurry."

"But more expensive, *n'est-ce pas?*"

"You're supposed to enjoy yourself during this trip," he told her, "not count its cost."

She readily assented, being too ignorant to accurately judge what he owed for their rooms and the dinner and stabling for the horses, or the charges demanded by the post-boys.

As soon as they finished eating, the valet summoned a waiter, who cleared the table with speedy efficiency.

"That will be all, Webster," said Gervase. "Consider yourself dismissed for the evening." He waited until his servant withdrew before saying, "Rosalie, don't look so terrified. If you'd rather not take advantage of our married state tonight, so be it."

"I don't feel quite as I expected to," she confessed, hating the way her voice shook.

"Happy, you mean?"

"Married," she explained. "I keep remembering that I'm as ill equipped to be your wife as I was to be your mistress."

He reached down to pull her out of her chair. "You are everything to me. I've never been so content as I've been all day, knowing that we shall be together for the whole of our lives. Nothing and no one can come between us." Taking her face between his hands he kissed her.

His lips convinced her that he what he said was true. "I never really believed in love until I met you, Gervais," she whispered. Almost breathless from bridal shyness, she let him lead her to the bedchamber.

Did he expect her to disrobe, or would he undress her? "I'm not sure about what to do," she confessed, her pallor giving way to blushes.

"Let me show you," he offered, reaching behind her to unfasten her gown.

When she was clad only in her chemise and he in nothing more than his shirt and breeches, she asked if he intended to blow out the candles.

He abandoned the task of loosening his cuffs to glance at her. "Would that make you feel more comfortable?"

Her heart raced and her legs felt as though they might give way. Sinking down on the bed, she answered candidly, "No," for at that moment she was incapable of feeling comfortable.

Laughing softly, Gervase pulled his shirt over his head. "Are you more reluctant to see me in a state of undress, or to let me look at you? Lest you forget, my darling dancer, those ballet costumes of yours left very little to the imagination."

Then he took her in his arms and attempted to restore her confidence with his kisses.

15

Then to the dance, and make the sober moon
Witness of joys that shun the sights of noon.
                                    —WILLIAM COWPER

Rosalie examined her left hand, which was lying upon the sill of the open window, and admired the play of sunlight on her ruby ring. Then she leaned out of the open window to draw in deep breaths of salt-scented sea air. A gentleman bather had emerged from one of several machines on Weymouth's sandy shore, and she watched him descend the wooden ladder and gingerly lower himself into the lapping water.

During the fourteen days since she and Gervase had exchanged their vows, they had occupied a suite in Stacie's Hotel on the Esplanade, indulging their desire for privacy and each other. When out of bed, her fond husband could sometimes be quite stubborn, but his determination to have his way was always rooted in his determination to give her pleasure or guard her from unpleasantness. After so many years of fending for herself, she was learning to enjoy being spoiled.

The previous night they had danced together for the first time, at a militia ball held in the Royal Assembly Rooms. At Gervase's request, Mr. Rodber, the master of ceremonies, had kept their identities to himself, and the company had therefore demonstrated scant interest in a tall distinguished gentleman and his graceful partner, who wore the same white and silver dress in which she'd been wed.

Over coffee that morning they had debated—not very heatedly—about whether to drive to Lulworth Cave in the morning or the afternoon. Rosalie abandoned her arguments when she remembered that it was his habit to visit the receiving office at midday. Because he had offered no explanation for this, she assumed he expected an important communication, probably from his mother.

"Had you quite given me up?" he asked when he returned from his errand. "I was detained at the stables, where I stopped to hire coach horses for tomorrow's journey back to town." Smiling, he held up a letter. "This arrived today, from Bibury."

"You've opened it," she accused him.

"Only because it was directed to me."

Puzzled, Rosalie asked, "Why would Aunt Tilda write you? What does she say?"

"She hopes you'll pay her a visit that she may felicitate you in person. Apparently I'm included in the invitation, because she adds that the fishing is excellent in the summer months. It's what she wrote in the closing paragraph that is most significant. Shall I read it to you?"

Curbing her impatience to set out on their expedition, she nodded.

"'In reply to your grace's query about whether the family received letters from my brother during the year preceding Rosalie's birth, I can tell you that he first informed our parents of his and Delphine's expectations in December of 1788, some four months after their marriage. I have the letter by me now, as well as the one he sent immediately after his wife's confinement. In describing his new daughter, he states with endearing certitude that she inherited *his* eyes, nose, and chin. How he could make such a claim about a newborn infant, I shall never know. And although my niece grew up to resemble her mother, the portraits of her in childhood remind me very much of David in his early youth.'"

Rosalie pried the letter from his hand and read the passage herself. Her eyes shone when she looked up at him. "I ought to have asked Aunt Tilda for information, but I was too afraid to admit my doubts about my parentage. I never guessed you might have done so yourself, Gervais!"

"It occurred to me that she was the only person who

could clear up the mystery that has been plaguing you. I daresay Lemercier never knew the precise date of your parents' nuptials, which is why he might conclude that you were his daughter."

"I'll have to tell him the truth, poor man." After studying the letter, she added, "Aunt Tilda also says I must collect the Fragonard and the three Greuze canvases. They are my dowry and must have some value."

His arms encircled her. "You, Rosalie, are by far my most valuable acquisition. But I shall be glad to have your Greuze paintings—we can put one in each of our houses, if you wish. Or would you rather keep them together?"

They continued their discussion during their drive out of Weymouth to explore the natural wonders a few miles to the east. The road wound through the verdant downs and patchwork farms of Dorsetshire. The rolling contours were dappled with sunshine and shade, and the thick grasses on the chalk hills rippled in the breeze coming off the sea. Rosalie was entranced by the beauty and majesty of the surrounding landscape, which affected her in the same way as beautiful and majestic music, and made her wish she could dance out her feelings.

Lulworth Cove was a placid pool of green seawater enclosed by steep limestone cliffs. After strolling along the pebbled beach, the couple climbed a steep, turf-carpeted hill where a man was gazing through a telescope.

"I'm watching the ships in the channel," he explained after introducing himself as Mr. Weld. "Here, ma'am, have a look."

He offered the instrument to Rosalie. Peering through its eyepiece, she saw sailing vessels large and small, gliding upon the waters.

Gervase asked Mr. Weld if there was a decent inn nearby where he and his wife might order some dinner.

"The Red Lion at Lulworth sets a fine table. Are you stopping in the neighborhood?"

"At Weymouth."

"Ah," the gentleman sighed. "I'm afraid it has been sadly quiet since the King ceased visiting. The townspeople erected the statue of His Majesty last year to commemorate the Jubilee, but he has never seen it. Nor will he, it seems. Well, sir, may you and your lady enjoy a fine dinner, and an uneventful drive through the countryside."

"Are there footpads in this district?" Rosalie wondered as she returned his telescope.

Mr. Weld smiled and shook his head. "Nay, only smugglers, and unless you're preventive officers in disguise, you've naught to fear from them."

Although the Red Lion was a small establishment, it lived up to the gentleman's good report and provided the duke and duchess with lobster and prawns, sliced cucumber, and gooseberry pie. At dusk they wandered back toward the cove, hand in hand.

"I wish we could remain at the seaside forever," said Rosalie.

"But if we delay our return to London, the world will say we're hiding ourselves in shame."

"Not 'we.' You."

"I'd prefer to take you Pontesbury," Gervase told her. "It is a true country house, comfortable yet unpretentious, and Shropshire suits me best in summertime. At Haberdine and Solway House I'm required to live *en prince*, but never at cosy old Pontesbury."

"It has been your home for many years, hasn't it?"

"Since I came of age. When we do go there, possibly in July, we can stop at Bibury to see your aunt."

After remaining silent for a short time, Rosalie said, "If we must live in town during the coming weeks, I hope you'll send for Lord Swanborough to join us. I'm eager to see him again and it sounds as though we won't be visiting Northamptonshire for quite a long time."

Gervase paused on the path and faced her. "Are you saying you want to take charge of Ninian?"

"He ought to reside with his guardian, Gervais. I know he professes to dislike London, but he must be lonely at Haberdine."

"He's got Duffield for company. And my mother."

His last three words resurrected the depression that struck her whenever she thought of the dowager duchess. For now that Matilda's letter had vanquished all doubts about her lineage, the existence of her formidable mother-in-law was the only blight on her happiness.

"If it's what you want," he said, "I'll send an express to Haberdine straightaway. But first you must promise me that you won't let Ninian drag you off to Sadler's Wells when you'd rather not go."

Tucking her arm in his, she asked, "Is that what he did to you?"

"Yes. At first I complained, but for some time now I've realized that I have cause to be grateful to him, young devil that he is."

He slipped his arm around her waist and they continued down to the beach. The night was clear and cloudless, and a multitude of stars twinkled overhead; waves crashed against the shore of the dark, deserted cove. Inspired by the romantic beauty of the setting, the Duchess of Solway lifted her trailing skirts and twirled about, performing an impromptu dance for her appreciative husband.

The scandal resulting from their hasty and private marriage had subsided before the newlyweds reached London, and they soon discovered that the chief topic of conversation among all classes of people was the forthcoming fête at Carlton House. The Prince Regent intended to acknowledge his father's birthday and mark his own rise to power with a grand celebration, and it promised to be the most lavish in the history of the monarchy. The guests of honor would be Louis Bourbon, the hereditary King of France, and members of his court of exile.

The public criticized the Regent for spending an excessive sum—fifteen thousand pounds, according to one report—on a single entertainment and many people believed its magnitude and expense was inappropriate during wartime. Others, recalling the poor King's illness, denounced it as an unfilial act. The outraged buzzing grew still louder when the date was changed to allow the painters, upholsterers, florists, chefs, and confectioners to complete their extensive transformation of Carlton House. The delay was welcomed by London's dressmakers and tailors, who worked day and night to accommodate those clients who had been favored with an invitation.

The day after their return to Solway House the morning newspaper announced that over fifteen thousand members of the British nobility had been so honored, in addition to ministers, foreign ambassadors, and princes. Rosalie's fears that she and Gervase were the only aristocrats excluded from the festivities ended with the arrival of a footman in blue and buff livery. But the receipt of the coveted card engraved with the Prince of Wales's feathers meant that she, like every other noblewoman in London, had to decide what to wear. No gown in her wardrobe was magnificent enough for the occasion, and she was unacquainted with the most elegant modistes.

The removal of her belongings from the lodging in Panton Street diverted her from thoughts of fashion for the space of one day. She readily shouldered the responsibility of finding new employment for Peg Reilly, who preferred not to follow her mistress to Park Lane.

"I'd not be comfortable around all them grand servants of the duke's," she said sadly. "Best that I seek a place in a smaller house."

Rosalie took her to Golden Square and had no difficulty persuading Mrs. Hughes to increase her staff.

Gervase, who had divided his day between his man of business and his club, brought home the latest *on-dits* about the fête and repeated them to his bride. The Queen and the royal princesses were not expected to attend. The Regent had not only invited Mrs. Fitzherbert, he'd even offered to pay for her dress, but after she learned that she would not be seated at his table she'd refused to go. Lady Wentworth, as eager as anyone to take part in the greatest social event of this or any season, had boldly questioned the delay of the invitation her rank entitled her to receive.

"Her friends told her that the Regent's secretary ran out of cards before he reached the *W*'s on his list," Gervase said. "To which her ladyship replied, 'That can't be the reason, for quite half the *whores* in the town have theirs already!' But the members of that sisterhood must be sadly disappointed," he added, "for the Regent's mother made him promise not to receive any ladies who had been un-faithful to their marriage vows."

"Well, that's a neat solution to my problem," Rosalie said merrily. "If I can find myself a lover I won't need a ballgown!" After her husband objected to this drastic plan, she said, "*Vraiment*, I don't know what I ought to do. This afternoon I visited two dressmakers, one in Oxford Street and the other in Bond Street, and both were too overworked to accept the commission. Why couldn't we have stayed in Weymouth until this foolishness was over and done? I'm tempted to beg assistance from Madame Ferrier, who used to sew my ballet costumes."

"Why don't you?"

"Perhaps I shall," she said thoughtfully. "She's the most skilful seamstress I know, and efficient. And I still have that length of gold-shot silk that was never made up."

The very next day Rosalie took the town coach to Pentonville. Gervase remained at home to study the reports from his land steward in Shropshire, but he was forced to set them aside at midday when his mother, Ninian, and Mr. Duffield arrived.

He received his parent cordially but with caution, and was relieved to find her in an amiable mood. But her desire for a private interview was made obvious when she sent Ninian from the green salon to wash and change out of his rumpled garments.

"You have been busy since we last met," the dowager duchess told her son. "No, don't worry, I didn't come here to fling recriminations at your head."

"I'm glad of that," he responded. "Which is not to suggest that I deserve any."

"It was very sudden, your decision to take a wife," she said, taking a seat.

"I've always known it was my duty to marry," he countered. "How many ladies do you suppose I've met since I attained my majority? Hundreds, I should imagine. I danced with all the pretty ones and flirted with the bold ones. I even believed myself enamored with a certain widow, greatly to your distress. So you will surely agree that I've had sufficient experience of the female sex to make a reasoned choice."

"And what were those reasons? You omitted them when you wrote the letter informing me of your intentions."

"After several months of uncertainty, I recognized that Rosalie de Barante was no passing fancy. I also discovered that my feelings were so strong that I could not give her up. To me, she is the personification of that line from the poet Cowper: 'Strength joined with beauty, dignity with grace.' I want her by my side for the duration of my life, and it is she who must be the mother of my children, not some lady I hardly know and cannot love." Impressed by his own eloquence, he hoped she would be also.

"The announcement in the 'Recent Marriages' column of the papers was a remarkable feat of brevity," she said. " 'The Duke of Solway wed Miss Lovegrove of Bibury, Gloucestershire' sounded well enough, but it makes me wonder if you meant to conceal the fact of her former profession."

"No, nor has it. I hoped that if people knew about Rosalie's English background they might accept her more readily than if they believed her to be French. Society as we know it may be surprised by our marriage, but I don't doubt that by end of this season my duchess will have proved her worthiness for that title. And after she has been seen at Carlton House, all doors will be open to her."

"You may be right."

Eventually they talked of other family matters, which occupied them until the dowager duchess decided to end her visit. "My sister expects me to bear her company for the next few weeks, and the retired situation of Hampton Court has a strong appeal for me. But I will see you again soon, I trust. And also your bride," she added with a fleeting but inscrutable smile.

Upon her return from her meeting with Madame Ferrier, Rosalie learned that Lord Swanborough and his tutor had arrived. Five months had altered Ninian, increasing his stature, and his deeper voice was another sign of maturity.

"Aunt Elizabeth decided to visit her sister," he explained,

"so she brought Jap and me in her traveling carriage. Even though *I* wanted to ride on the stage. After she and Ger talked she left for Hampton Court. Her sister has a grace-and-favor lodging there because she used to wait upon the Queen."

Rosalie was surprised that the duke had not persuaded his mother to stay at Solway House. Or had his invitation been refused? It was entirely likely, for the dowager duchess must be grievously disappointed in her son's marriage.

During an afternoon stroll through the gardens, Rosalie questioned the earl closely, trusting him to be candid. "Was your aunt disturbed by the letter Gervais wrote?" she asked.

Ninian hunched his broadening shoulders. "I don't know, she didn't say anything to me. Why should she be? For years she has wanted Ger to be married, and I told her there's no one nicer or prettier than you." He halted beneath the laburnum arch, laden with dangling clusters of gold flowers, and asked, "What do I call you now? You aren't a mademoiselle any longer."

"I won't be satisfied with anything but 'your grace,'" she said severely.

His dark blue eyes widened incredulously. Then he grinned at her. "Duchess you may be, but I can't believe you'll be as toplofty as Aunt Elizabeth."

"Tell me about your Easter visit to Cavender Chase," she encouraged him. "What do you think of your niece Juliet?"

"Everyone says she's going to be *beautiful*," he reported. "My mama was there, too. Justin and Mira gave a party, and an old gentleman told her she looked the same as she did on the day they met. That made her very happy."

He was still talking about his stay in Wiltshire when Robert brought her the news that a French gentleman had called and wished to speak with her. While Ninian embarked upon a nautical discussion with his favorite footman, she hurried to the green salon to meet Monsieur Lemercier.

Bowing deeply from the waist, he said, "Madame la Duchesse, I was honored to receive your messenger, and it is my pleasure to see you again. Words cannot convey my joy when I read the notice of your marriage in the newspaper. I only regret that your surname was given as Lovegrove."

"It was no error, monsieur."

She explained, as gently as possible, that she had incontrovertible proof of her parentage.

He was disinclined to accept it. "This woman you call your aunt is certain of these dates?"

"You may read her letter if you wish," she replied. "I never informed her of your claim, or apprised her of my recent doubts about my parentage. The duke sought this confirmation from her without my prior knowledge, and sorry though I am to cause you pain, I'm thankful that he did."

The Frenchman's powdered head drooped. "When I found you, I believed that you would accept me, in time. I wanted it more than anything, for I have no other remembrance of Delphine, *la grande passion de ma vie*. Perhaps this is a just punishment for my cruel desertion."

Rosalie looked to the delicate porcelain figurine on the mantel, having placed it there at Gervase's suggestion. It was one of her most precious keepsakes, but she also possessed the Fragonard painting, and many lesser relics which had belonged to her mother. Etienne Lemercier had nothing but the memory of her tears.

"Take this," she said softly, presenting her treasure to him. "*Certainement,* Maman would want you to have something of she treasured."

Gazing sadly at the object she had given him, he said, "Whenever I look upon it, I will think not only of my lost love, but also of the so beautiful *danseuse* who became a *duchesse*—and might have been my daughter."

Rosalie's pensive silence troubled Gervase later, when they left Solway House to attend a performance at the King's Theatre. It would be their first public appearance as man and wife, and he suspected she was nervous.

Fingering her necklace, a *rivière* of large topazes and small diamonds, she confessed, "It is so strange to be going to the theater with you, in your carriage."

"You've ridden in it several times," he reminded her.

"Yes, but this is different. And it will be stranger still to see an opera from your box seat rather than from the wings. I hope you don't mind taking me—fashionable people aren't expected to attend a singer's benefit. But Naldi was always so good to me that I owe it to him to be there. *The Magic Flute* is a Mozart opera, after all, and Armand is dancing afterward." With a little shake of her head, she said, "I must remember to call him Vestris now."

Despite the fact that it was a benefit performance, they found a long line of coaches in the Haymarket and a crowd in the box lobby. They reached their seats only moments before the overture began.

Gervase noted that Rosalie was rather pale, possibly because hundreds of people were studying her face, her dress, and her jewels. He shifted his satin-covered thigh closer to hers, seeking to reassure her with physical contact. The soaring violins matched his mood, for his mother had not berated him, and his wife did him great credit.

Now that their honeymoon was behind them, they were expected to maintain a stifling degree of propriety at all times except when they were alone. This was made even more difficult by his recurring impulse to take her to bed, which he was now lawfully permitted to do as frequently as he wished. He'd discovered that she was remarkably demure for a girl with French blood—but only up to a point. And while she gave every sign of welcoming his attentions, he didn't want her to think he regarded her only as a plaything. To him she was much more than someone he'd taken as his wife simply because she refused to be his mistress. That, he suspected, was what his mother believed.

He became aware of a change in Rosalie at the beginning of the opera's second scene. While the evil Monostatos preyed upon Pamina, she pressed her lips together and clutched the arms of her chair, entirely caught up in the action. And, Gervase realized in a flash of intuition, the heroine's situation had reminded her of Benjamin Beckmann's attack. Should he put their precarious dignity at risk by reaching for her gloved hand? He restrained himself, for her sake.

The subsequent entrance of Papageno the bird-catcher brought an appreciative smile to her face. Soon Tamino was playing the magic flute, enticing various wild creatures from the wood, and while bears, apes, and an ungainly crocodile cavorted about the stage, Rosalie's enjoyment was exactly as Ninian's would have been. Her spirits were as changeable as a child's, and he was learning to expect those rapid transformations from gravity to merriment.

Between acts she turned to him and said, "The Parisian productions of this opera were far more spectacular than this one. And except for Signora Bertinotti, the singers are sadly out of voice tonight."

"I'm sorry that you're disappointed. Shall we go, then?"

"Not before the ballet."

After the curtain descended upon the principals and the chorus, she exhibited signs of extreme agitation. "You're quite sure you wish to stay?" he probed, but her firm, decisive nod failed to reassure him.

His foreboding increased when the ballet began, and Rosalie's profound interest in what appeared to be an unremarkable piece of choreography wounded him. Her attention never left the stage, where Armand Vestris leaped and bounded with vigorous abandon. Did he imagine it, or were her eyes misted by tears of regret?

Watching his wife watch her former colleagues, Gervase felt guilty of a crime as foul as those Beckmann had committed against her. Marrying her had been an act of supreme selfishness. He had caged this airy sprite, and now she was earthbound, no longer free. In future she might hate him for it.

To his considerable relief, he detected no animosity in his bride when they drove through the lamplit streets to their Park Lane mansion. And the way she snuggled against him, seeking to rest her head upon his shoulder, soothed his alarms.

"Thank you for taking me," she murmured. "But I don't think I'll often ask you to."

"Was it so painful?"

"Yes. Because the opera was less than good, and Armand's ballet even worse—and the performers must have known it, too."

"I thought you were jealous of them."

"Oh no," she protested, "*pas du tout.* I felt only pity."

Stroking her curls, he said, "I have admired you as a mermaid, fairy, goddess, and nymph, but in none of your roles have you pleased me more than in that of duchess."

She sighed, then said softly, "*Cher* Gervais, you always give the answer I most need to hear."

16

My charmer is not mine alone.
—WILLIAM COWPER

June the nineteenth, the day of the Carlton House fête, dragged by for Rosalie. Gervase, who had always proved capable of calming her worst fears, decided to take Ninian out to Greenwich, no doubt thinking he was doing her a favor, but she missed them both terribly. It was well past dinnertime when they returned and she was already closeted with Madame Ferrier, who brought her finished ballgown to Solway House.

The gauzy turquoise silk of the overdress was lavishly embroidered with gold thread, and the Frenchwoman had appliquéd a chain of miniature golden cockleshells to the hem. She confided to her satisfied customer that it was the most magnificent garment she had ever created, and deserved to be seen by the Comte de Lille, the uncrowned brother of Louis the Sixteenth.

"It is a dress worthy of Queen Marie Antoinette herself," Rosalie said, a compliment which brought tears to the seamstress's eyes.

"When you see our King, Madame la Duchesse, you must tell him that all loyalists pray for our monarchy to be restored. It is dishonor to our country that he must live in exile here, while that Corsican *usurpateur* pretends to be our ruler!"

Madame Ferrier, after years of serving as a dresser in the theater, was as skilled with the comb as she was with her needle. She arranged Rosalie's curling tresses in an elegant coiffure, upon which she placed the heavy topaz and diamond crescent. She handed Rosalie the other glittering pieces of the parure, one by one, and fastened each clasp for her.

By nine o'clock that evening, carriages bearing more than two thousand invited guests clogged the streets of Mayfair. The congestion was increased by the crowds of common folk who gathered along the street to watch the procession. Gervase preferred to wait until well past ten before calling for his coach, and by that time Rosalie was almost paralyzed with anticipation.

Ninian had stayed up late to see them off. As he studied his cousin's court dress of dark velvet coat trimmed with silver lace, white satin knee breeches, and silk waistcoat, he commented, "I never saw you look so much like a duke. May I hold your sword?"

"Definitely not," Gervase said without hesitation.

"Why is Rosalie wearing Aunt Elizabeth's necklace and eardrops?" Ninian wondered.

"Because I asked her to."

Rosalie turned away from the pier glass. "The topazes belong to your mother?"

"At my father's death they became my property. You will have the use of them for as long as I live, and when I'm gone they'll pass to our eldest son." He picked up his *chapeau bras*, tucking it beneath one arm, and extended the other to his duchess.

After a meandering journey through the lamplit streets, the town coach discharged its passengers beneath the columned portico of Carlton House.

Gervase and Rosalie proceeded through the entrance hall, and upon entering the Crimson Drawing Room they joined a vast crowd of exquisitely dressed persons. Most of the gentlemen were clad in velvet and satin, and the coats of those in military dress displayed medals and sparkling decorations. The ladies wore silk and satin; white was the predominant color, making Rosalie conspicuous in her vivid blue-green gown. Jeweled tiaras supported their waving plumes, and Rosalie marveled at the number of emeralds, rubies, and amethysts that had been mined from the

earth to grace the necks and wrists of England's noblewomen.

Gervase conducted her through the Circular Room, the
Throne Room, and the Rose Satin Room, each one
crammed with people. An orchestra played continuously
but there wasn't enough space for dancing, and the music
was drowned out by the incessant hum of several thousand
voices. Rosalie knew no one, although her husband tried to
remedy that by occasionally introducing her to Lord This or
Lady That.

"Are you acquainted with everyone here?" she asked him
when they reached yet another anteroom.

"Oh no," he laughed, "nor do I want to be. Come, I must
present you to His Royal Highness."

The Prince Regent was receiving his guests in the Blue
Velvet Room. Its azure velvet hangings, carpet, and silk
chair covers were so liberally decorated with gold fleur-de-
lis that it was a suitable setting for the exiled Bourbons.

Rosalie curtsied to her host, who bore a disconcerting resemblance to the caricatures she'd seen in print shop windows. His scarlet coat was trimmed with gold lace and he
wore the shining star that designated his membership in the
Order of the Garter.

The Regent beamed at Rosalie, his broad smile plumping
his pink cheeks. "How delightful that such a charming creature has married into our nobility. You were born in France,
I believe—or so we have been told."

"I was, sir," she replied.

"Allow me to present you to my guest of honor, the
Comte de Lille." Turning to the portly individual at his
side, he said, "Monseigneur, here is one of your countrywomen, the Duchess of Solway."

The comte inclined his powdered head in dignified acknowledgement. He was a victim of obesity and gout, and
his movements were slow and ponderous. *"Et votre famille,
Madame la Duchesse?"*

Gervase replied for her, saying, "My wife's father was
an Englishman, and her mother was Delphine de Barante."

The Comte de Lille's sharp eyes studied Rosalie. *"La

Belle Delphine," he said, nodding again. *"Une artiste du ballet, une danseuse magnifique. Bon, bon."*

Rosalie forgot her disappointment in the titular monarch's appearance and manner when she met Marie Thérèse Charlotte, daughter and only surviving child of Marie Antoinette. A dignified woman in her thirties, she was handsome rather than pretty. Her small mouth and prominent nose were legacies from her Hapsburg forebears. Rosalie perceived a faint resemblance to the French Queen, whose face was more familiar to her from portraits than memory. She wore a diamond tiara of such great height that it resembled a crown of state.

Standing at her side was her husband and cousin, the un-prepossessing Duc d'Angoulème, elder son of the Comte d'Artois. The Duc de Berri, his more vibrant and flamboyant brother, bowed over Rosalie's hand and murmured extravagant compliments.

Her face was still pink with pleasure when the Marquis of Elston approached her. "My dear duchess, you've no idea how glad I am to have found you—and wouldn't believe how desperately I've been searching," he said, his alabaster face more animated than she had ever seen it. "Follow me, there's something you must see. You, too, Gervase."

They went with him to a corridor hung with gilt-framed paintings. One of them, which was achingly familiar to her, depicted a young girl in a scarlet cloak, her hair bound by a matching ribbon.

" 'Mischief,' " Rosalie gasped. "Gervais, it's the little Gypsy!" Tearing her eyes from the long-lost canvas, she turned to her husband.

"The Regent's most recent acquisition," Damon told them triumphantly, "purchased on the advice of Sir George Beaumont, who told him it had been privately sold by Monsieur Lemercier."

"Etienne Lemercier?" Rosalie asked. After a thoughtful moment, she said, "I suppose he decided to let it go after our conversation the other day. *Pauvre gentilhomme.*"

Said Gervase, "I only wish I'd had the opportunity to make an offer. I doubt that His Royal Highness will let the painting go now that it's in his clutches."

"To think that my face is hanging on the wall of a royal residence! Maman would be so proud!"

"And not merely your face," Gervase interjected dryly, focused on the low décolletage of the girl in the picture. "I'm not best pleased that the Regent can gaze upon my bride's charms whenever he chooses."

Unlike his friend the duke, Lord Elston was acquainted with the majority of the guests. While he and the Solways strolled through the extensive gardens behind the house, he entertained them with wicked gossip about many of the individuals thronging the grounds. Canvas awnings had been stretched over many of the walks, from which hung suspended illumination and fragrant festoons of flowers.

When Gervase went in search of some champagne and the marquis paused to greet an attractive female, Rosalie walked on alone, relieved to have a moment to herself. The combination of crowded, overheated rooms, the ceaseless buzz of voices, and the weighty crescent she was wearing had given her a fierce headache. Assuming that her husband was lost among the mob, she wandered toward a shadowy grove of trees in the hope of finding some cooler, fresher air.

While weaving among the well-tended shrubs and topiary, she met another solitary lady in gray silk and pearls, and politely stepped aside to let her pass.

"Those topazes become you far more than they ever did me," said the woman.

Rosalie stared up at the proud, well-preserved face she remembered so well. "Your grace," she choked, dropping a hasty, off-balance curtsy. "I—we didn't know you were here."

"In such a crush as this, it is no wonder," replied the Dowager Duchess of Solway. "What has become of my son?"

"I don't know," Rosalie admitted. "I was about to look for him."

"Let him find you," the older woman suggested. "I will keep you company until he does so, for I have many things to say."

17

When at their dance's end they kiss.
—ANDREW MARVELL

This woman, thought Rosalie miserably, was every inch a duchess. Tall and regal with patrician features, she possessed an impressive air of command and an enviable assurance. How disappointed she must be in a successor so small and ordinary, and only half English.

Having no other choice, she accompanied her mother-in-law to a pair of empty chairs at the edge of the terrace. She felt even more vulnerable than she had at their first meeting, and prepared herself for similar unpleasantness.

"I hope you haven't felt slighted by my apparent neglect," the older woman said as they sat down together. "I intended to pay my duty visit the day I brought Ninian to London, but you were out and Gervase discouraged me from awaiting your return. He felt you were not yet ready to meet me."

She would have voiced a polite protest had she not suspected that this grande dame preferred uncompromising honesty. "It is true, your grace, although I never told him so."

"Is it because you believe me opposed to the marriage? On principle I would have been, had anyone asked my opinion beforehand."

"I didn't entrap him," she said in a rush, determined to clarify that point, "for I never imagined that he would want to marry me."

"It's just as well that he did. I much prefer having a for-

mer opera dancer for my daughter-in-law than I would the
Princess Charlotte of Wales. You have spared me that indignity. As antecedents go, yours are respectable enough.
According to Gervase, your father's family were Gloucestershire gentry."

"Yes, but the Lovegrove properties are not extensive,
and my future inheritance consists of a few small farms and
a house in Bibury village. I have nothing in the way of a
fortune. My father was a professional musician, and Aunt
Tilda taught singing at a Bristol seminary. Of my maternal
relations I know very little. My French grandfather was a
wealthy *avocat,* but I wasn't told any more than that. He
disowned Maman when she went on the stage."

"Your mother performed at the Paris Opera, I have been
informed. And also Versailles?"

Said Rosalie with pride, "She did, your grace. The Queen
admired her very much. She had a great interest in children,
too, and often invited Maman to bring me to the Tuileries. I
was little more than a babe, but I do remember her holding
me." Lifting her chin, she added, "This occasion is not the
first time I have been presented to royalty."

For the first time the duchess smiled. "My dear child,
you needn't be so uncomfortable. I'm not your enemy, and
there will be no repetition of that deplorable scene at Haberdine. I admit, at that time I was concerned that my son's
feelings for you would result in sorrow, or worse, bitter dis-
illusionment. His happiness is of paramount importance to
me."

"*À moi aussi,*" Rosalie murmured.

The fine silvery eyes studied the younger woman's face.
"What I should like to know, if you can answer so intimate
a question from a virtual stranger, is the reason you accepted his marriage proposal."

"I was so tired of refusing him. More than once he asked
me to be his—his *fille de joie,* but I could not. It was agony
for me to hurt Gervais."

"Had you not been in love before?" the duchess asked
gently.

"No more than a little. And never with one such as he. If
he had proposed to me at a time when I was able to think

more clearly, I might not have agreed to marry him. I knew it was not *comme il faut* for dukes to marry dancers. But I was *très désolée*. My career had ended so badly and stupidly and, I didn't know what I would do except go back to Paris, and that he would not permit. I think to him I was *l'âme perdue*—a lost soul. So when he said that he wanted me to be his wife, I consented. We were married the very next day."

"It cannot have been easy making so swift a transition from performer to peeress. You haven't regretted your choice?"

"*Jamais*. How could I, when I have Gervais to love me, to help me? Before knowing him, I did not like to think of a life without dancing, and now I could not live without him. I have discovered that I have a talent for marriage also. It is very like a *pas de deux*," Rosalie elaborated. "There is a need for a sense of balance and timing. One must give support to the partner, and also rely upon his support. Gervais and I are learning each other's moods and habits just as dancers learn their music."

The duchess surprised her by saying, "I would have liked to see you perform. My nephew says that you are exceedingly gifted."

Smiling reminiscently, Rosalie said, "Everything is his fault. My meeting Gervais was the result of Lord Swanborough's mania for the aquatic spectacles at Sadler's Wells."

"He *is* a naughty boy. Has he been behaving himself?"

She laughed. "I wouldn't say that, your grace. He can be an exacting charge, but I enjoy having him at Solway House. My childhood was so odd that I have no notion of how to manage children properly. It is something about which I will require much advice."

"You'll find your way, I have no doubt. And I suspect your theatrical past will serve you very well in your new position, for it also demanded discipline and courage. Now that we have become better acquainted, I realize that Gervase has done very well for himself. And though I'm sure he'd rather spend the summer in seclusion, fishing and reading and doting on his bride, I hope he will remain fixed in town."

"He has said we will."

"Excellent. Otherwise our friends and acquaintances will believe you are an embarrassment to the Marchant family, or worse, some sort of adventuress. Although five minutes in your company would quickly disabuse them of that notion."

Following the other woman's lead, Rosalie climbed to her feet. "You will visit us, then?"

"As often as I may." The duchess took both her hands, clasping them firmly. "Had you remained on the stage, you would never have been more than what you were, an opera dancer. Now you are a wife and a duchess, the mistress of many houses. One day you will become a mother. And already you are a daughter I am proud to have."

Rosalie began another curtsy, but the duchess shook her head.

"No, no, I do not wish for formality between us." Patting the young woman's cheek she said, "After tonight, I hope you will cease to fear me, Rosalie. Gervase is wise enough to let us find our own way to friendship, and he's very patient. He gets both virtues from me."

And also his *beaux yeux*, thought Rosalie, answering her mother-in-law's smile with a radiant one of her own.

Two hours after midnight the Regent's guests assembled in the rooms on the garden level and under the marquees for their dinner.

Rosalie was amazed that she and Gervase should be seated so near their host, among the foreign princes and ambassadors, British ministers of state, and such honored female guests as the Duchess of York, Lady Hertford, and Lady Charlotte Campbell. The high table, extending the whole length of the Gothic conservatory, was laden with gold tureens, covered dishes, and goblets.

The upper servants of the royal household were clad in dark blue livery, and while they served the wines for the first course Rosalie examined the principal decoration. A channel of clear water flowed from the large basin near the Prince Regent's place and meandered down the middle of the table, exciting the admiration of the diners. Several picturesque bridges adorned this miniature river, which had a sandy bottom and was banked with rocks and green moss.

When Rosalie noticed the gold and silvery fish swimming about, she leaned close to Gervase and whispered, "Poor creatures, they'll not survive the heat from all these candles."

The meal was composed of innumerable delicacies, mostly French and all of them rich and heavy. It began and ended with toasts—to the Regent, his guests, the armies in the Peninsula, and the future restoration of the Bourbons. Rosalie, uncomfortably aware that the hands of the great clock marked the fourth hour of a new day, prayed that no more speeches would follow.

The Regent rose, glass in hand. "We would be remiss if we failed to acknowledge a marriage which lately took place," he announced. "It is a union symbolic of the great friendship between the hereditary rulers of the two greatest nations of the world, England and France. Your Majesty, my lords and ladies, I give you the Duke of Solway and his lovely duchess!"

Several hours later, when the newlyweds lay in bed discussing the event, Rosalie asked her husband, "Why would the Regent make such an announcement? You might have married his daughter, after all."

"There was never any chance of that," Gervase contradicted her. "The toast was simply one of the Regent's attempts to appear affable and charming. And it was a masterly way of acknowledging the Comte de Lille. More of a compliment to him than to us," he mused as his fingers drifted through her unbound hair.

"Well, it's something to tell our children, and our grandchildren. That is what your mother said afterward."

"I'm quite sure they'd rather hear about Clown Grimaldi, and your adventures in Paris—posing for the painter Jean-Baptiste Greuze, and dancing for Napoleon Bonaparte."

"I danced for you *aussi*," she reminded him.

"And also for me."

Their lips touched in a protracted kiss.

Resting her head upon the pillow they shared, Rosalie observed wearily, "The sun is already rising, Gervais. Do you think Ninian will let us lie in bed all day?"

"If he doesn't, I'll make sure he regrets it," the Duke of Solway replied, closing his eyes.

Historical Note

The personnel and productions at Sadler's Wells and the Italian Opera House are authentic, based upon descriptions from newspapers of the period and theatrical memoirs. The collection of London's Theatre Museum in Covent Garden provided a wealth of historical and visual information and contains many Grimaldi artifacts and memorabilia.

Joseph Grimaldi retired from Sadler's Wells on 17 March, 1828, during his forty-ninth year. His farewell performance took place at the Theatre Royal, Drury Lane, on 28 June, his final appearance on any stage. During the following season his son Joe performed some of his most popular parts at Covent Garden. Three years after his dismissal from that company the young man injured himself on another stage and died shortly afterward, aged thirty. His mother Mary, already in poor health, survived him by only two years. Joseph Grimaldi the elder lived until 1837.

In 1813, Armand Vestris married the sixteen-year-old performer Lucia Bartolozzi, and the following year he was promoted from *premier danseur* to ballet master at the King's Theatre. After separating from his wife he continued to work in various European capitals until his death in 1825. Madame Vestris later became wildly popular with early Victorian audiences as an actress, singer, and theater manageress.

I would be remiss if I failed to acknowledge another source of inspiration for *Dangerous Diversions*, the works of Jean Baptiste Greuze in the Wallace Collection, Manchester Square, London.

I dedicate this work to the many individuals who made a meaningful contribution, little though they may realize it. The following have earned my abiding gratitude:

Michael Deep—actor, musician, comedian, playwright, lifelong friend, and modern incarnation of Joseph Grimaldi, about whom he, too, has studied and written.

Marilyn Darling, an inspiring teacher of ballet, who opened my eyes to the fascinating history of dance. And Linda McInnis, at whose side I struggled and sweated through many a session at the barre.

Robert and Margot Pierson, for a memorable visit to Bibury. And my cousin Justin Evans, who kindly gave me a tour of Harrow.

My patient and supportive parents, for all those years they transported me to and from rehearsals and classes.

Lastly and mostly, my husband Christopher, for his involvement and encouragement.

Toast of the Town

Good my lord, will you see the players well bestowed?
Do you hear, let them be well used, for they are
the abstract and brief chronicles of the time.

—Hamlet, II. ii.

Prologue

A curtain of mist lay over the city, and Drury Lane was a tunnel of darkness in which streetlights, carriage lamps, and linkboys' torches glowed eerily. It was March, a two-faced month when wintry weather frequently marred the gentle greening and timidly colorful displays of spring, and the damp and chill in the air urged pedestrians to hurry along the famous thoroughfare, driven by a desire to take shelter from the elements.

The presence of two unescorted ladies was unremarkable in this part of town, the traditional haunt of wantons, pickpockets, and stage performers. But if they were making a harlots' progress, it was destined to be unsuccessful, because the older woman's expression was more forbidding than encouraging to the male passersby, and however shapely the younger lady's figure might be, it was concealed by a long cloak.

With each brisk, purposeful step, her hood slipped back, permitting the crossing sweeps and chair men who loitered on the greasy pavements to admire her heart-shaped face and dark curls. As they began to call out lewd compliments, the middle-aged female reached over and replaced the hood, dispelling the impression that she was a local bawd displaying her lovely protégée.

Paying no heed to her unruly admirers, Flora Campion walked on. Her pink lips moved as if in prayer, and she clasped and unclasped her gloved hands in nervous accompaniment to her whispered soliloquy. "Oh, sir," she said softly but audibly, "I will not be so hardhearted, I will give out divers schedules of my beauty. It shall be inventoried, and every particle and utensil labeled." The woman plodding along beside her made no reply, nor did she seem disturbed by being thus addressed. After a thoughtful moment, Flora added, "I think that's correct."

"Well, to be sure, ma'am, I don't rightly remember."

"Over a year since I've played the Lady Olivia." Turning bright green eyes toward her chaperone, she asked, "But where, Margery? Was it at Chichester that we last performed *Twelfth Night*?"

"Portsmouth," corrected Margery, once more adjusting Flora's hood.

"Both," said the actress positively. "I must try and find a copy of the playbook when we reach the theater—I'm hopelessly rusty. Still, I suppose it's something," she went on, "this chance to play a principal role again. I can scarcely believe it."

Margery's plain face was set in stern lines as she announced grimly, "What *I* can't believe is how Mrs. Ellis waited the whole day before deciding she wouldn't play tonight. You could've done with a bit of rehearsal."

"It doesn't matter. If I become muddled, I can always go back to Shakespeare's original text. Ben didn't alter the play too much, thank heaven."

But Flora's thankfulness was tempered by her displeasure, despite being the recipient of that stroke of fortune every understudy yearned for. A leading player had been felled by illness, but if only it hadn't been at the last minute, she fumed. However fond she was of her employer, who was her mentor and benefactor as well, returning to the theater was most inconvenient; she disliked going without dinner. And in all likelihood the play would not be repeated, which only added insult to the original injury of surrendering a favorite role to Mrs. Ellis when, at the first of the year, the company had come to London. After Benedict Forster had pointed out the necessity of subordinating one's personal ambitions for the common good, Flora had regretfully relinquished Olivia and Ophelia, Kate Hardcastle and Lydia Languish, roles she had long considered her personal property.

Her destination this foggy night was a minor theater tucked into an obscure corner of Drury Lane. It was not, as many mistakenly supposed, named for a member of any royal family, past or present, but had originally been the Saracen Princess, a popular but semi-disreputable tavern. After a damaging fire a century ago it had been rebuilt as a playhouse, and a succession of managers had struggled to make it go. The Princess had languished in the shadow of older, more illustrious theaters down the street and had long been a venue for musical burlettas and spectacles, the only offerings legally permitted the non-patent playhouses. And then she had been rescued from obscurity by fate and a determined fellow named Forster.

Flora hoped his bold venture would succeed, for remaining in one place was an unaccustomed luxury. During her six years with the troupe of players, she had lived as a vagabond, picking up and moving every few weeks.

In her eagerness to reach the warmth of the green-room fire she quickened her pace, leaving the slower Margery behind. Familiar habit had already replaced annoyance, and by the time the stage-door keeper closed the portals behind the actress and her faithful servant, Flora had quite forgotten that she'd deserted the same dilapidated building barely two hours before, in happy anticipation of a night of unaccustomed liberty.

1

'Tis beauty truly blent, whose white and red
Nature's own sweet and cunning hand laid on.

Twelfth Night, I.v.

In the fashionable district of St. James's, three well-dressed gentlemen emerged from the sacred precincts of White's Club. Two of them were actively engaged in a debate and paused on the rain-slick paving stones to continue it. When the youngest man stated his desire to visit the theater, the eldest shook his head in adamant protest and extolled the merits of a particular bottle of spirits he'd been saving for just such a night as this.

They made an appeal to the third gentleman, who towered over them. His brown hair, worn longer than the prevailing fashion, framed a patrician countenance which was both proud and noble. In a low and well-modulated voice, he informed his companions that although he had no preference for one plan over the other, he would appreciate a quick decision, as the damp was slowly but inexorably permeating his garments. In fact, he added, he would await the outcome of their discussion in his carriage.

His retreat prompted them to settle their argument. The youth called out the direction to the coachman, and issued a triumphant order to the footman at the door of the vehicle. He climbed in and announced to its owner, "I've sent your man ahead to secure a stage box, Trevor. You can sample Rupert's cognac *after* the play."

Trevor John Cotterell, 3rd Earl of Leafield, directed a smile at the gentleman seated across from him. "Well, I suppose if your fine spirit ages for a few more hours, it can only be to our advantage."

"Just so," agreed Mr. Rupert Harburton. "But I doubt our young friend has any intention of passing the evening with what lies in my cellars."

Turning to the youth, Trevor asked, "Didn't your last experience cure your partiality for opera dancers?"

Lord Edgar, taking instant exception, bestowed a disdainful glance upon his friend. "I'm ages wiser now, and I won't have you teasing me about my—my—"

"Backstage friendships," Trevor supplied.

"Well, yes. But it's no opera dancer this time. She's an actress, a leading actress—but Rupert knows. Tell him about Louise."

Bowing to the young man's insistence, Mr. Harburton said languidly, "Louise Talley, for whom this stripling has conceived a grand passion, is a featured comic actress at the new theater which has caused all the furor of late. But Baron Allingham is also laying siege to the lady, and I'm afraid the odds are decidedly—and quite naturally—in his favor. Haven't you looked into the betting book at the club lately, my lord?"

Lord Edgar's eyes blazed. "I ought to call you out for that, Rupert—by God, I shall!"

"On what pretext?" was his friend's damping reply. "No insult was intended, I was merely stating a fact. Allingham is precisely the protector La Talley has dreamed of since the day her dainty foot first trod the boards. Young, handsome, reasonably rich—"

"But he's engaged to be married," the youth protested, causing the other two gentlemen to exchange glances yet again.

Mr. Harburton shook his head, and his eyes were faintly contemptuous. "It's money and a carriage and jewels she wants from him, not a wedding ring."

"And noblemen don't marry actresses," Trevor pronounced coolly, in case Lord Edgar had failed to mark Mr. Harburton's subtle warning.

He regretted his words, because the young man immediately embarked upon a catalog of every nobleman who had ever wed a lady of the stage, as though he'd spent the past week studying the subject. Such idealism was refreshing to one who had attained the sophisticated and somewhat jaded heights of his early thirties. Without having set eyes on Miss Talley, Trevor knew she would be exactly like the jolly little opera dancer who had spurned the lordling's advances to bestow her favors on a gentleman with a fortune rumored to be one of the largest in the realm.

The crush of traffic in Drury Lane was impossible to avoid, so the gentlemen chose to abandon the earl's carriage near the top of the street and walk the rest of the way. With hours of dramatic entertainment before him, Trevor was glad of the opportunity to stretch his legs.

"Edgar is young yet," Mr. Harburton reminded him, "and a fellow is expected to cut his milk teeth on a playhouse wench."

"But not to marry her," Trevor said.

The playbill affixed to a front column of the theater informed him that the main offering was to be *Twelfth Night*, and the loud ovation from within heralded the conclusion of the curtain raiser. He would have preferred a night of drink and conversation to the proposed entertainment, having outgrown any enthusiasm for attending the play long ago.

Inside the theater, prostitutes paraded along the shabby corridors and lurked in the corners of the box lobby and saloon, their gowns barely concealing their abundant charms, while pickpockets tried to blend in with the crowd, sharp eyes and itching fingers at the ready. The Princess was prime hunting ground; her manager's unpopularity in political circles had cost him the services of Bow Street Runners, who warned the playgoers at other theaters to mind their pockets. Those persons unable to procure a box at either Drury Lane or Covent Garden had chosen the rival theater by default; the gallery was nearly full, and the exquisitely dressed bucks and dandies crowded the pit.

The earl's footman had taken possession of a stage box with worn chairs and chipped gilding. When the new arrivals took their places, the fashionable young damsels gazed hopefully at his lordship, sighing over the chiseled lips and square chin with its hint of a cleft, and noting how the chandeliers burnished the waving brown hair with a coppery brilliance.

The hazel eyes which figured so prominently in the debutantes' innocent heartburnings fell upon the coterie of married society ladies in the adjacent box. All were friends of Trevor's former mistress, whose irate spouse had removed her from town in an effort to avoid an incipient scandal.

He glanced down at a smudged sheet of paper Lord Edgar had pressed upon him, and after reading the titles of the pieces to be acted that night, he let it waft to the floor to join those left from the last night's performance. He was not altogether pleased to learn that the manager had the funds to produce a triple bill.

Trevor had heard of Benedict Forster, for he had been a popular topic of discussion ever since announcing his intention of producing the legitimate forms of drama denied to all theaters except Drury Lane and Covent Garden, which held royal patents. At first no one had placed any confidence in his plan, for without a license he couldn't open his decaying playhouse. No magistrate of Westminster, the domain of the Theatres Royal, was likely to support a possible rival.

But the provincial manager was more clever than anyone had guessed. It turned out that the Princess sat outside of the boundary separating Westminster from the adjacent borough of Holborn and therefore fell within the jurisdiction of a different magistrate. Forster was also fortunate in having several influential well-wishers so eager to have a third legitimate theater in London that they had prevailed upon the Lord Chamberlain to interpret the Licensing Act more liberally than his predecessor. Armed with a special dispensation to produce serious drama for a probationary period of one year, Forster was regarded as a miracle worker by the public, but his disgruntled competitors viewed him as a threat, for he'd made an unprecedented breach in a long-unbroken theatrical monopoly.

Trevor looked toward the stage as the talk of the town marched out from the wings to deliver the prologue in a powerful and highly trained voice. The green curtain rose, the play began, and he was able to judge for himself the charms of the creature who had so inflamed his friend's youthful ardor. Louise Talley was a round-faced girl with ginger hair, a high-pitched warble, and the habit of directing her speeches to the stage box containing the predatory person of Baron Allingham. When she made her exit at the end of the scene, she gave the nobleman a final, melting glance, as if inviting him to follow her into the wings. This caused a murmur in the pit; the bucks nudged each other knowingly as the odds in Allingham's favor rose even higher.

Louise appeared next in masculine dress, a shirt and breeches that revealed her greatest assets, a full bosom and shapely legs. Trevor understood why she was so popular, even though her speaking voice was barely adequate and she possessed no remarkable degree of beauty, but still he was confounded by Lord Edgar's penchant for her. Evidently it was common to all the young men, for Miss Talley's every appearance was greeted with calls, whistles, and stamping feet.

The audience roared its approval of the stock comic characters, Sir Toby and Maria, Feste the Clown and Sir Andrew Aguecheek, but nothing had the power to amuse the earl, who sank deeper into his chair and wished he dared close his eyes. The various Forsters acquitted themselves nobly, but Miss Talley was the weakest link; her meager talents didn't meet their uncommonly high standard. Hoping to be diverted by Benedict Forster's portrayal of the obsequious steward, Trevor lifted his head when Malvolio and the Lady Olivia made their entrance. And when his numbed brain finally accepted what his eyes told him was only too true, he joined in the collective sigh of appreciation that rose from the crowd.

The actress who had caught his attention—and held it—had the face of an angel, and the figure revealed by her blue gown would be envied by any courtesan. Her hair was lustrous and black, arranged in long curls, and her veil of delicate, spidery lace trembled as she moved across the stage.

He leaned forward, resting one arm on the edge of the box as Shakespeare's poetry was spoken in a clear, musical voice which carried across the proscenium. Its possessor displayed a very real gift for acting, to the extent that he wondered what manner of person lay beneath the meticulous characterization. Unlike Louise Talley, who was in all probability the strumpet she seemed, this actress gave no hint that she was anything other than the melancholy Olivia, her sorrowing heart closed off to mortal man.

But Miss Talley's coarser charms had won the hearts of the gentlemen in the pit. Impatient for her return, they shifted in their seats and talked over the dialogue. The scene ended, far too quickly in Trevor's opinion, and after the lovely lady glided off the stage, he looked down for the bill of the play he'd discarded so carelessly.

Mr. Harburton, guessing his purpose, saved him the trouble and indignity of sorting through the debris by handing over his own. "She must be the understudy," he whispered. "Mrs. Ellis is advertised as playing Olivia, but she's forty if she's a day. That girl is no more Mrs. Ellis than I am the Prince of Wales. Lord Edgar might be reduced to jelly by La Talley, but to my mind, there is more to admire in the dark lady's performance."

Trevor's eyes glinted with amusement and something more. He murmured, "There is more to admire in the dark lady's person, her performance aside. Who the devil is she?"

His friend shrugged unhelpfully. "I can't say, but our friend Skiffy Skeffington must know—he rubs shoulders with every actor in London."

"Quiet!" came a pained request from the other side of the box. Lord Edgar was sitting as stiffly upright as Trevor had been a few minutes earlier: once again Miss Talley had claimed the stage.

When the curtain fell, marking the first interval, the Earl of Leafield joined in the ebb and flow of humanity as playgoers went in search of refreshment and paid visits to friends seated elsewhere in the auditorium. As he maneuvered his way across the lobby, he avoided the beauties from the adjacent box, and passed by the hopeful mamas and their offspring without a glance.

As he approached a group of dandified *literati* who visited the London theaters every night, a thin gentleman in a rose satin coat and white silk breeches waved his quizzing glass and greeted Trevor in an affected drawl. "I was just telling Jones here that it's been an age since Leafield was seen in the environs of Drury Lane—the street as well as the theater." Lumley St. George Skeffington, crony of the Prince of Wales, sometime playwright, and devotee of matters theatrical, tittered at his own wit and stroked the distinctive side whiskers that were often held up to ridicule by the caricaturists. "Accompanying young Fleming, I perceive. Certainly he has been a regular visitor of late."

Trevor wasted no time in coming to the point, and asked his foppish acquaintance if he knew the name of the young actress playing Olivia.

"Ah, yes," said Skeffington on a sorrowful sigh. "Flora Campion, poor dear. An unfair world it is, for she's only the understudy, more's the pity, and takes the part tonight because Eliza Ellis is indisposed. But there's a delightful part written especially for her in Mr. Jones's new play—Forster commissioned the piece for her. Come here, Jones, and make your bow to the Earl of Leafield." At his urging, a pasty-faced gentleman moved forward from the outskirts of the group to be presented as the author of *In Praise of Parsimony*.

"They called him Gentleman Forster down in Portsmouth," Skeffington continued, abandoning the subject that most concerned his listener, "and I'll grant you he's deserving of the title, for all he's an actor. I went to Lord Dartmouth in support of his cause, and see what has come of it! Another theater, more or less legitimate, and she the old Princess. Poor Sheridan is mad as fire and nearly cut me t'other day, and as for Kemble, he and his sister Siddons are still reeling from the Master Betty business a year or so back and don't welcome a new rival."

Master William Betty, a child actor, had once been the rage, and Trevor vaguely recalled the mass hysteria the prodigy had produced during his heyday. But the theatrical nature of the conversation was beginning to bore him, and after suffering through a spate of backstage gossip, he was glad to escape Mr. Skeffington.

Strolling across the crowded lobby, he congratulated himself on his good fortune. The lovely actress was new to London and probably had no protector as yet. Even better, she was only a supporting player, not yet so established in her profession that she would object to retiring from it for a brief period. Trevor smiled so warmly that one of the painted prostitutes in his path was emboldened to approach, but he was intent upon calculating the expense of the venture he was contemplating and therefore ignored her. It would be necessary to provide

Miss Flora Campion with clothes and jewels, and she would probably expect him to offer her a generous settlement—all in all she would be expensive. But he was a man of substance, and whatever her demands, he would satisfy them. She was more than satisfactory for his needs; she was perfection itself.

Flora Campion, observing the crowd milling about the green room, feared that the audience for *The Marriage of Feste*, the evening's afterpiece, was sadly diminished. At the final fall of the curtain, a host of bucks and beaux had swarmed into the anteroom where the performers passed their time offstage and received their well-wishers after the play.

For six years Flora had trod the path to modest prominence in country towns, and now she was in London, where actors' reputations were made. Consigned to playing secondary parts, she had been ignored by critics and public alike but had received marked attention from the young men prowling backstage, ever on the lookout for a pretty and complaisant actress. She was neither: her spectacular beauty was no mere prettiness, nor did she desire a protector.

She'd retired to a corner to wait for Ben Forster, but no sooner had he made his entrance than his supporters gathered around him and his brother, preventing her from bidding them good night. Both actors still wore stage costume, although Horatio had already removed the blond wig he wore as Sebastian and was running his fingers through his black hair.

Resigned to a longer vigil than she had expected, Flora observed Louise Talley, still clad in her form-fitting breeches. Her face was flushed with compliments and champagne, and as she flirted with her partisans she spoke hardly a word to the adoring Lord Edgar Fleming and saved all of her smiles for Lord Allingham. The baron stood somewhat apart, evidently sure enough of his conquest that he saw no need to assert himself.

How would he react, Flora wondered, if she informed him that she was his kinswoman? It must be true—mere coincidence couldn't account for the upward slant of Lord Allingham's eyebrows, or the way his hair grew from a peak on his forehead, as did Flora's and her brother's. Even if the baron's complexion was olive and both Campions were fair-skinned, and although his eyes were brown and theirs green, she was inclined to believe the family legend about shared blood. Would he be shocked to learn that he had a pair of cousins on the wrong side of the blanket? Probably not; he was no model of the virtues.

Lord Leafield, piqued by Miss Campion's obvious and intense interest in his fellow peer, waited until she was no longer distracted by Allingham's presence before accosting her.

Although she regarded him curiously, he could perceive no come-hither in her green eyes, nor did she simper or flutter her amazingly long lashes at him. "I beg leave to introduce myself, Miss Campion," he began, "for Skeffington, our only mutual acquaintance, is elsewhere occupied and I'm uncertain of the etiquette that prevails backstage. I'm Leafield."

"Any friend of Mr. Skeffington's is welcome here," she answered politely. "We are honored that you should have visited our theater."

"The honor is all mine."

The carmined lips parted in a delightful smile, showing teeth that were pearly and even. The graceful contours of her cheeks were enhanced by the rouge, and the sparkle in her green eyes was more genuine than that of the false gems she wore.

When Trevor told her how much he had enjoyed her performance, she laughed softly. "You are kind, but if I acquitted myself no more than adequately tonight, I am fortunate. Mrs. Ellis, our tragedienne, has acted the part of Olivia since our company came to London."

He expressed the certainty that no one could have surpassed her in that role, all the while wondering how to broach his business. There was no delicate way to go about it, although at the very least he could do her the kindness of waiting until they were not surrounded by a pack of interested onlookers— his friends and her colleagues.

"You may deem it presumptuous of me, as we have only just met, but I hope I have permission to call upon you tomorrow, Miss Campion. I wish to discuss a personal matter, and in privacy. I have a proposition to make—on first seeing you tonight, I was convinced that you are the very lady I've been seeking. And," he added, more to himself than to her, "the odd thing is that I hadn't yet begun to look for her."

The actress's face went white beneath its light coating of cosmetics. "Pray say no more, sir," she said hastily, "for what you ask is impossible."

Trevor hastened to correct her false impression. "No, no, it's not that sort of offer—I swear it."

She eyed him doubtfully. "You said it was something personal—what did you *expect* me to think?"

"Forgive me, I hadn't considered my words very carefully. I do come to you with an offer of employment, but not in—" He saved himself from saying "my bed" by substituting quickly, "Not in the way you supposed."

As she a drew a calming breath, the taut muscles in her neck relaxed. "My lord, I'm sorry to disappoint you, but I'm not at liberty to accept any professional engagements at present."

He shook his head. "You don't yet know what I want, and I can't explain myself fully here and now. Will you permit me to call on you?"

Flora, unnerved by his aristocratic air and the intensity of his hazel eyes, would have refused outright, had he not been someone whose influence might in some way benefit her employer and her theater. With regret, for Sunday was her only day of freedom from work, she replied, "Very well, my lord, I will receive you tomorrow. After church."

"And where does one find Miss Campion at home?"

"On Great Queen Street. On the south side near Lincoln's Inn Fields." After she gave him the number of her house, he thanked her, bowed, and withdrew. As she watched the tall nobleman weave his way through the crowd to rejoin his friends, she regretted that it was too late to rescind her impulsive invitation.

Seeing that Ben and Horatio were still occupied with their backers, she deserted the green room, her brow furrowed by frustration. She wandered along a dim backstage corridor until she came to a rickety wooden staircase. She had begun her ascent when she heard the sound of clattering heels behind her and a familiar voice calling, "Wait, Florry!"

Sally Jenkins, who played chambermaid roles with great verve, placed one hand on her heaving bosom and the other on the banister. "I'm due onstage any moment, but I had to speak to you—I saw what happened in the green room. The Earl of Leafield! I vow, Florry, if Louise hadn't snared Allingham, she'd be livid!"

"He claims his interest isn't amorous at all, merely a matter of business."

The other actress tipped her head back and a peal of derisive laughter rang out in the narrow hallway. "A matter of business—and you believed him? Oh, love, I daresay it's perfectly true, but just fancy his calling it that from the start! *Business*!"

Flushed and chagrined, Flora shook her head in vigorous denial. But Sally dashed off as quickly as she had come, still chuckling, her fingers toying with the ribbons of the maidservant's cap perched atop her bright red head.

2

I beseech you, what manner of man is he?

Twelfth Night, III. iv.

The backstage area of the Princess Theatre, a confusing maze of corridors, went unseen by the public. On the topmost level of the building a long attic with skylights had been partitioned to create the carpenter's shop and the scenery-painting room. The floor immediately below consisted of storage areas for stage properties and wardrobe, and the closetlike treasury where the evening's receipts were counted and to which the players flocked on Saturdays for the doling out of weekly salaries. Tucked into a dim corner of the same hallway was Flora's dressing room, which boasted a small window overlooking the courtyard. The effluvium of dust and cobwebs which had greeted her two months ago had been swept away, but the tiny cubicle was still grimy about the edges.

That night marked the end of a week that had seemed to contain double the usual number of days, and Flora sighed in relief as her dresser stripped the brocade gown from her aching body. As usual, the brazier in the corner failed to warm the drafty room, and she donned her own clothes in haste before sitting down at her dressing table, where a clean towel and a basin of steaming water awaited her. She began the routine task of removing her paint while Margery unpinned her elaborate coiffure and combed out the long black curls.

Within a few minutes the actress and her dresser descended to the ground level where they found Madam Forster, the grande dame of the company, occupying the stage-door keeper's humble wooden chair as majestically as she sat upon Queen Gertrude's gilded throne. An impressive and regal figure in or out of costume, she had long been a mentor and surrogate mother to Flora, and because they lived on the same street, she always shared a carriage with the younger actress.

The three women exited the building, taking care to lift their skirts as they crossed the muddy courtyard to the waiting hackney. As it moved forward, Flora peered through the dirty window and saw that Drury Lane was thronged with traffic again, a sure sign that other theaters were also emptying. The fog still hung thick and low over the city.

A yawning manservant admitted her to her abode, one of the last houses in Great Queen Street. "Home at last, Frank," she announced, removing her cloak for the final time that night. "Is everyone abed?"

He shook his head. "Mrs. Drew is in the small parlor, ma'am."

She took the candle he gave her and lit her way to the room at the back of the house. The solitary young woman seated there looked up from the book on her lap to say softly, "High time you were home."

"Don't I know it."

"I've got the key to the larder—would you like something to eat? You'd only just sat down to dinner when Mr. Forster's message came."

Esther Drew preceded Flora into the dark kitchen, and within minutes she produced a loaf of bread, a round cheese, and a bottle of wine. The house was still and silent; the only sound to assail their ears was the muffled cry of the night watchman, whose voice faded with his progress along the street.

Flora ate a mouthful of bread and cheese, chewed thoughtfully, and after swallowing said, "Tonight was our best night since coming to London—the theater was almost full. How is Hartley?"

Smoothing a stray lock of brown hair in a harassed fashion, Esther said, "Poor little man, he's resting comfortably at last, and I hope he'll sleep the night through—for his sake and mine."

"What a pity his papa isn't here to see these fine teeth that cause so much trouble."

Esther's husband and Flora's brother both served on His Majesty's Ship *Vestal*, presently stationed in the West Indies. Letters from the naval officers were infrequent, newspaper reports about their maneuvers were vague, but they were in no great personal danger and the ladies were resigned to going weeks, often months, without tidings.

"I expect our brave seamen will be returning before long," Flora commented.

"With prize money spilling from their pockets," Captain Drew's fond wife said hopefully as she cut another slice of bread.

These midnight, post-performance conversations were something of a ritual by now, and both women found solace in meeting thus across the table to talk of their very different lives and wholly dissimilar aspirations.

As Esther filled Flora's wineglass she said, "To escape my fretful boy for half an hour, I accepted our neighbor's invitation to tea."

"How *is* Julie?"

"Much better, although she's disappointed that she isn't with child again."

"I can't think why—she always complains that during both pregnancies her sufferings were far in excess of what the usual female undergoes. Madam declares she was a better actress in the straw than she ever was on the stage."

"That sounds like something a mother-in-law would say! My dear Flora, I hope someday you'll experience the rigors of childbirth—then you'll learn how very ignorant you are about the subject."

Eyes dancing, Flora murmured primly, "Why, Esther, you know I'm not that sort of girl."

"I mean when you're a married woman. Julie hasn't given up hope that you'll wed her rakish brother-in-law."

Flora set down her wineglass so forcefully that some of its contents washed over the rim. As she blotted the puddle with her napkin, she said impatiently, "That boy-and-girl nonsense between Horry and me was over years ago. Besides, I've no time for a husband."

She was perfectly satisfied with her lot. At twenty-five she was no longer prey to the foolish fancies of extreme youth, and her years in the theater had taught her not to yearn for what was impossible. Her contentment was rooted in her ability to keep a roof over her head, clothes on her back, and food in her stomach. Miles, who had sailed the high seas since boyhood and was an infrequent visitor to England's shores, accepted her choice of profession and was proud of her success.

After six years of working so closely with the Forsters, she felt as much a part of the clan as if a tie of blood bound her to them in addition to a shared past and a strong mutual affection. Her intimacy with the manager's family was a consideration that far exceeded any payment or promotion. In the months since the company had arrived in London, she'd watched with amusement as its tragedienne tried to out-Siddons Mrs. Siddons and newcomer Louise tried to scale the heights of popularity attained by the much-loved Mrs. Jordan of Drury Lane. Unlike Mrs. Ellis and Miss Talley, who emulated others, Flora was bent on making use of the qualities that set her apart from other actresses, and she hoped Mr. Jones's new work would allow her to shine.

"Have you chosen the play for your benefit yet?" Esther asked.

Flora said she preferred to wait and see how the new comedy was received by the public before making a decision. As a senior member of the company, she was entitled to a benefit performance at the end of the season; on that night the total revenue, minus the operating costs of the theater, would be hers. Her colleagues would take no salary, donating their time and talent *gratis*, in the expectation of receiving the same consideration when their turn came. But despite this do-unto-others policy, battles over the rights to a play could be fierce, and the most popular pieces in the reportory were hotly contested.

Smiling across the table, Flora continued, "Horatio, clever fellow, has already bespoken *Twelfth Night*, and for his sake I hope Louise Talley remains in the company. She may be a disruptive influence, but she's filling the theater quite nicely in the role of Viola."

"And fills her shirt and breeches, too."

"Eliza Ellis can't abide performing with her—anyone could have foreseen that. They detest one another."

Well-versed in the various backstage squabbles, Esther said,

"I don't envy Mr. Forster the job of keeping so many jealous actresses happy."

"He does his best, and Madam comes to his aid whenever necessary."

Esther put away the leftover food, leaving Flora to sweep the table free of crumbs, and emerged from the larder to ask, "Is it to be the early service tomorrow morning, Florry, or the late one?"

"Oh, Lord," the actress moaned, striking her forehead in a theatrical gesture that she would have scorned to employ on-stage, "we'll have to go to the early one. I'm receiving a caller—a very illustrious caller—at eleven o'clock. Unless he forgets to come, which I devoutly hope he may do."

"A he?" Esther repeated, with strong emphasis on the pro-noun.

"The Earl of Leafield," Flora intoned impressively.

Her friend failed to oblige her by falling into a faint or giv-ing any other evidence of surprise. "Should I know him?"

"Not unless you look at the Court Page in the papers."

"Well, I don't," was Esther's matter-of-fact reply. "The paper is of no earthly use to me except when it gives details of naval battles or describes the progress of the war on the Conti-nent, which news James expects me to communicate to him." When Flora frowned at her, she added swiftly, "But I *always* read the reviews and the theatrical gossip."

Taking up the candelabra, Flora said sourly, "Lord Leafield, whom you will have the opportunity to judge for yourself to-morrow, is an extremely well-favored gentleman of about thirty. He and that nice young lord who worships Louise came backstage after the main entertainment tonight, and he asked if he might call upon me to discuss a matter of business." She frowned as she recalled the nobleman's smile, not the least of his charms. "So I said yes, though I can't imagine why. 'I know not what 'twas but distraction,'" she quoted softly.

Esther, looking into her friend's grave face, said cheerfully, "Well, a young and handsome earl coming to our humble house! Knowing you does have its advantages."

"I daresay he's planning an evening of private theatricals,

and wants to engage a professional." When the other woman began to laugh, Flora demanded, "What's so amusing in that?"

"Just what sort of *professional* does he take you for? I can just imagine the sort of private performance a gentleman of title would expect from an actress!" Esther used her pocket handkerchief to stifle her next mirthful outburst.

"You are the most corrupt-minded female of my acquaintance, Esther Drew, and considering the company I keep, that's quite a condemnation!"

A faint cry sounded from some distant source and Esther held up her hand, tipping her head sideways to listen. She expelled her breath in a long sigh of relief. "I thought it might be Hartley."

"The kitchen cat, asking to be let in. Go upstairs, little mother, and cuddle your baby. I'll see to Puss."

She returned to the dark kitchen and opened the back door to a silent gray shadow that scurried inside. Flora's presence went unacknowledged and was clearly unwelcome at this hour, when the mice were stirring. Impervious to the snub, she made her weary way to the upper regions, seeking the warmth and comfort of the bed she'd been thinking about so wistfully ever since the final fall of the curtain.

Sunday was the servants' day off, so on the following morning the two young women helped one another dress, then hurried down to the dining room, clutching their prayer books and bemoaning the lateness of the hour.

Mrs. Tabitha Brooke, titular mistress of the household, had just finished her breakfast and was trying to coax her grandson into eating a bit of toast soaked in milk. Although her husband had been dead for more than a decade, she still chose to wear full mourning. Young Hartley Drew, fascinated by the lappets of her elaborate widow's cap, tugged at them with his chubby hand.

She stared in bemusement at the two young women frantically tying the strings of their bonnets. "Why are you in such a rush to be away?" she asked, her round eyes shifting from her lodger to her daughter.

"Flora must be home well before noon," Esther explained. "She's expecting a visitor."

Mrs. Brooke reached for her teacup, oblivious to the complicit glance the two young women exchanged. "I'll be gone by the time you return, my dears, for I promised to call upon my sister in Kensington. I mean to invite Mrs. Prescott to go with me—unless you have some objection, Flora."

"None whatever," Flora hastened to assure her. "Margery may do as she pleases."

Esther bent to kiss her son's plump cheek. When she begged him to be a good little man while she was out, he replied with a gurgle.

As they exited the house, Flora commented, "What luck that your mama and Margery will both be gone when the earl arrives! Aunt Tab would think me as abandoned as Louise Talley if she knew I'd brazenly agreed to receive a strange gentleman after no more than five minutes of conversation with him."

Esther reached up to clutch her bonnet as a fierce gust threatened to blow this highly prized article from her head. "I'll play chaperone to keep you safe from the evil earl, or you can leave the parlor door open."

"I would have done anyway."

"Oh, don't be silly, Flora, I was only teasing. You're well past the age of requiring a duenna."

"Indeed, but actress that I am, I so seldom have an opportunity to observe the rules of propriety." Flora said this lightly, but her face was troubled all the same. In general she didn't waste time worrying about her reputation, but she hoped Lord Leafield didn't regard her as a loose woman.

She was aware that the public considered female stage performers to be little better than the painted creatures prowling outside the theater and decorating its lobby. Often it was true, as in the case of Louise Talley. But not even the highly respectable Mrs. Siddons was immune to the scorn her profession received, and vicious rumors had circulated when she began living separately from her spouse. Although Flora had managed to preserve her virtue, this fact didn't deter friendship with those of her colleagues whose lives were less than

chaste. During her years in the provincial circuit she had with-
stood the advances of many a backstage gallant, a breed she
judged more amusing than threatening. And as a result of her
special relationship with the manager and his family, not even
the boldest or most persistent of the actors in the company
dared to offend her by pressing unwanted attentions.

Until the encounter with Lord Leafield, her only admirers
had been harmless fops like Lumley Skeffington, or elderly
men who went no further than pinching her on the cheek and
telling her how she reminded them of some pretty actress they
had known in their salad days. Baron Allingham, everyone's
idea of the stage-door lothario, had attached himself to Louise
Talley.

She hoped the earl wasn't seeking to fill his bed, because
however comfortable it might be she had no interest in a liaison with a nobleman. Nevertheless, for a brief, titillating moment she pictured herself swathed in silks and laden with
jewels—until she realized her thoughts were most unseemly
for someone on her way to church.

When she and Esther scurried along Drury Lane past Princess
Alley, she direct a fond glance at the theater. They followed a
circuitous route, for even on a quiet Sunday morning it was necessary to avoid the disreputable alleys and side streets of Seven
Dials, the slum district lying near St. Giles-in-the-Fields.

The bells gave forth a resounding peal as the two latecomers
reached the church door. Squeezing into a pew at the back, the
ladies lifted voices in a familiar hymn about processions and
palm branches, its cheerful refrain punctuated with hosannas.
Flora's clear soprano soared exultantly as she remembered the
many things she had to rejoice about: a comfortable lodging,
money of her own, and good friends with whom to share her
joys and sorrows. And there was just enough strife at the theater to spice up an otherwise untrammeled contentment.

Yet she could not quite repress a pessimistic certainty that
something distressing would soon occur. Now that the sturdy
bark carrying her through life was moving along effortlessly
and independently, it was inevitable that the rocky shoals
ahead would show themselves, possibly with unsettling results.

3

What is to be said to him, lady?
He's fortified against any denial.

Twelfth Night, I. v.

The Earl of Leafield spent the night in a bed other than his own, the result of an encounter with a fair-haired beauty in the vestibule of the Princess Theatre. When she had confessed to him that her husband was absent from town, her azure eyes extended a bold invitation to the delights that had followed. And although he might have preferred to return to his own house afterward, Clarissa had prevented it by reminding him of her fear of sleeping alone. Presumably her husband, a portly and affable viscount, was aware of her aversion and cared not who comforted her when he was away.

Within a few hours of returning to Leafield House he set out once more, guiding his horses and phaeton out of gracious Mayfair and toward the less fashionable part of town where Miss Flora Campion lodged. A prevailing west wind had dissipated last night's fog, and there were patches of blue sky overhead. When the sun peeped out from behind the clouds at last, the neat plots of grass bounded by the town squares suddenly seemed greener and the daffodils yellower. Trevor was heartened by this sign that spring had not forgotten London after all.

Great Queen Street was a genteel thoroughfare extending from Drury Lane to the green oasis of Lincoln's Inn Fields, and the facades of its parallel rows of town houses were uniformly decorated with Corinthian pilasters. As Trevor approached the door bearing the number he sought, he heard feminine voices. Looking over his shoulder, he saw a pair of ladies coming toward him. Both were attractive, and their flowery bonnets and pastel spencers provided color to the somber street scene.

He smiled and bowed, expecting them to pass him by, but the prettier one halted, crying in dismay, "I was hoping to arrive before you did, my lord, but this morning's sermon was endless! Can it be eleven o'clock already?"

The breathless, fresh-faced creature staring up at him bore no resemblance to the woman he had accosted in the theater green room last night, and when he followed her inside, he wondered how it was possible that she could be even more beautiful than he remembered.

She introduced him to the other lady, who excused herself and went up the stairs. Trevor handed his hat to the actress, and she placed it gingerly on the hall table before removing her bonnet and tossing it carelessly onto a chair. As she led him into a front parlor, she asked if he would like a glass of wine.

"Yes, thank you," he replied, never dreaming that she would murmur something about the servants' day off, much less that she would dart from the room like a hare pursued by a pack of hounds.

Nothing about her was as he'd expected, and he didn't know whether to be sorry or pleased. He had been thrown off balance by the striking dissimilarity between his flustered hostess and the cool, painted creature of last night, to say nothing of the fact that she had actually attended matins—pious actresses were quite beyond the realm of his experience. The surroundings in which she lived and her companion's quiet respectability were equally puzzling. He wandered about the room, inspecting the prints on the walls, framed representations of crumbling Greek and Roman temples; a small but well-executed oil painting of a ship in full sail hung over the pianoforte. The silence of the house was pierced by an infant's wail, and to his great relief it was of short duration.

Flora Campion soon returned, bearing a tray and two glasses of what he guessed to be an indifferent sort of claret. In the interim she had smoothed her dusky curls and removed her spencer, thereby exposing the niceties of her figure. Hers was the smallest of waists, accentuated by the high, rounded bosom above, and she had the advantage of being so slim that she appeared taller than she really was. But her porcelain-perfect

face was her most arresting feature. The slanting brows were
as black and graceful as a quill stroke, her clear green eyes
were fringed by inky lashes, and she had an utterly entrancing
rosebud of a mouth. Trevor, who judged himself a connoisseur
of her sex, considered her one of the most beautiful women
he'd ever seen. But her apparent nervousness surprised him,
and as he accepted her invitation to be seated, it never occurred to him that he was the cause.

Flora was desperately trying to convince herself that she had
no more to fear from him than from Benedict or Horatio
Forster, the only male callers she had received since coming to
town. Unlike her actor friends, however, Lord Leafield seemed
out of place in Mrs. Brooke's parlor. He deserved a more
splendid setting, one of carved mahogany chairs and richly
colored tapestries. He would also look well mounted upon a
fine thoroughbred—he must often be outdoors, she thought,
because his skin had a warm golden tone and the waving
brown hair was lightened by the sun in places. It wasn't until
she met his hazel eyes in a glance of mutual appraisal that she
realized she was as much an object of curiosity to him as he
was to her. The strange mixture of trepidation and uncertainty
churning in her breast ebbed away, and her rather forced smile
broadened into something more genuine.

Said he, pleasantly, "The other lady—Mrs. Drew, I believe—is this her house or yours?"

"It belongs to neither of us," was Flora's equivocal reply.
"Esther's husband is away at sea, so she and her baby son
make their home with her mother. They very kindly offered to
let me and my dresser stay here as lodgers for as long as we
wish."

"How long have you been on the stage, Miss Campion?"

"Six years. I have performed at theaters in Hampshire and
Sussex, mostly in the coastal towns, and our company has
toured Ireland as well."

Her experience was yet another surprise, for Trevor had
supposed she was a neophyte. Not from any lack of talent,
quite the contrary, but because she looked so young and fair in
her flowing muslin; her face, free of cosmetics, was as appealing as a child's in its utter flawlessness. Untainted—the word

kept coming to mind, although given her profession, it was quite an illogical description. "You aren't offended by my curiosity, I hope," he said, seeking to thaw her with a warm smile.

"I've learned to expect it from strangers."

"I daresay, but I hope I won't be a stranger for very long, Miss Campion." He sipped his wine and observed her reaction to these words over the rim of the glass. She maintained her composure, and only by the swift fall of her eyelashes did she betray her agitation.

After a moment she said, "That remains to be seen. Now then, my lord, what business are you so eager to discuss with me?"

He placed his wineglass on a table. "Before I begin with explanations, I wish to know your real name."

Smiling faintly, she replied, "Is Flora Campion so very improbable? Nonetheless, that is how my parents christened me, so I can't help if it sounds like a stage name."

"It's perfectly charming," said Trevor, making a quick recovery. "To state my purpose as simply as I can, I wish to employ you as an actress, Miss Campion, and it would be a business arrangement, nothing more or less. You will impersonate a young female of quality. An heiress, to be precise."

"What is the play?"

He smiled. "One of my own creation, and it is to be enacted off the stage."

Without a moment's hesitation she answered, "I'm sorry, Lord Leafield, but I cannot help you."

"Will you tell me why? You may be quite frank."

"In the first place, I don't think I would care to pass myself off as someone I am not." When he started to speak, she held up one hand to stop him. "My profession requires it, I know, and that is precisely why I must refuse. Also, as I tried to explain last night, I am not free to accept any other work. I've signed a legal bond with Mr. Forster which stipulates that I must perform four times each week for twenty weeks, of which only half are behind me."

"But afterwards? When the period of your contract is over?"

She had to smile at his persistence, if not at the fact that her primary objection had gone unacknowledged. "Although Ben's—Mr. Forster's plans haven't been made public, I know that our company will spend the summer at Bath, where we expect to play for at least a month—with the possibility of an extension." She sat back in her chair with the air of one who had played her trump card.

The earl's request was not quite what she had anticipated, but it was almost as bad. She'd heard of such arrangements and had no desire to be party to one herself.

Some actresses made a secondary career of impersonating wife or widow, sister or sweetheart, for a handsome fee, though they sometimes risked being implicated in a minor crime, or being seduced by an enterprising employer. Prostitution usually followed, but anyone who fell that far rarely found her way back to the theater. Managers, constantly besieged by hopefuls, had replacements aplenty, and only for the most illustrious of female performers was a temporary retirement from the stage truly temporary.

Flora's first London season had been rigorous beyond guess, but she had no intention of giving it up, certainly not to help Lord Leafield play some practical joke. Lifting her chin, she said, "My lord, I fear you have wasted your time. I won't take part in this masquerade."

Apparently undaunted by her refusal or her faintly contemptuous description, he replied, "You haven't even given me a chance to explain."

She supposed she owed him the courtesy of listening, although she told him candidly, "Nothing you say can make me change my mind, Lord Leafield."

"I do hope you will," he said, "for this is a matter of great importance to me and my family, of which I am the head. Are you acquainted with my cousin, Mr. Hugh Cotterell? He is my heir and the dupe in our hoax."

She refrained from pointing out that he was taking her compliance for granted, as she had not consented to assist him. "I have not met him, but if he attends the theater he may well know about me."

"He's out of the country," Trevor reported. "And I'll tell you why, for I've no intention of concealing the truth. Hugh's character is not what one could describe as steady—quite the opposite. He is a libertine, a wastrel, and long before he came of age he had done everything in his power to drag the Cotterell name through the muck. My cousin, Miss Campion, is the black sheep of our family."

With a laugh, she confessed, "I was afraid it might be you."

"Oh? I think those who know me best would describe my wool as somewhat gray." Trevor's grin faded when he continued, "Even so, compared to Hugh's reputation mine is virtually spotless. A few weeks ago he was involved in a duel. Not his first—in fact, it was the fifth. I don't know the cause, only that it took place on the outskirts of London and the other principal was wounded in the exchange of fire."

Flora was beginning to understand why her visitor suddenly looked so perturbed. "Fatally?"

"No," he replied. "What resulted was something of a comedy of errors. Hugh's second was a gentleman reputed to be three-parts drunk at all times, Mr. Rollins, and he was foxed even at the impossibly early hour of the duel. When Hugh's opponent fell, Rollins mistakenly understood the surgeon to say the man had suffered a mortal injury. He encouraged my cousin to flee—misguided advice, as it turned out. The other fellow's wound was but a scratch, though it bled profusely."

"One can't help but feel sorry for your hapless cousin," Flora said, smiling.

"Hopeless is more like, and I feel no sympathy whatever!" he declared heatedly. "I was out of town when all this took place and knew nothing until last week, when Rollins thought to inform me that my heir is presently on the other side of the North Sea, in Copenhagen. When I learned why, I was more amused than angry. And then my visitor stopped sipping my finest Madeira long enough to make a curious and cryptic reference to Hugh's bride—he even boasted that he had been present at the marriage ceremony. From his garbled tale, I deduce that shortly before departing these shores, Hugh took a wife in flagrant violation of a codicil in our grandfather's will which stipulates that he must not marry without my knowledge and consent. If he does so—or has done so—he's cut out of the succession. By proving it, I would be able to designate another male relative as heir to my unentailed property, although Hugh would claim my title should I fail to produce a son. I'll do anything to keep Hopeton Hall and Combe Cotterell from falling into my cousin's hands—he would lose them at cards within a fortnight of my demise."

"But you do have proof," his listener pointed out, "if this man was a witness to the marriage."

"I wish it were that simple. Although he talked freely, ultimately it was unproductive because he was too drunk at the wedding to have more than the vaguest recollection of what I assume to be a hole-in-corner affair. Hugh could've been married by special license, or he may have made use of some illegal mock ceremony. That would be more in character, but I hope he did tie the knot properly. My solicitor is making inquiries, but as you can imagine, it may well require the search of every parish register in London to uncover the truth. And I will, however long it takes."

Flora, noting the stubborn thrust of his jaw, did not doubt it. "Have you considered asking Mr. Cotterell if he's wed?"

"He wouldn't admit it. I believe Rollins, who is an honest man in or out of his cups. Hugh is not and never has been. And now, Miss Campion, I come to your entrance into this sordid scene. Not even Hugh would commit bigamy, or so I hope, and by arranging his marriage to a lady of my own choosing, I'll force him to disclose the existing union."

"And to properly bait the trap, his prospective bride must be an heiress."

"Oh, absolutely. A young lady rich in money and looks, and even more important, one who rejoices in my guardianship."

"Your lordship's plan has a flaw," she pointed out, purely from a spirit of good fellowship. "Won't your cousin expect you to have designs on this paragon yourself?"

"As I am popularly believed to be a confirmed bachelor, I doubt it very much. It may be that he will confess as soon as I propose this marriage to him, in which case you would not be involved. But if I should resort to this stratagem, I depend upon your cooperation." He resumed his seat before telling her, "I have decided that your introduction to Hugh must take place out of town, at my estate in Devonshire."

"But I've already declined the honor of becoming your ward," she reminded him. "Besides, I'd never be convincing as a minor—I'm all of twenty-five." No stranger to flattery, she was nevertheless gratified when he said bluntly that she didn't look it.

"Last evening you proved that you are adept at portraying a young female of refinement and breeding," Trevor continued. "And you are no less believable now—if I didn't know better, I would swear you really *are* a—" He hesitated as a flush suffused his gold-toned face.

His implication that she wasn't a real lady was unfortunate, because Flora had begun to be fascinated by this compelling and determined gentleman. Now his condescension had soured what had turned into a thoroughly enjoyable contest of wills.

Gravely he said, "Miss Campion, you must be aware that you are quite different from—well, from Louise Talley, for want of a better example. In a variety of ways, all of which are readily apparent to me."

"You are right, I'm nothing like Louise." But she didn't elaborate on how, or ask him what he perceived those differences to be. She would not parade her virtue before this arrogant aristocrat—in all probability he wouldn't believe her, for clearly he considered every actress a slut.

Going from bad to worse, he added, "I'll pay you handsomely, Miss Campion, you have only to name your price. And I intend to provide fine clothes and a pearl necklace and all the other outward trappings of a young heiress. You may keep or sell them as you prefer. I'm also willing to use my influence in your behalf if you care to try your luck at Drury Lane or Covent Garden. I'm acquainted with Dick Sheridan, and a friend of mine is one of Kemble's investors."

Flora's patience was beginning to wear thin, and she said witheringly, "Your lordship's offer of patronage is unnecessary. I could never leave Mr. Forster, not for another theater— or for a working holiday in Devonshire. Truly, Lord Leafield, you would be wise to seek out another actress, one who might be tempted by the offer of clothes and money and such."

"As far as I'm concerned, there is no other," he interrupted. "When I arrived on your doorstep, I was prepared for either of

two outcomes: that you would jump at the chance to earn a
tidy sum for very little trouble on your part, or that you would
not. One thing you will learn about me, ma'am, is that I do not
easily despair, and I trust you will permit me to discuss this
matter with you again when you've had sufficient time to consider it."

"My refusals will always be stronger than your entreaties,"
she maintained, "so it would save us both a great deal of time
if you would accept my decision as irrevocable. I have three
roles to make perfect by the week's end and will therefore
have no opportunity to concern myself with your lordship's
difficulties."

She was relieved when he abruptly abandoned his efforts to
sway her and brought his visit to an end. At least he hadn't had
seduction in mind, she thought, surreptitiously watching his
departure from the parlor window. The high-stepping bay
horses moved forward, drawing the phaeton and its handsome
occupant out of sight.

Now that the sun was showing its face, the broad street was
crowded with Sunday afternoon pleasure seekers making for
Lincoln's Inn Fields. Eager to join them, Flora let the curtain
fall and went upstairs to discover if Esther was interested in
accompanying her.

4

I warrant thou art a merry fellow and carest for nothing.

Twelfth Night, III. i.

Early in the week Flora had believed there was ample time to put the finishing touches on *In Praise of Parsimony*, but as the days slipped quickly by she had to wonder if the play would succeed. Tumbling into her bed at night, exhausted from a late rehearsal, she sometimes remembered Lord Leafield and his bizarre proposition, but work was her primary concern. Even in her dreams she could hear the callboy's constant refrain: "You're wanted onstage, Miss Campion."

On the day before the first performance, Flora reached the theater early, neither fully rested nor completely refreshed by her Easter holiday. She sent Margery off to inspect all the seams of her new costumes, a necessary precaution ever since a memorable moment during *The School for Scandal*, when she'd drawn breath for her opening speech only to be rendered mute by a dozen pins poking into various parts of her anatomy.

She'd learned a great deal during her years on the stage, she thought, adding a few coals to the green-room fire. Backstage conversation was frank, spiced with phrases that would have horrified her sailor brother. Bawdy songs and jests abounded, drunkenness was common, but she quickly learned to accept these facts, and so much more.

Shortly after joining the company, she'd had visible proof that actors lived by a different code than most mortals. One day she had entered a deserted wardrobe room and found a couple entwined on a makeshift bed of cloaks and robes. When the nature of their enterprise had dawned on Flora, she had slipped out unnoticed, but for some time afterward she worried that she hadn't been as shocked as a decently raised young woman should have been.

At nineteen, the world had seemed so full of exciting possibilities, and she'd often imagined how it might feel to lie with a man. There was a deeper meaning to those lofty speeches she heard onstage each night, and she looked forward to the time when she, too, would experience the all-consuming passions described by the playwrights and poets.

She sat down at a scarred wooden table, spreading out her "lengths," pages of foolscap on which were written her cue lines and each of her speeches. Her study of the playwright's latest revisions was broken by the entrance of a gentleman whose dark good looks and bold movements proclaimed him a Forster.

"Hullo, Florry," he greeted her, and though his voice was a trifle husky from the earliness of the hour, it retained its rich resonance.

"Hullo, Horry." She acknowledged the actor's presence by offering her cheek for the brotherly kiss it was his practice to bestow every day.

"Jones has made *more* changes?" Horatio Forster asked sympathetically, collapsing into the empty chair beside hers.

"Yes, and all of them in the final scene. Why doesn't he ever alter the beginning? Then we'd be over the hurdle at the start of the play, instead of having to endure agonies of uncertainty all the way through to the last act."

"If you hold off learning your new words for a few hours, you'll save yourself a lot of bother. He's sure to change everything back to what it was." After discharging this advice, Horatio took up one of the pages and read it over, humming a tune under his breath.

Flora, her eyes glued to the sheet before her, said severely, "You're ruining my concentration, you know."

"That was my object," he returned, with a notable lack of contrition.

She looked up, frowning, and his red-rimmed eyes and heavy-lidded aspect told her how he had passed his evening. Flora was all too familiar with the unfocused stare that indicated a night of carousing, and she was dismayed to see the flush brought on by a bout with the bottle. But unlike some of their colleagues, Horatio had never forfeited her respect by appearing onstage in a drunken state.

"Does my appearance give you pause?" he asked. "And after I wore this coat—your favorite, is it not?"

"You were wearing it yesterday."

He dropped his jet-black head into his hands, heaving a deep sigh. "Ah, well, the truth is that I never went to bed. But don't fret, love, 'twas nothing more than a bit of holiday merrymaking and no harm done."

"I do wish that before you indulge yourself that way you'd think of me. You know what I must undergo as a result of *your* excesses! Julie will come dashing over to our house and beg me on bended knee to reform your character."

"I did think of you—longingly," he said, grinning. "My busybody sister-in-law isn't the only one who hopes you'll make an honest man of me. What say you, my mouse of virtue? It only takes a word."

"Never!" she cried, returning to the pages of dialogue.

Horatio's tone was wickedly suggestive when he murmured, "A new pantomime opens at Sadler's Wells tomorrow, *Jam-Ben-Jan, or Harlequin and the Forty Virgins*. Why don't we attend this promising spectacle, and consign Ben and the rest of 'em to the devil?"

The notion of deserting on their own first night made Flora smile. "Can't you just see his face if we did? He'd give us the sack! Or murder us."

"If our poor effort is damned by the public, never to be repeated, I'll take you to Drury Lane on Wednesday to see Monk Lewis's latest melodrama, *The Wood Demon*. Michael Kelly wrote the music, always a recommendation."

"Even if we could go, I wouldn't. Whenever I attend a play, someone always seems sadly miscast, or a clumsily staged tableau catches my eye, and I take no pleasure in it." When Horatio stretched out in his chair and closed his eyes, Flora judged it safe to return to her work.

Five years ago Benedict Forster had made a move counter to theatrical tradition and paired his wild brother with the virginal Campion lass in *Romeo and Juliet*, letting youth play youth. To the astonishment of the entire troupe, the hero and heroine began keeping company off the stage as well.

For a whole summer the two were inseparable, sitting only a whisper's distance from each other in the green room, romping together between rehearsals. They walked unchaperoned along the shingle beaches near Portsmouth, the romantic backdrop for a succession of kisses, eager on Horatio's side, shy on Flora's. Because his experience of life and love far exceeded hers, he wasn't long satisfied with so tepid an affair, so out of curiosity and a strong desire to please him, Flora permitted liberties she had denied to other swains. But even though she felt positively weak when he touched her breast or stroked her leg above her garter, she always stopped short of that great sacrifice he demanded as a proof of her love. Not even an offer of marriage could persuade her to give in; Flora had no real desire to be his or any man's wife, and told him so. They quarrelled, bringing the three months' idyll to an abrupt end. She was regretful but wiser, Horatio was resentful, and the other Forsters were vastly relieved.

There followed a period of coolness, during which Flora devoted herself to her work and Horatio consoled himself with drink and lively Sally Jenkins. Less than a month after claiming his life was blighted, he moved into lodgings with the redhead. Despite his many subsequent liaisons, he never failed to refer to Flora as the single great love of his life, making no secret of the fact that in his mind, at least, their rift was temporary.

With the passing of time they had established a less volatile, more secure friendship, but it was only marginally less physical than their short-lived romantic attachment. Flora never failed to offer her embrace as consolation for failure or disappointment, or to reward a success. He would often pat her cheek in delighted response to a joke, and during the first reading of a bad play, they kicked at one another under the table like a pair of ill-behaved children.

The dozing actor, roused by the babble of voices in the courtyard, sat up and said, "Lord, but I'm glad we're finally done with *Twelfth Night*."

"Why is that?" Flora asked absently. Other players were filtering into the room, and she still had four long speeches to memorize.

"Because Sebastian is an idiot and a fool. And I'm sick of that damned blond wig that's supposed to make me a twin to Louise. Won't you play Viola for my benefit, Florry? We match so well that I could dispense with the blasted toupee!"

"Louise is the one who can guarantee you a full house. And I won't play breeches parts."

"You could if you wanted," he said. "Even Madam played her share of 'em when she was younger." Both Forster sons referred to their mother in this respectful fashion, even when speaking to her directly.

"It's Ben's rule for me: no male characters, no Viola or Rosalind, or even Peggy in *The Country Girl*. He promised Miles never to display my nether limbs onstage."

"'Fess up, Florry, it's really because beneath your skirts you've got crooked legs, with knock knees and thick, ugly ankles."

"There's nothing wrong with my legs and you know it," she flared.

"Watch your tongue, madcap—you'll give everyone the wrong impression. What should a rake like myself be knowing about the legs of the proper Miss Campion, now?"

"Wretch!"

"Prude!" he shot back, for this was an infallible provocation.

"Wastrel!" she cried wrathfully, shoving at him.

"Gypsy!" And so they continued until both became bored with the exercise, much to the disappointment of their amused audience.

The callboy, whose title was belied by his advanced age and thinning gray hair, hurried into the room. "You're wanted onstage, Miss Campion, Master Horry," he wheezed through a pair of lungs that had inhaled the dust of old theaters for many a decade. "Mr. Jones has arrived with the revisions for the opening scene, and Mr. Forster is ready to begin rehearsal."

With an exchange of martyred glances, the actor and actress left the comforts of the green room hand in hand, and followed the rheumy messenger toward the scaffold of duty.

* * *

The master of Leafield House sat in a comfortable chair in his handsomely appointed study, reading the London news and occasionally looking out the window to watch the boys at play in the square gardens.

According to his paper, the actors of the Princess Theatre—Forster's Folly, as it was described—would perform a new comedy tomorrow evening. A week and a day had passed since Trevor's visit to Miss Flora Campion, and in the interim he'd often recalled that brief, inconclusive interview.

Her cool dignity surpassed that of Lady Derby, the former Elizabeth Farren, who had once trod the boards of Drury Lane in fine-lady roles. Derby's first countess was hardly in her grave when he married his longtime mistress, and from the moment he placed the ring on the actress's skinny finger, she'd wiped the past from her mind. Nowadays her ladyship held herself aloof from all but the highest in the land and looked down her long nose at anyone of lesser rank, as if she'd been born into the nobility. These actresses, Trevor thought with amusement, never seemed to give over playing a part. According to the strict standards of his class, Flora Campion, with her precise diction and elegant manners, was no lady; the trappings of respectability with which she surrounded herself were meaningless because her profession negated them.

Undaunted by her refusal to assist him, Trevor intended to persevere. He envisioned a pleasant association with Miss Campion, one not entirely founded upon business, for no doubt the lovely player had other talents than those she displayed in public.

Folding up his paper, he set it aside and reached for the letters on the table beside his chair. Now that Easter was past, the social Season had begun in earnest, and London's hostesses had showered gilt-edged cards upon him weeks in advance of their entertainments. Many of his fellow peers employed a secretary to take care of all but the most personal correspondence, but Trevor preferred to read and respond to it himself. After sifting through the invitations, he found a letter bearing a Bath postmark.

His aunt's ill health restricted her activities, and communicating with him was one of her primary occupations. However disappointed to find that her latest missive was only a few paragraphs long, he was intrigued by an unusual request: that he attend a party in Berkeley Square. "It will be the very first ball of the season, on Easter Monday, and is being given by Lord and Lady Batsford, whose daughter is being presented this spring," Lady Ainsley had written. "Now, dearest, as a favor to your favorite aunt, please send me a faithful report of how Lady Caroline Lewes conducts herself."

Her reticence was remarkable, for she hadn't even described the girl. Although her greater concern appeared to be the success of her friend's party, her nephew knew better. And because he had no particular plans for the evening, he decided to have a look at—he glanced at the note to make sure of the name—at Lady Batsford's daughter Caroline. His matchmaking relative knew his tastes better than anyone, and if she felt this young lady was worth pointing out, her reasons must be sound.

A springtime crop of gently reared, innocent young misses had come to town, many of them destined to become spoiled, adulterous society wives. Season after Season Trevor had watched flighty young noblewomen discard and acquire new lovers as they did ballgowns, seeking in vain for one that would wear really well over time. And even as he dallied with them, he pitied them from the bottom of his heart.

Although his father and an uncle had died in their prime, until lately he'd felt no sense of urgency about taking a wife. The late earl, his grandfather, had lived many years—too many, the old man had opined as he'd waited for death to claim him. But the troublesome heir thrust upon Trevor by that same stubborn, long-lived gentleman was reason enough to contemplate matrimony. If he acquired a well-born bride, and the requisite male child, Hugh Cotterell could no longer plague him.

But it was difficult to concentrate on the necessity of marriage this morning, when his mind kept returning to the heart-faced lady of the stage. Advancing age must have broadened his preferences, he concluded, for there was no other way to account for his eagerness to seduce someone with midnight locks. Formerly he'd had a taste for blondes. Not saucy Nell Gwynne types like Louise Talley, but the flaxen-haired, rosy-cheeked epitome of English maidenhood, which he hoped Lady Caroline Lewes would turn out to be.

"My lord."

Looking up, he saw his butler standing on the threshold. "Another invitation, Cochrane?" He sighed, spying a square of folded paper on the small silver tray.

The man entered the room shaking his silvered head. "It came from Mr. Linton's offices in the Strand."

Trevor reached for the letter and ripped the seal. The solicitor's bold, definite script leapt up at him, and the message it conveyed was troubling. "Does the man wait for a reply? I have none."

Cochrane cleared his throat. "My lord, there is another matter. Master Hugh is here and wishes to see you."

"Send him in at once. And," Trevor called after the butler's stiff, retreating figure, "I've changed my mind about answering Linton. Tell his clerk that I'll call in the Strand this afternoon."

"Very good, my lord."

Trevor crossed to the window overlooking Cavendish Square, and when a wiry young man stepped into the study he turned around and said calmly, "Don't worry, I'm not going to scold, there's no point at this late date, and your opponent did survive the duel. How was Copenhagen? Did you have a pleasant stay?"

"No, blast it!" The wiry young man flung himself into the nearest chair. "It's a cursed unpleasant place, and Denmark is beastly—I don't think the sun shone once in the fortnight I was there. I didn't even mind that spell of rain last week—it was London rain, thank God!"

"Exactly how long have you been in town?"

Mr. Hugh Cotterell ran his fingers nervously through his brown hair, a shade lighter than his cousin's. "After Jack Rollins wrote to say I might return, I boarded the next ship bound for England."

"You should have visited me sooner," Trevor said. "We

may not be close, but I'm always interested in knowing your whereabouts."

"I wasn't at all sure you'd receive me—black sheep of the family and all that. After my last duel, you said I was a disgrace to the Cotterell name. I'm here because I want my allowance. It was due at Lady Day."

"And was paid. In your absence, I instructed Linton to settle your outstanding debts."

"You did *what*?" When Trevor repeated his statement, Hugh's bony face went rigid with anger. "I never heard of such a damned scurvy trick! You had no right—on what, pray tell, am I expected to live?"

"On my bounty, I should think," Trevor said wearily. "What else could I do? Linton was being dunned to death by your creditors. He's *my* man of business, yet your tangled affairs were thrust upon him when you came of age four years ago. I empowered him to do as he thought best, he did it, and you should be glad to know that you've returned to your native shores unencumbered by financial obligations."

"How can I be glad, when all I have to my name is a few shillings and a single pound note?" Hugh grumbled. "I trust you can advance me some money—I'll pay you back next quarter-day, I promise."

"By then you'll be in debt again," Trevor predicted. "You need some form of employment, Hugh. I've always thought Grandfather did you a disservice by keeping you out of the army when you wanted to join."

"Then why in God's name didn't you persuade him?"

"I tried, but he never cared that much for my opinion. He only listened to one person."

"His holiness our Uncle George, the dutiful youngest son." Hugh glared at his cousin. "I daresay my exploits have prompted a sermonizing letter or two from the vicarage at Hopeton. Lord," he said heavily, "what an odd lot we Cotterells are. There's you, the paragon. And me, the prodigal. And the parson who never leaves his parish."

"Uncle George couldn't help being the favorite. Our fathers married women Grandfather disliked and offended him further by dying before their time. George took holy orders and wed the squire's daughter and remained on the estate."

"I wonder Grandfather didn't leave him the Hall and Combe Cotterall. There was no entail to prevent it."

"He who is last shall be first in the kingdom of heaven," Trevor murmured.

"Well, our uncle is last in the succession, with you and me standing between him and the family fortune," said Hugh in a voice of satisfaction. "And our male issue would come before old George and that band of cherubs living a stone's throw from the gates of Hopeton Hall."

Trevor said mildly, "Unless you married without my consent, in which case you would inherit nothing but the title."

"I don't give a damn about all those houses and farms and investments, nor do I want some lawyer telling me what to do when Consols go up or down. All I need is a regular allowance and the freedom to do as I please."

"Well, as we both know, you inevitably fall into a scrape when left to your own devices," Trevor reminded him. "But I am willing to lend my assistance, if not my money." Trevor regarded the expectant Hugh unsmilingly and said, "You may stay at Leafield House. But in return you must tell me where and with whom you've spent the last week."

Hugh swallowed twice. "Is it so important? If you must know, I've been with Rollins."

It was necessary for Trevor to count to ten, silently, to calm himself. He knew Hugh was capable of telling falsehoods to cover his sins, but this one was outrageous. "Rollins lodges just off Piccadilly, does he not?" he asked. "Clarges Street?"

"Near there—White Horse Street, Shepherd's Market."

"And you've come directly from his house this morning?"

"Of course. It's too early in the day to call on anyone but a relative."

"Your sojourn abroad seems to have exerted a beneficial influence," Trevor observed. "You never used to be so concerned about etiquette."

"If I'm to reside in Leafield House, I'd best mind my manners, hadn't I?" his cousin retorted.

Trevor reached for the decanter and poured two glasses of wine. Handing one of them to Hugh, he continued, "As long as you behave circumspectly, I think we'll rub along well enough. I suggest you visit my tailor—at my expense—and have him outfit you with less haphazard raiment. I don't think much of Rollins's valet if he lets you go out in public looking as you do now."

Hugh glowered at him but made no reply.

"I've hired a stage box at the Princess Theatre for the remainder of its season, and tomorrow evening we'll attend a new comedy, which I trust will entertain you." He paced the length of the room, then faced his cousin. "Tonight there's a ball at Lady Batsford's, her daughter's debut. She's the sort of Bath tabby who'll report your doings to Aunt Belle, so if you're wise you'll abstain from deep play or deep drinking."

"Trying to reform my character?" Hugh sneered. "I daresay I shall be worn out by all these dissipations—visits to the tailor, a seat at the theater, society balls."

"Don't be provoking," Trevor warned.

Reading the danger in the hazel eyes, Hugh felt a frisson of alarm. "I was only jesting."

"Oh, and I must ask that you refrain from mentioning to anyone that you've been with Jack Rollins for the past week. I'm afraid he isn't very likely to corroborate your story."

Sitting up a little straighter, Hugh asked, "What do you mean?"

His cousin extracted a folded sheet of paper from his coat pocket. "I've just received some tragic tidings from Linton, who has been so busy on your behalf. Two nights ago your friend was found lying dead in an alley near St. James's."

Within an instant, Hugh's countenance was as white as his rumpled cravat.

"No foul play suspected," his lordship continued, "but he received a fatal blow. The coroner ruled that Mr. Rollins, so often in an inebriated state, sustained the injury in a fall. But the unfortunate and untimely accident does raise a few awkward questions about your recent activities, to say the least." He handed over the solicitor's note.

Hugh clutched it, his hand visibly shaking, and he stared helplessly down at the handwritten obituary. Rollins, the one man who knew all his secrets, would carry them to the grave.

5

I delight in masques and revels sometimes altogether.

Twelfth Night, I. iii.

The Earl of Leafield and Mr. Hugh Cotterell were among the last to enter the Berkeley Square house Lord and Lady Batsford had hired for the Season. Her ladyship was one of Bath's leading hostesses, and her London connections had served her well; if not exactly a crush, the ball had attracted a respectable mix of the fashionable, the political set, and several unattached gentlemen of title and fortune. As she greeted Trevor, he perceived the glint of triumph in her eye.

Still haunted by the disturbances of the day, he was amazed that Hugh had recovered so quickly from the shock of hearing about his crony's death. When his cousin disappeared into the library, where the card tables had been arranged, Trevor prayed that Linton and his minions could work a miracle and quietly uncover tangible proof of the alleged marriage before Hugh guessed his suspicions.

The dancing had already begun; a dozen couples were gliding about the polished floor to the soft strains of a popular tune. Trevor couldn't guess which of the young ladies was the daughter of the house, but a swift inspection told him that three could lay some claim to beauty. When the music ended, Baron Allingham's partner, a slim creature in lemon silk, hurried to Lady Batsford's side like a tiny yellow chick seeking the security of the mother hen. She was quite pretty, with chestnut curls and a slim, graceful figure. Best to begin with the papa, he thought, looking around for Lord Batsford, who would doubtless be more than happy to perform the introduction Trevor desired.

Not long afterward, he lured Lady Caroline Lewes over to a sofa, preferring to converse with her rather than join her in the exertions of a *contre-danse*. His aunt's name was sufficient to inaugurate a dialogue between them, and Trevor gently quizzed her, saying, "I suppose you find London quite different from Bath."

In a shy, breathless voice, Lady Caroline said, "Bath is also busy. And I did visit London last winter, when Mama brought me to visit her dressmaker. We didn't attend any parties then, but we went to the theater."

He thought of Flora Campion, and dispelled her recurrent appearance in his mind by focusing on the bright face across from him. Her ladyship had blue eyes and a sweet smile; a pity she wasn't blonde as well, but one couldn't have everything. "You enjoy going to the play?"

"All our family like theatricals, my lord."

"Then perhaps you and Lady Batsford will help make up a theater party some evening."

Lady Caroline ducked her head. "That is for Mama to say, but I would enjoy it very much."

He smiled. Biddable, he thought, and very well-trained. Aunt Isabelle had not erred in bringing this little miss to his attention. "You may be sure I will speak to your lady mother," he said as her next dancing partner came forward to claim her, ending their tête-à-tête.

The viscountess, whose house and bed he had frequented ever since their encounter at the theater, stood nearby with Lord Allingham, and Trevor went over to greet them. The baron, casting an appreciative glance at the young lady in yellow, commented, "Pretty chit."

"Leave her to Trevor, Allingham; you're already engaged," said Clarissa, rapping his arm with her closed fan.

"Not any longer, my dear. Haven't you heard? I was jilted."

"Are condolences or felicitations in order?" Trevor asked.

"Either or both," was Lord Allingham's diffident response.

Smiling up at Trevor, Clarissa said, "Planning a match, are you?"

"As I never met the child before tonight, the question seems a trifle premature."

"Lady Batsford doesn't think so—didn't you see her hopeful expression when you approached her cherished daughter?"

"*I* was not so fortunate," the baron interjected. "I say, Trev, was that Hugh I spied in the card room? Where the devil has he been lately?"

"Why don't you go ask him?" Clarissa suggested pointedly. When Lord Allingham had withdrawn, she said, "Poor boy, his penchant for play actresses shows no sign of abating. I wonder what made him think he was ready to marry."

"I can't imagine."

Fluttering her pale eyelashes at Trevor, she asked, "What brings *you* to so insipid an affair as this, my friend?"

"I looked in as a favor to my aunt."

"As did I, in compliance with my absent husband's request. Reggie's mama is a second cousin once removed from Lord Batsford. Or is it third cousin twice removed? I never can remember those things. Just think, Trevor, if you do wed Lady Caroline we'll be related by marriage."

"Barely, from the sound of it."

Drifting closer, she whispered, "Shall I see you later? Henrietta can let you into the house."

Trevor hesitated before answering, "Very well, but only on the condition that I need not stay till dawn."

She pouted. "Trevor, you know I loathe sleeping alone."

"I know you always say so."

She accepted the compromise, but with obvious reluctance. "As you prefer, but I never dreamed you could be so cruel. Lately I've relied upon bachelors because they don't *need* to rush away. I detest frantic, hurried encounters. Married men glance so often and so furtively at the clock that I always feel like a—" But Clarissa failed to complete her analogy, leaving it to Trevor to supply the word for himself.

The next afternoon there was a frantic, last-minute rehearsal at the Princess Theatre which left the prompter hoarse from shouting lines to the forgetful.

Flora ate her dinner in her dressing room, her head bent over a fresh set of speeches. Even for this frothy comic role, her preparation was far in excess of what was common. Most players read through their new parts once or twice at most, attended rehearsals as required, and left it at that.

Earlier in her career she, too, had viewed acting as nothing more than an endless game of charades. As a consequence she had been a failure in her first speaking role, undone by insufficient study, shattered nerves, and an audience more enthusiastic about her physical attributes than her acting ability. Chastened by the experience, she had rehearsed subsequent roles more thoroughly, but still hadn't excelled as Juliet; Horatio Forster had been too great a distraction. Only after their romance ended had she set about remedying her primary faults: a lack of stage presence and a speaking voice over which she had an imperfect control.

Madam Forster had supplied the necessary instruction, imparting the various tricks that had served her well during her long career. In time Flora was able to maintain her concentration when riots broke out in the pit, or even if an unruly crowd threw objects onto the stage. She struggled to achieve the proper placement of her voice, and learned to move gracefully yet purposefully.

The reward for her hard work had finally come, and now she was about to face a London audience in a play written expressly for her. The success or failure of Mr. Jones's latest effort depended upon her, for a mediocre script might be hailed as a masterpiece if brought to life by a Siddons, a Kemble, or a Jordan. She was determined to please as Letty Loyal, for by creating the role she made it her undisputed property. And her several hours' traffic on the stage would be more of an adventure than usual, because many of her scenes were with Louise Talley, whose joy in upstaging other actresses was no secret.

Flora was posing before the mirror in her first-act gown when flame-haired Sally Jenkins, wearing her customary maid's costume, bounded into the dressing room.

"What a row took place a moment ago, Florry," the actress cried exuberantly. "The things you miss by hiding up here instead of loitering in the green room like the rest of the common herd! I thought it best to warn you that Louise will be after you tonight—beware."

Flora began applying her paint. "Why? We've been on the very best of terms all week."

"No longer. She accuses you of going behind her back to

Mr. Jones. Wouldn't you know, our illustrious playwright locked himself in a closet this afternoon to do a bit more slashing, and it was Louise's part that suffered the most. I gathered from the way she was shrieking that he's whittled it down quite a lot."

"Oh, Sal, no."

"Oh, Florry, *yes*! That scene in the third act, when you confess your love for Horatio, has been altered. Jones has altered that bit completely. Your humble servant, and I mean that literally, is now the recipient of the speech. Letty Loyal addresses it to her maid, not Selina. When Mr. Jones told Louise, she started screaming and threw her fan at the poor man—missed him by yards, but the fan hit the wall and broke to bits, which only made her more furious. She went on and on about what a scheming little hussy you are, and how Jones is your dupe, and to crown all she says she can't abide her costumes because they aren't new like yours. Ben is with her now, trying to calm her, but I wouldn't wager too much on his chances of success."

Flora turned back to her mirror. She dipped a hare's foot into the powder, saying, "Ben will prevail, he always does. What about our parts, Sal? They must be affected by these last-minute changes."

Sally shrugged dismissively. "The prompter is copying out our lengths for the scene right now, and they'll be brought up directly. We can read them through if you like, or just take our chances when the time comes."

Flora announced a strong preference for the former, and persuaded her diffident friend that they ought to rehearse. When a stagehand came to Miss Campion's door with a sheaf of pages still wet from the prompter's quill, the ladies sat down to commit the new material to memory.

Both were quick studies, and before long they went downstairs to the green room. The other principal players were there, huddled in small groups and discussing the recent contretemps. There was no sign of Miss Talley. When the various threats of vengeance were imparted to Flora, word for word, she felt more than the usual first-night flutter. The prospect of spending several hours onstage with a woman of Louise's uncertain temper was most unappealing.

"I told Ben that La Talley would be trouble," Madam Forster announced as she swept into the room wearing a feathered headdress which made her appear taller and more imposing than usual. She took possession of the most comfortable chair in the room, hers by right according to the rigid code of etiquette that prevailed backstage. Smoothing the puce gown she wore as Mrs. Loyal, Letty's mama, she reported, "When my son emerged from her dressing room a moment ago, he said the breakages will be deducted from her wages, which leads me to suppose that she fired a few rouge pots at him. He looked none the worse for it."

Mr. Osric Logan, the grand old man of the company, said from his place at the hearthside, "He should fine her for insubordination. That one would do better to give more attention to the substance of her part and less to the size of it."

The woman next to him murmured, "And so ungrateful, too, after all Ben has done for her." The speaker was universally, if unlawfully, acknowledged as Mrs. Logan in recognition of having borne the old actor five children, and because she had shared his lodgings and his bed, if not his name, for the past twenty years.

The pit was always crowded when Miss Talley was featured, but on this night, when new productions at other theaters competed for playgoers, it was a coup to have the galleries and even the box seats filled as well. From the moment the green curtain rose on the opening tableau, Flora forgot the audience and Louise and concentrated on remembering her lines. In the ballroom scene she flirted and fanned herself and tried not to panic when one of the speeches addressed to her by Horatio turned out to be fully three versions old.

Her next trial came in her first encounter with Louise, who played Selina, Letty's rival for Mr. Prodigal's affections. But the addition of costumes and scenery and an appreciative audience conspired to put her at ease, and she parried all attempts to upstage her with skill and not a little enjoyment.

After the final act, a weeping Mr. Jones was pushed to the

fore of Mr. Lumley Skeffington's stage box to acknowledge the crowd's noisy appreciation of his new work.

Benedict Forster bestowed a few words of praise upon his leading players, pointedly ignoring Miss Talley. As he gave orders to the stagehands about the proper assembly of the scenery for the pantomime, Louise flounced off the stage, her pert features set in a mask of rage.

"Never mind her," Horatio whispered in Flora's ear. "It's your play entirely."

They dodged a group of dancers tricked out as Harlequins and Columbines for the pantomime, and Flora said, "She hates me. And Eliza Ellis hasn't spoken to me since I took her part of Olivia a few weeks ago. It was bad enough when the two of them were at each other's throats, and now I'll be the target of their malice."

The green room was redolent of savory roast beef and pastries hot from the oven of a nearby chophouse, and the actors were eagerly partaking of the first-night supper. As Horatio led Flora through the crowd blocking the doorway, he said, "Ignore them."

Flora didn't care for the constant bickering that characterized backstage life, but to stand silently by and let herself be abused was equally disagreeable. "But that's so spiritless!"

"Oh, everyone knows you're a bold piece, for they've seen you ripping up at me since time out of mind."

"That's different," she said, smiling. "You deserve it. But at least you don't resent me, like Louise and Eliza."

"Only because they know you can act them into flinders. You've got more in your left eyebrow than Louise has in that precious body she's always flaunting in front of Lord Allingham's box. And as for Eliza—well, she improves with age, but Siddons ain't got nothing to fear. Why, when I made that blunder in the ballroom scene you scarcely batted an eye, and before I knew what you were about, we were bowling right along. So for that, Miss Campion, you deserve at least one of these lovely cheesecakes before they're devoured by this pack of starving rogues and vagabonds."

They filled their plates with much more than just the cheesecakes and sat down with Sally Jenkins, whose current sweetheart was at that moment sawing away on his violin in the orchestra pit.

Flora suddenly discovered she was ravenous. Although she was usually in a rush to get home, tonight she lingered, assuaging her appetite and joining in her friends' cheerful discourse. When Horatio suggested that everyone repair to a tavern to continue their revels, she realized that it was high time she removed her costume and paint and made her way home.

As she bounded to her feet, the actor caught her hand. "What, won't you join us?"

"When have I ever visited those disreputable cock-and-hen places you frequent? I haven't the strength to carouse, and if you want to drink ale and sing ballads till sunup, it's your own affair." When she tried to jerk her hand away, he pulled her down to sit on his lap and planted a smacking kiss on her mouth.

"Give over, love," he crooned, "and come along."

"Horry, let me go—you're crushing my new gown!" Flora squirmed in his embrace, but upon discovering that she was trapped she joined in the laughter.

Her levity was short-lived. Conscious of an uncharacteristic silence in her companions, she looked up to see the Earl of Leafield standing before them. When she met his hazel eyes, she flushed from her crown to her toes, embarrassed to be found sprawling across a man's lap like some common trull. Horatio released her, and she was thankful that at least he had refrained from slapping her on the backside as he so often did.

Lord Leafield bowed. "Miss Campion, I predict that the critics will hail you as the latest sensation."

"And I hope they keep a rein on their enthusiasm," she replied with outward calm, although her pulse was fluttering. "A sensation seldom lasts in London, I have heard, and lives on only to be reviled by the very public that created it. I'm surprised to see you tonight, my lord. During our last conversation I received the distinct impression that you're not a habitual visitor to the theater."

"Ah, but that was before I made your acquaintance," was his smooth reply. "Didn't you see me sitting in my box? I would swear you looked up at least once during the play."

With damping frankness, Flora told him that she took very little notice of the individuals in the audience, adding, "It is their collective response that concerns me. And I have so few friends in town that the likelihood of my recognizing anyone is very slight."

"Well, that puts me in my place," he observed. Holding out his arm, he said, "Permit me to enlarge your London acquaintance by making you known to someone who desires an introduction."

She let him lead her over to a young man standing in the corner, whose sharp features were oddly familiar to her. One swift upward glance at the earl's similarly aquiline profile was enough to support her suspicion.

His next words confirmed it as truth. "Miss Campion, here is another member of my family who admires your many talents. My cousin, Mr. Cotterell. Hugh has lately been visiting Denmark."

"How interesting," Flora murmured, both surprised and pleased that he'd apparently given up his elaborate plan to pass her off as his wealthy ward. The young man, who didn't appear to advantage beside his cousin, had a lean and hungry look. Of medium height, he had brown hair somewhat lighter than Lord Leafield's; his eyes were darker and set under heavy lids.

"You are fortunate indeed to be able to go abroad, sir," she said. "With the Continent in such disarray, few people have the opportunity to travel."

Hugh Cotterell's lip curled, and his tone was unpleasant when he replied, "My journey wasn't made under circumstances which I would describe as fortunate."

Momentarily at a loss, Flora decided that Lord Leafield had not exaggerated when he'd described his heir in an unflattering light; he might even have erred on the side of kindness. In fact, she was inclined to dismiss the likelihood of Mr. Cotterell's secret marriage on the grounds that no female could possibly consider him an agreeable prospect for a husband.

His lordship turned to her and asked, "Do you have a desire to travel, Miss Campion?"

She detected the mischief in his expression and was instantly on her guard. "No more than the average person," she said stiffly.

"I wish I might introduce you to the beauties of Devonshire. I have an estate there, Combe Cotterell—I believe I mentioned it the other day? Alas, it is too far, but perhaps you will permit me to show you some of the pleasant views to be found nearer London." Then he flashed his most winning smile, the one Flora could not resist, and said he hoped he might have the honor of driving her to Richmond Park in his phaeton.

The refusal was forming on her lips when she became aware of Horatio's jealous presence. He was glowering, an unsubtle indication that he didn't approve of her consorting with gentlemen other than himself.

Determined to give him a much-needed lesson and with no thought for the possible consequences, she shifted her gaze back to Lord Leafield, forgetting her earlier determination to resist him. Smiling back at him, she gave a reply that Horatio would be sure to hear: "I would be delighted to accept, my lord, and look forward to the engagement with all my heart."

6

Trip no further, pretty sweeting,
Journeys end in lovers' meeting.

Twelfth Night, II. iii.

Several days of rainfall encouraged Flora's hope that there
would be a postponement of the proposed expedition to Richmond, but on Friday a footman arrived on the doorstep with
his master's brief note, which fixed the hour. Saturday dawned
gloriously fair, sealing her fate, and she prepared for her ordeal by bathing in a tub of rose-scented water, wishing she
could remain there all day. To be at home was to be at peace,
for the atmosphere at the theater was strained at best, bellicose
at worst.

As Horatio had predicted, Miss Talley and Mrs. Ellis had
joined forces against her. They united in giving her the cold
shoulder in public; when there was no danger of being overheard, they sneered insults. But because they behaved circumspectly during performances, she made no effort to retaliate
and suffered their snubs and sulks in silence. Louise continued
to upstage her whenever possible, but Flora was experienced
enough to turn this ploy against her, and often the other actress
was the more discomfited.

She was soaping her arms when Esther barged into the bedchamber, holding a newspaper aloft. "You're mentioned in the
theatrical review!" she cried triumphantly.

Flora's sense of modesty was greatly diminished after her
years in the common dressing room, but she drew up her knees
to cover her bare bosom.

Her friend climbed upon the unmade bed and spread out the
paper. " 'The Princess Theatre, often called Forster's Folly by
those with pretensions to prognostication—' "

"Spare me the long-winded rhetoric," Flora intervened

hastily, "I've already heard it *ad nauseum*. Every paper in town has joined in the endless debate about whether our theater should be licensed, and Sheridan has mounted a fierce campaign against Ben. The insults and broadsheets are flying thick and fast the length of Drury Lane. What does the reviewer say about the *play*?"

"'With his new work, *In Praise of Parsimony*,'" Esther read, "'Mr. Jones marks the return of comedy in its genteelest form. On Tuesday last the play was received with approbation by the faithful worshipers at the Temple of Thespis.' He goes on to describe the plot—I shan't bore you with that bit—but somewhere he mentions the actors. Oh, yes, here it is: 'Mr. Horatio Forster, in the role of Prodigal, exhibits those qualities of person and performance that must delight the fair sex and be not unacceptable to the discriminating playgoer. Mrs. Forster, having won the admiration of provincial audiences, bids fair to enjoy a similar reputation in the Metropolis and shines as Mrs. Loyal . . . Mr. Logan, in a genuinely comic performance . . . Miss Talley as Selina, the coquette, has the unfortunate habit of dropping her character at the end of the scene.'"

"Only when Lord Allingham is present," Flora said fairly, resting her head against the rim of the tub. "Go on."

"'As Letty Loyal, Miss Campion demonstrates not only her histrionic talents, but also a naturalness of expression and movement. She excels in the role of the lady of quality as has no other since Miss Farren retired from the boards a decade past to wed into the Peerage, thus continuing her onstage roles in the Play of Life. Miss Campion satisfies; nothing in her performance is distorted, and laudable consistency appears to be her watchword. It is to be hoped that the Management of the Princess will continue to feature this lovely lady in future works of comparable merit.'" Esther started to fold the paper. "That's all."

"How gratifying."

Esther puckered her mouth in a moue of displeasure. "I think he might've been more enthusiastic. I was at the theater on Tuesday, and it seemed to me that the play was a considerable success."

The actress expelled a long sigh. "Oh, the critics will ever regard tragedy as the very pinnacle of dramatic art. The best a comedy can hope for is, 'All very well in its way,' or, 'a fine effort, for a comic play.' But the managers know that the surest crowd-pleaser is some vulgar burletta or spectacle, like the ones at Astley's or Sadler's Wells. Give the public a dancing horse, or a dog that saves a drowning female from a tub of water, or a precocious boy like Master Betty in an adult role, and you'll have a success in the theatrical realm of London."

"What will you wear today?" Esther asked, folding up the paper.

"I don't know," Flora replied gloomily, and she sank deeper into the water as though to escape what lay ahead. "I wish I dared to send his lordship word that I've succumbed to an ague and am too ill to join him today."

"You'd look mightily foolish if he happened to visit the theater tonight and saw you playing Letty Loyal."

"True," she acknowledged regretfully as Esther peered into her wardrobe.

"This sprigged muslin walking dress with the scalloped hem and blue underskirt is vastly becoming."

"He's only taking me to look at some trees and flowers, not to call upon Her Majesty the Queen."

The young matron eventually managed to rouse the indifferent actress from the tub. Flora put on the muslin gown as suggested, and a matching blue spencer, and let Esther select a fetching hat. Despite her extravagant show of unconcern, the sudden thump of the door knocker caused her to give a little jump, and shriek that she wasn't yet ready.

"He's frightfully early—by nearly half an hour," was Esther's comment as they hurried downstairs.

But Frank had opened the door to someone far more welcome than Lord Leafield, and Flora, seeing her employer standing in the hall, took the last steps at a skipping pace. "Here's a pleasant surprise!" she cried. "I hope there's no trouble at your house, Ben."

"Oh, no," Benedict Forster replied as she ushered him into the parlor. A stockier version of his swarthy younger brother, his graying temples and the faint lines at the corners of his shrewd, dark eyes attested to the fact that he had spent his forty years busily. "I'll not stay long, for I understand that you're expecting a visitor."

"Did Horry tell you so?"

"Yes," Forster said, taking a seat. "And my better half persuaded me that the news I have for you couldn't wait." His mouth twisted humorously.

Flora smiled. "Julie wanted you to act as her spy, and sent you here in the hope that you and Lord Leafield would collide on the doorstep. Apart from her curiosity, what brings you across the street this morning?"

"Theater business," he announced promptly. "Our management committee held its weekly meeting last night. I've made some necessary changes in the distribution of roles in *Hamlet*. Madam has given up Queen Gertrude, pleading fatigue, and Mrs. Ellis will replace her."

"But you're playing Hamlet, are you not?" When he nodded, Flora said on a choking laugh, "Yet you and she are much the same age."

"It will be no more singular than other such pairings in the history of our profession. When we begin rehearsals on Monday, you'll resume your former role of Ophelia."

"But why *Hamlet* so soon? I thought *The Critic* was to come next, with the tragedy to follow."

Her visitor struck a pose that she recognized as his cunning Richard the Third. "So it would've been, but I changed my mind in order to deliver a mortal blow to that damned cur Sheridan. He'll be offering a comedy at the Lane next, and after that, according to my spies, he's mounting Monk Lewis's new tragedy. I'll present the opposite: a tragedy followed by a comedy. By the by, did you read that scurrilous piece in the paper?"

"Which one?" she murmured. "I believe the latest called for you to be placed in the public pillory, and suggested that Forster's Folly be closed down immediately."

"I published a notice of my own yesterday, offering a hundred pounds to anyone who came to me with the identity of the author of such a foul libel. And what do you think was the result? Old Sherry comes 'round to the Princess, as cool as could be, to confess that he wrote it himself! Worse yet, the scoundrel demanded payment on the spot!"

Poised between dismay and high delight, Flora asked, "And did you give it to him?"

"What else could I do?" he replied testily. "Well, for all he has no head for business, he's got a deal of charm. I hope he'll use the money to pay his actors—they go whole weeks without their wages, poor devils—but it's more likely he'll lose the whole sum at cards or on some wager, or spend it all on drink."

She didn't believe for an instant that her employer was anything other than vastly proud of his quarrel with the great Sheridan of Drury Lane.

"I'll have my revenge on him for libeling me, Florry, you see if I don't," he declared. "By providing a counterpoint to his next two plays, I'm assured of making a stir—and I'll regain my hundred pounds at his expense. Even better, he wrote *The Critic* himself, which will make my triumph all the sweeter. You're to play Tilburina. Louise will be Tilburina's Confidante, and she can try to upstage you with a vengeance, because that's her character."

"So I must go mad and rave on and on about wildflowers in both plays, the tragedy and the farce. Lovely," said Flora with gentle sarcasm.

"I want you to spoof Mrs. Siddons in your portrayal of Tilburina. Madam my mother will undertake to instruct you; she knows the woman well." He rubbed his hands together and said gleefully, "It'll be a slap in the face to those damned Kembles at Covent Garden—I'll knock their long noses out of joint, see if I don't. And then, after we've made them uncomfortable, we'll retire to Bath. London is a theatrical desert in the summer, there's no getting 'round it, and I won't waste my investors' money on the four most useless months of the year. In the autumn, I'll return to take on the two patent theaters in a head-to-head contest on their own ground, I will, and it'll be a three-way race, you mark my words."

He kissed her cheek at parting, and took both of her hands in a firm grip. "You're not too much troubled by that pair of spiteful vixens at the theater, I hope? Oh, yes, Horry keeps me informed about all the doings in the green room. I prefer not to meddle in my actors' affairs so long as they appear onstage as expected, in a more or less sober state, but if matters get out of hand—"

"They won't," she said positively. "Horry, like all Forsters, is overprotective. Do you think I could have survived so long in this profession if I couldn't take care of myself just a tiny bit?"

"I suppose not. Remember, my Julie will have her nose pressed to the parlor window all morning, waiting to see this earl of yours. Have a pleasant time, my dear."

"I'll try," she promised.

The two occupants of the open carriage said very little to one another as it traversed Piccadilly and passed through the turnpike gate near Hyde Park Corner. Trevor was concerned with his restive horses, but they calmed down on the Fulham Road, preferring market gardens and pasture to city traffic.

Glancing over at his passenger, he saw that the long ribbons of her wide straw hat streamed behind her, and offered to slow the pace if she preferred. "I'm afraid that I tend to give them their heads as soon as they're clear of the crowded streets," he explained.

"I like traveling along so briskly," Flora told him, clutching her headgear. "It's a novelty for me, as I've never ridden in a phaeton before today."

"Mine is honored in being the first. Is that the reason you accepted my invitation? At the time I had the impression you did so to pique one of your fellow performers, the one who plays Mr. Prodigal."

"How the devil did you guess that?" Instantly regretting her unladylike exclamation, she said contritely, "I must remember to mind my tongue when I'm not in the green room. But yes, I *was* trying to put Horatio in his place."

"I look forward to future opportunities to assist in that effort," he replied.

Flora chose to leave this hopeful remark unanswered and said hastily, "I wish you'd tell me something about Richmond, for I'm as ignorant of what lies outside London as I am about the city itself."

She was relieved when he embarked upon a monologue in which he detailed the town's associations with royalty, pausing long enough to show his ticket to the keeper of the Queen Elm Gate.

When he told her how the grieving King Richard had razed the Palace of Sheen after his first wife's tragic death, Flora said, "I played his second queen once, in Chichester. Not a large part, for it's very much a man's play. The Duchess of Gloucester has the best of all the women's speeches, the one beginning, 'Finds brotherhood in thee no sharper spur?' Madam Forster was most impressive, and so was Mr. Logan as old John of Gaunt." As the phaeton drew up before the Star and Garter, an ostler hurried forward to take charge of the temperamental bays.

"You must know the whole of Shakespeare's works backward and forward," her escort commented after they began the ascent of Richmond Hill.

"I don't think anyone does," she replied, "because nowadays managers hack and alter the texts mercilessly. In general I prefer acting the comic plays, although the tragedies are more popular with audiences. In fact, we'll be busy with *Hamlet* soon, so I shall be obliged to go mad and get me to a nunnery and all that." Eyes twinkling, she added, "Of the thirty parts I possess, a quarter of them are Shakespeare."

He asked curiously, "What does it mean, to possess a part? Are thirty a great many?"

After discovering his superior knowledge of history, she was not sorry to have an opportunity to display her own small area of expertise. Looking away from the magnificent view of the Thames, she said, "When an actor possesses a part, in theory it's his for life, unless he voluntarily relinquishes it to someone else. At the end of his career, the great David Garrick possessed over ninety."

A short time later, as they strolled through the Old Deer Park, she commented, "It's remarkable, the sense one has of being in the country, and yet we aren't so very far from London. I didn't realize how desperate I was to see fields and trees, as well as the river itself. I've never lived in a city so large that I couldn't easily escape it when I wished."

"I, too, find London wearisome," he answered. "So much so that I recently purchased a rural retreat at Twickenham. It can't compare to Combe Cotterell, of course—my part of Devonshire is delightful at all seasons, and the estate is near enough to the sea to enjoy a pleasant breeze on the most uncomfortable of summer days."

A smile teased the corners of Flora's mouth. "I hope you aren't about to repeat your invitation of a fortnight past, my lord. But as you have introduced me to Mr. Cotterell, I suppose that you no longer contemplate the 'fictitious ward' scheme you outlined to me."

"It seemed best to me that Hugh know you for what you are—or perhaps will be," he said obliquely. "As for proving his marriage, I'm at a standstill. Do you remember I told you about Rollins, the fellow who was Hugh's second in the duel and witness to the wedding?"

"The man who is generally three-quarters drunk."

"Well, now he is four-quarters dead." She stared at him, and he nodded. "My only real evidence against Hugh died with him. It's frustrating, to say the least, because my cousin's behavior more than hints at concealment. He is disturbed by something—whether the enormity of his deception, or Rollins's demise, I can't be sure. But I didn't ask you to come with me today to talk about Hugh."

At a turning in the path they came upon a group of deer, and Flora halted, staring at them in fascination.

"They are quite tame and would feed from your hand," Trevor told her. "In the days of the Tudor and Stuart monarchs, the deer at Richmond were hunted, but now they are left to themselves and the care of the park keeper."

When they walked on, he posed several questions about her life before she came to London. Flora set aside her usual reluctance to talk about herself and proudly informed him that her father had been an instructor in mathematical sciences at the Naval Academy in Portsmouth.

"He was not a navy man," she elaborated, "but my brother is. He serves on His Majesty's Ship *Vestal* in the West Indies.

Papa was born in Hampshire. My mother was Irish—she loved to sing and dance, and had a wonderfully expressive speaking voice. I think she might have made a fine actress."

"And how did you come to be one?"

"Mama was a needlewoman—she had been apprenticed to a seamstress—and she sometimes sewed costumes for old Mr. Forster's theater. He became quite fond of our family, and let Miles work as a stagehand during his school vacations, excellent training for a seaman, because of the ropes and knots used for the scenery and mechanical devices. I often attended the play, with my brother or my parents. Perhaps because the theater was so familiar to me, it didn't hold the same romantic fascination it does for most young girls." She shook her head over the great tides of time that had ebbed and flowed since those long-ago days when her only experience of the theater had been from the audience side of the footlights.

"Mama and Papa died suddenly of a fever," she continued. "Miles was in port at the time, and we decided to give up the house, sell the books and furniture, and invest the capital in Consols. The Forsters had offered me a home, you see, so by the time Miles received his orders to sail I was settled. It seemed foolish to live on my allowance when I could so easily earn my keep on stage, but old Mr. Forster wouldn't hear of it. But it wasn't long before Ben, the elder son, inherited the theater and employed me at eighteen shillings a week. My first professional appearance was in a crowd scene."

"What was your brother's reaction?" he asked.

"By the time he learned what I had done, he was on the high seas and couldn't do a thing to stop me. So I served my apprenticeship and worked my way up from utility performer and walking parts to speaking parts."

Her removal from the Forsters' household, the painful result of her break with Horatio, had occurred next, but she chose not to disclose this bit of her past. "Eventually I took lodgings of my own, and by then I had Margery to take care of me. She had been dresser to another actress, and one day she came to me and said, 'You're young to be taking to this work, miss, but you'll do well enough if you live as respectable as you can and keep away from face paint whitened with lead, because it's poison. Rice powder will save your complexion, you mark my words.' I invited her to be my companion on the spot."

Her tale came to an abrupt halt, and she resisted his lordship's efforts to draw her out further. "There's nothing left to tell, except to give you a catalog of performances. We actors mark the passage of time by the order of the roles we play and the towns where we appear."

While they waited for the ostler at the Star and Garter to harness the horses to his phaeton, she thanked Lord Leafield for an excursion that had been far more enjoyable than she had expected, adding, "How I hate to leave all this behind for crowded, noisy London!"

"We needn't return yet," he said smoothly. "At what hour must you be at the theater?"

"Six o'clock."

"Then we've half the afternoon left to us." He helped her into the vehicle and climbed up to sit beside her. "I know a pleasant place along the river, only a couple of miles distant. I think you'd like it very much."

In no time at all they were bowling along a stretch of road that followed the curves of the Thames. Flora sensed an urgency in him, a kind of suppressed excitement, as if he knew a lovely secret and looked forward to sharing it with her.

Their brief journey ended at a gatehouse. An elderly man, whom the earl greeted by name, emerged and took charge of the phaeton.

"We'll walk the rest of the way," Trevor told Flora as he helped her down from the high carriage.

Wildly curious, she went with him down the drive until they came to a domed white building set in a miniature park. Behind it were flower beds, a trifle overgrown but profusely colorful, and the grassy bank of the river. Taking her by the hand, he led her to the willow grove at the water's edge.

"Faith, but you're a beauty," Trevor breathed, untying the ribbons of her hat and lifting it from her head. A fringe of black curls decorated her brow, and the long ringlets, caught up on either side of her face with silver combs, fell to her shoulders. The coiffure was slightly out of date, but its simple classical lines suited her. "How everyone stared at Richmond—do you ever get used to it? When you look in your mirror, do you see what I do?"

"I'm usually too busy covering my face with rouge and powder to take much notice of how I look," she answered.

Trevor touched her cheek, her temple, then traced the curve of her ear with a gentle forefinger, murmuring, "I was right in thinking this garden a proper setting for you." She was a flower in more than name, for her skin was as white and soft as the petal of a lily, she smelled of roses, and her carnation lips were an invitation to do what he had dreamed of doing for weeks. Her hat slipped to the ground when he took her in his arms, pressing his mouth against hers in a deep, desperate kiss. She moaned softly, and he held her closer still, never thinking she meant to protest his actions.

Pulling away, she asked breathlessly, "Whose house is this? Yours?" He affirmed it with a smile. "And you brought me here for—for this?"

"And a great deal more. My caretaker assured me the painters and plasterers and upholsterers are gone for the day—lucky for us, is it not? Otherwise, it would be necessary to repair to the village inn, where the beds are so lumpy and ill-aired, and complete privacy hard to achieve."

His hand left Flora's waist, trailing slowly and deliciously upward along her torso to cup her breast, and her nipple drew itself into a bud of sensitivity. Standing chest to chest with him made her feel faint; she couldn't think properly. He took advantage of her impaired state and began kissing her again.

For a brief, mad moment she submitted, but then his questing tongue flicked against hers. Shocked and confused, she tried to break free of his embrace. "No—you mustn't."

"Now that I've seen you in the garden," he whispered, "I want to see you in my house. In my bed."

Gazing up at his eager, golden face, Flora said vaguely, "I hardly know you."

"You will. Come, let's go inside."

Flora shook her head in emphatic denial, adding, "I can't—I won't. Did you expect me to lie with you simply because I let you kiss me? If so, you were sadly mistaken." She bent down to retrieve the broad-brimmed hat lying on the grass. "Thank goodness it's not spoiled—otherwise I would have made you buy me another."

"I'll buy you dozens of bonnets," he vowed, "and gowns to go with them. Whatever you ask, Flora, shall be yours."

"I won't be taking anything from you, I don't accept your *carte blanche*," she answered. "Because I am a woman of the world, five-and-twenty years old, and an actress besides, your suggestion doesn't shock me. But I state this very clearly, so you will have no doubt: I've no intention of entering your house. If I'd known your purpose in bringing me to this all but deserted place, lovely though it is, I would never have come. I refuse to be your paramour, Lord Leafield, not even for the space of an afternoon," she declared, standing her ground as he approached her again.

"Is there nothing I can do to change your mind?"

Ignoring his question, she announced coolly, "I wish to return to London."

They walked back to the lodge gates in silence.

"Is there someone else?" Trevor asked. "On the night we met, I saw you watching Allingham in the green room—do you mean to snatch him from Miss Talley?"

"What a poor opinion you have of me, and I can't think what I've done to deserve it." She sighed, tying the bonnet ribbons beneath her chin. "I don't fancy Lord Allingham as a lover, and he interests me only because I knew his grandfather, who dandled me on his knee when I was but a child."

Trevor, disappointed by her unexpected rebuff, was relieved to know that he had no rival. "At the outset of our acquaintance, I warned you that I don't give up easily—I hope you remember that."

"*You* may regard your tenacity as a point of pride, my lord, but in my opinion, it's a most regrettable flaw of character."

Laughing at this sharp assessment, he assisted her into the phaeton.

At dusk that evening, a shabby hackney coach followed the direct route from the West End of London, halting before a vast expanse of market gardens. The passenger, a solitary gentleman, climbed out of the vehicle and said sharply, "Wait for me, and I'll make it worth your while." The driver mumbled unintelligibly and reached for a flask hidden in the folds of his greatcoat.

It was almost dinnertime; the laborers had tied up the last of the young plants and were gathering up their hoes and spades. The young man hurried along one of the pathways that dissected the garden plots, breathing in the scent of damp earth and listening to the murmurs of the menials.

A female voice called out from the shadows, "Oh, Hugh, you did come!"

"Did you doubt me, Emmy?" he asked the girl who materialized in his path.

Her worried face reminded him of the morning she had found him lying in Goodman's Fields. Half drunk he'd been, his face bruised from a fight—the usual coda to a night of carousing—and she had taken him home. She wasn't exactly pretty, for her features were ordinary and her dark hair was thick and unruly. Sometimes, when they lay together in the dark, he could strike sparks by stroking it. Her eyes were big and brown, she had a wide mouth, and even now, with so much on his mind, he was wild to kiss her.

After satisfying his urge, he asked hoarsely, "Did you bring it?"

"Is that the only reason you came? After so many days apart, I thought you'd be glad to see me."

"Glad enough to wish I could see more of you." He reached beneath her figure-concealing shawl, placing one hand on her breast and the other on the leather pouch she clutched. "You've been well? No more sickness in the mornings?"

"No, it passed. But oh, Hugh, I've missed you so!"

Hugh was too busy tipping the contents of her purse into his hand to reply in kind. "I say, Em, is this all?" He frowned down at the jumbled coins and banknotes.

"I used to think five pounds a fortune till I met you. My da's an honest working man, and a thrifty one—p'rhaps I should give it to him."

She snatched at the money, but he had closed his fingers over the cash. "It's mine now."

"And if you keep my money, you'll have to keep me as well, won't you?"

"We'll see about that." Hugh pulled her close again, and she twined her arms around his neck. Eventually he said, "I mean to settle with my former landlady, and I'll pay her enough so she won't remember either of us, if anyone comes asking. We can't continue to meet this way, Em. Trevor isn't above having one of his servants spy on me." Scowling, he released her.

"What is it, Hugh?" The girl placed a consoling hand on his shoulder. "It's not only the earl troubling you."

"Jack Rollins is dead, poor old rogue. What makes it even worse, I told Trevor I'd been staying with him on White Horse Street to cover the fact I'd been with you at my old lodgings. That was enough to make him suspicious. Of what, I can't say, but I don't like his finding out about Rollins so soon—he knew before I did."

"I can't hide my belly from Da much longer."

Hugh patted her arm. "I'll make things right with him as soon as I can, I promise. Here's one piece of good news: Trev is dangling after a pretty chit named Caroline, and he may well have serious intentions. His marriage will set me free, for he'll turn his attention to the begetting of a son and heir who'll make me redundant. Just be patient, Em, and we'll be together soon, you'll see." He gave her a swift parting kiss.

She stood staring after him for a long time. Nearly all the laborers had departed, but the few who remained eyed her so curiously that she ran blindly down one of the paths, hoping none of them had recognized her. If word of tonight's meeting, or its purpose, ever reached her da's ears, he would put a stop to her pin money. Without it, Emmy had no hope at all of seeing Mr. Hugh Cotterell again, whatever right she might have to his visits. And, she reminded herself bitterly, to his support.

7

When came he to this town?

Twelfth Night, V. i.

In spite of working in a theater where impulsive hugs, sly pinches, and playful slaps were common coinage, Flora was unable to dismiss the incident in the riverside garden as readily as she had supposed she might. Her mind often returned to that episode in Twickenham, and she was disturbed by the memory of his lordship's firm embrace and searing kisses. She'd made a mistake in accepting his invitation on such slight acquaintance, and now that she recognized the true purpose of his pursuit she would avoid him.

But he was making that difficult, and the repercussions of his regular appearances in the green room were as uncomfortable as they were unwelcome. Backstage gossip, fueled by Mrs. Ellis and Miss Talley, was so rife that the manager's wife felt it necessary to call upon Flora.

After taking a chair in the front parlor, Julie Forster arranged her fashionable draperies in graceful folds about her and turned her golden head this way and that to give her hostesses a more complete view of her white silk turban. "What do you think?" she asked.

"Charming," replied Esther, somewhat preoccupied with helping her mother hand the cups around.

"It comes from Madame Felice's establishment," Julie said grandly. "You must go to her, Florry, and be sure to tell her I sent you so she'll reduce the price of my next purchase." Leaning forward, she said slyly, "I heard that Lord Leafield is courting you."

Mrs. Tabitha Brooke gasped, her eyes round with amazement. "Oh, my, I had no idea!"

"And Sally Jenkins told me he seems positively smitten."

The widow's mouth dropped open. "You don't say," she murmured, glancing at her lodger. "Flora, dear, is it true?"

Flora assured her landlady that these allegations had no basis in fact. "Fie, Julie," she scolded the tale bearer. "You of all people ought to know better than to trust green-room gossip."

Julie pouted. "Well, you might at least tell me more about Lord Allingham and La Talley. Has he made her an offer yet?"

"Not to my knowledge, but Louise and I aren't in the habit of exchanging confidences." Flora hastened to divert her by asking, "What day has Ben chosen for your removal to Bath?" This was a successful gambit; Julie, distracted by the question, quickly forgot Lord Leafield and began describing the dresses she considered necessary for a stay at the fashionable spa.

That evening Esther Drew revived the discussion of the impending journey. As soon as Flora returned home from the theater she declared, "Ever since Julie was here, I've been thinking how much I, too, would like to exchange London for Bath, which would certainly be healthier for Hartley. My mother plans to visit Margate with my aunt, and I have no strong desire to go with them or to remain in town alone. We might take a nice house together, and I believe Mama has a friend there who can inform us about what's available at this season." They discussed the scheme at length, and after a day of departure was agreed upon Esther asked, "Was Lord Leafield at the theater tonight?"

"With a party of ladies," Flora reported sourly as she massaged her temples. "Louise, who can't keep her eyes off the audience, told me his stage box was crammed with females—a countess and a viscountess and the daughter of one or the other, I forget. She was furious, because during the first interval Baron Allingham left his seat and joined the earl's party and none of them stayed for the afterpiece."

"Your admirer didn't come backstage to pay his respects?"

"No. Thank goodness," Flora added rather belatedly, her cheeks pink.

"I think the Evil Earl is extremely clever. You'd best be careful."

"What do you mean?"

"If Lord Leafield had visited the green room tonight, you'd have forgotten all about it by morning. By not doing so, he has ensured that you will puzzle over his actions, and thus he keeps himself alive in your memory."

With unwonted sharpness, Flora declared that Bath was looking better to her all the time.

Hamlet had enjoyed a mild success, and the new production of *The Critic* was receiving even greater acclaim. It had provoked the ire of its author just as Ben Forster had hoped; vitriol poured forth from Sheridan's pen to be printed in the columns of the newspapers and theater journals. Several of Forster's most prominent performers, Flora among them, suddenly received flattering offers of employment from Drury Lane. Those who had no particular loyalty to their manager decamped for a higher salary at one of the permanently licensed theaters. Most of them remained, choosing the security of a smaller but regular weekly wage over a larger one paid out at irregular intervals. Salaries at the Princess might be less than at the patent houses, but at least the treasurer never fobbed off the players with excuses and false promises when Saturdays came around. Drury Lane was especially notorious for forcing its actors into debt, that state so familiar to its proprietor.

The comings and goings at the smaller theater were so frequent and so many that the company treasurer's ledger began to resemble a schoolboy's mussed copybook as he crossed out the names of the departed and hastily scrawled entries for newcomers. By the week of the actors' benefits, there was much consternation and speculation over who would or would not be on the roster.

Flora chose *In Praise of Parsimony* for benefit night; its cast was still intact. She placed a notice of advertisement in the newspapers and visited all the shops that enjoyed her custom, offering her tickets for sale.

The play had lain dormant for several weeks, so she bullied Ben Forster into scheduling a rehearsal on the day of performance. She set out at her usual hour, and along the way met Sally Jenkins, who emerged from the rutted side street where she lodged with her violinist.

The redhead matched her bouncing, leggy gait to Flora's even steps and with an ostentatious lift to her brows observed, "What, no watchdog Margery trotting behind you today?"

"She and Esther are packing."

Pointedly ignoring the leering drayman who flung a ribald comment in their direction, Sally asked, "Are you nervous about tonight?"

"Nervous, hopeful, fearful—the whole gamut of emotions. I'm only half awake as well, because Horatio's drunken cater-wauling woke me at dawn. He must've made a great deal of money from *his* benefit—he was singing beneath my window, and later I heard what sounded like an altercation with the watchman. I don't expect to see him till tonight."

"He'll be at rehearsal, no matter what the state of his poor head," Sally prophesied. "He'd drag himself out of bed for you—or through the gates of hell."

"I fancy this morning they're one and the same." After side-stepping a burly individual, Flora turned to her friend and said, "I'm thoroughly sick of London—nothing but dirt and crowds and noise and smells from the market." She wrinkled her nose in distaste.

Sally laughed. "You can't measure the whole city by Covent Garden! I like London, it's so very gay—especially at night, when every other town comes to a dead halt." She chat-ted merrily until they reached the theater courtyard, when she suddenly placed one hand on Flora's arm, bringing her to a standstill. "Look," she breathed, her voice tremulous with emotion, as she pointed out the object that had so excited her.

An elegant landaulet with a coachman on the box stood in the muddy yard, its body gleaming with coat upon coat of paint and varnish, the pinnacle of luxury. The actresses watched in fascination as a spectacular vision in primrose silk emerged from the stage door and made her mincing, pouting way to the waiting equipage. It was Louise Talley, who was followed by the stage-door keeper and a liveried footman, both burdened with what Flora and Sally recognized as the personal properties and costumes that had formerly been scattered about Louise's dressing room.

While her minions stowed her belongings in the carriage,

Louise called out, "Good morning. Rather, it's good-bye," she amended, her round face taking on the quality of a feline who had been at the cream. "From now on I'll be performing at the Theatre Royal, Drury Lane. I've been engaged by Sheridan, with the assistance of Lord Allingham," she added with a simper.

A grin replaced the amazement on Sally's freckled face, and she drawled, "Is that so?" She made a sweeping, all-inclusive gesture. "And might this fine turnout be another example of the baron's kindness?"

"Perhaps." Louise lifted her dimpled chin, daring Sally to say more. Then she turned to Flora to say grandly, "My dear, I'm desolated not to be able to take part in your benefit tonight, and of course Allingham will miss it too—I'm making my first appearance at the Lane, and he wants to be there to support me. But you simply *must* come to tea one afternoon to tell me about it. I'm living in Bloomsbury now in a charming house, with servants and everything."

This was no great surprise; Flora had heard the same words many times from the lips of other actresses. And she knew that Louise had no intention of inviting an old rival to her new abode but was merely puffing off the fact of it.

Sally chortled. "The baron has been *very* kind indeed: a house, a carriage, servants, and even a job at Drury Lane. We must congratulate you on your great success, Louise. And Allingham, for I'm sure you'll be worth every penny he pays for your upkeep." Her voice was laced with sarcasm when she added, "But let me offer a little friendly advice: don't give up the stage, or if you do, be sure to put by a few pounds and shillings for a rainy day. He's reputed to be fickle, your baron, and since you've begun with him, you won't want to slide down the social scale too rapidly. Will it be a viscount next time, or only a baronet? And what will it be next year—a brothel?"

"How dare you! Why, you're nothing but a common, draggle-tail slut, Sally Jenkins!" cried Louise, her full bosom heaving with wrath and the effects of too-tight lacing. "Everyone knows you live with that violin player, that Fred Stafford person, so you've no cause to insult me!"

"I'm not ashamed, for I've never sold myself, and that's what makes a whore a whore. Good-bye, Louise, and good luck to you. You'll be needing it."

Watching the elegant carriage slog through the thick ooze, Flora sighed, "Poor thing, I almost feel sorry for her."

"What a stupid girl you can be sometimes," was Sally's exasperated comment as the doorkeeper ushered them inside the dim theater. "Louise chose her path and I don't condemn her for that, only for doing you an ill turn. And Ben, too. She came to him with nothing more than a good figure and a saucy manner, and he was clever enough to make her popular. Now she repays him by going over to the enemy, and I have no patience with such base treachery! *Sorry* for her? You ought to be furious, for now she won't be playing Selina in your benefit tonight. And the understudy's voice squeaks so badly that half the sense of the words will be lost."

None of the players received the news of La Talley's defection with regret, and many were heard to mutter, "Good riddance." But everyone echoed Sally's opinion: the most grievous wrong had been desertion at benefit time. Theatrical tradition decreed that all personal disputes should be set aside, and for a brief time camaraderie and general good-will reigned at the close of the season.

Madam Forster, Louise's chief critic, summed up the general feeling by predicting that the actress would soon be earning all of her living on her back and none of it on the boards. Flora's rehearsal suffered a necessary delay—a messenger was summarily dispatched to the understudy's lodgings—and her colleagues entertained themselves with gossip and tea and games of whist.

The postponement was fortunate for Horatio Forster. When he lurched into the green room, Flora was energetically rubbing a piece of bread across a white satin slipper to clean it. "Never mind," she said, interrupting his profuse apologies, "it doesn't matter that you're late. Louise has bolted—to Allingham's bed and Sheridan's theater."

"Has she now?" Horatio glanced around the room. "Then why the long faces? She won't be missed, and this means she won't be going to Bath with us, the tiresome wench."

"Suppose the people demand their money back?"

Flora's companions assured her that these fears were unfounded. The understudy arrived sooner than anyone had expected, harassed and unkempt, as if she'd been dragged from her bed, but when the rehearsal was over even Flora had to agree that Louise would not be much missed. It was far easier to work scenes with an actress who remained in her appointed place instead of constantly creeping around the stage to gain the most advantageous position.

She declined Horatio's playful suggestion that she accompany him to a tavern on Maiden Lane for a feast of oysters and ale, and returned to Great Queen Street. She found Esther in the nursery, and was describing to her the tumultuous events of the morning when Frank intruded, his arms overflowing with flowers.

"Carried here by a footman, ma'am, in a blue coat with brass buttons as large as shilling pieces," he said impressively and not without envy.

Flora, by now familiar with the blue and buff livery of the Leafield House servants, examined the bouquet. Hidden among the hothouse specimens were several white campion blossoms, and she was irrationally touched by the play upon her name. While her friend read the card that accompanied the tribute, she turned to the manservant. "Tell Mary to put these in water—there must be quite enough flowers here to adorn all the downstairs rooms." As he left the room she muttered ominously, "The earl bought up most of the box seats for my benefit."

"Can Julie be right? What if he *should* offer what Louise Talley has—a house and a carriage and—"

"You sound as if you think I ought to accept!"

"Of course not, but you can't deny that it's exciting."

With studied offhandedness, Flora replied, "I am not the least bit flustered—or flattered—by his persistence. Next week I'll be on my way to Bath, Lord Leafield will likely go to Brighton with the rest of society, and the curtain will be rung down on this bizarre episode."

On this defiant note, she swept out of the room, leaving Esther to frown over the earl's card and to inhale the sweet fragrance still lingering in the air.

Four days later, a post coach carrying four weary women and a fretful child arrived in Bath.

After two days on the road, the entire party was exhausted, particularly young Hartley, who had proven himself to be an uncomfortable traveling companion. The vehicle halted before a long row of connected residences, the trunks were deposited on the pavement, and a cook-housekeeper emerged to greet her employers. Mrs. Meeks, a stout soul with a broad, friendly face, dutifully showed them the drawing room, dining parlor, and storerooms on the ground floor. The bedchambers and linen closet were upstairs, with a garret above. The furnishings were simple, neither new nor terribly worn, and the beds were sufficiently comfortable to induce sleep almost at once.

The new day was young when Flora and Esther received their first caller. Horatio Forster found them at the breakfast table; Flora was still wearing her paisley dressing gown. He bussed her cheek, then demanded the same privilege of Mrs. Drew. "Your first day in Bath, and you haven't made your pilgrimage to the Pump Room? Our Julie is there now, you may be sure."

"I'm more interested in seeing the theater," Flora said candidly.

"Dearest one, I would be delighted to escort you to Orchard Street," he told her. "In fact, Ben is waiting for me there—the wagon carrying our properties and stock wardrobe is due to arrive this morning. Let us go at once."

His black eyes included Esther, who shook her head, saying all she cared to do was to laze the morning away and perhaps call on her mother's friend in the afternoon. Flora excused herself to change, and when she returned Horatio was describing the farewell dinner given to his brother by the management committee.

"Have you heard?" he asked Flora jovially. "We're going on holiday soon. Julie has persuaded Ben to spend a month at Brighton, and you're invited to join us."

"Hasn't she seen enough of the seaside?" Flora wondered. "We used to play at the theater on Duke Street every winter."

"Oh, our Julie was a working girl in those days," he reminded her with a broad wink. "Now she's a lady of leisure, wife of a rising theater manager, and as such will command respect at a fashionable resort."

Esther Drew shook her head, smiling at Mrs. Forster's pretensions. "I suppose she means to be very genteel while in Bath, if she's taking the waters every day and parading in the Pump Room."

This program sounded dull to Flora, but it was also the sort of nonsense that most appealed to Julie Forster, whose retirement from the stage, subsequent motherhood, and love of fashion left the two women with nothing in common but a fondness for Ben Forster.

The elegant matron had cut short her visit to the Pump Room to accompany her husband to the theater, and she greeted Flora with pleasure, casting her knowledgeable eyes over the actress's attire.

"But my dear," she declared in shocked accents, "you mustn't go about in that plain pelisse! And that antiquated fichu—really, now! That's last year's gown, too, don't bother to deny it."

"No one else in Bath will know," Flora murmured, adjusting the white neck-handkerchief tucked into the bodice. Her cambric gown was a favorite, and she was too accustomed to this sort of criticism to take offense.

"I'll take you to the shops," Julie said decisively. "Ben says you cleared over a hundred pounds from your benefit, so you can't plead poverty as an excuse for going about so shabbily dressed."

"My money is safely deposited with my banker in London, so neither you nor the Bath shops will tempt me to loosen my purse strings. A subscription to the circulating library and a new trimming for my best bonnet will be the limit to my expenditures."

"Oh, do let's go to Milsom Street! I depend on you to keep me company today—Madam is visiting old Mr. Siddons, and Ben will be here for hours yet. I can show you our house on

Trim Street—the children will love to see you. Sam asked me this morning when Florry was coming, and baby Julia is saying whole words now!"

Only five days had passed since Flora had last seen the two young Forsters, but she raised no objection. Horatio went with them, and where the pavements were narrow or too crowded for three persons, he fell behind and sauntered along in their wake. When they paused at a library so Flora could pay her subscription fee, the actor joined the other gentlemen loungers.

After touring the shops and taking tea with Julie, Flora returned to her own lodgings. Upon being informed by Mrs. Meeks that Esther and Margery were away, she gathered up some writing paper and carried it to the sitting room to compose a letter to her brother.

Because it had been many weeks since Flora had written Miles, line after line flowed from her pen. She described her recent activities, told him of the riches her benefit had provided, and even described the enmity of London's theater managers, for she invariably told him the bad along with the good. Despite this habit of full disclosure, she sat idle for several minutes, tickling her chin with the point of her quill as she pondered whether or not to tell him about her most notable admirer. In the end, she wrote only that she had encountered several distinguished persons, the Earl of Leafield and Lord Allingham among them.

The more impressive of the two titles stood out on the page, and she stared down at it with strange fascination. Had he truly been determined to prove his cousin's marriage, or had that only been a ruse to lure her to his bed? Was he presently chasing after some other, more willing female? She had no way to know. In which case, she chided herself, she ought not to care.

After she finished her letter she left it unsealed, thinking Esther might add a few lines to Captain Drew at the bottom. She reached for a pen wiper as the door knocker sounded below. Supposing that it heralded the return of Horatio, she told Mrs. Meeks to admit her visitor and send him upstairs.

A few minutes later she looked up to find a tall gentleman silhouetted in the doorway, watching her. The quill fell from her fingers. "What the devil are *you* doing here?" she cried as the Earl of Leafield executed one of his polished bows in her direction.

"From your expression, I assume that the devil would be a great deal more welcome. I actually hoped you would be *glad* to see me."

She rose hastily, outraged to find him in Bath just when she had been thinking herself well and truly free of him. Raising one hand to her head, as though she had received a stunning blow, she moaned, "Oh, no." She wavered slightly on her feet, then crumpled to the floor.

8

If you can separate yourself and your misdemeanors,
You are welcome to the house.

Twelfth Night, II. iii.

Kneeling beside the fallen lady's limp form, Trevor parted the snowy scarf tucked into her bodice. When he placed one hand on the warm flesh of her bosom, it rose and fell erratically, indicating extreme agitation, as did the strong and tumultuous heartbeat. Her face was unusually flushed for an unconscious person.

"Is this an attempt to hoax me?" he murmured before bestowing a restorative kiss.

Flora struggled to sit up. "How could you—the housekeeper might have walked in!"

He released her with a regretful sigh. "Still so cruel?"

The ready answer fell from lips still throbbing from the firm, familiar pressure of his. "Still so constant, my lord," she replied, trying to appear as cool and composed as Countess Olivia, whom she had quoted. She avoided his amused and mocking gaze as she straightened her fichu and smoothed her tumbled hair.

"You are unhurt?" he asked.

"I learned the trick of falling years ago. The only damage will be to my gown, as I don't usually expire without the carpet of tragedy." Seeing that he was puzzled by her reference, she explained, "The green baize cloth that covers the stage floor during a tragic play has a practical use: it keeps our clothes from being soiled in the death scenes. In *Hamlet*, or *Macbeth*, the bodies pile up fast and furiously, and the carpet is a necessary comfort. Costumes are costly." She twisted around to get a rear view, which eluded her. Presenting her back to him, she asked worriedly, "Did I dirty my gown?"

After a very thorough inspection of her posterior, Trevor informed her that she had not.

"I shouldn't have greeted you by falling at your feet, but I couldn't resist the temptation. I've played so many madwomen lately that my own wits have become somewhat addled." After inviting him to be seated, she gazed at him curiously. "How did you know where to find me? *My* name wasn't included in the list of new arrivals in the morning paper."

"I chanced to meet Mr. Forster—the younger one—on Bath Street today, and he gave me the happy news of your recent arrival. Hugh and I are playing a long overdue visit to our aunt, who resides on Sydney Place. A most convenient circumstance, now that you are also here." He placed one hand over his heart.

His loverlike gesture alarmed her only a little less than the kiss. In a carefully disinterested voice, she asked how long he would be in town.

"That depends upon you."

"I don't understand."

Said he, a trifle impatiently, "If you recall our discussion at Twickenham, you'll know why I've dragged myself to Bath at this benighted season."

"And if you do the same," Flora shot back, "you would remember that I was firm in my refusal." She crossed to the window, striving to maintain the frigid disinterest she'd cultivated ever since their impromptu excursion to his riverside villa, where he'd made his intentions plain. After marshaling her thoughts, she faced him again and said, "I didn't take to the stage for the purpose of parading my wares to noblemen. I'd have made it clearer to you when we first met, but I never supposed that you would carry me off to your house without a by-your-leave, as if I were a common strumpet."

"I scarcely gave your reputation a thought, not being aware that it was so much at risk."

Deeply affronted, she gasped, "What a horrid thing to say!"

"I didn't mean it unkindly." He extracted a piece of paper from his pocket and held it out to her. Smiling, he said, "Not *carte blanche*, my dear Flora, but a notice for the newspaper. I'd like you to look it over."

"'To the young woman who contracted a secret alliance with a young gentleman, Mr. H. C.,'" she read aloud. "'The aforementioned lady, by presenting herself at the offices of R. P. Linton, the Strand, with proofs of the marriage, may lay claim to a handsome reward, entitling her to a future of independence and security.'"

When she returned the paper to him, he told her, "That advertisement will be printed in the *Times* and the *London Gazette.*"

"Both are easily had here in Bath," Flora pointed out. "Suppose Mr. Cotterell sees it?"

"The risk was one Linton and I chose to take, knowing that Hugh seldom reads the papers. Of course, his wife may be similarly disinclined. In the meantime, I've formed yet another plan to spur his confession, which requires your assistance. I offer the same terms I did last time—name your price and I'll meet it. You shall have new clothes, fine jewels, whatever you desire if only you'll visit Combe Cotterell and encourage my cousin to ingratiate himself with you."

"Are you so sure that he would try?"

Trevor's lip curled. "Married men are the most debauched fellows of all, surely you know that without my telling you. Yes, I'm convinced you can coax the truth out of him within a very short time."

"You want me to be your spy!"

"I suppose that's an accurate description," he agreed.

"I can think of others, all of them equally base."

"Oh, I don't mean for you to become his mistress," he said audaciously. "Not when I continue to cherish hopes of my own."

Flora approached his chair. "Lord Leafield, won't you *please* call a halt to these games of yours and let me be? In a few weeks I depart for Brighton with the Forsters, and until then I'll be very busy at the Orchard Street theater."

"But you won't always be working, will you? Like me, you'll surely need a pleasant diversion while you're in Bath."

"I don't want to be your 'diversion.'"

"Couldn't you be my friend?" he persisted.

"People would be bound to talk, as they did in London, and

I loathe being the subject of gossip and speculation. Don't you?"

"No one gossips about Lumley Skeffington. He haunts the theaters, and not only does he pay court to the actors and actresses, he also passes himself off as a playwright. Not," he said consideringly, "that I have any ambition to do the same. You're an intelligent and talented woman—that's just as obvious as your valentine of a face—and I happen to prefer your company to that of Mrs. Siddons."

"Mrs. Siddons could be your mother, my lord. Not a soul will say that of me, you may be sure." Placing her hands on a chair back, she continued, "You speak as if you can suddenly decree us friends and it is done, but friendships can't be forced, or ordained. They grow."

But she was already weakening. Didn't her long association with Horatio prove that a man and a woman could sustain a platonic relationship? To say nothing of the great Dr. Johnson and Mrs. Piozzi, or Mrs. Siddons and Thomas Lawrence. But perhaps the latter pair made a poor example; some mildly suggestive rumors had circulated about the famous tragedienne and the noted portrait painter, although at one time he'd been suitor to her daughters.

"Oh, very well," she said at last, "I accept your offer of friendship, but only conditionally. You must forget everything that happened at Twickenham, and you will cease to badger me about joining your summer house party in Devonshire."

Trevor stepped forward to clasp her hand, pledging himself to uphold these terms. "As you wish." She must have been satisfied, for he had no difficulty convincing her to accompany him to Sydney Gardens the next day, after her rehearsal.

When he left Westgate Buildings he made his way through the town to the graceful Florentine bridge over the Avon. Pulteney Street extended to the park, bounded on each side by Sydney Place. As he approached one of the newer houses its door was opened to him by a footman who relieved him of his hat and cane, saying, "Her ladyship is in the sitting room, my lord."

The strong resemblance between the Countess Ainsley and her nephews could be traced in the firm jaw, aquiline nose, and hazel eyes, but ill health had taken its toll of her looks. Her complexion was sallow, and her mouse-brown hair was liberally flecked with gray.

"My dear Trevor, you've been away quite a time," she observed as the earl entered her sunny sanctuary. "What have you been doing?"

"I looked in at the Pump Room, stopped at Meyler and Sons, and wandered about the Abbey Churchyard. And then," he added on a triumphant note, "I called upon Miss Flora Campion."

Lady Ainsley sat up straighter in her chair, her blue-veined hands gripping the arms. "You have come to terms with her?"

"Not yet." Lowering his voice, Trevor asked, "Is Hugh at home?"

"Heavens no, he's hardly the sort to sit with an ailing lady all day," she replied, but without a trace of self-pity. "Tell me about Miss Campion."

"She's as lovely as ever, and just as stubborn. I believe her contract with Forster expires at the end of July, and it could well take me till then to convince her to visit Combe Cotterell. At present she is contemplating a trip to Brighton instead."

"When shall I see her?"

"If you peek through your drawing-room window tomorrow afternoon, you might catch a glimpse of her. She agreed to walk with me in the gardens, and if I can overcome her inherent distrust of designing noblemen to that extent, I think we need not doubt a happy conclusion to this business."

Her ladyship's fond expression gave way to a concerned frown. "Trevor, you will have a care, won't you? The creature may be playing a game as deep as your own."

"Never fear, ma'am, the little play actress can't do me a particle of harm. I have everything to gain and nothing to lose, whereas she, poor girl, must always be on her guard against me. I have influence, I have money, and I am a man. Any one of those would be enough to ruin her, and the combination is formidable if used against her—or exerted in her favor." But he rather doubted that Flora Campion feared him, and she appeared to possess more good sense than he would have liked in his victim.

In the firm voice that was at odds with her frail appearance, Lady Ainsley warned him, "Whatever your position, it's not wise to make a policy of turning other people's lives upside down to suit your convenience. If Miss Campion won't help you, hire some other pretty actress to seduce the truth from Hugh, or alter the succession by some other means."

"How?" he asked grimly. "By proposing marriage to the first presentable female who crosses my path?"

"Well," her ladyship replied, "you might at least wait until the Batsfords return from London. I have heard that their daughter Caroline is still unattached."

By the end of Flora's first week in Bath, she was in love.

She could only suppose that those persons who had described the city as dull, staid, and gossipy were hopelessly hard to please, for she admired its architecture, from the abbey to the public buildings, and especially the terraces and crescents that draped themselves so gracefully upon the surrounding hills. London had been a hodgepodge of stone-built and stuccoed dwellings flung up beside brick ones in a mix of styles, but the buildings of Bath were characterized by a pleasing uniformity. Nearly all had been built in the last century from a local stone that gleamed like gold in the summer sun.

Lord Leafield met her on Orchard Street after her first rehearsal and escorted her across the Pulteney Bridge to the pleasure gardens on the other side of the Avon, which he likened to a miniature Vauxhall. This analogy fell short, for Flora had never visited London's famed gardens, but because she had no measure against which to judge, Bath's version couldn't suffer by comparison. It was composed of velvety bowling greens, several pleasant arbors, cool labyrinths of shrubbery, and swings. An outdoor concert was in progress, and they strolled the banks of the canal to the faint accompaniment of chamber music. Punts crammed with merrymakers glided across the water; pretty girls darted in and out of the trees, pursued by their eager swains. Lord Leafield explained that despite the spa's reputation for stodginess, its young people enjoyed a greater freedom than did their counterparts in London.

Bath was a melting pot of humanity, and no longer the resort of preference for the wealthy and titled. Merchants, half-pay officers, and professional men had settled there with their families, as had those persons whose ill health made them dependent on the medical men, mineral waters, and hot baths. Although Julie Forster searched the weekly papers for the names of new arrivals, the number of aristocrats in residence mattered little to Flora, who only hoped there were enough playgoers to fill the Orchard Street theater.

From the first night *The Rivals* played to a crowd, for its Bath setting made it popular with the locals. Flora considered Lydia Languish the most foolish of heroines, but at each performance the old theater rang with the public's appreciation of the even sillier Mrs. Malaprop and the many mistaken identities.

All in all she was content, but during one of Horatio's regular visits to Westgate Buildings, she voiced her single source of frustration.

"When will we ever be finished with this dratted play and move on to something else?" she wailed. "I'm sick to death of it, and so must you be, for I swear Captain Absolute is just as idiotic as Lydia."

"A good thing old Sheridan can't hear you!" The actor lowered the loose pages of the manuscript he'd been reading. "I'm afraid you won't like Mr. Jones's latest work any better. The author may claim that *Callista, or the Melancholy Maiden* is better than *In Praise of Parsimony* or *The Inconstant Lady*, but to me they're much the same."

She approached the sofa and Horatio handed her a few loose sheets. After a cursory glance at the speeches and stage directions, she sighed. " 'If 'twere played upon a stage, I would condemn it as an improbable fiction.' But I suppose if we think it stupid, it's sure to be a hit." She flung herself into a chair. "*Must* we sit about with nothing to amuse us but Mr. Jones's masterpiece? Let's go somewhere—I'm deadly dull today."

Horatio's black eyes hardened and his deep-timbered voice lacked its usual teasing note when he said, "I was forgetting that you are accustomed to more exalted society than that of a

humble actor. Should I deck myself out in pantaloons and
fancy waistcoats and drag a gold-topped walking stick around
every time I step out of my door? I'm not sure I can keep up to
your new standard in gentlemen friends, Florry love."

"I only meant—"

"And naturally," he interrupted with his expert sarcasm,
"like your other admirer, I ought to shower you with compliments and spout quizzical nonsense all the day long."

"That's exactly what you *are* doing," was Flora's acid comment. "Am I to infer from this invective that you are jealous of
Lord Leafield?"

"Have I some cause to be jealous?" he asked, his voice rising with the question. "I can't help worrying, for I've always
had the impression that you abhorred the sort of connection
that Leafield clearly has in mind."

"You can't judge every other man by your own depraved
self," she pointed out venomously. That Horry, who knew her
best, should be the first to sully her new intimacy with Lord
Leafield with suspicion was more than she could bear. And he
had reminded her of the earl's attempt to seduce her in the garden of his villa, an incident that still figured prominently in her
traitorous memory. "Why must you imagine the worst? I'm a
grown woman, not some ignorant little child to be guarded
from the whole bad world by a pack of Forsters!"

"Is that so? Well, I thought it right to give you a hint that
some people—your *true* friends, I might add—are beginning
to wonder at the curious change in your attitude," he told her,
his face flushed. "And if you're not careful, you'll soon hear
me say, 'I told you so.' "

Flora's wrath blazed. Reaching for the nearest object, a calfbound book from the circulating library, she hurled it at him
with all the force in her arm.

He caught it neatly. "Practicing to play Kate the Shrew?" he
sneered.

"Go to the devil!" she advised him at the top of her lungs,
and without another word, he stalked out of the house.

The next person to court her displeasure was Esther Drew.

When she arrived home from the theater, burdened with one
of the generous bouquets Lord Leafield sometimes provided,

the young matron looked up from her needlework to remark, "Isn't it imprudent to encourage this friendship that seems to have sprung up between you and the evil earl like a mushroom in the night?"

Flora, knowing that to answer one question with another was a useful device, asked coolly, "You don't like him?"

"I don't know him well enough to form an opinion, and you can hardly know him much better," said Esther. "Oh, I grant you, he's a gentleman of distinction, and very attractive, but his following you to Bath and singling you out as he does encourages gossip."

"There's no scandal in walking with Lord Leafield in a public pleasure garden and driving up to Landsdown in his phaeton. Or letting him once—only once, mind you—escort me home when we chanced to meet on High Street."

"But he stayed quite half an hour afterwards. And if you've forgotten that he visited your dressing room three times this week and sat through a rehearsal, Margery hasn't; she told me." Esther stabbed her needle into the fabric. "You seemed reluctant to receive him the first time he called on you in London. And as I recall, the day he drove you to Richmond, I could hardly get you out of the house and into his carriage. When he engaged the seats for your benefit, you said—"

"Have you been keeping a tally?" Flora interrupted, feigning an amusement she didn't feel.

"I'm sure you care next to nothing for what I may think, or what Julie thinks—and she has been very vocal on the subject, you may be sure. But what about Miles? I don't think he would be pleased to know his sister is keeping company with a nobleman who pays her dubious court—no man would. Does he know?"

"Yes," Flora answered with quiet dignity. "I have nothing to conceal."

Esther reached for her scissors and cut a thread. As she smoothed out the new seam in her son's short coat, she said, "You think I'm meddling, but I do feel very strongly that you should keep away from Lord Leafield."

"What harm can he do? If you object simply because he's a

man and I'm not, I must remind you that Horatio and I are also close."

"You and Horatio share a profession, and you have the same interests and background."

"How inconsistent!" Flora trilled. "Horry has a *terrible* reputation—he's a notorious rake."

Esther said quietly, "He wouldn't compromise you. He still loves you, as I'm sure you know."

His erratic behavior seemed to prove this, but Flora shied from admitting it to herself. "I've never set myself up as an arbiter of morals, or criticized the way others choose to behave. Now that everyone is doing it to me, and over such a simple thing, I find it most disagreeable. The Earl of Leafield is witty and amusing, and very good company. I never imagined that someone unconnected with the theater could be so—so interesting."

And before Esther could make another irritating comment, or further disparage her new friend, Flora took herself off to bed.

9

Well, I will be so much a sinner, to be a double dealer.

Twelfth Night, V. i.

A ferocious storm descended upon Bath one morning, turning the creamy stone buildings to dull gray and wetting the streets and pavements. Pedestrians hurried home for their umbrellas, and many remained there, postponing their shopping expeditions and visits to the Pump Room.

The rain continued all week. On the first day of bad weather, Flora and a sneezing Esther huddled by the fire or took turns standing at the parlor window to watch the diminished traffic below. By the next day they were resigned to indoor pursuits, and passed the time reading the latest novel from the circulating library and playing with the baby. In the evening, Flora strapped on her pattens for the short but wet walk to the theater, with Margery holding the umbrella over both their heads.

One damp afternoon Mrs. Forster's manservant brought the ladies an invitation to an afternoon party, and Flora was tempted by the promise of tea and cakes and theatrical gossip. Julie's entertainment would be no different from any leisurely hour in the green room, except that the actresses would wear their best gowns and gentlemen would be absent. But anything was better than spending another day in Westgate Buildings, so she left Esther to nurse a sore throat and walked to Trim Street.

A babel of tongues—the Scots brogue, the singsong accents of Wales, the lilt of Hibernia, and the plebian dialects of London's boroughs—battled for supremacy as her peers welcomed her. Julie greeted her warmly, nodding approval of her lemon-hued gown, and accepting Esther's regrets with a sigh. Flora had no desire to sit down at a whist table, so she paid her respects to Madam Forster, impressively attired in maroon satin and her customary turban as she held court from a rosewood settee.

The great lady was describing her recent visit to William Siddons. "Poor man, his legs are very bad, and he's completely chair-bound, with only his cats and his memories to keep him company. But I told him, 'Siddons, the world may talk, but as I see it, your separation from Sarah was the wisest decision of your life.' And do you know what he said?"

Madam Forster's audience waited, hushed and expectant, but she was too experienced a performer to give immediate satisfaction. She sipped her tea, glanced around the room, and drew a breath before saying, "He answered, 'Eulalia, thirty years of marriage is a tie that cannot be broken, but 'tis best we live apart. I am a poor thing now, and she was ever too grand a creature for the likes of me.'"

Sally Jenkins chortled. "From all I ever heard, he was a worthless husband and not much of an actor, either!" Before Madam could rebuke her, she added defiantly, "Well, he did lose a great deal of his wife's money through poor advice and bad investments."

The older woman nodded her turbaned head and agreed that it was too true. "But he has been a support through Sarah's many trials—the deaths of their daughters were the worst of them—and he stayed by her side during a scandal or two. They're on friendly terms still, for he visits her in London when his health permits, and she comes to Bath between her professional engagements."

The topic of Mrs. Siddons's marital affairs was abandoned, and other items of theatrical dirty laundry were aired. Sally, who cared little for the past, only the present, sidled over to Flora and whispered, "Never once have I heard of a marriage that didn't make me vow and swear to remain single so long as I'm on the stage! I'll not hand over my earnings to a husband, or mother his bairns all day in addition to slaving on the stage by night. Far better to live in sin, if you ask me!"

Flora pointed out the flaw in her reasoning with a reminder that the absence of a wedding band didn't preclude the possibility of motherhood.

"Oh, there are ways and means," Sally replied, her blue eyes twinkling. "Just ask Eliza Ellis if you ever need to know."

"Pooh, I can't believe any of her tricks are infallible. Actresses in keeping send for the midwife regularly; it's an occupational hazard. Think of Mrs. Jordan: never wed and she has twelve—no, now it's thirteen children—ten of them by her royal consort."

Sally said carelessly, "Mrs. Jordan is as good as married to her jolly sailor duke. It's no secret he depends on her for money, his family is so stingy and he so expensive. I suspect she'd rather retire, but because his grace of Clarence hasn't the wherewithal to provide for so many offspring, she must keep slogging away. I'll bet a guinea he has the poor soul back on the stage come September."

"Done! For I believe she has already given up acting."

When Julie took up a newspaper and read aloud an account of a splendid private party at the Countess Ainsley's home on Sydney Place, Flora's conversation with Sally tapered off. The list of notable guests and the detailed descriptions of the ladies' toilettes elicited sighs of envy from the actresses, and her mind wandered back to Lord Leafield's brief, bored reference to his aunt's entertainment, which had kept him away from the theater one night. According to the paper, he'd opened the glittering ball by dancing with Lady Caroline Lewes.

" 'The young ladyship,' " Julie read in dulcet tones, " 'wore white sarsenet with a gauze overdress trimmed in seed pearls sewn in a floral pattern.' It must have cost her mama a fortune!"

One bright morning the earl called on Flora with the intention of taking her on a tour of the surrounding countryside. When she exhibited reluctance, he assured her that he owned no villa in the environs of Bath and further enticed her with a description of the famous standing stones at Stanton Drew.

During the drive, Flora played with her parasol uncertainly, as though it were a new and unfamiliar stage prop. From time to time she drew her eyes from their pastoral surroundings to look over at her companion, noting how the sunshine intensified the red tints in his hair and the russet coat complimented his broad shoulders. Keeping her lashes discreetly lowered, she traced the muscles of his legs, clearly visible through the doeskin breeches. As the product of a community in which physical attributes were noticed and commented on—and bartered—she couldn't help but be aware of the face and form of a man so splendidly endowed. His motive for continuing to seek her out was still a mystery, and she sometimes warned herself that her growing fascination with him was as foolish as it might prove dangerous.

"How does *Callista, or the Melancholy Maiden* progress?" he asked while they strolled among the massive rocks rising up from the village common.

"Slowly," she sighed. "There was a quarrel between Sally Jenkins and Mrs. Logan at our last rehearsal over a bit of staging more beneficial to one than the other."

"Your friend Miss Jenkins I know, but which lady is Mrs. Logan?"

"She played Mrs. Malaprop in *Rivals*, but under a different name," Flora explained. "On the playbill she's Mrs. Walsh, but we call her Mrs. Logan."

He looked away from the tallest and most impressive monolith to ask, "And why is that?"

"Despite the fact that she and Mr. Logan have lived together forever, he already has a wife in Ireland, and because he belongs to the Roman Church there is no possibility of a divorce. So Mrs. Logan is actually Miss Walsh, being a single lady, but we call her 'Mrs.' as a professional courtesy and 'Logan' for the sake of the children. They have five."

His hearty laughter made some of the grazing sheep move nervously away. "It's a wonder you can keep it straight. Not many of your colleagues are wed, are they?"

"Mrs. Ellis is, though I think she'd rather *not* be," Flora said frankly. "And Ben. Sally prefers not to marry into the profession, and like poor Mrs. Logan, who would if she could, she must live by a different code of behavior."

"And what is your code?" he inquired, no longer smiling.

"To give my best performance, and make Ben proud," she answered promptly.

* * *

Hugh Cotterell paced his aunt's parlor impatiently, desperate to know the outcome of his cousin's drive into the countryside. He'd remained at Sydney Place all afternoon in the expectation that Trevor would return as an engaged man, for his courtship of Lady Caroline had progressed to the point that this was entirely possible. Lord and Lady Batsford were giving a party at their Grosvenor Place mansion on that very night, a perfect opportunity to announce their daughter's forthcoming marriage.

Hearing his cousin's tread, he stuck his head into the hallway and called, "Come have some brandy, Trev, and tell me about your outing. Did you have a pleasant drive?"

"Quite," Trevor answered as he entered the parlor. "Miss Campion had a fancy to visit the Druidical stones at Stanton Drew."

"Miss Campion," Hugh repeated dully. "But I thought—damn it, Trev, what kind of game are you playing?"

The earl's face was impassive as he picked up the brandy decanter, and his voice was cool when he said, "I'm not sure I know what you mean."

"Lady Caroline Lewes, Miss Flora Campion, and Mrs. Martha Harris. You've danced attendance on all three of 'em since we arrived in Bath. If your intentions toward her ladyship are honorable, I can't fathom why you go to the widow's house every night, and continue to chase after that black-haired wench from the Orchard Street playhouse."

"Miss Campion is damnably elusive," Trevor replied. "So I have taken advantage of my unstructured but long-standing arrangement with Mrs. Harris."

Hugh shook his head in disgust, and a stray lock of hair fell across his brow.

"Do I detect censure in your countenance? Where the fair sex is concerned, *your* reputation can hardly be described as stainless, Hugh."

The younger man glared at him before charging out of the room.

If Hugh only knew the truth, his cousin thought, he would be even more confused.

Trevor had learned to value the chaste friendship he had sought so selfishly, for Flora Campion was an ideal companion—bright, entertaining, and capable of discussing weighty subjects as well as frivolous ones. She spoke her mind freely and never balked at expressing an opinion—not even when it ran counter to his—and he found her frankness appealing and attractive. But greatly though he admired her strength of mind and character, he was amazed by her devotion to her work, and the demands it placed upon her.

In the past, watching a play from the comfortable distance of a box seat, an actor's life had looked easy. He'd dismissed the popular stories about Mrs. Siddons fainting in the wings after a performance as apocryphal, the puffery of a greedy manager anxious to fill his house. But lately he had seen Flora's colleagues stagger off the stage, stunned by fatigue, concerned only with changing out of their costumes and returning to their lodgings for much-needed rest. Others, full of energy and exhilarated by the performance, would laugh and chatter away, and they usually repaired to the nearest tavern for food and drink and good fellowship. Trevor could never predict to which group Flora would belong on a given night. Sometimes when he met her in the green room she could hardly hold up her end of a conversation; on other nights she seemed quite unaffected by her labors.

During one visit to her tiny dressing room, he had shifted one of her costumes from a chair, a blue gown so heavy that he asked how she could wear it for nearly four hours. "No wonder poor mad Ophelia is dragged down to a watery death," he had commented. "This must weigh a full stone."

"By the end of an evening it seems like more!" she'd answered. "Ben has been infected with Kemble's passion for historical accuracy, and we players suffer in our velvets and brocades and stiff petticoats. Margery haunts the secondhand shops and hoards every scrap of interesting or antique material she can find. But the more trimming a dress has, the greater the likelihood that something will come loose or fall off. She earns her wage, you may be sure."

It troubled Trevor that Flora should feign insanity and death night after night, and though he could only guess at the effort required for the part of Ophelia, he suspected that there was an emotional toll as well as a physical one. But she joked about the mad scenes, and in reply to one of his queries she laughed and said, "I quite enjoy my funeral in *Hamlet*. While I'm stretched out on Ophelia's bier and Horry and Ben are dueling over me, I usually decide what I'm going to wear the next day!"

Ironically, the life she led was a sheltered one, the very antithesis of the wild romp he had once supposed it to be. And though Trevor coveted both the daytime and the evening hours she spent on Orchard Street, at the same time he had a contradictory desire to further her career, to help her reach the pinnacle of success that he believed to be the sum of every player's dreams.

After puzzling over the matter for some time, he finally decided upon the perfect scheme, one that had the added advantage of placing her in his debt.

Very early one starry summer morning, the Earl of Leafield and Horatio Forster exited one of Bath's popular taverns, arm in arm and laughing uproariously.

Grasping a lamppost to steady himself, the actor asked, "Where to next, m'lord?"

"Bed," was Trevor's reply.

His companion responded with a wicked grin. "If any man can find a brothel in a town as stuffy as this one, it's me. But you must swear not to mention it to my Florry, because I hope—because she might—well, you can't say anything to her," Horatio concluded sheepishly.

"I'm not going with you. I just remembered," said Trevor in a voice of wonder at having forgotten, "that I've got an appointment in the Crescent."

"Which Crescent? Bath has scores of 'em," the actor called after him.

The walk and the night air failed to improve his disordered senses, but Trevor managed to reach the heights of Lansdown Crescent without any mishap. Removing a key from his waistcoat pocket, he let himself into one of the terrace houses and ascended its curving staircase slowly and unsteadily, relying

on the handrail and overcompensating for the height of the risers.

A blonde female in a nightgown of nearly transparent material waited for him in her candlelit bedchamber. As she guided
him toward the bed, he mumbled an apology and stretched out,
his heavy eyelids shutting out the revolving walls and furniture.

Several hours later, Trevor was roused from slumber by a
shove. He turned unfocused eyes upon the person bending
over him—not the dark-haired beauty who had figured in his
fevered dreams. Her dressing gown gaped open, and while
Trevor waited for his vision to clear he inspected her voluptuous charms dispassionately.

Evidently she'd received the wrong impression, because she
shook her head, saying, "There's no time for that, my lord. I'm
expecting visitors, and if you meet them on the doorstep,
you'll ruin my reputation, you will."

Trevor knew it was too late for his hostess to harbor concerns of that sort. How his head ached—it was all Horatio's
fault, damn him. "What's the time, m'dear?" he muttered.

"Something past ten." The lady sat down at her dressing
table to brush out her honey-colored hair. "I thought it might
be best to let you sleep it off."

"Was I very drunk?"

"I've seen worse."

Too late he realized that it was most ungallant of him to
admit that he couldn't recall what had or had not occurred in
the widow's curtained bed.

He left Landsdown Crescent in a hackney, wincing as its
wheels met each rut in the uneven street. His discomfort went
beyond his throbbing temples and parched mouth; he couldn't
rid himself of the suspicion that he'd treated someone abom-
inably last night, perhaps several people, himself included. He
had failed his mistress by visiting her in an inebriated state.
The wisdom of keeping a mistress in so gossipy and insular a
place as Bath was questionable, particularly during his
courtship of Lady Caroline Lewes. As for Flora Campion—he
tried to convince himself that she was the only person he
hadn't betrayed, but the effort made his head ache all the

more. He needed to see her, to explain—but somewhere between High Street and Laura Place he decided it might be
wiser to let someone else deliver the happy news that had
prompted last night's celebratory excesses.

10

But come what may, I do adore thee so
That danger shall seem sport, and I will go.

Twelfth Night, II. i.

"I plan to accompany Julie to the Pump Room this morning," Flora announced when she joined Esther at the breakfast table. "Why don't you join us?"

The young woman raised shining brown eyes from the letter she had been reading. "James expects the *Vestal* to return in September—isn't it wonderful? He's been at sea a year and a half, he hasn't even met his son! And he's bringing back prize money, for they lately seized a French privateer and a pair of American vessels."

"What news of Miles?" Flora asked eagerly.

"My husband slanders him terribly, accusing him of having flirts in every port. Apparently a Barbados sweetheart has been supplanted by a pretty planter's daughter in Jamaica. I wonder if anything will come of it?"

"Not if they're sailing for England—my brother inevitably makes a clean break before weighing anchor."

Their conversation ended with the arrival of Mrs. Benedict Forster, splendidly attired in a jonquil bombazine pelisse and a feathered bonnet.

Many residents were required by their physicians to take a glass of tepid, sulphurous water in the morning, so the Pump Room was bustling even at that early hour. Flora was thankful when Julie wearied of promenading and edged toward an alcove with some chairs strategically placed for viewing the assembly, though the music coming from the orchestra gallery overhead hampered conversation.

"There's that dreadful Mrs. Harris—they say she sometimes receives a certain nobleman with whom you are acquainted."

The same disturbing rumor had reached Flora earlier in the week. Eliza Ellis, jealous of her success as Ophelia, had been the first to inform her that Lord Leafield had a mistress.

"Here comes the Countess of Batsford with her daughter, Lady Caroline Lewes," Julie announced. "There was a grand ball at their house on Grosvenor Place this week; did you see the notice in the *Chronicle*?"

Flora murmured a negative reply before asking, "Which is Lady Caroline?"

"The one dressed all in white. Such a lovely complexion, and the prettiest chestnut curls! I saw her in a millinery on Bath Street the other day, trying on hats."

Flora's eyes sought the lady so described, a fragile fairy figure in foamy gauze. Did the earl consider this acquaintance to be one of those boring social ones he often joked about? She couldn't imagine what a worldly, sophisticated nobleman found intriguing about a chit still in her teens, however pretty. As she watched the frail, elegant Lady Ainsley greet Lady Caroline, her spirits plummeted even further. Was Leafield thinking of marriage?

Suddenly the spacious room seemed more crowded than it had been earlier, crammed as it now was with ladies connected to the earl: his aunt, his reputed mistress, his prospective bride, and herself. And for the remainder of the morning, she devoted herself to the task of assuming a casual and impartial interest in the parade of humanity.

She returned to Westgate Buildings in a reflective state, and was rescued from looming melancholy by a visit from her employer.

Ben Forster gave her one of the warm and affectionate smiles he reserved for her alone, saying, "I swear you grow lovelier by the day, my dear."

"Alas, no," she replied in mock despair. "Would that it were so. I've reached an age where I can expect each day to diminish my looks, not enhance them. What do you want from me, Ben?"

He flicked her cheek with one finger and admitted that he had, in fact, come to discuss his plans for the forthcoming season in London. "I mean to open with a new production of

Romeo and Juliet." Ben paced the length of the room, and she recognized from his knit brow and unsmiling countenance that he was about to make another meaningful pronouncement. Turning slowly and deliberately, he intoned, "You're ready for Juliet."

"But Eliza—"

"Will play Lady Capulet," said Ben firmly. "She's too old to act the heroine and you know it as well as I. Now hear me out, Florry. *Romeo and Juliet* gives us the opportunity to shine. There are processions and dances and sword fighting— oh, it'll be a damned fine display! New scenery and costumes, all the trappings." He crossed his arms over his broad chest and nodded several times. "Yes, I rather fancy you in a blood-red gown for the crypt scene. Velvet, of course."

"Of course. Will I have the same Romeo?"

"Horry has a fancy to play Mercutio."

"Perfect," Flora murmured. "He *is* Mercutio."

"Well, what do you say?"

Flora hesitated, uncertain of how best to explain what was in her heart and mind. "I'm flattered, and I do hope I'll prove worthy of your trust in my ability."

"I have no worries on that score," he said, patting her shoulder. "I expect you to study your playbook while you're in Brighton, and Madam will be happy to school you if you ask her." He ran one hand through his dark, gray-streaked hair. "She and Julie and the children will go to the seaside as planned, and Horry with them, but I must return to London. The preparations for a production of this magnitude cannot be delayed." Beaming upon his protégée, the manager predicted, "The critics will hail you as the greatest Juliet of this or any age, better than Susannah Cibber, better than Bellamy, better than Anne Brunton. Your success will be the certain means of saving the Princess Theatre."

A frown of annoyance flitted across Flora's face. "Be careful how you coax me, Ben. I'm no Louise Talley, and I won't court the kind of public attention she craved."

"You'll reap the benefits as surely as any of us." Sitting beside her on the sofa, he took her hands in his. "Only think of the acclaim, the prestige you might win for yourself." When he detected no sign of enthusiasm, he added, "And money—you'll have that too. I'm granting you a share of our profits next season."

She stared at him, letting her breath out in an awed exclamation: "Profit shares!" That mark of honor was reserved for performers of the first rank and importance.

"Lord Leafield, the newest member of our management committee, has proposed it, and I seconded wholeheartedly."

"Lord Leafield!" she echoed.

"He has purchased some of my shares in the Princess, enough to warrant his sitting on our committee."

"You sold your own shares?" This was perhaps the most shocking of all his news.

He replied gruffly, "How else could I suddenly afford *Romeo and Juliet*? We needed another investor, fresh blood—blue blood—and Leafield came forward at just the right moment. Never fear, Horry and I retain the controlling interest. We've been meeting together at the White Hart for several days now, and last night the agreement was concluded, drawn up, and signed. From the way my brother looks today, I gather he and the earl had quite a celebration after I left them."

"He has mentioned none of this to me—Lord Leafield, I mean."

"I believe he'll prove quite useful to us," Ben continued. "Because he sits in the House of Lords and has some influence politically, I'm encouraging him to sponsor a third theater bill in Parliament next year. If it passes, we can continue playing at the Princess, but without it we'll have no theater come January. The earl would be a formidable ally, so I want you to cultivate your friendship with him." When confronted by Flora's shocked face, he hastened to say, "I wasn't encouraging you to lie with him! I regard you as a sister—I expect you will be before much longer. Horry is a good deal steadier these days, for which some credit goes to you."

"I'm sure it's only because Bath offers fewer dissipations than London." Avoiding the subject of Horatio, Flora asked, "If the bill fails, what then?"

"The provincial circuit has grown wearisome after all these years—and to you, I know it well. I want a permanent home for my little band of players, preferably in London, but Bath is frequented by the gentry and would be an acceptable alternative. I've considered purchasing the Orchard Street theater."

"With Lord Leafield's money?" she asked bluntly.

He nodded. "So keep him well amused, my beauty. Cater to him in those innocent ways you women use to keep us gentlemen dancing on a string. Mind you, I like him well enough, but I'm not above exploiting him. And you shouldn't be either."

Flora's reading of the situation was that she was the one being exploited, and by both gentlemen. "You are utterly ruthless when it comes to having your way, Ben. Just as *he* is," she added bitterly.

Puffing out his chest, he said proudly, "I was born into this profession. You saw how my father spent his life toiling and scrimping, plowing every penny and shilling into his company and his theaters. Even so, he never got to London. I did, and I'm determined to stay there as long as I can." Ben retrieved his hat from a table, then faced her to say, "Julie and Madam and Horry share my dreams, and I hope you do too. I can't achieve them without your help."

His stage performances had never failed to elicit her strongest emotions, and he was no less effective in a shabby sitting room, with an audience of one. In answer to the appeal in his dark eyes, she gave him her hand. "Yes, Ben, I am with you. How could I not be, after so many years and everything the Forsters have done for me?"

After her next rehearsal, when Lord Leafield met her at the stage door, she was tempted to cut him dead. Instead, she tersely informed him that she was cognizant of his arrangement with Ben.

"Well, I didn't exactly swear the Forsters to secrecy," he replied unabashedly, placing his hand beneath her elbow to lead her around a puddle in their path.

She jerked her arm away. "I won't have anything to do with proving your cousin's marriage, so you can save yourself the trouble of asking me to go to Devonshire."

"That wasn't my intention."

"Do you mean to say that ensuring my compliance wasn't your primary object when you entered into this partnership?"

With a smile and a shrug, he admitted, "Not my primary object—more like a secondary, even a tertiary one. The theater has become my hobby of choice, a harmless diversion from the unvarying round of London seasons, Brighton summers, autumn shooting parties, and winter hunts."

Flora paused in the middle of the pavement and turned accusing eyes upon him. "How can I believe you? First you came to Bath, knowing I would be here. Then you edged your way into my circle of friends, and now you have become one of my employers."

"I was afraid you'd construe my motive as unalloyed self-interest—that's why I postponed telling you about my pact with Forster."

"What I cannot accept," she raged, "is that you used your new powers to raise my status in the company. By granting me a share of the profits, you've placed me under an obligation that I consider as burdensome as it is distasteful. I can guess what sort of favors you'll demand in return!"

She was sadly aware that the years of stage training had taught her the arts of unleashing emotion, not how to control it. To argue with him in the middle of a public thoroughfare was as rude as it was foolish, so after a pithy declaration that she was perfectly capable of reaching her door without assistance, she stalked off.

Trevor knew better than to follow.

That evening he obediently escorted his aunt to a party in the Royal Crescent, and although no new or interesting faces met his jaded eyes, one of them seemed out of place. Baron Allingham explained his sudden and unprecedented visit to Bath with a jest about escaping importunate creditors, but Trevor didn't believe him. Nor did he fail to note that his friend seldom strayed from Lady Caroline's side, to the obvious consternation of Lady Batsford. Trevor cared very little about this development; his interest in the young lady had already waned. In London she had appealed to him because of her looks, her pedigree, and his aunt's long friendship with her mother, but now that he knew her better, he was less inclined to seek her company. He didn't examine the reason for this change, and chose to believe it was because she was too young for him.

Bored with his well-born flirt and his overly obliging mistress, Trevor was increasingly aware of Flora Campion's superior attractions. His mind was so full of her that he could muster no desire for Martha Harris, whose warm body and eager caresses would not soothe the sting of the actress's sharp setdown. The violence of her wrath worried him; he feared that he'd forfeited her esteem. Would he ever discover the source of that passion Flora exhibited on the stage? He had ample proof that she was not as pure and virginal as the ingenues she portrayed, for she spoke freely about subjects that would prostrate most females with shock, and on several occasions he had seen her romping backstage with Horatio Forster like a hoyden.

He left the party early, but instead of going to Landsdown Crescent, he returned to Sydney Place with his aunt.

During the drive, Lady Ainsley made an observation about Caroline Lewes to which her nephew agreed in a voice so devoid of expression that she said, "Why, Trevor, I thought you liked her, and at the risk of provoking you, I'll add that I'd hoped it was so."

The gentleman leaned back to rest his head on the upholstery. "There was a moment—perhaps several moments— when I thought I might have met my fate, but the feeling passed quickly. I'm reluctant to wed a charming face only to cut Hugh out of the succession. I've said so all along."

Fingering the fringe of her velvet cloak, she asked, "Did you see that wild-looking young baron buzzing about her tonight?"

"Allingham? The Batsfords could do better for her, but they could do much worse, so long as they don't object to the occasional actress or opera dancer."

"That reminds me of something I've been meaning to ask you, Trevor. When we travel down to Combe Cotterell, will it be ourselves and Hugh, or does your friend Miss Campion go with us?"

"I haven't the faintest idea."

His aunt gave him a sharp look. "Indeed? This is the first time in the thirty-two years I've known you that you've admitted being less than certain about anything. I'd like to meet the woman who has reduced you to so pitiable a state."

"Does that mean you are willing to receive a play actress?"

"Lud, the Siddons woman has been everywhere, from Windsor Castle on down. Why should I object? Tomorrow I'll send a note to Miss Campion, inviting her to tea. You are her patron, after all."

Flora's nervousness waned with the arrival of a pair of footmen, one of them bearing a tray of cakes and biscuits, the other a silver urn. To be sure, their liveries were far newer than the moth-eaten ones from the stock wardrobe, but there was a comforting similarity between this scene and those she'd played on the stage. And Julie Forster's fondness for tea parties had accustomed her to the ritual.

"Is this quite as bad as you expected?" Trevor asked softly as he presented Flora with a cup and saucer.

Taking it from him she confided, "It's very much like a play, except that I've got no script to go by. I'm not sure what passes for polite conversation in exalted circles."

"No matter. Aunt Belle would think you a dull creature if you treated her to small talk, and I'd be sadly disappointed."

When Lady Ainsley resumed her interrupted discourse, she asked Flora's opinion of the new houses in the Sion Hill neighborhood. "So much building during wartime cannot be wise."

Leaving the ladies to their discussion, Trevor removed one letter from the pile on the mantel. He ripped the sealed flap, and after a swift but thorough perusal he uttered a sharp curse.

"Bad news?" his aunt asked.

"The worst."

"Do speak freely. Miss Campion, being somewhat acquainted with Hugh, already knows the worst about the Cotterell family."

Trevor handed over his letter, explaining for Flora's benefit, "It's from Linton, my man of business. His clerks continue to search through every church register in London, and as yet they've found no proof of Hugh's nuptials. Could he have used a false name?" he wondered. "But that would make the marriage less than legal and no good to me."

"What about the notice in the papers?" Flora asked. "Did nobody come forward?"

"Oh, yes," he replied bitterly. "According to Linton, two very interesting ladies presented themselves in the Strand. Both claimed to have been secretly married, but only one was in the first blush of youth, and neither could supply Hugh's name."

Lady Ainsley abandoned her inspection of the letter to glance at her nephew. "The Devonshire scheme is still a possibility, Trevor."

This comment indicated to Flora that Lord Leafield had lured her to his aunt's house that they might join forces against her, and the absence of Hugh Cotterell confirmed her suspicion. Curiously, she was not offended by his tactic and could only suppose that she'd become inured.

He had done so much—and might do more—for her and her employer and their theater. But she was less moved by Ben's theater bill or any other practical consideration than by a sudden, insane desire to give this man, so powerful and yet so helpless, what he most wanted.

She said mildly, "My lord, do not look so dismayed. I've already guessed what you are about to ask me."

"How can you, when I'm not sure myself?" he replied, shaking his head as though perplexed by his own words. "First you must acquit me of backing you into a corner, for I never meant to."

A tentative smile flickered at the corners of Flora's mouth. "I won't acquit you, though I might be able to *pardon* you."

"Then I must be satisfied," he told her gravely, "for I am a desperate man. Will you help me, Miss Campion?"

She refused to acknowledge or heed the insistent voice at the back of her mind, which warned her that she would regret her decision. At last she gave him the answer for which he had battled so long, so hard, and so unfairly. "Yes, my lord, I will help. My services are yours to command."

11

She'll not match above her degree, neither in estate, years
nor wit.

Twelfth Night, I. iii.

Giving the Forsters no reason for her sudden change of heart,
Flora begged off from the trip to Brighton and judged herself
fortunate that they neglected to ask about her specific plans.
Julie had grown bored—Bath's more distinguished visitors
were trickling away—so Ben sent her, his mother, and the two
children to the seacoast a week earlier than planned. He and
Horatio were so consumed by *Romeo and Juliet* that they
failed to notice, as his nosy wife would have done, that Miss
Campion was a regular visitor to the Milsom Street shops and
a millinery in the North Parade frequented by aspirants to high
fashion.

When Lord Leafield had called upon Flora after her visit to
Sydney Place, she was dismayed to learn that he expected her
to purchase a new wardrobe. "To entice Hugh, you really must
achieve a more showy appearance," he explained.

Though he told her to spare no expense, when she visited a
Bath modiste she had difficulty overcoming her inborn thrift
and the effects of long years of penny-pinching. After one particularly shocking consultation, she returned home moaning
about the cost of her many purchases.

Esther Drew refused to commiserate. Eyeing the parcels
spread upon the sofa, she asked eagerly, "May I open them
and have a look? If you're about to embark upon intrigue and
deception down in the country, you must let me share in the
fun where I can!"

"Fun is hardly my impression of this afternoon," said Flora
with a sigh, wafting wearily into the nearest chair. "My feet
ache, my nerves are shattered, and my conscience is giving me

fits for having spent so much of the earl's money. Today it was shoes and stockings, scarves, shawls, chemises. Then I gazed at fashion plates and fabric swatches till my head swam. All the gowns will be so dashing and indiscreet—but they may prove useful as stage costumes someday. Tomorrow I'm returning to the milliner's to try on several new bonnets, and my temples are pounding at the prospect!"

She continued to complain about the rigors of shopping until the earl gave her another, far more strenuous assignment.

After an enthusiastic description of Combe Cotterell and its views of estuary and sea, he said he looked forward to showing her around the estate. "I have a steady roan gelding that will make an excellent lady's mount."

"But I don't ride," she told him. Before he could express the astonishment she read in his countenance, she hastened to defend what he obviously regarded as an omission in her education. "A few years ago Horry and I rode donkeys along the cliffs near Brighton, but I don't recall ever being on horseback."

"Never?"

"Does it matter?"

"Well, it's true that long rambles on horseback in Hugh's company would spur on your intimacy," he replied. "And selfishly, I'd hoped you and I might sometimes enjoy a gallop together on the moor. Would you object to having riding lessons?"

"To suit your own convenience or to further your plot?" she wondered.

"Both," was his instant reply. "Bath has a riding academy where you can receive instruction—I'll pay for it, of course."

The riding lessons were impossible to conceal, so she didn't even try. As she expected, Horatio teased her mercilessly.

"Planning to leave us for Philip Astley and his Olympic Pavilion, Florry?" he asked one day. "I never guessed you aspired to perform in equestrian spectacles."

Laughing, she replied, "I'm not nearly ready for Astley's—not yet! I'm learning equitation only, nothing so exciting as bareback riding or acrobatics. Why don't you come to the rid-

ing house with me and see for yourself? This is my last day."
She was determined to mend their rift before he departed Bath.

When her final hour of instruction ended, an impressed Horatio helped her to dismount. "Florry love, you've given me an idea for a new play," he told her as they left the ring together. "An epic history of Lady Godiva. And you, my poppet, shall play the heroine."

"Oh, no, I shan't!" she contradicted him. "It would be far worse than any breeches part I can think of." Fighting the urge to sneeze, for her horse's hooves had kicked up a wealth of sawdust, she tucked the tail of her green broadcloth habit over her arm.

"Don't worry," the actor said with a laugh, "I'll use the same device Sheridan does in *The Critic*, when Tilburina describes the approach of the Spanish Armada, with plenty of 'I see this, I see that.' The property man will be in the wings, clopping away with the wooden blocks. Over the sound of hoofbeats, the good burghers of Coventry will describe Godiva's progress along the street. 'A fine seat she has,' says one. 'Mark you, I like 'em plumper myself,' says another. Although now I think of it," he added wickedly, his eyes gleaming, "mayhap we should let the audience see you ride by—they always appreciate animals on the stage."

"Are you referring to me or the horse?"

"The wigmaker's bill will be exorbitant, because your crowning glory must be fully long enough to cloak your entire figure—more's the pity."

"Lud, you sound half serious!"

"People would come in droves, I tell you. We could puff it off in the papers to make them think female flesh will be publicly exposed. It would be a sensation."

"Ben would *never* stage it, and I would seek employment in a Temple of Hymen before I'd act in your version of the tale," she said with a derisive toss of her head.

The street outside, lit by a July sun, was a blinding contrast to the darker interior of the riding academy. As the actor and actress set out for Westgate Buildings they discussed playwriting, and Flora admitted her desire to try it herself, saying wistfully, "I've a wealth of ideas."

"Someday you'll find time to write them down." Horatio cocked his head at her like a blackbird eyeing a ripe cherry. "I wish you were going to Brighton, if only to keep me out of trouble. This holiday won't be much fun without my Florry."

She prayed he wouldn't ask why she had changed her mind about the trip, for he still harbored a strong resentment of the peer who had taken up so much of her time of late.

With a reminiscent smile he asked, "D'you remember that summer in Portsmouth, five years ago? I'd hoped we might relive those days—another summer by the sea, another production of *Romeo and Juliet* before us."

"I remember how young I was, and also that I'd no business playing Juliet," she said. "This time I'm determined to do better."

Horatio reached for her hand and swung it up and down. "We'll both do better. On the stage and off."

There was no mistaking the deeper purpose behind those confident, carefree words, or his ulterior meaning. Coming to a halt, Flora confronted him. "Are you making a declaration here, in the middle of the street? You might have waited till I was home, with a sofa conveniently nearby to receive my fainting form as I whisper, 'But, sir, it's so sudden!'"

His dark face was still and serious, and he chided gently, "Don't treat it as a joke. I thought you'd be pleased."

"Astounded is more like," she told him with perfect frankness. "But flattered, too." He had been her first love and her last, and she still cared for him, albeit with no more than a vestige of the wild passion he had once inspired. "But Horry," she began, afraid of saying too much but just as determined not to say so little that he would be discouraged, "I don't think we should—"

"We shouldn't," he agreed blithely as they approached her doorstep. "Not here, not now. But think on it. Come September, when we're in London again, I'll come calling on you, a flower in my buttonhole and hope in my heart."

She laughed, but her merriment was but a fleeting thing, and vanished with him as he sauntered down the street.

*   *   *

While lying in her bed that night, Flora considered the weighty subject her friend had raised so lightly. She knew all too well the troubles she would face by marrying one of her own kind.

Ben and Julie Forster never had a marital squabble that wasn't known and openly discussed by the entire company, for few secrets, particularly domestic ones, could escape nosy, prying colleagues. Romances, infidelities, pregnancies, and quarrels—everyone was conversant with someone else's business. Nor was this uncomfortable absence of privacy confined to the Forsters' troupe. The long affair between Dorothy Jordan and her Duke of Clarence and Mrs. Siddons's estrangement from her spouse were common knowledge. Any player, however innocent or discreet, could become the target of gossip and speculation, as Flora had learned since the night Lord Leafield had first approached her in the green room.

To banish the earl's intrusive and unsettling image, she tried to imagine her future as Horatio's wife. They were incompatible in some respects—he preferred disorder while she was fanatically tidy, keeping her abode clear of the debris of her daily work. Flora stored her playbooks in a bookcase, whereas Horry left them scattered across tabletops and piled them on the floor. She would have to share his lodgings with the favorite stage properties he sometimes carried home from the theater: capes, swords, pinchbeck crowns, and chains of office studded with false jewels. In due course, when Ben relinquished the role of Hamlet to his brother, Yorick's skull would likely find its way into Horry's collection. The grisly but inevitable prospect made Flora smile. Oh, yes, she would know her share of laughter and fun, but would it be enough to make up for the loss of her precious independence or the absence of romance?

Her passionate impulses, which had lain dormant in the years since their early experiments in physical love, were not so very far below the surface—her inward response to the earl's kisses had proved it. Horatio's prowess was legendary, for he'd sampled the favors of nearly every actress and dancer in the company and was reputed to be the most considerate, if inconstant, of partners. But dalliance was an ingrained habit with him, and she didn't expect him to change his ways, not even for her. She couldn't guess how long he might be content with the role of faithful husband. Was she prepared to spend many a night in lonely speculation, wondering whose bed he was in?

After a well-attended final performance, the theater on Orchard Street closed for the season. On the following morning, the Forster brothers bade Flora a fond farewell before following their separate roads, Ben to town, Horatio to Brighton.

She had little opportunity to miss them, for the earl was filling her days with long rides into the countryside. Guiding an unfamiliar horse along city streets and across open land was more difficult than working in the indoor ring of the academy, her mount on a lead and her instructor close at hand.

Prior to his lordship's departure for Combe Cotterell, he took her riding one last time. The day was overcast; an approaching shower scented the air and made their mounts skittish.

The grand new residences springing up in the neighborhood of Prior Park reminded Flora that she must soon find a home of her own, in London. There was no room for a married couple in the Forsters' narrow town house, nor at Mrs. Brooke's, and she had no desire to lodge on one of the crowded, filthy streets of the Covent Garden district. By pooling their incomes and shares of the theater's profits, she and Horry could afford to lease a small house in some attractive rural borough like Hampstead. Chelsea might also be pleasant, as it was so near the river.

Trevor commented on her silence. "You seem entirely oblivious to the beauties around us—that herd of cows, for instance. Are you still so troubled by your impending ordeal in Devonshire?"

"It isn't that. I was thinking of London, and trying to decide where to begin looking for a house. I should have asked Ben's advice before he left Bath, although I daresay he'd have told me to marry Horry sooner rather than later and let him choose where we should live." She had spoken without thinking and immediately regretted her choice of words.

"Is a marriage imminent?"

"Possibly. I'm not entirely sure. Horry has declared his intention of asking me." She had inadvertently given the mare her head, and tugged nervously at the reins. "Five years ago he courted me and I refused him. We weren't children by any means, but ours was a rather childish affair—I'm afraid I was very young at twenty."

"Will you accept him this time?"

"I haven't yet come up with a strong enough reason not to."

"In my experience," Trevor said wryly, "brides-to-be usually simper and blush when they speak of their nuptials. Your face is distinctly woebegone, and I can't help but wonder why that should be—unless Benedict Forster is pressuring you to wed his brother. I know he looks on you as his possession, a rare and precious object which he must guard carefully until he can display you in a way that will most benefit him and his theater."

"He's my friend," she reminded him, putting up her chin. "And so is Horatio."

"Both are businessmen, first and foremost. You would be unwise to let your dependence on them rule your life."

"I make my own decisions," she maintained. "I am entirely independent."

"Are you really?" he shot back so cruelly that she recoiled. "You are a most delightful compound of beauty and intellect, and you possess the talent and sensibility of a true artist, and I detect no vices in you. Your only flaw seems to be a disastrous tendency to be too trusting where Forsters are concerned. Can't you see what is so very plain to me? Your Horatio seeks to continue his brother's theatrical dynasty. If you marry him it will be the most shameful *waste*."

"I'm an actress, not a titled lady with scores of well-intentioned suitors, like your Lady Caroline Lewes," Flora retorted. She was silenced by a bitter envy of the proud man riding beside her, whose long lineage had no blot of shame upon it. "Horry and I share a profession as well as a romantic past, and our marriage will be the most suitable one I can hope to make. If you think I'm ignorant of his wenching and carousing, you're mistaken. He may not be the most faithful of husbands, or the soberest, but he is very fond of me." Ironically, her stalwart defense of her suitor reawakened many of the doubts she'd laid to rest. "For too many years I've been preyed upon by any man seeking a mistress in the green room. At the very least, Horry can provide protection from them."

Trevor said harshly, "You can't deter your admirers by changing your name to Forster."

"Perhaps not, but my husband can depend upon my loyalty." Her cool words were as clear a warning as his had seemed a threat.

"Yet you admit you don't expect similar consideration from him. You must be very much in love."

Flora flinched. "I am a realist. I daresay you expect actors to be guided by lofty ideals, not by a desire for comfort and security. But if we were so completely lost to the practicalities of this life, we'd soon starve. Aristocrats are not the only people who marry for the sake of convenience, Lord Leafield."

After a moment of silent scrutiny, he asked, "Did you tell me of your engagement in the belief that I would release you from your pledge to assist me?"

"Of course not—I would never go back on my word!" Furthermore, she doubted his ability to call a halt: letters had been posted, the necessary travel arrangements were complete, and she'd already packed her new clothes away in their trunks. Within a few days she would find herself in the remote countryside with an overbearing earl, a toplofty countess, and an out-and-out libertine. Only Margery, in her capacity as personal maid, would represent the familiar world of the theater, from which Flora had not intended to stray.

She said waspishly, "For weeks you plotted against me, you've wrecked my peace by involving me in this contemptible charade, and now you insult me. Even worse, you've managed to separate me from my closest friends."

"Not all of them," he interrupted.

"Don't flatter yourself," she said, each word a stiletto. "Margery Prescott will be the only *true* friend of mine at Combe Cotterell!"

* * *

Esther Drew returned from a long walk in Kingsmead to find Flora stretched upon the bed, dressed in her riding habit and clutching a damp, crumpled handkerchief that bore all the signs of recent employment. After listening to an impassioned and largely incoherent account of the recent altercation, she commented, "Your anger may be justified, but he's still your patron. And very soon he will be your host."

"He's the most odious, conniving, fiendish person I've ever known," Flora ranted, kicking the bedpost. "I used to have the sense to withstand his blandishments, but since coming to Bath I've been as soft and pliant as a lump of clay, and twice as stupid. In Lady Ainsley's drawing room the other day, he looked over at me, and I wanted to help him so desperately—I would have agreed to anything he asked. *Anything*! Oh, never before have I been such a dunce!" Rolling onto her back, she glowered up at the tester. "Very likely his horrid cousin will compromise me in some hideous fashion, or else I'll break my neck falling from a wild horse."

"I didn't realize it would be so hazardous a mission."

"If Leafield's nonsensical plan does succeed, he'll have no further use for me." Realizing that her last prophecy had more of the forlorn than the furious about it, she took a moment to stoke up her wrath. "He is completely heartless."

Esther sat down upon the bed. "Is the famous friendship over, then? Or will you patch it up, as you always do with Horatio Forster?"

Suddenly Flora sat up, her face transformed by a smile. "At least his lordship won't be able to bully and browbeat me after I'm married. Call me practical and unromantic if you wish—*he* very nearly did—but I've decided to have Horry for my husband."

Esther gave her an impulsive hug. "Oh, I'm so glad!"

"With Miles coming home so soon, there's no better time for a wedding. But you mustn't tell a soul, for nothing is definite. A fine figure I should cut if Horry meets some charmer in Brighton and changes his mind."

"He won't," Esther assured her. "Unless someone warns him about what a termagant he'll have for a wife." Laughing, she ducked as a pillow flew past her head.

12

I have unclasped to thee the book even of my secret soul.

Twelfth Night, I. iv.

Flora, accustomed to the wayside public houses that had sheltered Benedict Forster's players through the years, could appreciate the superior amenities of the Castle Inn at Taunton and the Half Moon in Exeter, where she and the countess spent their nights on the road. But comfortable as the beds were, she slept no better than she had since her parting quarrel with Lord Leafield.

As Lady Ainsley's traveling chaise crossed the South Hams, a prolapse of land between the Rivers Dart and Plym, she contemplated her imminent reunion with the author of her sorrows. Her infatuation with Lord Leafield had somehow survived her discovery of his perfidy, and she feared the effects of his caressing voice and endless capacity to charm. He would hurt her again, it seemed inevitable, but the next time might effect a permanent cure.

Despite her strong determination to find fault with anything and everything connected with him—his cousin, his horses, his taste in waistcoats—it was impossible to disdain his aunt's company and conversation. His country, too, was worthy of admiration. Scattered among green hills and hedged fields were small towns with narrow, crooked streets, their quaint buildings of thatch and stone standing in the shadow of an ancient church in the Perpendicular style prevalent in the shire.

After continuing for a mile or so beyond the village of Combe Cotterell, the chaise swung sharply into a long drive. The earl's property was bounded by an estuary on one side, and its focal point was a substantial dwelling of faded sandstone, roofed in slate. The old-fashioned leaded casements of the Tudor front faced westward; rows of sash windows on a

more modern facade overlooked gardens and lawn. The two
portions were distinct yet perfectly matched, the grace and
simplicity of one age wedded to that of another, and the thorny
arms of climbing roses embraced both the old and new wings.
This was no blindingly palatial residence along the lines of a
Blenheim or a Chatsworth, as Flora had feared, but a handsome manor house, impressive in its antiquity and entirely
welcoming.

She had very little time to absorb the ancient grandeur of the
timber-vaulted hall before the housekeeper led her past a suit
of armor and up an ornate wooden staircase. "Her ladyship
wants you to have the Rose Bedchamber," the woman announced, conducting her along a corridor hung with tapestries.

Flora was delighted with her room, which lay in the newer
part of the house. Its floral theme was carried out in the chintz
bed hangings and several still-life paintings; even the tall mahogany bedposts were surmounted with finials carved in the
shape of rosebuds.

With Margery's help, she changed out of her hot carriage
habit and donned a new, floating muslin, shuddering at the
recollection of its exorbitant cost. Avoiding her servant's
shocked gaze, she rouged her lips ever so slightly and unpinned one long black curl to let it fall forward across her
breast in an attempt to impersonate a female of dubious virtue.

She went downstairs in search of her hostess and encountered the butler, who stiffly informed her that it was Lady
Ainsley's custom to rest after a journey. He then showed Flora
to the saloon, where she found an opulence that matched her
imaginings, and left her there.

The tall windows were curtained with the same pale blue
damask of the giltwood chairs and sofas, and the bright light
streaming into the room made the lusters of the cut-glass chandeliers and sconces sparkle like diamonds. The fine carpet
under Flora's feet repeated the delicate cockleshell motif of
the plasterwork overhead. A self-conscious glance into the
massive looking glass showed how dwarfed she was by the
size and magnificence of her blue and gold surroundings. Even
in the bright afternoon light, and despite her painted lips, she

resembled a ghostly figure in her insubstantial gown, with hair too black and eyes too large for her pale face.

She managed to force some color into her cheeks, but the pinched-in roses faded with Lord Leafield's entrance. In his olive coat and buff breeches, he was every inch the country gentleman, with topboots as black as obsidian and just as shiny. The riding crop in his hand indicated that he'd lately been on horseback.

"I wondered if you would come," he said as their eyes met in the mirror world. Holding out his whip, he added, "You may use this if you wish—I deserve to be punished. I was greedy, I wanted your goodwill and your assistance equally. If I sacrificed one to gain the other, I can hardly count it a victory. Can you forgive me?"

Remorse was not what she had expected from him. Less than an hour in his house, only a few minutes in his presence, and already she was under his spell. "You *are* forgiven," she answered, facing him. "And I must beg your pardon for my rudeness at our last meeting."

"I provoked you, and will take care not to do so in future. Now, my dear Miss Campion, may I have the honor of showing you my house?" The twinkle in his hazel eyes belied his formality. After pointing out several objects of note, he guided her into the adjacent drawing room. "The great Robert Adam is responsible for all this rarefied beauty. My grandfather was never satisfied with the wing that his father added, so he engaged the finest of all architects to make improvements."

He took her through the original part of the house, built in the days of the Tudors and scarcely altered. Flora's favorite room was the wood-paneled library, with a door that opened onto a grassy courtyard.

"This is the Queen's Court," Trevor informed her, and he pointed out the marble busts mounted on three of the ivy-hung walls. "Each of the royal ladies represented here is prominently featured in the Cotterell history. The first Queen Mary knighted my ancestor, who wed one of her ladies-in-waiting, and after the victory against the Armada her sister Elizabeth ennobled him by creating the barony of Hopeton. Poor Queen Anne granted the earldom to my great-grandfather a century

ago. Come and sit down for a while. It's a long drive from Exeter, and you must be weary."

She let him lead her to one of the stone benches. "Everything is delightful—not only this garden, but the whole of
Combe Cotterell."

"You've only seen a small part of it."

"Did you grow up here?"

Shaking his head, he answered, "When not at school, I was
most often at Hopeton Hall. It's a fine estate, every guide book
extols its beauty, but the house is too large to be comfortable.
My grandsire preferred it, which gives you an idea of his character." He chuckled softly. "But he never failed to bring Hugh
and me to Devonshire in the summertime. This is my favorite
place in all England and the closest thing to home."

Flora was aware of how many properties might have been
so designated. In addition to the two country seats, he owned
Leafield House in Cavendish Square, a cottage in Leicestershire used only in the hunting season, and that pretty Palladian
villa overlooking the Thames. The expense represented by
each of these establishments was beyond her ability to calcu-
late or comprehend; she had to accept his wealth as an essential part of him, like the faint cleft that marked his chin. And
now, having seen Combe Cotterell, she could better understand why he was so desperate to keep every morsel of his
birthright safe from a wastrel cousin. It wasn't the fortune or
the title he was protecting so much as the precious property
entailed upon the Cotterell heir: the vast acreages and a pair of
residences long connected to a distinguished family.

When he excused himself to change his riding dress for dinner attire, Flora remained in the quiet courtyard, watching the
robin perched atop the stone wall until Hugh Cotterell passed
beneath the arched doorway and frightened it away.

His intrusion annoyed her, but she was mindful of her duty.
She smiled with captivating brilliance and invited him to take
the place his cousin had lately vacated.

"I might as well," he answered, adding morosely that he'd
already ridden to the village and back and therefore had nothing else to do.

Flora couldn't like him; neither did she know him well

enough to dislike him, but she was conscious of his loneliness and boredom.

As soon as Lady Ainsley recovered her strength, the neighbors descended—the squire's wife, the vicar's wife, the doctor's wife. Flora, conscious of her questionable status in the earl's household, learned to escape the house. At the first sound of carriage wheels or hoofbeats she retreated to the ragged cliffs blanketed with wild raspberry, rock roses, and toadflax, or descended to the sandy beach of the cove below.

She soon discovered that her hostess was an avid gardener, as knowledgeable about plants as any botanist or professional horticulturist. "I've had a great deal of time for study," she explained when Flora walked with her through rose beds full of treasured specimens. "I spend the long, cold winter poring over books and catalogs, and in the spring, when the rain falls on Bath, I write out my plans. In summer, Trevor brings me to our Devonshire paradise to carry them out. Hand me the shears if you will be so good. Here's a bloom that wants cutting."

As did the flowers, Flora's friendship with the noblewoman flourished in the warm sunshine. When the afternoon heat drove the countess indoors for her customary nap, Flora withdrew to the shade of the Queen's Court, where she sat upon the grass, her copy of Ben's adaptation of *Romeo and Juliet* open on her lap.

In Bath, Flora had labored while the earl had been at leisure; now it was the other way around. Each morning he disappeared immediately after breakfast to oversee the cultivation of the rich red earth, and he spent hours in his library consulting his bailiff about sheep and cows and other mysteries. Hugh, in his derisive way, said his cousin spent half the day with lazy tenants and the other half with aged pensioners. To Flora's ears it sounded very dull.

The days passed quickly and pleasantly, despite her relative lack of employment. For six years she'd been ruled by the clock, cramming her pursuits into the hours between the end of daily rehearsals and the rise of the curtain at night. Her present wealth of time was a greater luxury than the servants who did her bidding, the silver utensils she used at meals, or the silk-hung bed to which she repaired each night.

One afternoon she went to the drawing room to try out the harpsichord, having already devoted herself to the business of casting out lures to Mr. Cotterell. The instrument was different enough from Esther's pianoforte to present an interesting challenge, and she was wholly absorbed in her music when Trevor charged into the room, his hair wildly disheveled and his face rigid with anger.

Lifting her hands from the keyboard, she asked in alarm, "Whatever is the matter?"

"Horses," he answered cryptically, sinking into an armchair. "And heat. *And* Hugh, whose bad management of my second-best mount has resulted in a strained hock and inspired in me a strong desire to wring his miserable neck. How cool it is here—it's beastly oppressive outdoors. Jem Wallow, my head groom, says a storm is brewing."

"Does that mean we must put off the drive to Plymouth tomorrow?"

"Oh, no, the clouds usually blow over quickly—they should be spent by nightfall. That's my hope, as too much rain would be bad for the corn. Never fear, you shall visit the spiritual home of all seafarers, and I'll show you where Sir Francis Drake finished out his game of bowls before busying himself with the defeat of the Armada."

"Giving you another opportunity to show off your superior knowledge of history?" she quizzed him. "Be warned, I may retaliate by reciting all the pertinent passages about the Spanish fleet form *The Critic*!"

Trevor laid his riding whip on the marquetry-topped table at his elbow. "What were you playing?"

"Nothing but scales; I hadn't yet begun in earnest."

"Please do."

"Would your lordship prefer a sonata or an aria? My attempt at the first would be abysmal, and the latter merely lamentable. I might manage a ballad or a sea shanty, however." When he asked whether her repertoire was suitable for mixed company, she answered, "But of course!"

Grinning broadly, he said, "You astonish me."

"Well, I do know some highly improper songs," she admitted with a naughty smirk.

Trevor stretched out his long legs and regarded the tops of his boots. "Before you entertain me, I wish you'd tell me how your flirtation with my cousin progresses."

"It doesn't."

"Why not?"

"He mistrusts me. He seems to believe that I'm here to seduce you, not him."

Trevor lifted his head. "I wish I had cause to believe that."

To cover her confusion, Flora played "The Seeds of Love," a simple ballad in a minor key.

"You've an excellent voice," her listener remarked when she finished the last of its many verses. "You might earn your living as a singer."

"Not much of one," she said with a sigh. "My voice is sufficient for a drawing room, but not up to the demands of opera or oratorio." Abandoning the harpsichord, she moved to a window and stood gazing out at the dark clouds on the horizon. As she absently fingered a drapery tassel, she said, "I hope the storms in the Atlantic aren't too rough, just enough to make the *Vestal*'s journey home a swift one."

Her wistful words reminded Trevor that the long-absent Miles was the only relative she'd ever mentioned, and he asked curiously, "Haven't you any other family?"

"Not in England. My mother's people are connected with the linen trade in Dublin and I've met them once, during our only tour of Ireland. My aunts and uncles and cousins are most amiable, but there are so many of them that I can't recall their names! And all are quite prolific—I must have fifty cousins."

"And what of your father's family? You are surely acquainted with the Campions."

With simple candor she replied, "There are no Campions. Papa was an orphan, left on the parish when he was but a few days old. His mother died unwed, after being cast off by her protector. We know only her name—not her village or any of her history."

Trevor stared down at Flora, struggling to accept that half of her ancestry was a complete blank. It was incomprehensible to one who could trace his pedigree back to the era of William the Conqueror.

"You look so shocked."

"I'm a little surprised," he admitted. "You've told me that your father was an educated man. How is that possible?"

"He was monstrously clever, and he had a powerful and wealthy patron—Lord Allingham, one of the trustees of the orphanage. You will recognize the name, for he was grandfather to the present baron, and perhaps my own grandfather as well."

"An old gentleman who dandled you on his knee when you were small," he said, remembering something she'd said to him on that long-ago day at Richmond, when he'd questioned her interest in the wild young man who prowled the theater green rooms.

Flora inclined her head. "His lordship's support of my father gave rise to a rumor that he had been responsible for what happened to Susan Campion. Whether or not it's true, he did send my father to a school near his estate instead of letting him be apprenticed to a tradesman. That's the fate of most asylum children—the lucky ones. The rest simply waste away, or end up in a workhouse. Lord Allingham saw to it that Papa went to university and recommended him for the teaching position in Portsmouth. Later he used his influence to secure a commission for Miles. But if Papa was indeed his by-blow, I derived no benefits beyond a few pretty hair ribbons and a spinning top. He never admitted that any tie of blood existed, although Mama, who was remarkably intuitive, chose to believe in it."

So did Trevor, now that he was awakened to the possibility. The symmetry of her countenance was more than noble, it was sublime. From the widow's peak to the delicate chin, every inch had been molded by a master hand. Her colleen of a mother must have been the source of the fair, pure complexion common to the Irish, and the jet-black hair, but there was also a faint resemblance to his crony Allingham. But even if she were the granddaughter of a peer, it was on the wrong side of the blanket. Not only had this child of a humble seamstress and an illegitimate instructor of mathematics been bred in obscurity, she had voluntarily compounded the defects of her lineage by going onto the stage.

When the clock chimed the hour, she said, "So late—and I haven't yet studied my part today. If I'm not more diligent, I'll be sorry later."

"Haven't you played Juliet already?"

"Yes, but so poorly that Ben, fond as he is, admits that he was wrong to give me the role. He says I'm more capable now, yet even if he dresses me in velvets and devises charming tableaux and magnificent processions, the critics will be waiting to pounce. No amount of bribery or puffery or anything else will persuade them to be kind. I might be the greatest Juliet that ever drew breath—I hope I will be—but I'm still the upstart Forster's Juliet, and many will be eager to find fault. All the attention, the notoriety—how I dread it!" This was the first time she had spoken openly of her deepest fears, for she hadn't articulated them to Ben, or to Horatio either, however close their relationship.

"You're being absurd," he told her, smiling. "Forster would never stake his greatest treasure if he had any real concerns about the outcome of his venture."

"You spoke differently at Bath," she reminded him. "And you were correct. He'd risk everything for the chance to retain his license, because keeping the doors of the Princess open is and will ever be his first object. I am but a means to an end," she concluded forlornly.

He placed his hands upon her shoulders and slowly drew her toward him. The moment Flora felt his lips on her forehead, her body quivered and she leaned closer, seeking the consolation he offered. Afterward, when she found the courage to look up, his tender expression lulled her into an utter sense of disregard for plays or parts or problems. His kiss had been as brief as it had been chaste, but it was alarming in a way other more passionate kisses had not been. Horry, she reminded herself, would have comforted her in a similar fashion; it had been a friendly gesture, nothing more.

It was just as well that she put some distance between them, for a moment later Hugh entered the room.

"Ah, Miss Campion, here you are! I was hoping that you

would be so good as to join me in a game of piquet." He
turned to his frowning cousin and asked, "Still in a rage about
that business down at the stables?"

"What? Oh, that—no, I'd quite forgotten it."

After Flora and the young man sat down at the baize-covered table, the earl watched them for a few minutes before
making what she supposed was a strategic retreat.

Presently her adversary looked up from his cards. "Would
you mind telling me what the devil you're doing here, Miss
Campion?"

"Preparing to best you at this game," Flora replied
smoothly.

"I meant what are you doing here in Devonshire, as you
know very well."

"My patron invited me to his estate for a holiday, and I accepted."

"Patron?" He narrowed his eyes. "You can't be unaware
that he'd rather be your lover."

"If so, he would hardly have brought me to a house where
his aunt is also in residence," she pointed out. "He'll seek entertainment elsewhere, I suspect. He may not find any widows
in the neighborhood, but he is surely acquainted with some
friendly cottage girl or a pretty dairymaid."

The young man threw back his brown head and produced
one of his sharp barks of laughter. "*Les droits du seigneur*?
Not Leafield! I'd stake my last shilling on the probability that
he never diddled a dairymaid in his life. He's not one to take
his pleasure amongst the lower orders. So you knew about his
Bath doxy?"

"And also about his flirtation with Lady Caroline Lewes."

"It was rather more than that, until something—or someone—changed his mind about offering for her. It wasn't
Martha Harris, that much I know."

Flora stared at him, forgetting her discard. "You don't think
I was responsible!"

Hugh hunched his thin shoulders. "I can't pretend to understand my cousin, especially lately, and most especially in his
choice of female companionship."

Ignoring the slight, Flora lowered her lashes. "And you, sir? What manner of lady is your mistress?"

"What mistress?" he asked sourly. "I can't afford to keep one. The last time I was with a woman, I had to borrow money from her. That's a pretty way for a fellow to treat his—" He broke off suddenly.

"His what?"

"His ladybird," was the curt answer. "It's damned uncomfortable, being the poor relation. By God, if I had so much as fifty pounds, I'd book a seat on the fastest coach to London and—oh, never mind."

His burst of confidence ended there, and Flora was unable to draw him out further.

The next day Trevor neglected his estate business in order to drive Miss Campion to Plymouth in his phaeton. He led her around the Hoe, the great Citadel, and Sutton Pool Harbor as scrupulously as a paid guide, all the while striving to stifle yawns born not of boredom, but from lack of sleep.

All night he had tossed and turned in his bed, recalling their conversation in the drawing room. He'd wanted to kiss away all the troubles of the Forsters' making, and any for which he might be responsible, but caution had prevented him from giving her more than that brief, brotherly salute. Nowadays she could annihilate him with one of her cool rebuffs. But that moment of tender communion had revealed a startling truth: his need for her went deeper than desire. A thorough examination of his feelings revealed that this unprecedented yearning was mingled with respect and admiration. He was weary of self-delusion, sick of the charades he had played with his glacial, well-born blondes, and more recently with the widow of Bath. As his mistress, Flora Campion would be more than a convenience. He wanted to cherish and comfort and pamper her as he had no other.

He could not overlook her deflating refusal of him in his overgrown garden at Twickenham and therefore resolved to woo her with greater finesse than he'd demonstrated on that occasion. And when he had won her at last, he would never let her leave his side.

And then, as the sun had risen behind the curtains of his bedchamber window, he also remembered the one impediment to the glorious future he envisioned.

As he strolled with his inamorata along the seawall, he wondered if she was serious about marrying the libertine actor. And however reluctant to introduce his rival's name into their conversation, he had to know her intention, so he asked with studied ease, "Have you heard from Horatio Forster since your arrival?"

"No," she replied. "But I didn't expect to. Esther sees Ben now and again and passes the news along to me, so I know Horry is still on holiday."

"I'd willingly frank your letters to Brighton," said Trevor, although it was far from being true.

"Thank you, but it isn't necessary. If Horry or Madam—and Julie most especially—received a letter with your frank on it, my whereabouts would be secret no more. And if I posted a letter myself, without a frank, it would bear a Devonshire mark, quite enough to damn me. I'll see them soon enough— September is nearly upon us." Flora's bright smile faded and she turned her attention to the gulls gliding above the sparkling water. "How long will you remain here after I return to London?"

"I haven't decided."

During the night he had devised a short play of his own, one that featured Miss Flora Campion in a leading role. In this imaginative work she was installed in a house of his providing in Plymouth, conveniently near the small playhouse where he was certain she could secure employment. It was an easy distance from Combe Cotterell, and yet so very far removed from the distractions of London: Forsters, green-room bucks, and William Shakespeare.

It pained him to think she might not be capable of loving him to the exclusion of all else, but he accepted that she was unlikely to retire from the stage at his request. As long as she consented to receive his private attentions, he would never begrudge her the public attention she was due as an actress. All would be well if only he could convince her that she must break with Horatio Forster, and soon.

13

Fly away, fly away, breath
I am slain by a fair cruel maid.

Twelfth Night, II. iv.

After riding past the villages and mills along the banks of the River Erme, Flora and Trevor paused for refreshment at Ivybridge, a quaint hamlet on the edge of Dartmoor. They consumed cups of bitter tea and slices of brown bread smeared with clotted cream, then continued their journey, turning eastward. Neither the ominous gray clouds or her fatigue lessened Flora's determination to explore the changing countryside.

Neatly hedged fields gave way to a vast, bleak landscape brightened only by the yellow patches of gorse. Rough-coated ponies, as untamed as their surroundings, lifted their heads to observe their domesticated brethren but seemed unmoved by the intrusion.

"I've always been fascinated by the moor," said Trevor when they paused beside an ancient stone chapel, "but more than a few consider it menacing, particularly when the thick mists come sweeping across Black Tor. Storms can whip up in an instant, with lightning strikes and great crashes of thunder."

Flora envied his knowledge of the land, for she'd never lingered anywhere long enough to have a sense of place.

A misty drizzle fell from the leaden sky as they raced their horses across the stark terrain. Trevor's swift black thoroughbred easily outpaced her roan, and she followed fearlessly, not caring where he led her. She felt fully alive and entirely free, just like the rabbits skipping out of her path. She turned her head to look at a group of ponies huddled together at the base of a hill, flicking their scraggly tails and pawing the earth morosely.

The roan gave a sudden, heart-stopping lurch, and to keep

from flying out of the sidesaddle she grasped his mane. He quickly found his footing again, but his gait was so slow that she forced him to halt so she could climb down. Remembering how angry the earl had been when Hugh suffered a similar mishap, she prayed that the horse wasn't lame. Trevor had already turned back; the black stallion was thundering across the soggy turf.

Trevor dismounted swiftly. "When I looked around and couldn't see you," he said hoarsely, "I thought you'd fallen." His face was pale and his eyes unnaturally bright as he approached her. "Thank God you're safe—I love you too much to bear losing you."

She responded to this declaration and the subsequent embrace by clinging to him desperately and unashamedly, returning his kisses as he bestowed them, passionately and with no thought for the consequences.

"My darling Flora," he said at last, "how very *damp* you are."

"And you."

He pressed his lips against her forehead. "I wasn't speaking idly a moment ago—that confession came from the heart."

"I'm glad you saved it until we were here." She sighed, resting her cheek against his shoulder. "I wish we might stay on the moor forever. It seems so far removed from the rest of the world—your world and mine." This comment earned her another kiss.

"We'll come back, I promise, but I must get you home before you're entirely soaked." He knelt down to inspect the roan's forelegs, and after announcing that there was no swelling at the joints, he swung Flora up into the sidesaddle.

She paid less attention to the views during the rest of the afternoon, partly because the moorland was obscured by fog and rain, but also because her senses were too disordered. From their first meeting and forever afterward, she'd been sensible of her escort's charm, his laugh, the way the tight skin crinkled at the corners of his eyes when he smiled at her, which he did for most of their journey back to Combe Cotterell.

Later, when reminiscing about her first and last ride across Dartmoor, she realized that it was by far the longest period in which the theater had been absent from her thoughts.

"Here's a letter for you, Miss Campion," Lady Ainsley announced when the actress took her place at the tea table.

Flora, recognizing Esther Drew's neat script, said hopefully, "It must contain news of Miles." But as she began reading, her face clouded over with disappointment.

"His ship hasn't reached port?" Trevor asked, looking at her over his paper.

"Not yet," she replied in a subdued voice, her eyes focused on the second page. The mantle of joy she had worn for the past few hours slipped inch by inch, leaving her naked and vulnerable.

As soon as she could she found her way to the bench in the Queen's Court and read the letter once more. According to Esther, Horatio Forster had returned to town, and she described his outrage when he learned why Flora was not at the house on Great Queen Street, waiting for him. His very name shamed her, and she was flooded with guilt. London would be a purgatory, for somehow she had to atone for her betrayal of Horry during that insane moment of weakness on the wild moor. He had been her support through many a stormy rehearsal and exhausting performance. He understood her. He intended to marry her.

But all thoughts of Horatio, London, and the theater flew from her mind when Trevor invaded her place of retreat. Watching him make his way across the damp grass, she felt as though the butterflies hovering near the foxgloves were trapped in her breast. He could never be satisfied with a few kisses and caresses, for it was his nature to demand more than she could give.

"Don't run away from me, Flora."

Poised to do that very thing, she remained seated. A clean, swift break, painful though it would be, was her only hope of salvation and self-preservation. In a false, bright voice, she thanked him for a pleasant holiday, adding, "But it is time I returned to town and my work."

"Very recently you were glad that your world was worlds away," Trevor reminded her.

Her fingers crushed Esther's letter in a paroxysm of remorse. How could she explain that she did not belong in this rain-kissed garden, or tell him that he had no place in her life? "I was mistaken!" she cried in desperation. "I realize now that what happened on the moor is better forgotten." After a moment, she said more calmly, "Mr. Cotterell also wishes to leave Combe Cotterell as soon as he can. I don't know if it's in my power—or yours—to stop him."

"His lack of funds will keep him here. Tonight the squire and his lady are giving a ball, and if he doesn't return home drunk and in debt, then I do not know him." Gently, he smoothed the faint furrow in her brow. "Why do you frown?"

"Because you always speak ill of him, and I'm not sure he deserves it. He seems so unhappy that I pity him."

"I, too, am unhappy. Please stay, Flora. You have nothing to fear from me."

"I can't be dissuaded," she told him, "and I'll be packing my things tonight, while you're dancing at the ball."

"I'm not going. I don't feel like dancing, and I have no desire to watch Hugh make a fool of himself." He gazed down at her thoughtfully. "You know, if you were more cunning you could have taken advantage of his greatest weakness. Many a man spills his deepest, darkest secrets when tipsy."

"But by the time he comes home from the village tavern, I've usually gone up to bed."

"Tonight you'll wait up for him," Trevor instructed, "and you must wear the most beguiling of the costumes you bought in Bath." When she objected, he cut her off by saying bitterly, "If you can persuade him to admit the truth about his marriage tonight, you can be on your way to London tomorrow morning."

Her strong desire to do exactly that compelled her to follow his suggestion. When changing for dinner, she selected a gown of crimson silk with a tight bodice and a décolletage that Flora, no prude, considered excessively low-cut. The rich color threw her skin into pale relief, making her hair appear blacker and more lustrous.

"You look like a Jezebel, ma'am, and no mistake." The dresser sniffed, handing Flora a pot of rouge. "I suppose you'll be wanting this, just as if you was going on in the play tonight."

"Very amusing," she said mirthlessly. "You needn't wait up for me tonight."

"Which is as good as saying I probably should!" the older woman shot back.

Throughout the meal, Trevor's eyes were continually drawn to the tempting expanse of bosom on display. As soon as the cloth was removed the ladies retired to the drawing room and he followed them, choosing the chair nearest the harpsichord. A branch of candles cast a golden light upon Flora's face, and he noted the faint shadows the downswept lashes made against her cheeks. He drank several glasses of port as she played on, apparently oblivious to his presence.

On the moor, in his arms, she had been everything he had dreamed—warm, ardent, responsive. Afterward, when she'd done her dispassionate best to convince him that she regretted her actions, he had refused to believe that she meant it. But however frustrated he was by her determination to escape him, he dared not forget the lessons of the past. Each victory over her resistance and her scruples had been costly; he couldn't afford an error of judgment now, with so very much at stake.

He was surprised when his aunt, who had been plying her needle on behalf of the parish poor, sought her bed earlier than usual. One look at her wan face told Trevor that she was feeling unwell, but when he expressed his concern, she said tartly that she merely wanted to prepare herself for a busy day of gardening on the morrow.

Flora regarded him warily, as if afraid he might pounce now that they were alone together. Hoping to calm her, he blandly suggested a game of cribbage.

Her share of the ensuing dialogue was devoted to her professional concerns, and the important role that posed so many difficulties. He suspected that she'd raised the subject as a barrier against more intimate topics of conversation. "Juliet has become your obsession," he commented, moving his peg forward several paces on the board.

"Yes, I know," she said apologetically. "But it's worrying, the knowledge that the success of our theater rests on my shoulders."

"There's more to a season than a single play." Abandoning the game for a moment, he said, "I hope Forster doesn't plan to turn you into a tragedienne—his own version of Sarah Siddons."

Shaking her head, Flora reshuffled the deck of cards. "He couldn't even if he wanted, for Mrs. Siddons and I are worlds apart in age and experience."

"True, but in my opinion your talent far exceeds hers. You have that delicate touch she lacks, a quality of lightness that enables you to excel in comic as well as weightier roles."

"Comedy is more difficult to play than tragedy," she admitted, "because timing is so important. But no matter what the play, a first night is always the same—instinct and training take over. As soon as the curtain rises, I'm like any other cart horse when it's put into harness."

"You always manage to shatter my most romantic illusions about your art," he said lightly before inspecting the hand she had dealt him.

"I always notice the most inconsequential things during a performance," Flora continued reflectively. "A rent in the curtain, or an actor whose false beard is askew. But whatever my eye may see, my mind and body are engaged with the words and stage business." Her fingers fell slack and her opponent might have read every card she held, had his eyes not been fixed upon her rapt face. "It's so difficult to describe. Haven't you ever felt a strong sense of heightened excitement, a moment of exhilaration that's somehow physical and mental and spiritual and earthly, all at the same time?"

Trevor had known many such moments with the unnumbered, faceless partners in his amours, yet none of them had held so great a promise of fulfillment as the lady gazing back at him. He murmured daringly, "Yes, I've known that feeling, although not for some time, now. Too long, I think." But his dread of offending prompted him to add a plausible elaboration. "It has been many months since my last address in the

House of Lords, the closest *I've* ever come to performing in public."

"Then you do understand."

The glow in her eyes was not in reaction to his bold words or anything else connected with him, and the cold, unreasoning jealousy that gripped Trevor was stronger than he'd ever felt for Horatio Forster, his human rival. He battled the urge to fling down his cards and prove to her then and there that there were other joys in life, a greater passion than the one performing had inspired. Had no other man tried to seduce her from her absorption in her work? As always, he shrank from acknowledging the unpleasant possibility that the theater would always be her greatest love.

She was calmly adding up her points when the sound of carriage wheels outside caused her to exclaim, "He's here!"

Trevor held one finger to his lips. "Quietly, now. After you've put away the cribbage board and the cards, sit down at the harpsichord and begin playing. I must leave you, but I'll return later." He extinguished the candles in the wall sconces before exiting through the double doors leading to the saloon.

The faint strains of a minuet lured Hugh to the drawing room, and he paused on the threshold, grasping the door frame to steady himself. "A delightful performance as always, Miss Campion."

The actress looked up from the keyboard. "Did you have plenty of pretty dancing partners?"

"I didn't go to the ball to dance, and the only partners I had were at the gaming tables. And what d'you know, that fickle creature Dame Fortune sat in my pocket all night."

He lurched into the room, seeking drink, and took up a decanter from a console table. "Claret," he sighed mournfully. "Dismal stuff, fit only to wash down dinner. I suppose Trevor has drunk up all the port, greedy fellow." After presenting Flora with a full glass, he filled one for himself and held it high. "To my good luck, to my one hundred pounds, to my journey to London—to your fine eyes, m'dear!" He downed half his wine in a single gulp.

Flora sipped hers tentatively. "Your decision to leave

Combe Cotterell seems rather sudden." Her eyes were already accustomed to the semidarkness, and she had no difficulty judging just how inebriated he was. She feared she would never be able to manage Hugh as well as she could Horry in a similar state. The actor, however much he drank, never lost his endearing affability, a quality this young man had never possessed to begin with.

"I told you I'd be only too glad to brush off, if only I had the money. Now I've got it."

"But what if the earl—"

"The earl can go to the devil! He can't keep me here, and he ain't your jailer neither. I'll want some con—congenial company on the road, something sweet to warm my bed. Come with me, why don't you? Let's run off tonight!" He stumbled toward Flora and slipped his arm around her waist. "I'll show you a grand time, it'll be my last fling. For we must part when we get to town—someone is waiting for me there, and she's my love. My gypsy, my enchantress," he sang, slurring the sibilants. When Flora tried to free herself from his partial embrace, he tightened his hold. "Jealous of my Em, are you?" he taunted. "She's a dear, delightful witch, but you—why, you are a fairy, my fair Flora." He squeezed her. "Won't you fly away with me?"

There was enough strength in him to alarm her, but her protest was stifled when his mouth covered hers. The kiss was punishing, his breath was so potent that she reeled, and when she could endure it no longer she kicked his shins.

Muttering curses, he released her. "What the devil was that for?" When she wiped her lips in a gesture eloquent of distaste, he let out a sharp, humorless laugh. "Do I disgust you? Well, that makes us even. My little Emmy is worth ten of any woman who offers herself for public sale. You're destined to become Trevor's doxy, though I can't think why he'd want soiled goods."

Flora slapped his contemptuous face so hard that her eyes watered and her hand stung from the impact. "How dare you slander me! I wish to heaven I'd never met you—*or* your cousin!"

Hugh rubbed his cheek and looked down at her, frowning.

The blow must have acted as a restorative, for none of his words were slurred when he said, "I shouldn't have said that—it was the drink talking. I've no more interest in dalliance than you, and I know you're not a slut, because you've succeeded in eluding Trev. If you do come with me, I swear I won't lay a hand upon you." With a lopsided smile, he added, "We might as well share a carriage to London, don't you agree?"

Flora was tempted, but she would not repay the earl's good faith and hospitality by running off with his cousin, however innocently. "I can't," she said on a note of regret. She looked toward the window, her attention caught by the faint glow of lamps. "A carriage is coming up the drive—who could it be at this late hour? It must be past midnight."

Hugh took out his watch. "So it is, but not by much. They're on time after all." He crossed to the window and unlatched it.

"What are you doing?"

He repocketed his timepiece. "Escaping. Did you think I jested when I said we could leave for London tonight? I arranged my journey on my way to the squire's party—I had a feeling my luck was about to turn!"

Flora went to stand beside him, her fingers closing on the fabric of his sleeve. "But you can't go now!"

"Watch me," he retorted. "I'll leave it to you to express my farewells to Aunt Belle and Trev, and my thanks for such a *delightful* visit." With a mocking laugh, Hugh leaped over the sill, landing in the shrubbery below.

"Wait, please," she begged him, leaning out of the open window. "Stay until tomorrow."

"Trust me, it's better this way. Be a good girl now, don't raise a hue and cry." He grinned up at her and said, "Best of luck, Miss Campion, in all things."

She watched helplessly as he loped toward the waiting post chaise. He turned to wave at her before climbing inside, and the moment the door closed behind him the postboys spurred their horses.

Flora gasped as a warm hand covered her own, still resting upon the sill.

Trevor whispered, "Don't be startled, it's only me."

"Go after him!" she cried. "You can chase him down!"

"It's hardly worth the trouble of throwing a saddle across my horse," he said, calmly fastening the window and drawing the curtains.

He seemed not to care about the failure of the scene he had staged, the culmination of so much plotting and persuasion, and ironically she found herself in the position of trying to convince him not to give up so quickly. "He mentioned a woman, and might admit to being married if we persevere! You *can't* let him get away from you now!"

"I admit I'd like to thrash him for the things he said to you," Trevor said grimly, "but it's less messy this way."

Her eyes widened. "Did you hear—were you in the next room eavesdropping?" His nod confirmed it, and her bosom swelled with her wrathful intake of breath.

"I'm glad you didn't go with him." He smoothed her tumbled hair.

"Don't touch me," she said through clenched teeth.

He took a small backward step. "You didn't object earlier today, on the moor. Don't you know how much it meant to me, holding you close to my heart? That's where you belong, Flora."

"You've fallen into the habit of being with me—actors and actresses almost always fancy themselves in love with each other by the end of a season, but it's a fleeting emotion. You'll find that the recovery comes very quick."

"What a rake you are, breaking hearts with your warm kisses and your cool words. Someone should put a stop to you."

"Someone is going to," she said, lifting her chin.

"I hope it will be me."

Her laugh stuck in her throat, and when it finally emerged it was a feeble sound. "Not a chance of it. Why must you make it your habit to want what you can never have?"

"Because I usually get it. Remember, not so very long ago you swore you'd never come to Combe Cotterell."

"I wish I hadn't," she declared. Not to hurt him, which she obviously had, but because she couldn't come up with a more discouraging reply.

14

No wit nor reason can my passion hide.

Twelfth Night, II. iv.

Flora, waking from a troubled sleep, began the new day as she had ended the last one, berating herself for her failure to discover Hugh Cotterell's exact relationship to the female named Emmy. Was she his lawful wife or a favorite mistress?

The young man's flight was discussed by his relatives over breakfast. Lord Leafield, outwardly unruffled, said he did not despair of uncovering the truth in time.

Lady Ainsley, whose hands shook as she poured out the tea, advised him to inform his London solicitor of Hugh's abrupt departure. She had eaten only half of her boiled egg when she rose from the table, her face deeply flushed, and admitted that she was feeling a trifle weak.

"Don't let Trevor send for the doctor," she said a few minutes later, when Flora tucked her into bed. "He already has so many patients and is busy night and day—there's a fever running through the village."

After trying to make the countess comfortable, Flora hurried back downstairs and found the earl in the library, writing a letter.

"How is she?"

"I can't say," she answered helplessly. "I'm not familiar with her constitution, and I know next to nothing about illnesses."

"Well, Dr. Snell does know." Trevor continued to guide his quill across the paper. "I'm sending a message to him at once."

"She'd rather you didn't."

"And I'd rather she hadn't fallen ill here, so far away from her Bath physician. But because she has done, she must submit to Snell's authority."

"And yours?" she couldn't resist asking.

"And mine."

Dr. Snell arrived within the hour and was inclined to take an optimistic view of her ladyship's case, saying she had succumbed to the trifling malady presently making its rounds of the neighborhood. He prescribed bed rest and sustaining broths, and told the earl he would return the following day.

When Flora wasn't needed in the sickroom she retreated to the gardens, where she dead-headed the roses with great enthusiasm. She was thus engaged one afternoon when she heard the unmistakable sound of carriage wheels and hoofbeats crunching along the drive.

She stepped out from behind the bushes expecting to see the doctor's gig or the barouche belonging to the squire's wife, not the mud-splattered post chaise that had halted before the door. She held her breath in anticipation, wondering if Hugh had returned, but the gentleman who climbed out was a stranger of middle age. Because he carried a valise in one hand and a long black box in the other, she surmised that he was an illustrious medical practitioner summoned from Bath or London.

Flora had not seen the earl all day; since early morning he had been in the fields, overseeing the final stages of the harvest. She went down to dinner wearing the most flattering of her new gowns, a pale silk the color of young leaves, and found him in the saloon with the owl-like gentleman.

Her entrance marked the end of their discussion, and that it concerned her was made clear when Trevor observed cheerfully, "Here is the lady now. Miss Campion, allow me to present Mr. Linton, my man of business."

She was troubled by the censure she read in the sharp gray eyes; the solicitor had evidently drawn his own conclusions about her relationship to his noble client. Unable to refute them by word or action, she was therefore extremely self-conscious throughout the ensuing meal. As soon as the last course was over, she excused herself.

Trevor, with a nod at Mr. Linton, suggested that they remove to the library.

When they were settled in comfortable leather armchairs by the fireside, each with a full glass of wine, he said, "Well, I can't be other than satisfied with the outcome of your investigation, though it took far longer than I imagined. You are perfectly sure Hugh's marriage is legal?"

"My clerk found the proof at St. George's Church in Whitechapel last week, and the officiating parson verified it. Your cousin married Emily Marsh, spinster, in the last week of February, and she expects to be confined in a month's time."

Trevor added up the months in his head. "Then it is as I suspected—he married her under duress."

Mr. Linton lifted his shaggy brows. "It seems not, my lord. When Mr. Cotterell learned of the young woman's unfortunate situation, he was willing to wed her."

"Really?" Trevor sipped his wine thoughtfully.

"He admitted it to me, and the lady has shown me her marriage lines. When I received your lordship's letter informing me of his flight to London, I put Bow Street on the case with instructions to search for the Marsh dwelling. Within a day they found your cousin living over a butcher's shop on Batty Street—St. George's Parish—his father-in-law's establishment. Very outspoken the old gentleman was on the subject of the Runner sticking his nose into people's private affairs."

Frowning, Trevor said, "Undoubtedly a misalliance of this sort would have infuriated my grandfather."

With a grim smile, the older man said, "Mr. Marsh is also concerned about the match being an unequal one. He is willing to pay out his daughter's dowry, which is modest but respectable, but he had the effrontery to demand that you provide Mr. Cotterell with an allowance suitable for a married couple."

Climbing to his feet, Trevor said agreeably, "He'll also need a home for his wife and child, and some form of employment."

His attorney, taken aback, said ponderously, "That is hardly a punishment for the young man's transgressions."

"You may be sure that if I put him to work, he'll regard it as such." After a pause, Trevor asked, "Have you already drawn up the necessary papers?"

The older man opened his black tin box to remove several rolled-up documents, which he untied and passed to the earl.

Without even glancing down, Trevor ripped the sheets in

half, then held them up to the branch of candles on the mantel. When the flames began to lick at the fragments, he dropped them into the empty grate. Looking toward Mr. Linton, whose face registered shock and anguish, he said, "I have no further need of them."

"But the codicil to the late earl's will states clearly that if Mr. Cotterell marries without your knowledge and consent—"

"He has my consent," Trevor said inexorably. "You have faithfully discharged your responsibilities, Linton, and for that I am grateful. But that codicil doesn't *require* that I disinherit my cousin."

"That is true," the solicitor acknowledged reluctantly. "I hope you won't regard it as an impertinence, my lord, but I should like to know what made you change your mind so suddenly."

"I doubt you would understand—I scarcely do myself. Don't think you've come all this way to no purpose, for I need to review the monies I intend to settle on Miss Campion."

"Very well, my lord," said Mr. Linton in a voice heavy with resignation, and once again he reached into his document box.

Flora was sitting with Lady Ainsley when the housekeeper announced that the earl wished to see her. Going downstairs, she made her way to the older wing of the house and found him waiting for her in the library.

Before she could guess his purpose, he hurried to meet her, enfolding her in his embrace. After kissing her with considerable thoroughness, he laughed and said, "Don't be angry, I simply couldn't help myself and didn't even try. You look so beautiful tonight, and that perfume is too, too tempting. What is it?"

"Scent of bluebell."

"You must never wear anything else."

With a glance at the open door, Flora disentangled herself. "One of the servants might have seen," she reproved him.

"By this time everyone will be at the Harvest Home." He picked up a decanter from the table. "This ought to be champagne, but we had none on ice. Will you take a glass with me?"

"A very small one." She watched silently as he poured out the wine.

Replacing the crystal stopper, he said, "Poor old Linton, he must have thought my wits were addled. For the last hour I attended to no more than half of what he told me, and I'm afraid some of my replies shocked him very much. You've bewitched me," he accused her.

"I must have done," she said, striving for a light tone, "because you haven't yet told me what you learned about Mr. Cotterell."

Trevor handed her a wineglass, half filled in obedience to her wishes, and raised his in toast. "To the happy couple—my heir and his six months' bride."

"I'm glad, for your sake—and your cousin's. But what will become of him now that he's been disinherited?"

His joviality gave way to seriousness when he admitted, "I couldn't do it, Flora. When I learned that Hugh married a Whitechapel butcher's daughter to give their child a name, it occurred to me that he possesses honor enough to be an Earl of Leafield. I've undertaken to provide them with a town house and an income. And Hugh can take the position of land agent, which has been vacant for several years, in order to familiarize him with the management of my various estates."

"It may be that your show of good faith will steady him as much as the marriage and his other new responsibilities," Flora hazarded.

"I hope so. I was always so eager to think the worst of Hugh that he was afraid to come to me with the truth. I must have put him through hell by separating him from his wife—clearly he kept silent so long to protect her. I not only understand that, I have to admire it."

She was pleased by this speech, and favorably impressed by his change of attitude. The magnanimity he was showing to Hugh and the girl he'd married would have been out of character for the proud, unyielding man who had visited her at Mrs. Brooke's house so many months ago.

"And when you hear what else I have to say," he continued, smiling at her, "you'll find that we have still more to celebrate."

This remark raised hopes she hadn't dared to acknowledge until now. But his acceptance of his cousin's marriage didn't mean he would go down on his knee to a lowborn actress beneath the very noses of his Cotterell forbears, whose portraits lined the walls.

"I must not stay," she said nervously.

His voice was low and sonorous as he replied, "I know. Our present situation is painfully awkward, but we can begin making plans. I want you to live with me, Flora. For some time I've been thinking that my villa at Twickenham will answer perfectly—I always thought it would be the perfect setting for you, as I said on the day I took you there." He stroked the nape of her neck. "To set you up in some town house, to visit you discreetly between the hours of two and five, or after the play—no, that would never do. I know you haven't had a real home for years, and I'm not sure I have either, however many houses I may own. Linton and I have just concluded a lengthy conversation about settlements—you can depend on me to be generous. I'm not asking you to give up the stage, either. You'll have a carriage of your own, so you can come and go as you please, to rehearsals and—"

"No—oh, no!" she protested. "I will not be your mistress." She wouldn't take the first step on the path to sorrow and shame, however great the temptation. "It is impossible."

"I'll do anything to make it possible," he persisted. "Before I knew you, no woman was ever more to me than the plaything of an hour. When we first met and for a while afterwards, I hardly remember how long, I didn't guess you could be different. But you are. You surpass every female I've ever known—you are my friend and my love and my whole desire. And you're mistaken if you think I crave only your body. I want your heart and your mind and your soul, in exchange for mine, which you already possess."

"You ask too much," she said sadly, "you always do. Although no man ever asked so beautifully."

His sun-bronzed face wore a grave expression. "Have there been other men? No, don't answer that," he said swiftly, "I won't pry into your past. What matters is that you will share your future with me."

Flora pressed the backs of her hands to her hot cheeks to cool the flame his question had kindled. "You are mistaken," she began, but before she could explain that she had no sordid past to conceal, he gripped her shoulders.

"Don't you love me even a little?" he demanded.

She'd never told him an untruth and couldn't do it now. "I must, or my heart wouldn't ache so. But however much I might *want* to live with you, there are a thousand reasons why I cannot."

"So many as that?"

"How would your relatives receive the news that you and a play actress were living together without benefit of clergy? Lady Ainsley would be greatly distressed, and also your uncle—isn't he a parson?"

"That needn't concern you."

"I have a brother whose feelings I must consider," she went on. "And I couldn't bear to disappoint Ben and all the Forsters."

"Surely you aren't still planning to marry that actor?"

"My mind is such a muddle I can't plan anything. Poor Horry," she sighed. "When he learns how badly I've treated him, he may not want me."

Lifting the point of her chin with his forefinger, he chided gently, "Always so quick to offer your pity to others, when I am the one who most deserves it. Forster can seal his vows to you with a marriage ring, I cannot. I won't lie to you, or hold out any false hopes, though if I ever thought you could—'" Here he paused, and whatever words he'd intended to utter died a premature death.

"I never intended to be any man's wife," she told him frankly. "Except Horry's."

"If you do marry your Horry, he'll be unfaithful in time—as I could never be—and I presume he has designs upon your earnings, which naturally I do not. But only he can ensure that respectability you crave, whereas I, loving you and wanting only to make you happy, must destroy the reputation you guard so carefully. There is no way I can prevent gossip, though I will do my very best to shield you from it."

Of all that he'd said, one thing lingered in her mind. "You

would never be unfaithful to me? Yet one day you will want some highborn lady for your wife. When Lady Caroline Lewes or her like becomes Countess of Leafield, what happens to your fidelity to me?"

"Like you, I can't think of anyone else now," Trevor responded savagely. "I'm as reluctant to wed a giddy, unformed aristocrat as you are to enter into one of those plague-ridden theatrical unions you've described to me. And perhaps, with you at my side, I won't ever care to marry. I have an heir. It's you I want more than anyone or anything." He reached out to her again, and she backed away from him. There was an unpleasant edge to his voice when he asked, "Will you stubbornly fling away your happiness—and mine? Does my love mean so little that you can refuse it outright? To speak your own language, that is cruelty of the cruelest sort, Flora."

"How dare you lay such a charge against me!" she cried. "You don't know how I feel, how much I hate hurting you. It isn't easy to reject so tempting an offer, for I've no home, almost no family, not even what you consider to be a normal life—only my independence. And just because I live in a world where such liaisons are accepted doesn't mean—has never meant—that I would enter into one myself. I don't say that it is wrong, only that it's wrong for *me*, and I've always known it. Otherwise, I might have given myself to you that day at Twickenham. It would have been so easy—then, and many times since."

He didn't appear to be gratified by this painful confession. "Do you intend to live as a nun for the rest of your days? Or will you marry a man you don't love for the luxury of building a reputation no one will believe in? Don't bother to reply," he said, having by now worked himself into a rage. "You want to run back to that precious world of yours, more dear than any human except a Forster. You think yourself independent, yet you refuse to unravel the rope of dependency tying you to that family! And if you are so misguided as to wed your Horatio, you won't be marrying a man, just a rickety theater and an empty respectability."

"That can't be worse than becoming your lordship's whore!"

Trevor's tanned face turned a sickly white. A moment later he turned his back upon her and moved toward his desk. Sinking heavily into the chair, as if all strength had been drained from his body, he said quietly, "Many months ago, when I said you could name your price if only you would come to Devonshire with me, I never dreamed that our association would be so very costly."

"It's late," she said in a distant, detached voice, "and I promised to read to Lady Ainsley. May I go to her?"

"Still running from me, Flora? It has grown to be a habit with you. Oh, very well, but at least have the fairness to consider my offer more carefully before you decline it."

It was imperative that she leave Combe Cotterell, if not that very night, which was impractical, then early the next morning. She must hasten to London, where she would begin the painful task of trying to forget she had ever been desired by such a man. If he had the power to draw from her unwilling lips the admission of love she'd never wanted to make, what else might he not win from her in time? One possible answer to that question sent her running blindly along the dark corridor and up the staircase of carved oak.

15

Get him to bed, and let his hurt be looked to.

Twelfth Night, V. i.

Although Trevor was in no mood for the harvest revels, he owed it to his laborers to make an appearance at the great barn where the common folk were making merry. By the time he arrived, the food tables had already been cleared, but the home-brewed ale and potent cider still flowed freely. While he quaffed a brimming mug, he watched the young men and their sweethearts perform a lively reel and regretted that he couldn't teach it to Flora, with whom he'd never danced.

How could he change her mind? He'd never once been able to move her with clever arguments or soft kisses. She was answerable to no one; she had no parents whose feelings she must consider and no husband—not quite yet. She was free to take a lover or refuse one as she wished.

When Trevor returned to the house, he went directly to his aunt's bedchamber. Her face was wan and pale, etched with lines of weariness and something else he couldn't define until her first words told him it was pity.

"Oh, my poor boy—come and sit down so I can talk with you."

He sat down upon the armless chair which Flora occupied when reading aloud. "She told you everything, didn't she?"

"No, only that she must go away tomorrow, and that was enough. My traveling chaise will take her to the Royal Oak at Ivy Bridge, for the mail coach to Exeter and London."

"No doubt she's grateful to you for helping her escape my wicked snares," he said dryly.

"What else could I do? I admit, I'm surprised she turned you down, which I gather she has done."

"In no uncertain terms. But she isn't an ordinary creature,

Aunt Belle, as I have discovered to my delight and despair."
After a moment of silence, he remembered to tell her about
Mr. Linton's success. "He found proof of the marriage, though
I've chosen not to make use of it, and says that my cousin will
shortly become a papa." He clenched one hand into a fist, then
slowly released it. "To think that I should envy Hugh, of all
people. It seems I've fallen victim to one of fate's crueler
jokes."

His aunt smiled. "I don't object to your being in love with
an actress, but I really must draw the line at remarks like that
one. You sound like the hero of a very poor play. If you can't
have Miss Campion as your mistress, you might consider making her your wife."

"Even though her father, however wise and worthy a man,
was the bastard child of a peasant woman? Perhaps sired by a
noble lover, but just as possibly by the village blacksmith."

Said Lady Ainsley tartly, "You won't convince me that her
parent's illegitimacy, or even the fact that she was reared in a
playhouse, are obstacles to you."

"Perhaps not," he confessed. "But if I had asked Flora to
marry me, her answer would have been the same. I can't imagine she would willingly sacrifice what promises to be a brilliant career merely to become a countess, even mine. Not that
she'll remain single forever—she wants the respectability a
husband can provide. If she marries her actor, she can have
both her work *and* her good name."

"She'll find no joy in either one if she weds someone she
doesn't love," said Lady Ainsley. "A convenient marriage
isn't always the best one."

"Yet you encouraged me to dangle after Lady Caroline."

"Only because I didn't realize you'd already lost your heart
to another," she said in defense. "Well, whatever happens, you
may always count me as your friend—and hers."

He leaned over and kissed her thin cheek. "Thank you for
that. I'm sure that in time she'll understand that my proposal is
the best and only one I can make, given our circumstances."

* * *

Flora, who was at that moment frantically opening drawers and removing her belongings, understood only the necessity of immediate flight.

Margery Prescott, when informed that they would be leaving Combe Cotterell at daybreak, accepted the lack of explanation without a blink. Seeing that her mistress wore the wild expression of a rabbit fighting to free itself from a snare before the gamekeeper comes to dispatch it, she said soothingly, "You may leave everything to me, ma'am." Then she moved to the tall wardrobe and began taking down bandboxes in an unhurried, methodical fashion.

The garments Flora had purchased in Bath hung on their pegs, a rainbow of colors: crimson silk, blue cambric, green broadcloth, summery pastel muslins. All had been bought with his lordship's gold. A collection entirely suitable for a mistress, she thought with a pang, and he must have known it all along. To keep them would be to give the impression that her principles were variable—and vulnerable.

"Pack only my own gowns," she said with apparent nonchalance. "I'll leave the rest behind—they don't really suit me."

"I'll ask the laundress to press your gray traveling habit for tomorrow," Margery offered.

"Yes, it will do very well." Flora thought bleakly that the color would suit her mood to perfection. She removed her elegant gown and tossed it aside. After putting on her nightshift, she sat down at her dressing table and reached for her reticule. "Here are vails for the servants," she said as she sorted through a selection of gold and silver coins. "A half-guinea each for the housekeeper and the butler, and a pair of sixpences for the chambermaid and the laundry woman."

Margery promised to distribute them for her.

Flora unpinned her coiffure and raked the comb through her long curls. With her hair down she looked young and lost, not at all the twenty-five-year-old actress who should have known better than to let herself fall in love with an earl. But she mustn't think of him now, or she would never sleep; she'd have an excess of time for reflection on her way to London.

Her eyes fell on the battered trunk Margery was pulling out from under the bed, the companion of many a long journey

and a symbol of her profession. Each scratch in the leather and
dent in the lid marked a move—from one town to the next,
from one theater to another. Someday, she vowed, she would
stay in place for more than the length of a season. With maturity had come a dwindling of her resiliance, and a fitful longing for a life that was less public and more domestic. Her
would-be lover had known exactly how to tempt her, with his
promise of a shared home, a peaceful refuge from the hustle
and bustle of her workaday world.

After years of practice, Margery was efficient and thorough,
and she didn't take long to finish packing. "Is there anything
more I should do?" she asked, turning down the bed.

"No, I think not."

"Good night, ma'am. Don't sit up, now, if you mean to
make such an early start."

When Flora finished combing her hair, she bent forward to
blow out the candles affixed to either side of the mirror. The
money she'd intended to dole out to the household servants
still lay beside her purse—Margery had inadvertently left it
behind.

She shrugged into her paisley dressing gown, loosely tying
the sash, then scooped up the coins. She tiptoed out into the
stone-flagged hallway, and after making several wrong turns
she finally found the narrow wooden stairway leading to the
garret and Margery's quarters. The older woman scolded her
for wandering about a drafty old pile without her slippers
when she should be in bed.

Because Flora had left her room in darkness, she was surprised to see a light beneath her door. When she stepped inside, she saw a wax taper on the mantel, which cast a soft glow
over the curtained bed and the figure standing by the window.

She let out a startled exclamation when Lord Leafield
turned to face her. He wore no coat or cravat; the collar and
cuffs of his shirt were unfastened. "Did you mean to go without bidding me a fond farewell?"

"You shouldn't be here." Drawing her dressing gown more
closely about her, she fumbled for the sash, only to discover it
was missing. She watched with increasing alarm as he moved
closer. His expression was a compound of gentle amusement

and something she didn't feel comfortable meeting in her bedroom so late at night.

"How lovely you are." Placing one hand over the inverted
triangle of brown flesh revealed by the gap in his shirt, he recited, "And yet 'tis not your inky brows, your black silk hair,
your cheek of cream—you see I've been studying the Bard,
the better to woo you."

"My lord—"

"Use my name, Flora. That is a simple means of pleasing
me, and costs you nothing."

"My lord," she repeated firmly, "there is nothing more to be
said. I am departing early tomorrow."

"Wilt thou leave me so unsatisfied?" When she stared back
at him, he smiled and asked, "Don't you know your next line,
my sweet Juliet? You're supposed to reply, 'But what satisfaction canst thou have tonight?' "

"I haven't forgotten, it is only that I do not relish your jest,"
Flora replied, not altogether certain it had been one.

"Flora." He reached out for her, pulling her so close that the
short, curling hairs on his chest tickled her cheek. His lips
touched her hair and lightly brushed her temple before avidly
claiming her mouth, and the hot kisses melted her resistance.

He pushed her wrapper away from her shoulders, and it slid
to the floor, pooling at their feet. As he touched her breast,
now covered only by the thin fabric of her nightdress, she felt
her nipple contract and harden beneath his hand. Pressed
against him as she was, she sensed the tension in his lower
body and was aware of a liquid softness in the corresponding
region of her own anatomy.

"I know how to chase all your doubts away. Let me love
you—I can show you how it will be." His tone was restrained,
reassuring, but his eyes burned with passion.

Flora knew that if she rendered the secrets of her body she
would never be free of him—but was that what she really
wanted? Confused, half faint with desire, she did not protest
when he guided her toward the bed with the rosebud finials.

Trevor removed her gown slowly and deliberately, savoring
the first, ritual unveiling of her white body. She was a thing of
beauty, with contours so graceful that she resembled a piece of

marble statuary, an artist's idealized conception of woman-hood. With increasing urgency his hands explored the straight back and tapering waist, moving ever downward. He curbed his impatience as best he could, for although it had been many weeks since he'd had a woman, this one was far too precious to take a single moment before she was ready to receive him.

Gradually it dawned on him that she wasn't responding as eagerly as she had been a moment ago. Her eyes were tightly shut; her expression was one of resignation, not rapture. "Don't be afraid," he murmured.

"I can't help it," she said feebly. "Isn't it natural—the first time?"

His hands stilled, and he stared down at her, his voice hoarse with shock as he asked, "Have you never lain with a man?"

She buried her cheek in the pillow. "You'll have proof of it soon enough."

There was no mistaking her meaning, and Trevor was too astonished to say or do anything. Flora, who had trod the boards for half a dozen years, and had lived among actors for most of her life, had somehow managed to retain her virginity. And that, he realized, explained her characteristic elusiveness and her oft-stated reluctance to become his mistress.

"You might have told me," he chided gently.

"Perhaps I would have done," she replied, "if I thought you'd believe me."

"I'll always believe you, Flora." Taking her bare and trembling body in his arms again, he said, "My past behavior has made you doubt my ability to be patient, I know, but you have my word that I won't rush you. I can wait, and my consolation will be knowing that I'll be your first and only lover. You must go to London as we discussed last night, to my villa at Twickenham, and I will join you there as soon as I can."

He hadn't really changed, Flora thought miserably, he still had that old habit of backing her into a corner and trying to rule her as it pleased him. Was he going to ordain her entire future? It was a fearsome prospect.

"I will not live with you," she declared. "I'm returning to London because my duty lies there, but I shall never, ever go to Twickenham." She freed herself from his embrace and went to gather up her dressing gown from the floor. "There's more to life than lying together in a bed," she said, covering herself. "Suppose you got me with child? I know you, you'd shut me away, you would make me give up acting. What a slur it would be upon your lordship's dignity if your child—even your bastard—were born in some backstage corner! I don't want a protector, and even if you did make love to me it wouldn't persuade me to accept your offer."

As Trevor stared at her wild, white face, he fell prey to that persistent fear that he would always be the lesser of her loves. "Go to London, then," he told her harshly, for there was nothing else he could say.

He left her without a backward glance, and closed the door behind him.

Late in the afternoon a stage coach, heavily burdened with baggage and passengers, brought Flora and Margery to the cathedral city of Exeter. They took rooms at a quiet inn, and the actress ordered tea while her dresser visited the post office to book seats on the next mail coach to London.

"It leaves at dawn," Margery reported when she returned. "We'll make London by six o'clock the next morning, provided the coachman can keep to his time bill," she announced.

"A twenty-four-hour journey—what an exhausting prospect." Flora sighed.

She went to bed early, for she hadn't slept at all the night before, and all too soon Margery was shaking her awake again. Half conscious, her temples pounding, she scrambled into her clothes and tried to revive herself with a cup of tea. She and Margery arrived at the post office in time to watch the guards load the sacks of Royal Mail. A handful of bleary-eyed passengers had gathered in the yard, most of them still yawning; some stared at the sad-faced beauty in drab gray.

During the first stage of the journey, Flora spoke scarcely a word. Her headache worsened, and just before the coach stopped at Honiton to take on the mail, she felt a twinge of pain in her lower back.

When they stopped at Salisbury for dinner, she asked her companion how much time was allowed for the meal.

"Thirty minutes, according to the time bill, but we won't go till the cross-mail comes in from Shaftesbury," said Margery, who had become friendly with the older of the two guards during the course of the journey. "Sometimes it's as much as twenty minutes late," she added. "And if you're ailing for the reason I suspect, you'd do better to stop here and spend the night."

"I own I don't relish traveling today, but the journey will be over by morning."

"When the cross-mail comes in, then we'll see if you feel like being jolted around all night long," the dresser replied. She cast a knowing glance at the wan face, and a short time later slipped away to request that the guard remove their baggage from the coach. After speaking to the landlord and engaging a room, she led Flora upstairs and tucked her into bed with a hot brick and a glass of wine, her standard and infallible remedies for the onset of menstrual cramps.

"It's come a week early," she observed dourly, as if it were Flora's fault. "And you are regular as an old clock all these years. Well, they do say as how a shock can sometimes bring it on." And she sat down to bend her gray head over the tatting she had begun in the country, where her duties had been so limited.

Flora, buried under the covers, held her body immobile in the hope that by doing so the next wave of pain would pass her by.

For a day and a half she'd kept regret at bay, but as the wine took effect she could no longer avoid thinking about Trevor Cotterell. He loved her and she loved him, even if he seemed unable to accept her dedication to her work, and her dread of scandal and disgrace. She was unable to hover in the background of his life in some equivocal position, more than a mistress but less than a wife. It might have a certain romantic appeal, but in time that would be overshadowed by her shame.

In the morning she felt sufficiently refreshed to continue her journey by post chaise, a more expensive mode of travel but one which permitted her to call a halt if she wished. And consequently she reached Great Queen Street at a more civilized hour than if she'd remained on the mail.

Her arrival was unexpected but timely, or so Esther said as she lured Flora to the back parlor with the promise of a surprise.

Two gentlemen were waiting there, both so tall that their heads—one black, one golden—nearly brushed the low ceiling.

"Miles!" Flora cried, casting herself into the arms of one tanned giant. She shed a few happy tears onto the front of his blue coat, and it was several minutes before she regained her composure. "I'd forgotten you might be here, but how glad I am to see you—and you, dear James!"

Captain James Drew tossed his young son into the air, his laugh booming disconcertingly in a house that had long been the preserve of soft-spoken females. "She *forgot*—that's hardly a sisterly welcome!"

Miles Campion, as black of hair and green of eye as his sister, said, "Esther hasn't removed her arms from her husband's neck long enough to pen the happy news to you, Florry."

"I'm glad I saved her the trouble. Oh, Miles, how brown you are." Flora laughed, reaching up to touch his cheek. His complexion, once as fair as her own, was ruddier than ever from the harsh sun of the tropic regions.

Mrs. Brooke took her squealing grandson from his proud but unhandy papa. "How do you come to be in London so soon, Flora dear?"

"Indeed, you weren't due to arrive for another week, or so you said in your last letter," Esther observed. "That's what we told Master Horry when he dined here last night."

Flora blushed to hear Horatio's name but replied serenely, "Lady Ainsley's fever broke, so there was no reason for me to remain in the country. Perhaps I had a premonition of our sailors' return!"

As always after one of their long separations, Lieutenant Miles Campion was alert to changes in his sister, but he supposed her long journey was the reason she looked pale and tired. He was more disturbed by the fact that her former bright gaiety had been tempered by time, and the discovery that two years had made her so much older.

16

Some are born great, some achieve greatness,
And some have greatness thrust upon 'em.

Twelfth Night, II. v.

Flora hoped her brother would be an antidote to sorrow, but he was not completely free to devote himself to her.

The morning after she returned to London, he and Captain Drew departed for Portsmouth, where their ship was undergoing refurbishment, and Esther chose to go with them. After two long days on the road, Flora had little interest in another trip, and let Mrs. Brooke take her place in the carriage.

She was in the nursery, watching young Hartley toddle about on his sturdy and inexhaustible legs, when the manservant announced that Mr. Forster had come to call. Flora jumped to her feet. "Which Mr. Forster?"

"Master Horry, ma'am."

"Tell him—" She hesitated, fighting her craven desire to plead a headache. "Oh, tell him I'll be down at once." Abandoning the child to his nurse, she made her way to the parlor.

After kissing her cheek in his usual fashion, Horatio commented that the air of Devonshire seemed to agree with her.

This was a kindness, for Flora knew better; her looks had suffered in recent days. "I'm sure any bloom will fade quickly enough, from the combination of London living and company rehearsals." Thinking it best to cover the highest hurdle at once, she said, "I'm sorry I concealed my whereabouts from you, Horry—I was afraid to tell you beforehand, for fear you'd misunderstand. Are you terribly angry with me?"

"I was furious," he declared. "Just ask Esther Drew, who witnessed the explosion. To be sure, she wove a convoluted tale about evil cousins and masquerades, all the while swearing up and down that your sojourn in the country was the most innocent thing in the world. Do you know what disturbed me most about her muddled explanation? The fact that Lord Leafield's aunt was there. I could no longer assume he intended a seduction, but rather, a serious courtship. So I've been practicing saying 'yes, your ladyship' and 'no, your ladyship' ever since."

"You go too far, Horry," she said crossly, for this was not a subject she cared to be teased about.

"So he didn't ask you!" Horatio crowed triumphantly.

"How could he? He's an earl, and I—well, we both know what I am."

"A simpleton. Dukes have taken wives from the playhouse, though none lately. As for earls—why, only think of Lord Derby and his high-nosed countess, who used to be plain Elizabeth Farren of Drury Lane. And Louisa Brunton has been heard to say that she would wed the Earl of Craven if he asked her."

"If you seriously believe that I could be party to so unequal a match, then you don't know me, Horry."

"I know you well enough to suspect that you haven't returned to London as heart-whole as you'd like me to believe," he shot back. "Come here, love, and give us a kiss," he invited her, holding out his arms. When Flora scurried out of the way, the spark of mockery went out of his brown eyes. "I suppose," he said at last, "that if you can't bring yourself to kiss me, then you'll find it much harder to marry me. Did your noble patron make you forget my last words to you at Bath?"

This was close enough to the truth to make her flinch. "Just because I don't indulge in the sort of slap and tickle you delight in doesn't mean—" But she hadn't foreseen into what murky depths she was plunging until it was too late to save herself.

"It doesn't mean what? That you don't care for him? That you won't marry me? Don't toy with me, Florry! You owe me the complete truth, I've a right to it, as a friend and suitor." He sat on the sofa and patted the seat cushion invitingly. "Now be a good girl and confess all, for however naughty you've been, I'm hardly the one to look askance."

Flora knew he was right. Her wicked Horatio was the only

person to whom she could unburden herself without fear of censure. And perhaps by telling her troubles, she might be able to lay them to rest, which she'd been unable to do by keeping them to herself. "You're too perceptive for comfort, Horry, or else I'm not the actress I was trained to be." She sighed.

"Poor lass, doesn't he love you back?"

"He does, that's the whole trouble," she said miserably. "He asked me to be his mistress, but I said no. Even so, I didn't stop him from—that is, I didn't stop myself. I should have, I meant to, and now I'm afraid he thinks that someday I'll say yes." She pulled out her handkerchief, having discovered that the dangers of confession lay in not knowing what would come out, or how. She resisted the strong impulse to weep all over her confessor, and after a brief dab at her eyes, she continued more coherently. "He won't wed me—my birth and background are unacceptable. There was nothing to do but part. And oh, Horry, I can't marry at all, not anyone. Not now."

"Oh, my God." If the substance of her revelation was more than Horatio had bargained for, he nevertheless responded gallantly. Taking her hands in a firm grip, he said, "I'll marry you. Whatever he did to you, no matter what results from your—your liaison, I'll stand by you."

"I'm not *ruined*," she told him, blushing.

He digested this, then said firmly, "We can be married anyway."

"You are a good friend," she murmured, giving his hand a grateful squeeze, "and though I love you dearly, I refuse."

He asked quizzically. "Must I wait another five years just to round out a full decade from the first time I asked? I've been pining for you, Florry."

"That may be, but I doubt you lived the life of a monk while you were in Brighton."

"It never mattered to you before."

"Perhaps not, but loving someone else does matter. I couldn't be comfortable in a marriage of convenience now, not even with you." She turned the full force of her green eyes upon him, silently pleading for absolution. "I don't want to risk spoiling the affection we have for each other."

"What a wise woman adversity has made you," he commented.

"I'm an arrant fool," she contradicted. "And one who appreciates your not saying, 'I told you so.' Because you did warn me. You were jealous of Leafield, and I think it was that, and a kind of nostalgia for the sort of love we once shared, that prompted you to propose marriage."

"That may be true. It makes no difference now." His jaw clenched, and then he said, "Call me jealous if you like, but I wish your first lover had been worthy of you."

"He *wasn't* my lover," she said firmly, "and you've no cause to speak ill of him."

"Don't I?" he retorted.

But he was smiling again by the time he left. Kissing her on the forehead, he said gently, "You're a brave girl. I'm sorry about everything—not just for you and myself, but even for Leafield, little as I like him. I can guess how he must feel."

Though her conscience was clearer, Flora continued to experience an unprecedented malaise of spirits. Her long stay in the country had left her rested in body, but definitely not in mind. She reminded herself that suffering built character, but what good was strength of character when one repaired to bed each night to speculate on what might have been, if she'd been able, if he'd been able—but what was the use? Denied marriage to the one man she loved and unable to love the only man she could marry, she must prepare herself for a solitary but productive spinsterhood.

When Benedict Forster came to see her in the afternoon, she seized upon the legal papers he brought like a drowning victim taking hold of a towline, and signed her name to her bond with a flourish. "I'm yours to command," she told him with a false smile.

Within a few days she was back at the theater, but even there she couldn't forget Trevor. In Bath he had often met her at the stage door to walk her home, listening patiently to her litany of professional joys and sorrows.

Her brother guessed that a deeply troubled soul was hiding beneath the mask of contentment. To Miles she seemed altogether different from that Florry of furloughs past, who had gushed and giggled about her colleagues and her conquests. Although she demanded the names of all the flirts he'd left behind in the port cities of the Caribbean, she hadn't disclosed the names of her admirers. He was aware that her present salary was handsome, but money was evidently not the source of delight it had been earlier in her career. She seldom laughed, and the songs she played on the pianoforte tended towards a minor key. And the fleeting, wistful expression that crossed her face sometimes when the Drews billed and cooed together led him to suppose that something crucial was being withheld from him, probably a failed romance.

One night she returned from the theater to find him the sole occupant of the back parlor. "Is everyone abed already?" she cried in dismay. "Never say it's *that* late!"

He folded his paper and laid it aside. "Not quite. James and Esther and Aunt Tab are dining across the street with Julie Forster. Poor girl, she never sees her family any more than we do you, so she imported some company. That was her excuse, but we all suspect her of wanting to show off the talents of her new French chef." Two pairs of green eyes met as brother and sister exchanged smiles. "You were a long time at the theater," he said. "Have you dined?"

Flora gave him a lopsided smile. "I recall Margery pushing something foodlike in front of me during a lull, but whether I finished it, I can't say."

"Poor little Florry, was your day so bad as that?"

"Worse!"

"Tell big brother all," he invited.

"Well, first there was the riot. Someone—probably Sheridan—orchestrated a nasty little demonstration outside the theater this morning, so Ben postponed rehearsal. Then I had to stay late because he arranged for one of the scene painters to make a sketch of my face. He thinks I'm going to be the rage as Juliet, and wants to sell my portrait to the booksellers and printshops. As always," she concluded, "he won me over by saying it will benefit the theater. Tell me about your day—didn't you and James call at Somerset House again? What news from the Navy Office?"

"Nothing definite," he answered, going to the fireplace to add a few more coals against the late September chill. "The *Vestal* is still being refitted for battle, and James and I may go to Portsmouth again to mark the progress. I was scanning the war reports in the paper just now, until I was diverted by the libelous descriptions of Ben in the back pages. Why doesn't he bring a suit against the publisher, for damages?"

"Controversy is good for business," she explained. "I suspect him of writing half of what appears in print and submitting it anonymously. The trick must work. Horry told me there's hardly a place to be had for the first performance, except in the one-shilling gallery. He peeked at one of the seating ledgers."

"Aren't you nervous, knowing there will be a crowd?"

"I would be if I'd the time to consider it!"

But on the day of the opening she had something more than the prospect of a full theater to overset her, and that was the news she had been dreading: Lord Leafield had returned to London.

Horatio, her informant, had attended the grand dinner he'd given for the theater's managing committee. "If Julie's new cook is true-born French, then I'm a Chinaman," he said sourly. "The food at her table is nothing like what was served last night in Cavendish Square! I lost all count of the courses—we had a different wine with each one. Oh, I should've told you at once—Leafield asked about you. I wonder he had the nerve." He reached into his coat pocket and pulled out a packet tied with a red ribbon. "*And* he bade me give you this, which I was sorely tempted to toss into the gutter."

She took the parcel without a word and carried it to her new dressing room, a refuge from well-meaning friends and curious colleagues. One of several benefits she'd derived from her promotion to leading player, it was large and had easy access to the stage, but in her opinion it was too near the noisy green room for peace. She also missed having a window. But for Margery's sake she was pleased; the dresser presided over their prestigious new quarters with a pride that far exceeded her own.

Flora sat down, her fingers shaking as they untied the gay

ribbon and tore at the paper wrapping. The object that fell into her lap was familiar: Trevor had found and returned the missing sash from her paisley dressing gown.

The sight of it revived the memories sweet summer had left with her, the strongest and most recurrent being the night a man had taken her in his arms, proving that she was capable of passions more real than those she simulated on the stage.

As she tucked the sash into her reticule, she pondered the significance of its return. Was this a sign that Trevor accepted her decision and had forgotten her, or did it symbolize his determination to win her?

On that all-important day, the Princess was a small city possessed by a frantic population as everyone from the lowliest scene shifter to Benedict Forster himself made the final preparations for the first performance. The utility players raided the stock wardrobe for trimming and lace to make themselves stand out in crowd scenes. Aproned workers swept out vestibules, planting virgin tapers in the brass sconces in the saloon and the box lobby, while the coffee-room attendants did the same in their humbler domain. At midafternoon several of the actors and stagehands left the premises in search of dinner or to down a mug or two of sustaining spirit; others ordered food and drink from a nearby tavern and ate at the theater.

A full two hours before the doors would be opened, a crowd began to form outside the pit entrance. Within, an expectant hush fell over the building. In the lamplighting room, the workers poured oil into the globe-shaped footlights. The chandeliers over the pit were lowered and their candles lit; the liveried footmen from the great households, admitted early to guard their employers' seats, gossiped together as they watched this ritual.

Flora dined in her dressing room with Sally Jenkins, whom Ben had promoted to the roles left vacant by Louise Talley. As always on a first night, the redhead was restless and talkative, and she chattered away uninhibitedly.

After clearing away the plates, Margery withdrew.

"How lucky you are to have your own dresser!" Sally sighed enviously. "I should have asked her to rearrange my

hair, but you've got clever fingers, love—can you help this
poor mop?"

Flora sorted through her finery and produced some silk
flowers to match her friend's costume. As she tucked them
into the cluster of copper curls, Sally glowered into the mirror
and muttered, "Devil fly away with Ben Forster!"

"What's he done now?"

"I had my heart set on a new short crop, but he says I must
keep my ringlets. They're such a bother to dress."

This complaint was a familiar one, and Flora nodded,
adding another sprig to the elaborate coiffure. "I've been
dressed and undressed, curled and poked and pulled about so
often this week that I feel like some stupid, helpless doll."

"But a beautiful one—that's all Ben cares for." Sally took
up a hare's foot and tapped it against the edge of the table to
remove the residue of rice powder from the fine hairs. With
studied indifference, she announced, "Fred Stafford and I have
parted."

"Oh, Sal, why?" But Flora understood only too well her
friend's probable state of mind and possible reluctance to
dwell on the rift, and she added gently, "Or would you rather
not talk about it?"

"I think I must tell someone or go mad," Sally declared. "A
week ago he asked me to marry him—that's how all the trouble began. Lud, Florry, can you believe it? I know he's hardworking, and that any musician is worth two actors, but I
won't be fettered. And then last night I told Fred my secret."
Her great blue eyes clouded over.

With grave delicacy Flora asked if she was increasing.

"No, and that's what set him off. I've been taking certain
precautions. And you needn't pretend to be shocked, because
you know perfectly well that they exist."

Indeed, Flora and every other actress knew a variety of preventive measures, and so did the bawds and the prostitutes of
the district. In murky alleyways near the theater, wizened
crones hawked foul nostrums which were guaranteed to cure
the pox or pregnancy, or both. But it was also common knowledge that these concoctions could have worse effects than in-
ducing miscarriage.

She said fearfully, "Not drugs? But they can do more harm than good—it's not worth the risk. Oh, please don't say you've been taking something dangerous!"

"Nothing so chancy, I swear. I used—well, never mind what, but it's a harlot's trick. Eliza Ellis began doing it after her last confinement, with some success, and I went to her a year ago when Fred and I began living together. I never told him—I didn't dare—till our row last night. But he was so damnably smug when he said if I were breeding I'd marry him quick enough. And I said not bloody likely." The freckled face screwed into a mask of pain. "He called me such names, Florry. Unnatural, unwomanly, depraved—I wanted to die."

"You did as you thought best."

"And you don't disapprove?"

After a moment's consideration, Flora gave the only possible answer. "I'm a woman too, Sally, and can't find it in myself to condemn you. But men are very different."

The other actress acknowledged the truth of this with a nod. "He and I had some jolly times, and I'll miss him—till the next likely chap comes my way. So tell me, how does that dashing brother of yours feel about ladies of the stage?" Sally had asked this in a jesting tone and was therefore startled to see that Flora was rather damp about the eyes. "You mustn't cry, love—I've always been too careless and selfish to keep a lover for very long. Here, take this or you'll spoil your face." And the comforted became the comforter as she pressed her handkerchief upon her distraught friend.

Using the edge of the white square, Flora carefully soaked up her tears before they could splash onto her painted cheeks. When she was done, she gave Sally a tremulous smile. "Why are all the unfairnesses in the world heaped upon actresses? Eliza Ellis and Mrs. Siddons must make room in their busy lives for everything other females take for granted—a husband, children, managing the household. Anyone who goes into keeping, like Dora Jordan or Mrs. Logan, gains an everlasting reputation of easy virtue no matter how faithful she may be to her protector."

"Well, all I know is that I want to live my little bit of life away from the theater on my own terms. And you must feel

the same," Sally hazarded, "if you've turned Horry down
again. He's already dangling after that little dancing girl, the
one with the lisp."

"Is he? I hadn't noticed."

"That nor anything else."

Flora shrugged, offering no explanation or excuse.

"That's how I knew he'd proposed to you again—every
time he does you refuse him and he has to find a new flirt."
The redhead rose and shook out her frothy blue skirts. "I really
must go, or your dragon Margery will give me a scold for imposing too long. You're a dear to listen to my troubles, and if I
can ever return the favor—" There was no glimmer of response in Flora's still face, so Sally said brightly, "Remember
that wager we made at Bath? I have it on good authority that
Mrs. Jordan is engaged at Drury Lane for the season, so you
owe me a guinea. And mind, don't you and Horry eat all of the
first-night supper while we comedians slave away in the
farce."

On her exit she nearly collided with the callboy, who stuck
his gray head through the door to say respectfully, "You're
wanted, Miss Campion, Miss Jenkins. 'Tis time for His
Majesty's hymn."

The two actresses immediately joined the flock of players
hurrying toward the stage. Through the curtain they could hear
the last frantic cries of the orange women out front, calling,
"Apples! Oranges! Bills of the play, good sirs, a penny
apiece!" When the orchestra struck up, the green draperies
began to rise slowly, and the assembled company sang "God
Save the King." The audience chimed in, more or less rever-
ently, and afterward the stage was cleared of all but Horatio
Forster, who spoke a lengthy prologue on behalf of the players, begging the indulgence of the audience.

Flora waited in the wings on the prompter's side, drawing
deep breaths to calm herself. Her feelings were, as ever, contradictory: she was impatient to begin acting the part she had
studied so long, and she wished she might turn tail and flee the
premises. And then there was no more time for rational
thought because Madam Forster, as the Nurse, was calling for
Lady Juliet. Flora's entrance inspired an approving murmur

punctuated by a few catcalls from the partisans of the royal patentees, but these protests were quickly hushed.

She had studied the part all summer, had lived and breathed it during the rehearsal period, and now the legacy of her own impossible love gave her new insight into her role. She had a strong empathy for any lovers who struggled to overcome the odds stacked against them by an unkind fate, and because her own personality was many-faceted, so was her Juliet's. As the play progressed, the character matured before the eyes of a captivated audience, which saw first the winsome child, then a trusting adolescent in the throes of first love, and finally the strong-willed woman, capable of fighting for her happiness and doomed to fail.

At last came Ben's great moment, the funeral procession. The focal point was Juliet's flower-bedecked bier, carried aloft by mourners and followed by grieving Capulets, the Nurse, the Friar, and lesser characters. Bringing up the rear were three dozen utility players decked out as priests, monks, nobles, and Veronese peasants, all singing mournful dirges. This magnificent display received a thunderous ovation; even John Kemble's supporters, inured to spectacle, were greatly impressed.

The volatile groundlings demanded to see the entire parade a second time, shouting boisterously, "Again! Again! Give us the funeral!"

The manager, fearing some damage to his theater if he failed to appease the mob, stepped forward, bowed once, then ordered his players to begin the scene again.

Afterward the pit settled down, and the play continued on toward its melancholy end. The suicides of the lovers evoked sobs and sighs, and all but the most case-hardened wept as Flora, clutching her happy dagger, made her final speech, and sank to the ground. She did so thankfully, although Mr. Warren, on whose bony form she had fallen, was a most uncomfortable resting place. Never before had she been so glad to expire: her entire body throbbed with weariness, and the oppressive heat made her feel faint. The oil-filled footlights, candle-lit chandeliers, and roomful of tightly packed bodies had turned the theater into an oven. When the curtain fell on the final tableau, a unified sigh of relief went up from players and public alike.

The corpses sprang to life and Flora faced her next trial, speaking the epilogue. She stepped past the curtain and walked out to the stage apron to begin the rhymed speech Ben had composed, but she could scarcely hear her own words.

The gentlemen in the pit shouted her name; the ladies wept and waved their handkerchiefs. Those few souls brave enough to contradict the consensus of opinion found themselves in danger of being attacked. Flora curtsied as they heaped their noisy adulation upon her, and as her ears grew accustomed to the din, she could hear Ben hissing from the wings, "Make your obeisance to the boxes. The pit be damned, woman—curtsy to the *boxes!*"

Obediently lifting her heavy crimson skirts, she presented herself to the boxes on her left and sank downward, rose, and turned to the right. And then she saw him.

He sat in the forefront of his stage box, the man who filled her thoughts, the one she had last seen when he had left her bedchamber. As the Earl of Leafield leaned slightly forward, his face was the only recognizable one in that sea of hundreds. Assailed by paralyzing memory, she scarcely heard Ben's next command—he was telling her to curtsy again. Although she tried to obey, her legs failed to respond to her will.

The roar of the crowd was more deafening than ever; it seemed that the mob was about to hurl itself at the stage. She turned a beseeching face toward the prompter's box.

The two Forsters rushed forward to take her by the arms. As they led her off the stage, she cast one final, fleeting glance at Trevor.

Suddenly Ben was kissing her and Horry was kissing her. Strangers approached her and addressed her in reverent tones, as though she were some royal or divine being, while she wondered vaguely who they were. The mob had chased her down, right into the green room, and she forced herself not to shrink as it pressed closer. Not even Margery Prescott could fight her way through to drape the shawl across Flora's shoulders, and Miles was trapped on the far side of the room, with Esther and James beside him.

Ben squeezed her waist. "Ah," he said gleefully, "Dick Sheridan and John Kemble will be green when they hear of this night's work. My beauty, you have conquered London in a single night—not since Siddons's appearance back in 'eighty-two has there been such a debut. We are made, Florry, *made*!"

Her answering smile was weak, for nothing that had occurred since the fall of the curtain seemed real to her. The crowd's approval had been gratifying, but its animal intensity had frightened her. Now she felt isolated from everything and everyone around her, cast adrift in a sea of well-wishers. It was as if she still played a part, albeit an unfamiliar one; she knew none of the lines and was wholly unprepared for her next cue. She wasn't Juliet any longer, but she wasn't Flora either. While the foppish Mr. Skeffington fluted his extravagant praises at her, she told herself that this was a dream and tomorrow everything would be as usual.

Only Trevor, who finally forced his way through the crush of bodies, seemed real to her. Or was he? Because when he bowed over her hand, his handsome, golden face was inscrutable, his voice detached.

"My felicitations, Miss Campion."

"Your lordship is kind," she replied in a wooden voice, thinking that his kindness was of the cruelest sort.

"I wish you joy in your great success." And with that he moved on to speak to the Forsters.

Her unconscious hopes had gone unanswered: she'd received no smile, not a glance, no proof whatsoever that she still held the preeminent place in his heart. In the very moment she had counted on him to put everything in its proper perspective, she was made to feel more alone than before.

And it was his coolness, not weariness, not her frayed nerves, not even joy in her great triumph, that caused Flora Campion to cry herself to sleep many hours later on this, the most important night of her career.

17

How the hours have racked and tortured me,
Since I have lost thee!

Twelfth Night, V. i.

"Your trick, Trevor," said Mr. Rupert Harburton, announcing what was perfectly obvious to the rest of the gentlemen at the card table.

Lord Edgar Fleming commented, "Well, one does visit Brooks's Club fully expecting to be fleeced."

"The game isn't over," his mentor reminded him gently.

"Faith, it might as well be," huffed the viscount who was Trevor's partner. The most rotund member of the foursome, he was seated in the place that had formerly belonged to Charles James Fox, leader of the Opposition. A substantial portion of the baize-covered table had been cut out to make room for the late Whig's ample belly.

After inspecting his remaining cards, Trevor led with a trump.

The Great Subscription Room of Brooks's was lit by a single chandelier hanging from the center of a curved ceiling. The pale green walls were almost bare of ornamentation, save for an intricate plasterwork border and a tall mirror above the plain mantel of marble. Four oval frescoes of gods and goddesses were situated high above the doorway and windows, in order that the gamesters should not be too much distracted by Zucchi's artistry.

When the rubber was played out, the gentlemen ordered another bottle of claret and discussed the news of the day.

"Did any of you invest in the new gaslight scheme?" Lord Edgar wanted to know. "Every soul in London has put his money in Mr. Winsor's Light and Heat Company. I heard that twenty thousand shares have been sold."

Said Mr. Harburton, "Perhaps someday Trevor will illuminate the interior of his theater with gaslight."

"It would be an expensive undertaking," Trevor replied, "and Benedict Forster has talent enough for spending my money as it is."

"The Prince of Wales is a fond playgoer—has he visited your theater?" asked the Viscount.

"Not yet. He's been too busy amusing himself with Lord Hertford's wife."

Trevor's companions laughed.

While they continued talking among themselves, Trevor's thoughts returned to the theater—indeed, these days they seldom left it.

Last month he had attended the initial performance of *Romeo and Juliet* in a fever of excitement that had nothing to do with the play. And that night he discovered that fortune had turned her back upon him, being so busy showering her bounty upon the Forsters and Flora Campion.

Still smarting from the blow London's new darling had delivered in Devonshire, he had no choice but to watch helplessly as she was buoyed up out of his reach by the tide of fame. When the reviewers praised the purity of her speaking eyes and crystalline voice, or acclaimed the natural spontaneity of her performance, or said that the pathos of her playing made butchers weep, he felt equal parts pride and pain. Whenever he walked to his club, her likeness gazed back at him from the bow windows of the print shops in Oxford Street and St. James, and the serenity of her painted smile wounded him.

He wondered if she was haunted by the memory of the brief time they had lain so close that their hearts had beat as one. Or was she too busy congratulating herself on her near escape from an entanglement that would only be a nuisance to her now?

From the night of her debut she had been the latest sensation. She was mobbed on the streets. Nobles and nobodies alike fawned upon her. She had only to be seen wearing a particular color for it to be immediately seized upon and sold by dressmakers as Campion Blue or Pink or Yellow. A variety of portraits and flattering representations of her as Juliet sprang up in shop windows, and London's most reputable artists lined up to limn her newly famous face. Tributes from the conservatories and hothouses of the elite found their way to her door. Flower markets did a brisk trade in the campion; the humble wildflower had risen to sudden prominence, and was cultivated for the adornment of the buttonholes of the beaux and bucks who professed themselves in love with the actress.

Richard Sheridan reportedly coveted her for his theater, as did John Kemble, and both had made overtures in the belief that the contract binding her to the Princess Theatre was only as durable as Benedict Forster's disputed license. Drury Lane and Covent Garden were suffering a period of artistic sterility; their offerings were mediocre at best, for their famous actresses had grown older and stouter by the year and increasingly improbable in youthful roles.

Each time *Romeo and Juliet* was announced, the long lines outside the Princess Theatre attested to its popularity; everyone wanted to view the theatrical triumph that was on all lips. Trevor went there every time Flora performed and always visited the green room to pay his respects. Her manner was polite but stiff, and there was always some other gentleman at her side, usually Ben Forster, often Horatio. Sometimes her brother was in attendance, a tanned seaman whose resemblance to Flora was startling.

Lord Edgar's piping voice cut across his thoughts. "I say, Trev, did you know the rich Miss Drummond was married to Peter Burrell a fortnight ago, in Edinburgh?"

"Was she indeed? I thought it was a settled matter between her and William Beckford."

"It quickly became unsettled," the younger man reported. "He wrote a letter which she considered impertinent."

"Marriage is most definitely in the air," said Mr. Harburton in his dry way as he poured another glass of wine. "I've heard of half a dozen betrothals this week. The betting book lists Frederick Byng and Lady Harriet Cavendish, as well as Lord Henry Petty and Margaret Beckford."

"Wish I'd laid a few guineas on the chance that Allingham would become engaged," said the viscount glumly.

"It's not too late to bet on the marriage, Reggie," Rupert

Harburton comforted him. "The odds are against his ever getting to the altar."

Trevor, who had been tracing his finger across the green baize, looked up to ask, "Has Allingham got himself engaged again?"

"To Lady Caroline Lewes," his friend replied.

The viscount's fat face puckered in a grin. "I want to know what'll become of his ladybird, the bosomy little actress at Drury Lane."

In a proprietary voice, Lord Edgar announced that Miss Louise Talley had availed herself of his protection.

This development surprised Trevor far less than the news of Baron Allingham's betrothal. The whole world was pairing up, he thought gloomily, and before long he would be the only one alone.

Leaning closer to Trevor, Lord Edgar muttered, "Don't look now, but Sheridan has just wandered into the card room. Louise tells me he's vexed by your partnership with Forster."

A few minutes later Mr. Lumley Skeffington delivered a similar warning when he emerged from that room.

"You here, Leafield?" he cried, throwing up his hands in an extravagant show of dismay. "Be forewarned—old Sherry may cut you dead, he's that annoyed over this third theater business. Not that he thinks such a bill could ever pass," he concluded, patting his scented tresses with a slim white hand.

Knowing the dandy to be a good source of theatrical anecdotes, which interested him far more than society gossip these days, Trevor invited him to join the party.

Mr. Skeffington confirmed the persistent rumor that John Philip Kemble was interested in Miss Campion. "He knows he can have her if Forster loses his theater—unless Sherry and Tom King snap her up first. They desperately need to boost the profits of Drury Lane. Mrs. Jordan has been ill lately. At least Kemble can rely on Grimaldi the Clown—his decision to repeat *Mother Goose* at Covent Garden has brought the crowds, as I'm sure you know."

Trevor did know, for Benedict Forster had been very careful not to play his triumphant tragedy on the same night as the

popular pantomime. "And how does your playwriting proceed?" he inquired politely.

"Very well indeed," Mr. Skeffington replied. "I'm hoping
the piece will be acted at Drury Lane in the New Year. It's
called *The Mysterious Bride*." He turned his perfectly coiffed
head as a party of gentlemen passed through the doorway link-
ing the card room and the Subscription Room. "Here comes
Sherry. No offense intended to your lordship, but he mustn't
see me talking with you." He rose from his chair with ludicrous haste, and Trevor watched his spindly form mince across
the carpet toward the manager of Drury Lane.

Richard Brinsley Sheridan, his face flushed from drink, his
clothes disheveled, grasped Mr. Skeffington's frail arm. Before making his exit he cast his eyes toward the table where
his old friend Fox had held court until a year ago.

A hush fell over the tables as the gamesters waited to see
how he would react to the Earl of Leafield's presence.

"Damned meddlesome fellow," the illustrious playwright
and politician declared in a loud voice before permitting Mr.
Skeffington to lead him away.

"It might have been much worse," Rupert Harburton commented as he and Trevor descended the iron-railed stairway
leading to the entrance hall. "By tomorrow he won't even remember that he insulted you."

Laughing, Trevor replied, "I wasn't offended, for he spoke
the truth—I *am* a damned meddlesome fellow. And I wouldn't
challenge old Sherry to a duel even if he had been sober."

"I'm glad to hear it," his friend said seriously, "for I hardly
think this new hobby of yours worth risking your life."

While waiting for the porter to fetch their greatcoats, Trevor
expressed the hope that Mr. Harburton would support the bill
he intended to sponsor. "I already have an ally in the House of
Commons who has agreed to introduce it, but I rely upon you
to help him win votes from other members. Sheridan's position is strong, for even those who dislike him most won't want
to alienate him. He's close to the Prince of Wales and is still a
power in the Opposition."

"I'll do what I can," Mr. Harburton assured him. "But you
must know how unlikely it is that such a bill will pass on the

first attempt. The Theatres Royal have held their patents since the time of Charles the Second, and their proprietors are far better known than your friend Mr. Forster."

"I never said he was a friend," Trevor protested. "But I do share his belief that another legitimate theater would benefit the public. The success of the Princess thus far has proved that London can and will support one."

"Save your arguments for the House of Lords," the other gentleman advised him. "You'll need every one of them."

It was Trevor's painful duty to attend the meetings of the theater's governing body, where virtual strangers erected barriers that would forever close Flora away from him. As much as he resented it, he had no right to protest their methods or their motives. By allying herself with the Forsters, Flora had empowered them to organize her life.

Wild-eyed Horatio brandished her name like a weapon, treating Trevor with a coolness that told him Flora had confided the most pertinent and personal details of her weeks in Devonshire. The actor's churning resentment was palpable, but Trevor empathized; they stood on common ground now. Although his former rival currently shared his lodgings with a ballet girl, there was no evidence that Flora's pride was hurt by his defection. She remained on the best of terms with her friend and seemed not to resent the fact that he'd found consolation elsewhere.

Trevor sought no consolation. He'd made his bed; it was an empty one, and he knew why. "Noblemen don't marry actresses," he'd said once to Lord Edgar Fleming. Those lofty words, spoken so many months ago, constantly echoed in his mind. If he had offered matrimony to her at Combe Cotterell she might have accepted, and though theater-going London would be the poorer for it, his own life would be complete, not the empty, aching thing it was without her. The irony was that if he could wed the lady he loved, which he was now so desperate to do, the scandal would be far greater than if he made her his mistress.

Trevor began meeting Flora socially at parties to which they had each been bidden, he as guest, she to provide entertain-

ment. The same elegant ladies with whom he had danced and
dallied for so many years were eager to receive Miss Campion
into their homes, for she lent a cachet to the genteel parties of
the autumn's Little Season. Benedict Forster, forever at his
protégée's side, showed her off proudly, accepting compliments on her behalf and seeing that she exchanged a few
words with the most influential persons in the room.

At one particularly lavish soirée in Hanover Square, Flora,
exquisitely gowned in white silk, delighted the assembled
company with a heart-wrenching recitation of Portia's "Quality of Mercy" speech. Afterward she was so besieged by admirers that when Trevor approached her, she looked toward
him in desperate appeal.

Pushing his way past the crowd, he placed his hand beneath
her elbow. She recoiled at his touch, but he paid no heed and
conducted her out of the crush before releasing her. "I think.
you'll be more comfortable in the supper room," he said. "It is
quieter."

As she accompanied him downstairs, Trevor kept his eyes
on her profile, which still looked as if it had been carved from
the purest, whitest marble. Her fine eyes were faintly shadowed by fatigue—Forster was working her too hard. Or was it
some other trouble that disturbed her? he wondered, guiding
her to a refreshment table. Flora rejected all of the many delicacies there, but he persuaded her to try a strawberry ice.

They sat down on an empty sofa in an alcove, and he
watched her toy self-consciously with the dessert. In hopes of
easing the constraint between them, he embarked upon an
uninspired commentary on the various notables present, but
she cut him short to ask how Hugh Cotterell was faring.

Taken aback by this unexpected query, Trevor replied,
"Mrs. Cotterell presented him with a fine daughter several
weeks ago, and Hugh's besotted with both. I had a letter from
my aunt today," he went on. "Bath has heard of Miss Campion's great success, and she counts herself fortunate to have
met the lady whose name is on all lips. She hopes you enjoy
your good fortune." After a short pause he asked, "Do you?"

"The money is agreeable," she told him. "Miles has been
very provoking—he won't let me share a bit of my new wealth

with him. But I did make a contribution to the orphans' asylum at Portsmouth in our father's memory."

Trevor knew her salary down to the penny—and her share of profits—and marveled that she should judge them sufficient for her own support, much less a pet charity's. "Rumor says that the Prince of Wales has become the latest of your admirers, and without yet having seen you perform. Ben Forster must be elated by the prospect of receiving support from that quarter."

"I don't refine too much on the possibility." Flora shook her head, and the silk flowers woven among the dusky curls trembled. "If His Royal Highness should visit our theater, it would be a slap in the face to his papa, by whose authority Drury Lane and Covent Garden hold their patents."

"Ah, but our prince is known to show favor where it will most displease the king. He's a byword for filial opposition. Forster had best refurbish his Royal Box—I'm sure it will soon be filled with Prince Florizel's portly person."

With an unexpected show of humor, she laughed. "More fodder for the caricaturists, then! I can just imagine what they'll make of it: 'Prinny at the Princess,' or 'Florizel visits Forster's Folly,' or some such. It's worrisome enough to see my face peering back at me from shop windows, but the satiric cartoons are the worst aspect of success. No," she said meditatively, lapsing back into her pensive mood, "that's not true. *This* is the worst by far."

Surely, he thought in anguish, she wasn't alluding to his presence. How much of this kind of torture did she think he could bear? "This?" he repeated hollowly.

Looking him full in the face for the first time, she explained, "These dreadful parties."

Trevor was caught off guard by this hint that her experience as a public figure had not been as roseate as he believed it to be. "Come now, you must like being the rage."

Waving an agitated hand, she said, "In some ways it has been gratifying. But—oh, I don't know how to explain."

"I wish you would try," he prompted.

"Uncivil as it sounds, I'd rather be at home with Miles. Now that England has declared war on Denmark he expects his sailing orders to come through, and time is precious. But Ben must drag me out to put me on display like some tame beast in a menagerie. People stare and exclaim and all but pat me on the head—it's the whole Master Betty phenomenon all over again. He was another nine days' wonder, and where is he today?" she asked, her voice filled with anxiety. "Playing in the provinces, basking in the fading glow of a former fame. He, who had the advantage of youth, cannot hope to retrieve his position in the London theaters. Sensations have a very short life here."

He said soothingly, "You do yourself a great disservice, describing your success as a nine days' wonder. The whole of London agrees that you are a Siddons and a Jordan combined, and those ladies have enjoyed a lasting reputation in their separate spheres of tragedy and comedy."

Flora shrugged. "I'm hardly human any longer, I'm just a— a creature, a draft horse, plodding along in harness, working for my supper and a kind word at the end of the day."

Once he had been amused by her favorite analogy; now it saddened him.

"Last week I attended a party much like this one," she continued, "and after I sang my songs and recited my speech, Ben led me around the room to curtsy and smile. He introduced me to Lord Dartmouth, the Lord Chamberlain, and presented me to our hostess. She handed me a purse with such a condescending air that I wanted to shrink, one so heavy that I knew it held a great deal of money. Fifty guineas—an outrageous sum for a few ballads and a poem! But against a fee twice the size, I'd have chosen a quiet night at home with my brother." She glanced down at her plate to find that the strawberry ice had melted away entirely, so she swirled the pink liquid with her spoon.

"I never guessed this was so difficult for you," Trevor confessed, wondering how he could have been so mistaken as to believe she reveled in her fame. "I might have known. I *should*, knowing you as I do." Determined to cheer her whatever the cost to himself, he said bracingly, "You'll grow accustomed in time."

"I hope I won't have to. Every day I wake with the expectation that all this fuss will come to an end. It's so distracting—although very good for business," Flora added, catching sight of her mentor on the other side of the room. "Ben is beckoning—pray excuse me, but I must go to him." They both rose, and she smiled up at him uncertainly.

"Thank you for rescuing me. And you've been very kind to sit here and listen to my troubles. It seems I hardly have time for any of my old acquaintances these days, there are so many new ones."

Acquaintance, Trevor repeated to himself as she drifted away. It was the unkindest cut of all, for with that remark she had driven the knife in, and twisted it, too. But remembering the strain she had exhibited, he was inclined to forgive her. Her face had pleaded for assurance that she was something more than a curiosity to be viewed by anyone who paid the price, be it a shilling for a gallery seat or fifty golden guineas for a ballad. Look at me, her eyes had mourned, I am that thing I refused to be for you. I have prostituted myself, and for what?

The party had dwindled down to a few conversation groups when Flora noticed her employer's absence. When she went in search of him, a footman informed her that Mr. Forster and Mr. Skeffington had departed a quarter of an hour earlier. Concealing her displeasure at being abandoned, she asked him to secure a hackney for her, that she might go home.

She was standing in the vestibule fastening her velvet opera cloak when the Earl of Leafield materialized at her side for the second time that evening.

"Forster has already gone," he told her. "When Skeffington invited him to a tavern to discuss his latest play, I offered to escort you home. My coach is waiting."

Flora's hand trembled as she worked the silken frog at her throat. "That won't be necessary," she replied, instantly suspicious of his knowledge of Ben's plans.

"But it is," he declared triumphantly, "because I intercepted the servant and said you'd changed your mind about the hackney. The famous Miss Campion must ride in style and comfort, you know, and my carriage offers both."

Flora experienced a familiar outrage, but she permitted him to lead her out of the house and down the front steps.

As soon as his footman closed the carriage door upon them, she loosed her pent-up fury. "You *arranged* for Mr. Skeffington to lure Ben away, didn't you?"

"Yes. I needed to speak with you once more, in private."

"I've nothing whatever to say to you," she warned him.

He reached for her hands, gripping them tightly as he said, "I don't care a damn for your foolish attempts to give me the cold shoulder—did you hope they would keep me away? You act as if you despise me, when not so many weeks ago you were lying naked in my arms." She gasped, but he continued ruthlessly, "I've noticed that you're not entirely yourself, and I want to know the truth. Are you regretting the decision you made that night?"

Her rigid control dissolved. Pulling her hands away, she hid her face in them, her shoulders shaking as she gave way to sobs. She'd never wept in his presence and feared he would think the worse of her for it. In a broken voice she said, "I am not pining for you, and there's nothing wrong that a good night's rest won't cure."

"Is it Horatio Forster? Are you so unhappy because he deserted you?"

Flora lifted her head so swiftly that the hood of her cloak slipped back. "Horry did *not* desert me. He offered for me, even after I told him how I had compromised myself. But I refused," she said on a sigh. "I would have been wrong to marry him."

"Because you still love me."

"Please don't make me say that." She ran her tongue over her lips nervously, then said, "I don't belong to you and never will, there is no lasting connection between us. I thought I proved that by leaving Combe Cotterell."

"And were you trying to prove it to yourself or to me?" he wondered aloud.

It was a question she dared not answer; if she told the truth he could twist it around to his advantage. "I don't have the strength to fight you any more, honestly, I am so tired of—of troubles and tribulation. Please, Trevor, lay the past to rest. If you care for me, leave me alone."

"To stand aside and let you ruin both our lives seems to me a very poor way of demonstrating my love."

"My life isn't ruined."

He leaned back against the cushions and said thoughtfully, "No, not in the same way as mine. You have your work, after all. I have nothing."

Flora very nearly cried out that there was no consolation for her either, that she loved him desperately, that she was sorry. But it would be most unfair to push him away with one hand and cling to him with the other, although that was precisely what she wanted to do. "I think," she said faintly, "that you should consider leaving London."

He did not reply at once, and appeared to be thinking over her advice. "Perhaps so," he said as the carriage turned sharply into Long Acre.

Flora reached for the leather strap, but not in time to prevent herself from falling against him. His arm closed around her waist, and even as she asked that he release her, her treacherous body thrilled at his touch.

Dipping his head down to hers, he said, "If I must go, at the very least you owe me a proper good-bye kiss."

But it was a most improper kiss he had in mind, as Flora discovered an instant later. She might have expected that, if he'd given her the opportunity to think at all before he drew her into his embrace. She felt dizzy—whether from his passion or her own, or from the odd sensation of being made love to in a moving carriage, she knew not. The certainty that she was better off apart from him evaporated at his touch; there was no happiness except within his arms. And when his caresses grew even more intimate, her response was stronger than her strongest vow not to be swayed by them. Unable to evade his insistent hands, she sighed as they stroked her into a welcome state of oblivion. When his fingers teased the bare flesh of her neck and shoulders, and the portion of her breasts exposed by her low-cut gown, she murmured softly, but not in protest.

Suddenly, with no warning, he pulled away. "Are you playing games with me, fair cruelty? How can I believe you really want to be rid of me when you offer such eloquent encouragement?"

Flora was too ashamed to reply. Now that she was separated from the heavy warmth of his body, she felt cold again despite the thick cloak she wore. Looking toward the window, she saw that they were on Great Queen Street; she could see Mrs. Brooke's house.

The conveyance came to a full stop, and without even waiting for the liveried footman to open the door, she wrenched the handle and pushed with all her might, uttering a wretched jumble of good nights and thanks and apologies.

During his solitary drive home Trevor leaned his head against the velvet cushions, inhaling the faint scent of bluebell that lingered in the air. He smiled when he recalled Flora's sighs of pleasure at his kisses, then frowned over her suggestion that he leave town. Not now, not yet—and never alone, he vowed.

A tiny white object lying on the seat caught his eye: one of the silk flowers she'd been wearing in her hair, which had been dislodged by his roving fingers. He picked it up and held it gently between his fingers, careful not to crush it. It was as pale and vulnerable as the lady he loved, and like her, it belonged to him.

18

A solemn combination shall be made of our dear souls.

Twelfth Night, V. i.

At the weekly meeting of the management committee, Lord Leafield had taken a firm stand against the manager's plan to stage *Hamlet* and had prevailed upon him to revive *In Praise of Parsimony* instead. Ben Forster agreed, saying that would whet the public's appetite for Flora's next portrayal of a tragic heroine. When she heard the story, it confirmed her suspicion that he would do anything to appease the earl, his powerful and noble ally.

The demanding repertory, particularly *Romeo and Juliet*, had left her depleted and depressed, and how Trevor had guessed it was a mystery to her. But she was grateful to him, and welcomed the respite from the rigors of Shakespearean tragedy.

The managers of other theaters, with Sheridan overtly luring them on and Kemble doing so covertly, had declared open warfare on the Princess Theatre. The furor was so great that Lord Dartmouth had been heard to say publicly that until the Forsters closed their Folly and left London, the city would know no peace.

Controversy swirled around Flora yet somehow never touched her. Her sense of isolation was exacerbated by the very people on whom she depended to cure it. Horatio, now that he had his dancing girl, was the most casual of cavaliers. Esther Drew was wholly occupied with her James and their child. Miles might have been her greatest solace, but with the outbreak of the very real war against Denmark and Portugal, he expected to return to his ship at any moment, and she didn't like to burden him with her problems.

After a considerable period of soul-searching, she finally

admitted to herself that all joy in her work had been taken away, bit by precious bit, by her fame.

The critics admired her in comedy but cried out for her to essay Desdemona or Cordelia, or heaven forbid, Cleopatra. If she must act Shakespeare, she countered whenever Ben raised the subject, let it be Kate the Shrew, or feisty Beatrice, or wise Portia. Certainly the adoring public cared not what she did so long as she appeared on the boards regularly. Her cult of worshipers came from all walks of life, and included the Prince of Wales. Before dashing down to Brighton, he had attended one of her performances with Lady Hertford, the latest in a succession of middle-aged royal mistresses.

Success had shaken up her quiet, ordered existence like nothing else had done since the night when Lord Leafield entered her life, changing it so dramatically. In reaction to her present lack of peace and privacy, she looked back fondly on the nineteen happy years she had passed in comfortable obscurity in Portsmouth. Before embarking upon a stage career she'd lived quietly and contentedly with her parents and Miles, looking to her friends and her books for fulfillment. And because her present was so distasteful and her future uncertain, she tended to regard her uneventful youth with nostalgia.

One night, after a well-attended performance of *In Praise of Parsimony*, Ben Forster called his actors and actresses into the green room and announced his intention of purchasing the Orchard Street theater in Bath.

Groans of dismay went up from the assembled company, and Mr. Warren, a young firebrand who had won modest accolades as Flora's Romeo, jumped to his feet. "Bath!" he cried scornfully. "Well, I shan't be going back there. It would be demeaning for me—for *all* of us—after our great success."

Madam Forster eyed him with disdain. "There is nothing demeaning in honest work, sir. And if you would take a walking part in a London theater over a leading role in the provinces, I think very little of your ambition."

Her son Ben stood in the middle of the room, observing the disappointment in the circle of faces. "There's no cause for alarm," he said, "for the Lord Chamberlain hasn't yet decided about our license. But even if he rules against it, I pin my hopes on the third theater bill which our illustrious patron, Lord Leafield, will introduce after Parliament's Christmas recess."

Flora, who had not intended to speak, suddenly looked up to ask, "If we go to Bath, what will become of the Princess? You do still own it, after all."

"And I'll retain my ownership of the property, in the expectation that we will return after the theater bill passes. Another manager has expressed an interest in leasing it for his productions of burletta and pantomime."

Flora accepted Madam's usual offer that they share a hackney, and as it traversed the fog-shrouded thoroughfares, she reflected on her earlier sojourn in the spa town and reminded herself that she had found it exceedingly pleasant. But would she like it so well in gray wintertime, without Trevor there to make her laugh?

When they reached Great Queen Street, Ben helped the two ladies out of the carriage. Flora hurried toward Mrs. Brooke's front door and had reached the area railing when she heard Ben Forster say, "Just a moment, Florry—I'd like a word with you."

Pausing on the pavement, she waited for him, shivering in the cold.

"I forgot to explain earlier that the lease of the playhouse will be drawn up to include the stock wardrobe, to save us the expense of transporting everything back and forth. If, as I suspect, our company will be somewhat diminished by the first of the year, we won't need it: leading players provide their own costumes. I know you and Sally and Eliza store your personal properties in the wardrobe room, so you'll want to be sure they're removed before the theater closes."

"Oh, Ben, I'm so sorry about everything."

In a valiant approximation of his confident manner, he replied, "It's only a temporary setback. Now listen, my dear, for I have some advice for you. I think you should make a tour of the provincial circuits before joining us in Bath so you can reap the benefits of this season's success. Mrs. Siddons and her brother Kemble make their progress every year to keep themselves solvent, and you would do well to follow their example. A tour to the Birmingham, York, and Edinburgh circuits, and some smaller towns would be lucrative, and I want you to consider it."

"Oh, very well," she replied, immediately shoving the unwelcome notion to the recesses of her already troubled mind.

One Sunday afternoon Flora set out for the theater dressed in a serviceable gown of faded kerseymere, ready to take on the difficult task of sorting through her belongings. The timeworn building wore a deserted, shuttered look on this day of rest. The elderly doorkeeper, who also acted as custodian, shook his grizzled head when she stated her purpose.

" 'Tis a sad thing when a body is forced from home, Miss Florry." He patted her shoulder, adding, "But Mr. Forster will find us another one, eh?"

As she made her way to the topmost level of the building, she was struck by the echoing silence. She missed the sound of hammers from the carpentry shop and the gentle swish of brushes in the scene-painting room. This was the Sabbath, of course, but those who labored high above the stage weren't overly assiduous in their observation of the holy day. Nothing could have said more clearly that the season was drawing to a close.

She went directly to the musty loft where many of the costumes and stage properties were stored, and found the usual jumble of court gowns and doublets heaped upon the floor. Crowns and scepters were piled unceremoniously in a corner, and a few stray pieces of furniture—beds, chairs, chaises, and plaster statuary—were scattered among the mounds of clothing. Her own costumes were hung neatly on pegs in one corner; Margery had wrapped some of the rich velvets and brocades in holland cloth as protection against dust and sunlight. And there she found a pair of wooden trunks.

Flora knelt down on the floor. Taking a key from her reticule, she unlocked the first one and lifted the lid.

On top lay her fans, covered in tissue. One had sticks of ivory, intricately carved; the other was spangled silk. She laid these aside and burrowed deeper through a collection of shawls, too threadbare to be worn in company but acceptable for stage use. Next she found a ballgown that she'd recently acquired from a dealer in secondhand clothing. It was almost new, a shining russet tabby; Margery hadn't altered it yet. Working her way through to the bottom of both trunks, she reviewed every scrap of lace, each petticoat and set of whalebone stays, with a view to what could be discarded.

But not even a pair of cheap, gaudy buckles with paste brilliants could be cast aside, for Horry had given them to her in the heyday of their affair. Something else that should have been rubbish was the sunshade with a broken ferrule. Long ago she had almost destroyed it in a fit of pique, but it might be mended. And how could she throw away the lovely, hand-worked apron she had worn so often as Miss Hardcastle in *She Stoops to Conquer*? There was a rent down the front, not even Margery's nimble fingers had been able to repair it, but it was a precious reminder of one of her favorite roles. Each item, however battered or useless, was a treasure. These trunks held memories, which had outlived the applause at the end of long-forgotten performances. Their contents were tangible proofs of her unremarkable, unalarming past.

When she had replaced all of her keepsakes, she climbed nimbly to her feet. The light was fading—it was December now, and the days were as short as they were chilly.

She had intended to return home, but instead she wandered around the room, picking up some of the familiar props. She unsheathed a dagger and stabbed the air several times, then tried on a pinchbeck crown. She wrapped herself in robes of office and tried on wigs, wistfully recalling the childlike joy she had known at the outset of her career.

The sound of footsteps along the corridor was thunderous in the sheer silence of the place, and she looked up from a stack of playbooks expecting to see the custodian.

Trevor stood in the doorway. "I came seeking you," he explained, looking about curiously as he entered the loft, "to discuss a subject of considerable importance. I went to Great Queen Street first, but the manservant seemed to think you'd come here. That old fellow downstairs let me in. Have you a fancy for gloom today? This place is a tomb."

"I know," she said. "I had to see to a bit of packing—a necessary evil when one faces a move."

"Ah, yes, Forster's return to Orchard Street."

"But have you heard the latest? He's encouraging me to undertake an extensive tour of the provinces before joining the company at Bath. According to him, I should journey the length and breadth of England, and enrich myself in the process."

"And will you?"

"I haven't decided what to do. I'm afraid my choices are rather limited."

"So it seems," he agreed. "If you don't return to Bath with the Forsters, you must desert them for the endlessly insolvent Sheridan of Drury Lane, or those tragedy-loving Kembles of Covent Garden."

She shook her head, saying adamantly, "I won't turn traitor. Anyway, Ben has spoiled me so, I'd never be comfortable with any other manager." How strange, she thought, that she was able to talk to him so candidly, without any constraint. Was it because they were at the theater, where she felt most at ease, or simply because all this time she had shunned him she had also missed him terribly?

He was a constant in a changing universe, and a certain source of comfort. "Help me, Trevor," she pleaded. "Hold me." And when he gathered her close, she hid her face in his chest.

"I wish I *could* help you, Flora, because I want you to be happy. But having learned the unwisdom of meddling in your life, I know you'd oppose any remedy I suggested."

At that moment she couldn't remember why she had been so perverse. Sorrow had softened her, and loneliness compelled her to reach out rather than close herself off from him. Whatever else he might have wished her to be, and however often his actions had disappointed her, he cared for her. And curiously, the man who had so often wrecked her peace was now giving it back to her.

Contact with his solid, familiar form changed her despair into a desire for greater intimacy, and she wound her arms around his neck, melting against him. He kissed her deeply, and she parted her lips for him, permitting his tongue to brush hers. And when he shifted his hands from her waist to her hips, drawing her still closer, she felt the proof of his arousal through the fabric of his breeches.

He looked down, his voice a rough, urgent whisper when he asked, "What am I to do now?"

She glanced uncertainly toward the jumble of furniture against the wall.

"You are sure, Flora?"

"Yes—oh, yes."

Sweeping her off her feet, he carried her over to the one unobstructed piece, an ancient bedstead. Its mattress seemed to contain more dust than down, for as they lay down upon it a great cloud rose to choke them.

Flora helped him remove his coat. He pulled off her slippers, then untied her garters, slowly peeling away each stocking. He unfastened the cloth-covered buttons at the neck of her gown with agonizing deliberation until he had bared her breasts.

All sensation seemed to reside wherever his lips and fingers moved across those parts of her body that were exposed. She felt no shyness or shame, and gloried in his appreciation of her as he lifted her long skirt. His hands caressed her legs, trailing their way to the place where her desire was centered.

Tugging at his hair, she forced him to look up. "Promise me," she begged him.

"Anything, dear heart."

"No expectations, Trevor. No demands this time."

"As you wish," he assured her.

The gentle stroking ceased while he unbuttoned his breeches.

She gasped when he entered her, her muscles tensing involuntarily as he eased his way past the barrier nature had raised against his sex. Murmuring endearments, he rocked against her, and her discomfort gave way to new, increasingly pleasant sensations. She arched upward to meet him, until, at the moment of his violent release, he drove himself against her.

She supposed he would turn over and go to sleep—that was what the dressing-room chatter had taught her to expect—and she was elated when he continued holding her. It seemed so

natural to lie so close, to feel the furious pounding of his heart
and rise and fall of his chest beneath her cheek. Soon she slept,
her head pillowed against his shoulder.

Flora woke with a start to discover that the wardrobe room
was completely dark.

When Trevor looked over and she smiled at him, he required no further encouragement. Her pain was less this time,
and vanished completely in the heat she felt deep within her as
he urged her into that mystical rhythm once more. The tiny
flame leaped and danced, growing higher and hotter, and she
cried out as a powerful tremor rocked her body.

Afterward she lay beneath him, stunned, and he murmured
against her ear, "You make me very happy, Flora, even when
you most confound me."

Her fingers plucked the damp fabric of his shirt, separating
it from his warm skin. As she held her sated lover in her arms,
she thought that her favorite poets had been too restrained in
their descriptions of fulfillment, and her female friends too
matter-of-fact. In the past she had believed that to give herself
to him would be nothing short of ruinous, but she didn't feel
ruined. She felt more serene than she had for many months. If
he should beg her to live with him as his mistress now she
would say yes, and gladly.

Her rapturous expression faded when she became aware of
peculiar sounds coming from outside—tramping feet, shouts—
and she lifted her head. Then, in fearful recognition, she sat
up, saying, "Listen, do you hear? It's coming closer all the
time—they're coming *here*!"

"Who?" he asked, perplexed, when she left the bed. "Who's
coming?"

Looking down from the window, she saw that a crowd of
people was marching down the dark street, slowly but purposefully. Many of them brandished cudgels; some carried
torches. "It's a mob," Flora announced woefully.

As soon as he discovered that she spoke the truth, he
grasped her arm and dragged her back, saying furiously,
"You've no business standing there—they might throw stones
or bricks. Has this happened before?"

"Last spring some hirelings threw rotten fruit and vegetables. And we were disturbed again just before the first performance of *Romeo and Juliet*. But these men are carrying torches, and they must know the theater is deserted on Sunday. Do they mean to burn it down?"

"They're making a token protest against Forster, nothing more."

"But why now, when he is about to have everything taken away from him? It's too unfair!"

Running his fingers through her tangled curls, he murmured, "There, there, I'll go down and—"

"Don't leave!" she begged, clutching at him.

"Only for a moment, just long enough to send the old man to Forster's house to warn him." Trevor led her back to the bed, and gently forced her into a sitting position. "Stay here—and don't you dare go near that window again. I'll be back before you can finish putting on your stockings and shoes."

When she heard him vaulting down the wooden steps, she swallowed past the lump in her throat and began to look for her discarded garments. But her hands were shaking so badly that she could hardly tug her stockings up, and tying her garters with nervous fingers was a nearly impossible feat. She was almost done when a brick sailed through the window, shattering the pane. It landed with a thud on the wooden floor, only a few feet away.

When Trevor returned, she was standing near the door. Pointing at the brick, she said ferociously, "See what they've done—the knaves!"

"I sent the doorkeeper for Forster and some reinforcements—officers from Bow Street, I hope. The crowd is fanning out around the building, from the front entrance to the back courtyard. I took the precaution of barring the stage door."

"So we're trapped. Oh, I do hope Ben comes soon." She was startled when he suddenly reached out as if to fondle her breast. "Trevor, not now!" she cried in admonition, before realizing he had done so in order to fasten her bodice. She pushed his hands away. "I can do it myself. Try to find my shawl and my bonnet."

He returned with the requested articles. As he shook them, a glistening shower of glass shards fell to the floor. "There must be some other outlet from the building that our visitors don't know."

Thinking quickly, she said, "Downstairs, the machine room beneath the stage. There's a door to the side yard. The scene shifters go there to drink and smoke during the performance. The yard is connected with a back street, and it leads directly to Drury Lane."

"I think we should at least make an effort to get away," he said, holding out his hand. "Come along and show me how."

She gripped his hand tightly as they descended the three flights of rickety stairs to the stage level. The auditorium was an empty cavern, and her whisper seemed loud in the black silence when she told him, "We'll have to climb down through the stage floor, it's the only way. The large trapdoor must be pushed open from below, but the grave trap lifts up by a cord." She showed him the smaller of the two doors in the planking.

A slight tug was sufficient to lift the trap, and they gazed down into the seemingly bottomless pit. "How much of a drop is it?" Trevor asked.

"Only a few feet. Just a short jump for you, your legs are so long." She watched him ease his body into the narrow opening, and begged him to hurry. "There's a ladder lying on the floor somewhere," she said, peering down at his disembodied face.

"I can swing you down more easily than I can find a ladder in the dark."

Flora sat down at the edge of the hole in the floor, and was about to push off when she cried suddenly, "My trunks! I can't leave without them!"

"You most certainly can," Trevor told her sternly. "Come along now."

She took a deep breath as she pushed off the edge, as if plunging into water. His strong arms closed around her, and her feet grazed the floor. She couldn't see him—her eyes had trouble adjusting to the greater darkness beneath the stage—but she felt his breath on her cheek when he asked her, "What about those damned trunks is so important that you would risk your neck?"

"Only my whole past." She sighed.

"Which way to the door?"

"It's in the far wall. But go carefully—heaven knows what machinery and stage pieces lie between here and there." Together they groped their way past pulleys and gears, canvas flats and coils of rope, making a tentative progress until at last they stood on the other side of the door. The world was dark and damp, and a freezing drizzle fell from the sky.

With a shaky laugh, Flora said, "I feel as if we've escaped from the Tower of London—or the Bastille."

"You *look* as if you have," he retorted. "What a pair we make. Ah, here come the reinforcements—it seems Forster is depending on his brother and the navy for assistance."

She looked around and saw Miles and Horatio running down the alley toward them.

"Flora—thank God you're safe!" her brother exclaimed.

"But where's Ben?" she asked.

"He and the Runners went 'round to the pit entrance," Horatio told her. "You shouldn't be here, Florry—best let Miles take you home."

When Trevor offered to escort her, Miles glowered at him. "What the devil are *you* doing here? My lord," he added belatedly and with scant respect.

"I have made a substantial investment in this theater, Lieutenant Campion," was the nobleman's calm reply.

The feeling of communion Flora had known when she and Trevor had lain together was slipping away. Other men who loved her had closed around her, cutting her off from him. "Perhaps it would be better if I go with Miles, Lord Leafield," she said, her eyes pleading for his understanding. "You and Horry will both be needed here."

He bowed, his courtly gesture at odds with the state of his attire: his cravat was in wild disorder and his dark coat defiled by dust and grime. Watching his and Horatio's retreating figures, Flora regretted not giving him some small token of assurance—a parting glance, a tender smile—so he would know how reluctant she was to be separated from him.

"What *was* he doing here?" Miles repeated as they proceeded down the alley.

"I was sorting through my trunks and—and he helped me."

"You had an assignation," he accused.

"We did not," she defended herself. Chin high, she said, "You've spent the whole of your life on the seas, and very soon you will sail away again. Do you feel you have a right to dictate to me during your few weeks on shore?"

"You're my sister, Florry, and you can't be so muddleheaded as to think I'll let some damned nob seduce you right under my very nose!"

"Really, Miles, there's no cause for histrionics." Not yet, she added silently, knowing how outraged he would be when she found the courage to admit that she intended to live with the earl.

When they reached the house on Great Queen Street, Flora evaded Esther's and Mrs. Brooke's questions and closeted herself in her room, refusing Margery's offers of tea or toast or hot bathwater. She changed her petticoat and carried it over to the washstand, knowing she would have to remove the rusty stain her innocence had left upon it. The dull ache between her legs was another reminder of her initiation, but she suspected it would soon subside.

The dresser eventually coaxed her out with the news that Horatio Forster was downstairs and wanted to speak with her.

"The theater still stands," he informed Flora when she joined him in the parlor. "Some windows are broken and a door or two will have to be replaced, but otherwise the Princess is in one piece."

"What do we do now?"

"Continue our work. Would you expect my brother to do anything else? Business as usual tomorrow—we'll begin with the reading of Jones's new play. Ben intends to have it ready for Christmas week. An armed watchman will be posted at the theater for the remainder of our stay in London, at Leafield's expense. I must say your admirer has his uses."

"You mean he has money," she said bitterly.

"His high and mighty lordship is damned officious where you're concerned," he continued. "You should've heard him—

wouldn't let me go home to my dinner till I'd promised to bring you those blasted trunks. They're out in the hall, and I had the devil of a time getting them in and out of the hackney."

"What a good, sweet Horry you are," she declared, standing on tiptoe to kiss his swarthy cheek. "Your errand is accomplished, and now you may go home to your supper—and your pretty dancer."

But before the actor departed, Miles Campion demanded a private audience.

Flora was in the hall instructing Frank about where to stow her treasures when the two gentlemen emerged from the back parlor. Their serious faces and heavy, portentous tones warned her that something was amiss, but they left the house before she could demand an explanation.

19

Be not amazed. Right noble is his blood.

Twelfth Night, V. i.

Flora hurriedly buttoned her thick, fur-trimmed pelisse, an extravagant purchase and a necessary one. The weather was typical of early December, gray and cold, it was Monday besides, and the morning would be devoted to the first reading of Mr. Jones's new play. Only the deeply ingrained habit of half a dozen years of punctual attendance prevented her from sending a message that she was ill. She picked up her muff, and after a swift glance in the mirror to be sure her furry hat was on straight, she left her room.

Miles was waiting for her in the vestibule, his large figure obscured by a greatcoat. Drawing on his gloves, he announced that he was escorting her to the theater, his tone indicating that he would not yield to any argument.

As they followed Great Queen Street toward Drury Lane, she essayed a laugh and said, "Lord Leafield is hardly likely to abduct me between here and the theater, Miles."

"I mean to make quite sure of that," Lieutenant Campion told her, each angry syllable a puff of vapor hanging in the frigid air.

What could he mean, she wondered, trying to keep up with his brisk stride. Knowing that gentlemen held strict notions about protecting the chastity of their female relations, she could only hope he was too prudent to resort to violent measures. She hated concealing the full truth of her relationship with Trevor Cotterell, but if she chose to enlighten Miles while he was in such a disagreeable mood it wouldn't be a question of a gentlemanly duel, but out-and-out murder.

The green room was less crowded than usual; several players had already sought places at other theaters. When Ben

Forster and the playwright entered, the actors and actresses took their places at the table. During the scramble for seats, Flora asked Horatio what he and her brother had discussed the night before.

"Nothing that need concern you," he answered dismissively.

"Don't try to bamboozle me," she whispered furiously. "I realize Miles is suspicious of Tre—of Lord Leafield—and if you reveal a word of what I confessed to you upon my return to town, I'll never speak to you again! A duel would be the ruination of his career, you know that. Trust me to tell him what he needs to know in my own good time."

For the rest of the day her recurring vision of her brother—or her lover—felled on the field of honor made her insane with worry. As soon as she was home she sat down to pen a hasty and only marginally coherent note to Trevor, begging him to come to her. Perhaps if they faced Miles and admitted their attachment, a dangerous and potentially fatal confrontation could be averted.

Miles would simply have to accept her decision to become Lord Leafield's mistress. And if he accused her of depravity, she would simply point out that as an officer in the Royal Navy he had no cause to look down his nose at her, for corruption and cruelty were by far more prevalent in his world than hers. He might be surprised by her choice to live in sin, but she couldn't believe he would be shocked, especially when she convinced him that Trevor would be a kind and generous protector. Everything a woman could ask would be hers—except a marriage ring.

Mrs. Brooke's manservant carried her letter to Cavendish Square, but he brought back no reply.

"Surely you gave it to someone," she said impatiently.

" 'Twas the porter took it, toplofty as he could stare," Frank grumbled. "His lordship is leaving town, and granted most of the servants a holiday."

There was nothing to do but thank her messenger and dismiss him. Staring into the fire, she wondered where Trevor might go, and why. Her first fear, that he had discarded her now that he'd finally seduced her, was foolish and had to be discounted. He wouldn't, he couldn't cast her off after what had happened yesterday, and certainly not if he loved her as much as he professed.

Honesty compelled her to acknowledge that she had given him no clear signal, and had even imposed silence upon him. Had her own foolish words driven him away? She had confused him time and again by her unpredictability—and her seemingly endless rejection of his love.

At the end of the week she played the Countess Olivia in *Twelfth Night*, always a reminder of the first time she had seen Trevor's golden face. Her mood was one of despondency and forboding, and she left the theater as soon as she could, hoping the long-awaited message had come during her absence.

The street was lined with town carriages. One highly varnished door bore Lord Leafield's crest, and she approached it in the expectation of finding him inside. But the brown head that emerged from the window belonged to a different Cotterell.

"Trevor let us have his stage box tonight," Hugh explained, climbing out to greet her. "And his coach as well." He looked very fine in his evening clothes, and there was no trace of his sullen expression when he spoke of his cousin. "You must let us take you home—I'll be most disappointed if you refuse. And Mrs. Cotterell is eager to meet you."

Flora was surprised to discover that the lady who had enslaved Hugh was no beauty, and the recent confinement had left her a trifle plump. Her accent was unrefined but not unpleasantly so when she said shyly, "Every time my husband sees your name in the papers, Miss Campion, I must hear all over again how greatly he admires you."

Flora felicitated them on the recent happy event and asked the name of the new addition to the family.

The proud young papa described his Arabella as the most beautiful child in all England. "My cousin stood as godfather. He has been most generous—we've got a snug house of our own, and he even offered us his carriage while he's away, thinking Emmy would like it. Which she does, I can tell you. And he said we might use his box at the theater."

"Do you know when he means to return?" Flora asked.

Hugh shook his head. "He paid us a call on his way out of

town, but never even said where he was going. He drove off in
his phaeton—I remember thinking it was frightfully cold for
an open carriage. He left on Monday, didn't he, Em?"

"Monday," Flora repeated blankly. The day after their encounter in the deserted theater. She wondered if he'd left London before or after receiving her letter.

When they reached her house, Hugh escorted the actress to
her door. In a low voice he said, "Truly, I'm glad to see you
again, Flora. I suppose you know that Trev and I have made
our peace, and I wanted to do the same with you—I was so
rude to you at Combe Cotterell. At the time I regarded you as
an enemy because you distracted him from that Lewes chit.
But everything turned out for the best. Have you heard? Lady
Caroline is engaged to Baron Allingham."

"Is she?" Flora smiled to think of that volatile nobleman,
possibly her kinsman, as a husband.

Before saying good night, Hugh told her, "Trev said your
success hadn't changed you a bit, and I see that he was right."

She chose not to dispute the allegation, false though it was.
Her three months of fame had altered her beyond description,
and she continued to feel cut off from the mainstream of activity, increasingly an observer, seldom a participant.

With the arrival of December, the weather took a turn for
the worse. The accumulated snow made Flora's walk from the
theater seem longer, and as she trudged toward Great Queen
Street she hoped it would not last.

The morning's rehearsal of the new play had ended abruptly
when Ben had been called away, and unlike her fellow players, she'd been sorry. Everyone else seemed to have someplace to go, some pressing business to take care of—even
Sally Jenkins, who had declined an invitation to tea. Flora,
wishing that she had some useful occupation, paused at a
linendraper's establishment on the way home, but none of his
wares tempted her. It wasn't long before she left the warmth of
the shop to continue her journey through the snowy streets.

When she entered the house, she could hear laughter from
belowstairs, and she envied the servants their daily tasks. And

because this was one of her nights off from the theater, she had
no hope of alleviating her ennui.

She was therefore delighted when Sally appeared on the
doorstep later in the day, her cheeks rosy from the cold and her
blue eyes bright with excitement. "Such an afternoon as I have
had," she exclaimed as she dropped into a chair in the parlor.
"I'll have a cup of tea, love, if you're still offering it."

"Of course," replied Flora, before going to tell Mary to heat
the kettle. She returned to find her friend resting her feet upon
the grate, her skirts bunched up to reveal a pair of bright yellow stockings. "And what have you been doing with yourself?" she inquired, taking a seat.

"Paying calls. Our acquaintance Miss Talley has a new
lodging, you know. Her current paramour, who has neither the
wealth nor the title of the one who cast her off, has provided a
modest set of rooms in Bolton Row. You should hear her complain of having to take a hackney from there to Drury Lane!
Well, I predicted her slide down the social scale months ago,"
said Sally with satisfaction. "Lord Edgar Fleming may be the
son of a duke, but he's still a commoner. She'll throw him
over as soon as she can, you mark my words—she'd rather be
a nobleman's doxy than anything."

"I suppose so," said Flora, wondering if she would be so described in future.

Frank appeared with the tea tray, and Sally's flow of gossip
ceased until Flora had poured two cups and passed the cakes.

"But I didn't spend the whole afternoon on Bolton Street,"
she went on. "I also went to have a look at Louisa Brunton's
trousseau—you do know she's to marry Lord Craven in a
week's time?"

"Yes, I heard that."

"Oh, the gowns she has! So fine—the sleeves of one of 'em
cost all of five and twenty guineas! Lord Craven has settled
five thousand pounds a year upon her, as though she were a
lady born and not a Drury Lane actress. He's not a bad sort,
though I've heard that Harriette Wilson was bored to tears
when she lived with him. I say, love, these cakes are grand—I
make do with stale biscuits and a scrap of toast, now that I'm

living alone in my hovel. That reminds me, would you like to share rooms when we're in Bath?"

"If you don't find someone else," Flora said diffidently.

Sally chuckled. "A gentleman, you mean? Mr. Warren *has* been attentive lately, but I'd have to convince him to stay with the company and I'm not sure he's worth the effort."

She chattered on for some time, seeming not to notice or care that Flora had little to contribute.

When Sally was gone, Flora determined to study her new part in the privacy of her bedchamber. Halfway up the stairs was a landing with a window seat, presently occupied by the gray house cat. Feeling the need of physical contact, Flora sat down to cuddle the dozing feline.

She watched the occasional carriage pass along the street, and the people huddled in their heaviest garments, trying to keep from slipping. The flakes were falling thick and fast, and soon darkness would cover the city; the lamplighter and his assistant were already at work.

Absently stroking the purring cat, she noticed a town coach moving through the dense haze of snow and fog. As it came closer, she recognized a crest that was as familiar as her own signature. Had Hugh and Emmy Cotterell come calling?

Her hand stilled when the vehicle came to a stop before the Forsters' house. Horatio climbed out, followed by Trevor, and Flora watched in bemusement as the two men shook hands in the middle of the street. The actor moved toward his brother's front door, while the nobleman—suddenly she bounded up from the window-seat, not even bothering to lay the cat down on the cushion where she'd found it.

She dashed down the stairs to the hall, and without even waiting for his knock, she flung open the door. A blast of cold air struck her, blowing her curls into disarray.

"Do come in," she invited him breathlessly, as the creature in her arms struggled to break free. In order to take his lordship's hat and stick, Flora had to let go of the cat. "Daft moggy," she muttered, as it dashed outside.

"Shall I chase after her?"

"No, she'll come back for her supper." Leading him into the parlor, Flora said, "How glad I am to see you—it seems an age

since I sent my note, though of course Mr. Cotterell told me
you went away."

"What note?" His startled question cut across her excited
greeting.

"Last week I sent a message to Leafield House. Isn't that
why you're here?"

"Not exactly," he admitted. "I haven't been to Cavendish
Square yet and don't employ a secretary to redirect my letters
when I'm out of town. I've been at Twickenham."

"Oh."

"Is Lieutenant Campion here?"

"He and James took Esther and Aunt Tab to an exhibition."
She noticed that her visitor wore a campion bloom in his but-
ton-hole, proclaiming him one of her admirers, and many of
her concerns faded.

"So I find you quite alone and unprotected. Fate is kind indeed, but I can't rejoice—actually, I came here seeking your
brother."

Flora tried to conceal her agitation, but it crept into her
voice when she said, "My lord—Trevor—if you love me, or
have ever loved me, *please* don't do it."

With a laugh, he said, "I hope you mean to tell me what has
unsettled you so much that you continually speak in riddles."

"I saw you with Horry just now," she explained. "And I'm
asking you not to be angry at Miles, whatever he's done. I
couldn't bear it if he—if you—if either of you should be
wounded, perhaps killed, and all because of a stupid misunderstanding." She was astonished when her caller began to laugh
even harder. His flippant response unnerved her, and she
reached out to shake some sense into him.

"Stupid misunderstanding indeed!" he crowed, holding her
off. "You think I have come here to issue some kind of challenge—or to accept one? Calm yourself, Flora, there's nothing
in my business with your brother to alarm you, but yes, you
are concerned in it. His presence will be considered necessary
at some point. Have you any idea when he will return?" She
shook her head. "No matter. You're of an independent spirit, I
know it all too well, and as a grown woman you hardly require
his consent, just his blessing. For I have come a-wooing," he

said tenderly. "Will you do me the very great honor of becoming my wife?"

"Your wife," she repeated on a choking gasp. "But I thought—that is, you once said it was impossible."

"I was mistaken. Be assured that it is very possible, so long as you are willing."

Her heart lurched in the most peculiar fashion, for he appeared to be serious. "Are you doing this because we—because of what happened at the theater?"

"I intended to ask you then, though I never had the chance. Is my proposal unacceptable?"

"No—that is, I don't think so, but—oh, dear, I was prepared for the other offer, never this one," she wailed.

"You know how greedy I am," he said lightly. "Each time I told you how much I wanted you, you fought back, saying no, and no, and no again. In Devonshire you used your innocence as a weapon against me. Then you tortured me by leaving me for the theater and the Forsters. When I chased you down to London, you battled me with silence and avoidance. Haven't you realized love is impervious to such tactics?" He extended his hand to stroke her cheekbone, then buried his fingers in the black curls.

"But marriage! Trevor, it would be a scandal."

"I don't give a damn for any opinion but yours."

She read the truth of it in his face.

"I came to town with the intention of making you my wife, but as soon as I set eyes on you again, you became a public figure. For a time I thought you happier in that than you could ever be with me. And then you made it quite clear that you weren't happy at all." He was about to claim a kiss when Flora placed her forefinger over his lips.

"I'm not the stuff of which countesses are made," she said simply. "Not so much because I'm an actress, but because my father was baseborn."

"Your father's father might have been a Baron Allingham or a stone picker, or anything in between. I am determined to marry you, Flora."

"But our children—"

"You will be their mother, and that is all the pedigree I require for my heirs. Now, what is there to amuse you in that?" he asked quizzically when she smiled. "Don't you believe me?"

"Yes," she replied. "And I just realized that ours would be a most equal marriage despite the differences in birth and status, because of the concessions each of us must make. You are prepared to accept my mongrel children, and if I accept your proposal, I must give up the stage."

"I can't pretend that you will find the same sort of fulfillment in the many things that I can provide. You aren't tempted by the title and fortune, or the houses and carriages and servants. I won't promise you an easy adjustment, either, or approval from my family—though Aunt Isabelle and Hugh will be delighted. My Uncle George and Aunt Grace will be cool at first, though they'll also be endlessly civil. But we'll have each other, and tears and tantrums and laughter—everything else we've shared already, although not enough. Never enough for me, Flora."

"Nor for me," she whispered, for she had realized it long since.

She knew she would willingly sacrifice her work and anything else to ensure that he would continue to hold her close and whisper such gratifying things into her ear. Her eyes were beacons of pure emotion when she lifted her face to his. "Here is your answer, Trevor—yes, and forever yes." Anything else she might have said was lost in his kiss, so she gave him the balance of her reply in an uninhibited response to his ardor. When he nuzzled the column of her neck, she closed her eyes and a beatific voice in the back of her mind told her never to look back with regret. All promise of happiness lay in the future, and she left nothing behind her but a triumph that had been hollow because he'd had no place in it.

When he interrupted his explorations of her face and form, it was to ask if she was quite sure of her decision. "For if you abandon something so important only because I have pressed you, you'll resent me again, and that I could not bear."

"How could you ever think I delight in this horrid, lonely life?" she wondered. "I hate it. I'm not even an actress now."

"Only a cart horse," he said, turning the words into a caress. "But a very beautiful one."

"On Sunday I made up my mind to be your mistress after all. But I probably shouldn't admit it, lest you retract your marriage proposal!"

"Never," he murmured.

"And then after we—afterwards, you left town and I was in agony."

"I was encouraged to absent myself," Trevor explained. "Horatio Forster called at my house on Monday and interrupted my breakfast to warn me that Lieutenant Campion is as hotheaded as his lovely sister. He promised to do his best to keep Miles at bay, but I saved him the trouble by retiring to the country. Theater business kept me in close communication with the Forsters all week; I assumed one of them would tell you where I had gone, and why."

"Damn Horry," Flora moaned. "He might have told me he was trying to soothe Miles, not stir him up."

"And how, mistress mine, will your brother accept the news of our engagement?"

"With relief, I should think, for he probably expects the worst. My only real qualm is on poor Ben's account. He won't like my leaving him."

"I wondered how long it would be before you'd recall poor Ben." He sighed.

"Trevor, is there any hope that he can keep the Princess?"

"None in the world. He knows it now."

She gripped his arm. "Where did he go when he left the theater this morning?"

"The committee was summoned to Lord Dartmouth's house. The Lord Chamberlain has apologetically but firmly denied Forster's petition for a renewal of the license. He was already opposed to it, and the mob action last Sunday was the final straw." Looking down at her, he said sternly, "I don't want to hear about your obligations to *poor* Ben, who will benefit more from our marriage than if you remain in his employ. He depends on me to promote a third theater bill in Parliament, so he'd better not oppose me when I demand that he release you from your bond."

Flora had forgotten that her tie to the theater was a legal one. "And if he refuses?" she asked hollowly.

"Where you are concerned, pure selfishness is my watchword. I'll present him with an ultimatum: only if he sets you free will I introduce his precious bill after the Christmas recess. If he won't let you go—and I wouldn't blame him, for you're more valuable to him now than ever before—he'll regret it. What chance is there that your friend Horatio will join my cause? Wouldn't he support your happiness over his brother's ambitions?"

"It won't come to that," Flora replied positively. "Winning a permanent license is more important to Ben than any actress."

When Trevor sat down on the sofa, his betrothed perched upon his knee and declared, "When I'm ancient and infirm, with a dozen grandchildren gathered 'round my skirts, I daresay I shall make much of my days on the wicked stage and sigh over how I was bullied into respectability by one very determined gentleman."

"Yes, you had my measure from the outset, didn't you? But I was altogether mistaken in my judgment of you, that first time you received me in this room. Little did I suppose then that on my next visit I'd be so intimate with the aloof Miss Campion." He tweaked a curl.

"And when are you going to make an honest woman of me?" she inquired.

"As soon as you let me. Why not today? In fact, it's the perfect solution to our dilemma. We'll present Ben Forster with a *fait accompli*. I acquired a special license weeks ago, and it's waiting at Leafield House. All we need is a parson. And witnesses, but that will be simple enough, for you'll want your brother and your friends—and Margery Prescott. I don't imagine our union would be quite legal if she weren't there to see the knot tied. The more I think on it," he said with a broad smile, "the better I like the notion. You need only decide whether the deed will be done in this parlor or at a church."

"Church, if you please, preferably my own. St. Giles-in-the-Field is where my idol, the great David Garrick, was wed," she informed him, swinging her legs back and forth.

"I require no further recommendation. St. Giles it must be.

Will you be content with my signet for a makeshift marriage ring until I can purchase a proper one? It might take considerable time to find something suited to your exalted station, and I'm too impatient to embark upon a shopping trip just now."

Flora, in spite of being pleased by her bridegroom's impatience, made a great show of being put upon. "I do hope you'll give me time to change my dress."

Trevor kissed her forehead. "I'm prepared to take you as I find you, but I accept that I must let you have your way once in a great while. Run along, then. I'll fetch the license and visit your church to arrange the ceremony. Be sure to tell your good Margery to pack whatever you need for a visit out of town—I intend to spirit my wife away from London as soon after our wedding as is decent."

"Combe Cotterell?" she asked hopefully, scampering down from his knee.

"Alas, too far." With a devilish smile he said, "I am admittedly eager to make love to my bride, but not in a roadside inn. The beds are so ill-aired." He continued in a more serious vein, "I would happily install you in Cavendish Square, but that might give rise to a worse kind of publicity than has already been inflicted upon you."

"Where do we go that is neither too close nor too far from London?" she wondered, following him to the front door.

"To a place I know," he said with so mysterious an air that Flora instantly took umbrage. "No quarrels today, if you please—wait until we're safely married."

"I must be mad to consider spending the rest of my days with a—a marble-breasted *tyrant*!"

Laughing, he retrieved his hat from the hall table. "Your experience of my ruthless methods should have led you to expect something of the kind. But I shall strive to be a better, more reasonable husband than I've been a lover."

When he was gone, Flora ran up the stairs, her slippers barely skimming the risers, and after giving Margery the happy news asked her to press and lay out a white gown sprigged with forget-me-nots. Then she sat down at her dressing table to reflect as calmly as possible on her drastic and delirious decision to exchange her present lowly status for that of Lady Leafield.

Much better that she leave the stage as quietly and unobtrusively as she had found her way there six years earlier; there was a pleasing symmetry about it. A gala farewell performance held no appeal, nor did laudatory verses composed in her honor; that sort of parting from the old life would be too public and too funereal to suit her. Her final night before an audience had been uneventful, hardly memorable, but it was tucked away in a corner of her mind and that was sufficient.

The stage, once her only home, had become a platform where she displayed herself to the curious in an increasingly mechanical and joyless fashion. She had given up Trevor to tilt with fame, but had found no consolation for her heartache. Sacrificing a potentially brilliant career might not be a painless prospect, but it wouldn't destroy her peace. She had found a more comfortable, more private home within the circle of her lover's arms.

The throngs that had flocked to see her perform had set her on a pedestal, declaring her to be a goddess, a nymph, a genius. Flattering but quite untrue, she thought, emptying her drawers in search of a lace veil to lend a bridal touch to her best bonnet. The noble Earl of Leafield had spent the better part of a year proving to her that she was all too human, just as she had shown him that she was a woman of integrity and independence. She'd argued with him and thwarted him in ways no other person, male or female, had done before, and he'd angered her beyond reason. She had laughed with him and teased him and told him things she had never admitted to another soul. She had run away from him more than once, only to discover in the end that she had been running toward him. And through it all his love had been unwavering.

The occasionally tempestuous nature of their relationship and the unorthodox way she'd earned her living would ensure that theirs would be no ordinary union. And Flora, whose experience of the truly ordinary was limited at best, knew she would have it no other way.

20

Here comes the Countess. Now Heaven walks on earth.

Twelfth Night, V. i.

The night was still young, but the Earl and Countess of Leafield had already retired to their bedchamber, where the mussed bedclothes and general disarray of the great fourposter testified to what had lately occurred there. A cravat draped negligently upon a chair bore the appearance of having been hastily removed, as did the lacy chemise lying upon the floor.

Now the newlyweds, clad in their dressing gowns, sat at the fireside. Trevor occupied a wing chair, his brown head bent over the newspaper, and Flora reposed at his feet, her legs tucked beneath her.

As her husband's fingers played with her tousled curls, she gazed thoughtfully into the flames.

They had exchanged their marriage vows a fortnight ago in a hurried ceremony at St. Giles-in-the-Field, in the presence of her brother and the Drews, and the moment the register was signed the wedding party had returned to Great Queen Street for an impromptu celebration. Before Flora's eager lord had carried her off to Twickenham, she'd composed a note to Benedict Forster, crammed with explanations and apologies.

Upon arriving at his Palladian villa on the Thames, Trevor sat down to write out the formal announcements for the London papers, but the task of folding and sealing them was abandoned for other, more pressing matters. His subsequent preoccupation with his bride made him forget the notices, still gathering dust on a writing table downstairs.

Flora displayed very little interest in the world beyond their wintry, snowbound retreat. When it occurred to her that her days would never again be regulated by the familiar round of rehearsal and performance, she didn't repine; her husband was taking great care to fill her time and her thoughts.

He heaved a deep sigh, and the newspaper crackled as he folded it in half. Reaching down to hand it to Flora, he said, "I believe you will want to read this."

There was no doubt about which paragraph he deemed worthy of her notice, for it was embedded in a column generally devoted to theatrical gossip.

LONDON'S LOST ACTRESS

Public curiosity, excited by the disappearance of that ornament of her profession, MISS CAMPION, has been gratified. MR. BENEDICT FORSTER has announced that the Lady's retirement is as certain as the imminent closing of his Theater, where she delighted playgoers this season. Never again will her like be seen upon the London stage. Her portrayals of Juliet, of Ophelia, of Letty Loyal, and her brilliant execution of Comic and Tragic roles, will not soon fade from the memories of those who were privileged to view them in London or at Bath.

In the wake of Lord L——'s absence from the Metropolis, rumors of an Alliance are rampant amongst the lady's former colleagues. If she has joined the rank of the countesses, she follows the example of both LADY DERBY and LADY CRAVEN, who formerly trod the boards.

The Managers of the Theatres Royal, Messrs. Sheridan and Kemble, assuredly regret their failure to steal the esteemed Actress from FORSTER, their Professional Rival, and will be saddened to learn that a Nobleman has plucked this fair flower from the stage.

"It sounds as though I was buried, not married," said Flora when she finished reading. "Ben wrote it, of course. He eulogizes me most handsomely, but shows his hand in that last bit about Sheridan and Kemble. Such spiteful stuff!"

"You might have known he'd find some way to discomfit

them, but certainly you deserve the praise," said her husband with fond pride.

"Poor Ben, even though he expected to lose the license, he has suffered a terrible blow. And only a few hours later he received the news of my desertion." She shook her head in regret.

Trevor reached down to stroke the white shoulder peeping from her dressing gown, which had slipped. "I daresay poor Ben is already planning his next assault upon Bath. And the campaign for the third theater bill will keep him busy."

"I know, but it's sad to think of the Princess closing her doors."

"Do you miss the theater so much? We've shared a great deal during this brief, glorious time, but never your feelings on that subject."

Flora searched for the best words to communicate the mix of emotions she experienced, determined to give the truthful answer he would expect of her. "Of course I'll sometimes miss my friends, and all the excitement of a first night, and the camaraderie of benefit week. And the acceptance—actors are so open-minded, they care nothing for background or breeding, and base their judgments on talent alone. But I won't miss the quarrels or the petty jealousy or the lack of preparation for a new play, or the endless packing and unpacking during a tour. At Combe Cotterell I discovered I could be happy living away from the theater—*and* the Forsters."

"I wish you'd told me at the time," he said, running his hand through his shaggy brown locks.

"I didn't know it myself until I returned to London," Flora replied. "But in Devonshire I think I began to suspect what I now know, that my stage career was an interlude, the curtain-raiser that comes before the main piece. And though I was on the stage for more than six years, the whole time I was but standing in the wings waiting for the real play to begin. And it finally did, Trevor, at St. Giles."

Smiling down at her, he said, "For the past fortnight I've wondered what we ought to do next, and you've just supplied the answer. Our stay here has been delightful, this is the per-

fect love nest and will always be, but we can't stay here forever."

"Are we going to Hopeton Hall?" she asked, concealing her
trepidation at the prospect of meeting his clergyman uncle and
saintly aunt.

"Eventually. First, however, I want to see you acting the
part of mistress at the Combe, especially now that Christmas
draws near. Would you like to travel to Devonshire?"

Jumping to her feet, Flora flung her arms around his neck
and pressed her lips to his cheek. "Yes, please," she breathed,
"as soon as possible." She spent some time convincing him of
her delight, to his immense satisfaction and her own, and afterward she found herself seated upon his knees, her head on his
shoulder.

"Trevor," she murmured, her eyes half-closed, "I don't yet
miss my work, but I can't help worrying sometimes that one
day I will feel a void. And I've already decided what I'll do, so
don't object too strenuously."

"And what is that, dear heart?"

"I think I might like to write a play," she confessed, suddenly feeling shy. "Horry and I always talked about trying it,
but we never had the time, being busy with other people's
plays. Which were usually so stupid that I ached to improve
them." She turned her earnest face toward him to judge his reaction, and was puzzled and a little hurt when he gave a shout
of laughter.

"But of course," Trevor agreed, to her great relief. "For you
must have some outlet for those creative fires, and I can't expect marriage to quench them. Why should I object, Flora? I
can see that you might require an endeavor that is your very
own, some accomplishment that is quite unconnected with me.
I have made a firm vow not to stifle the very quality that is so
attractive in you."

"My independence? Why, Trevor, have you been reading
tracts on the emancipation of females from the tyranny of
males, on the sly? I never guessed that you, of all men, could
be an admirer of Mary Godwin and her ilk," she teased.

"To be honest, I never gave the subject much thought, but I

think I'd better if your ladyship is going to be the next Aphra Behn or Joanna Baillie."

"Or Mrs. Inchbald," Flora added thoughtfully.

"As your patron, for so I still consider myself, perhaps I will commission a play from you." But Trevor's bride apparently hadn't heard his playful suggestion, and he recognized that familiar, fervent light in her lovely green eyes. She was leagues away from him already, and he almost regretted his foolhardy words about cherishing her creative impulses.

But by this time he knew perfectly well how to recall his presence to her with only the slightest exertion on his part, so he tightened his hold on her waist and let his free hand slide up and down one of the shapely legs draped across his knees.

His tactic was eminently successful; Flora abandoned the discussion of her playwriting scheme. But something else occurred to her, and she drew back from her ardent spouse. "Trevor, you asked me if I had regrets, and it's only fair that I ask the same question. Are you disappointed in me?"

"After two weeks of living with you, my dearest love, and becoming more intimately acquainted with your finer points, I can say with great certainty that you could never, ever disappoint me," he told her, his hazel eyes gleaming.

She pinched his earlobe. "I didn't mean in that way, and you know it. I meant because I'm not a dignified lady, only a common play actress whose dresser is her personal maid. I brought you no lands or dowry."

"I care nothing for the dignity of the Countess of Leafield, as I have been proving to you this fortnight," he replied, "nor do I give a snap of my fingers for land, having quite enough of my own. Your first play can be your dowry, if you feel the lack of one. I regret nothing, Flora. If you had accepted me as your protector when you were the toast of the town, I might never have discovered which had the greater share of your affections, the stage or my humble self. No, don't interrupt, I'm not done yet," he said, despite the fact that she hadn't spoken a word.

For Flora had simply turned her melting eyes upon him, giving him a loving look that thus far in their marriage had resulted in her being stripped of her garments and chased

mercilessly into bed. She might have forgotten this, or she
might not, but she continued to gaze at him in just that way.
"Why, Trevor—"

But further speech was prevented by his eager kisses. Already his hands were gently working at the sash of her dressing gown, and she permitted him to untie it. She sighed with
anticipation, for he was granting her yet another opportunity to
prove to both of them how very little she blamed him for enticing her away from that other world to make her queen of
his.

Historical Note

A third theater bill was introduced in the House of Commons but was defeated during the Parliamentary session of 1808. Later attempts in 1810 and 1813 met with similar failure.

The theater in Covent Garden burned to the ground in the autumn of 1808, and reconstruction took place soon after. John Philip Kemble's decision to raise the admission charges for the 1809 season sparked the "Old Price" riots and forced a temporary closure. Early in 1809, Sheridan's Drury Lane playhouse was destroyed by a blaze that lit up London, and until the costly rebuilding was completed three years later his company used the Haymarket Theatre and the Lyceum. The patent privileges granting the Theatres Royal exclusive rights to produce "serious" drama were abolished with the passing of the Theatre Regulation Act of 1843.

One particularly enjoyable aspect of my research for The Toast of the Town was studying the collections at London's Theatre Museum in Covent Garden and attending performances in provincial theaters.

Bath's Theatre Royal of 1805 has been painstakingly restored to Regency splendor. Its predecessor on Orchard Street was long ago converted to other uses, but the structure still stands.

The neighboring city of Bristol possesses the oldest working theater in Britain and an auditorium virtually unchanged from what was typical of the Georgian age. I hereby express my gratitude to my friends Margot and Robert Pierson for taking me there regularly.

Abundant thanks to my parents, who had to endure my youthful preoccupation with the stage, and to Christopher, my companion during so many hours spent in "box, pit, and gallery." M.E.P.